JUMPING
THE GREEN

a novel

LESLIE SCHWARTZ

Simon & Schuster

SIMON & SCHUSTER
Rockefeller Center
1230 Avenue of the Americas
New York, NY 10020

SIMON & SCHUSTER and colophon are registered trademarks of Simon & Schuster, Inc.

Designed by Karolina Harris

Manufactured in the United States of America

10 9 8 7 6 5 4 3 2 1

Library of Congress Cataloging-in-Publication Data
Schwartz, Leslie.
Jumping the green : a novel / Leslie Schwartz.
p.   cm.
I. Title.
PS3569.C5666J86   1999   99-33486
813'.54—dc21   CIP
ISBN 0-684-85589-5

Walter Arndt's translation of "Before the Summer Rain" by Rainer Maria Rilke
was first published in *New England Review*, Volume 4, No. 3, Spring 1982. It
subsequently appeared in *The Best of Rilke*, translated by Walter Arndt,
University Press of New England (Hanover, N.H., and London), 1989.
Reprinted by permission.

A c k n o w l e d g m e n t s

I wish to express my thanks and gratitude to Marysue Rucci, Elizabeth Sheinkman and my dear friend Werner Hoeflich. Thanks to Chuck Lande and Tom Passios for letting me write on their time and to Hedgebrook and the Ucross Foundation for space and solitude. Thanks also to the James Jones Literary Society for its support.

For Jim

ONE

1

M y discovery of masturbation is accompanied by the sudden epiphany that lovers slap each other around. Passion and love are fraught with this delight between the legs, this slap in the face, this wedding of pain and pleasure.

It happens one summer day, my discovery, three weeks shy of my ninth birthday. I am lying on an air mattress, floating in the Kowolskis' swimming pool. This is not unusual since the Kowolskis are our neighbors—our parents' best friends—and as such, share everything with us as we do them.

The air is hot, still and dry. Furry seed pods drift gently on the afternoon winds. I bob in the water, drunk on too much sun and the prospects of yet another orgasm that night. I have discovered my downthere has a toy button that when manipulated in just the right way creates an astonishing response. I have become addicted to this new discovery the way I once was to chocolate milk, though I have yet to fully understand its power.

Floating, buoyed by the clear water and my heady imagination, I conjure up the ways I will touch myself, what tools and gadgets I might find around the cluttered house to put inside me, when I hear Mr. Kowolski begin to shout.

Elaine Kowolski, his daughter who is three years older than me, is inside the pool house with my brother Martin. I can hear Elaine whining. "Quit it, you dork." Words like *dork* only bolster Martin's desire to annoy people. I can picture him pulling at Elaine's bathing suit, trying to get a peak at her booblets. That is what he calls undeveloped breasts.

The window to Mr. and Mrs. Kowolski's bedroom is wide open. The sights and sounds of one of their notorious fights penetrate my thoughts. I am aware of a slight moistness between my legs and the smell of my sweat. Mr. Kowolski is telling Mrs. Kowolski that she is a stupid, goddamned idiot and if she doesn't write down the fucking check numbers in the goddamned checkbook then he'll fucking teach her a goddamned lesson. Martin and Elaine Kowolski are silenced by this fight for a moment, but when Mr. Kowolski lapses into a stream of Polish obscenities, they break out into peals of laughter.

As I watch this fight unfold from my spectator raft, Mr. Kowolski sets his drink down on the table by their bed and smacks Mrs. Kowolski across the face. It is methodical, iron-cold. It is the work of a machine. The violence of a drone. She stumbles back and cups her cheek with her beautiful white hands. Her eyes fill with a kind of sorrow and pain that is mixed with a kind of arrogance. Mr. Kowolski is instantly contrite. He puts his hands around her, unzips her dress and buries his face in her breasts. She takes her beautiful hands and puts them around his head and holds him as if he is a baby. I see that her breasts are enormous, strikingly white with large reddish nipples. Her eyes close for a long time and her face smooths out, though a lingering attitude of disgust and hatred stays parked around the lines of her mouth. I watch them for a minute more until Mrs. Kowolski opens her eyes, sees me staring at her and smiles slightly, leaning over to shut the blinds.

I swim lazily in the pool, adrift in strange forbidden thoughts of the private parts of animals and the naked images of natives I have seen in the Time Life series of books our parents keep on the living room shelves. When Martin tells me he has had enough of Elaine and her retarded whining, I drag myself from the pool and follow him home across the street.

That night, Maggie and Harold engage in a drunken, nasty fight

over dinner. That is when they usually reserve the time to argue. My
brothers and sisters leave the table one by one. I am the last to go. I
generally stay for as long as I can to try and glean some meaning from
the volley of insults our parents hurl at each other. Maggie is calling
Harold an imbecile and wonders how he can call himself a father to
his children. Harold tells Maggie that if she spent as much time on
him and the kids as she did on her *fucking* hair then maybe they'd
have something resembling a family.

I leave the kitchen and shut myself in my room, succumbing finally
to the dangerous vision of Mrs. Kowolski's bursting red nipples. When I
come, the shrieks of my parents' argument drift through the walls and
into my room, where they float around in the sweaty, shameful aftermath of a hundred butterflies alighting from my exhausted, naked body.

We are the progeny of an interfaith marriage. Catholic mother, Jewish father. Five children, meeting both the Orthodox and Catholic requirements for a large litter of heirs to our parents' gene pools. The
older three are generally raised New Testament, with a little High Holidays thrown in for solemnity. By the time I roll out, an afterthought of
nostalgic love, Maggie's passion for Jesus and the Virgin Mary has
waned almost entirely and I learn to worship test tubes, the Big Bang
theory and a god of mythic proportions—half Jewish in His wrath and
fury, half Catholic in His conditional forgiveness; a God who surfaces
only when I am in need of an explanation for the unexplainable.

I spend most of my childhood roaming the neighborhood, a neatly
arranged network of wide streets and ranch-style homes, bordered by
old leafy trees good for climbing. Outside in summer, it smells like
metal and lilac, peaches and skunk. The ground is a gold mine of buttons, pennies and other shiny, castaway pocket fodder. I collect. I
gather. I accumulate. I have boxes of street gems—odd bits of suburban flotsam—which I glue together, erect and reinvent into enormous,
forbidding shapes. Faces made of pennies. Moons made of broken
glass. Hearts made of rocks and cement.

My sister Esther calls our house Monsoon Goldblum. A one-story
ranch with a haphazard add-on—my sad, dilapidated room that leaks
in winter, roasts in summer—in the back. Books and furniture are

everywhere, almost alive, disordered and breathing. You do not ever find things in our house, you stumble across them in your journey. Entire closets are jammed with board games, bathrobes, priceless silver, basketballs. Drawers in dressers are a treasure chest of watches, panties, foreign coins and scented sachets. Pets include Harry the Dog, a cat Martin named Bilbo Fucking Baggins after he read *The Hobbitt* and several fish in a glass bowl. Remnants of our parents' fights lie in pieces throughout the house, broken vases and dishes waiting to be glued, never thrown out, evidence of their brawls. You never know when you might step on broken glass. You never know when you might sleep with a hairbrush.

But the world outside is clean and open. There is logic to stepping on a burr or a rusty nail. There is sense to wilting flowers, new spring leaves, deflated tennis balls. The junior high school borders our backyard, a long field of low-slung buildings, drooping and insolent, made of concrete and wood. In the winter, left untended, the field grows wild with weeds that are hacked off in spring and left to dry out under the sun. We use the dried weeds to make igloos and sometimes you might see six or seven weed igloos scattered across the field, like Monet's haystacks in the burnished light.

Every summer I take on several jobs. The first is to capture lizards and garden snakes on Mr. Milton's land, several acres of apricot and cherry trees down the street from our house. The second is to flee from the salt pellets Mr. Milton fires at me from his drafty old upstairs window. I steal fruit, which I eat nonstop. As a consequence, I have diarrhea all summer.

Meanwhile, my brothers spend their energy erecting a tree fort. They conduct secret meetings that involve blood rituals and double dares. I am not allowed to participate because I am a girl, an accusation against which I heatedly argue. When they're not around, I sneak up the tree and invade their secret fort. My heart is a cannon. I face certain torture if I am caught. The walls are wood painted blue. There are girlie magazines and packs of cigarettes stolen from the half-full packs of Winstons Maggie and Harold leave absentmindedly around the house. I take a cigarette and pretend to smoke it. I look at the naked women. I am repulsed by pubic hair and pray that I don't grow any on my own down-there.

My brothers, Eddie and Martin, and their friends develop a secret alphabet so they can write cryptic notes to one another. One day I walk by the tree fort and there is a mystifying sign posted on the trunk: CYYTRILWS OLP TTHOOFLEPM. OYLT MNLLT!!! I have no idea what these words mean, but my brothers and their friends are notorious for their creative torture techniques and I am certain the words forebode a secret agony for all trespassers. I don't dare climb the rungs they have nailed into the burly trunk of the tree.

Instead, I float for hours in the pool, until my skin is pruney and my eyes turn red from the chlorine. Sometimes my sister Mary, who is one year older than me, swims with me, but watching her get in is torture. One step, one squeal. "Quit being such a girl," I say. If circumstances are right, I throw her in. My other sister, Esther, who I forgive for being in love with the neighborhood thug, refuses to get her hair wet. She spends most of her time with Danny Franconi, stealing cigarettes at the variety store and making out inside churches and movie theaters.

I play with the boys on the street. They smell of dirt and sweat, of the things that grow wild: oleander, rosemary, ice plant. Eddie and Martin allow me to play with them and their friends, all of whom are five or six years older then me, on the condition that I don't go act like a girl and cry. I make a profession out of kick the can, hide 'n go seek, tackle football and dodge ball. We play dodge ball in the street hoping there will be blood or broken bones. I rarely bleed. I rarely fall. I am allowed the privilege of fist fights. I swear freely. "Fuck you, you turd brain," I say. Eddie and Martin laugh till they cry. "Fuck you, you monkey shit," I say.

Then the dark days arrive. Laser-sharp arrows of pain come unbidden out of some poisonous swamp inside my head. The most I can bear then is the blue light of TV, no sound. The curtains are drawn in my bedroom—the half-assed add-on in the back—and I believe in an abstract, disjointed way that I too am nothing more than an add-on. The headaches get worse.

"You are just a child," Maggie screams. "You are not entitled to migraines." She brings in the fan. She puts cold rags that smell vaguely of dish soap across my forehead.

"She is just a child," I hear my mother say to no one as she leaves

my room, trailing perfume, cigarettes, vodka. The medicine, extracted
from her ubiquitous pill bottles, makes the world lopsided, makes my
heart labor, my eyes turn to glue, my body limp and disobedient but
also strangely civilized, at rest.

Maggie goes around the house saying no one is to disturb me. She
alone has visiting rights. Time vanishes, to be replaced by the instances
of her boozy, magnificent presence. She emerges from the gloom and
the murk, a shard of glass glinting in sunlight, with 7-UP and toast. Her
body miraculously lies down beside me. I am a comma in the recesses
of her womb. I am a hand in the glove. The seawater world flows
around me. I am the shore, she is the tide. I think, *Don't disappear.*
The blue night sweeps down and my mind dances to the tune of my
pulse, which has made its home inside my head. Thud, thud, thud.

Usually by the next morning, I am better. And Maggie treats me
with resignation, a slight annoyance, as if she liked me more when I
was sick. "Go on, dear, and leave me alone," she says, her voice filled
with drama and irritation, smoke surging from her mouth.

Harold, a man older than his years who travels through the house in
a cloud of thoughts, is not involved in the illnesses of his children. He
is a man haunted by science, terrorized by reality. If I come up behind
him suddenly or we bump into each other rounding the corners of the
house, he jumps as if startled and gazes at me for a moment as if trying
to remember who I am. He is a man who prefers to worship the myth
of theory over the certainty of facts.

He builds elaborate dollhouses from scratch in his garage. They are
beautiful, orderly homes, devoid of humanity. I gaze at them from
time to time, wishing I were small enough to live inside such cool, tidy
elegance. Sometimes when I can't sleep, I imagine that I am the sole
resident of whatever dollhouse he happens to be working on. I live
alone. I sit in the kitchen and read the newspaper, sipping from a
beautiful coffee cup. There are no parents, no brothers, no sisters.
There is no booze and no pills. There are no pool parties. I spend my
days wandering from room to room, the silence at my back. Nothing
breaks. No one screams. Sometimes Maggie or Harold knock on the
door, but I don't answer it. I hide behind the curtains and wait for
them to go away.

Usually, when Harold is finished with one of his houses he turns his back on it, donating it to a charity or letting it rot in the yard. For some reason, the finished product always disappoints him. It is as if he is searching for something that, to his dismay, can never be found by the gluing down of miniatures.

Our parents are poolside with the Kowolskis, getting soused on watermelon nui-nui and sangria. I hide out in the living room and peer at them from behind the drapes. If I don't keep vigil, something is bound to happen, something is bound to break. Someone is bound to get hurt.

Maggie is sitting in her chaise lounge, her long, beautiful legs crossed at the knee. In her right hand she holds a cigarette, extended cartoon-fashion by a cigarette holder. With her left hand she nervously taps a cocktail glass filled with vodka. Mr. Kowolski is telling everyone that Mrs. Kowolski has a fascination for the milkman.

"She is always doing this and that with her hair on Mondays and Wednesdays. Irene, tell them," he says.

"He's darling, Maggie. A little Mexican boy from over there." Mrs. Kowolski, who is all gold lamé and bouffant hair wags her hands in a vaguely southerly direction. She appears to be having a difficult time focusing on Maggie. But Maggie has that effect on people. Her presence insults. It mocks. It mystifies.

"Stupid spics," Mr. Kowolski says in his Polish accent.

"Don't be so damn German," Harold shouts from the other side of the pool.

"He's not German, *mon cher*," Maggie says, laughing. Her laugh is like water rushing over smooth rocks, water that goes on forever, like an echo of itself, water in a deep pool that broadcasts back the sound of a stone skimming upon its surface.

"Okay," says Harold. "Stop being such a damn Nazi."

"Now, now," Mr. Kowolski says. "One had to live there. Fit in or be killed."

I peer around the drapes in order to see my father. His tuft of hair, a white unruly patch that dominates his forehead, dangles forward and he pushes it gently aside. I can tell he is braving about a three-drink melancholy. Though I don't understand their conversation—I have a theory that our parents and their friends were dropped to Earth by a race of aliens happy to be rid of their outcasts—I know something has frightened Harold. He is easily spooked, easily jarred. He is a man who cries.

I watch the way Maggie dangles her legs, wiggling her toes. I stare at the glamorous splotches of blood-red nail polish on her toenails. Mr. Kowolski is telling her that most women her age have dimples on their ass, but that she, Maggie Goldblum, does not.

"*Ferme la bouche*, David, darling," Maggie says, pronouncing *David* like *Daveed*. She has a habit of speaking dramatically, like an American stage actress attempting British or French accents. And nothing ever seems to embarrass her. She is not the least bit ruffled that Mr. Kowolski is referring to her ass in front of Mrs. Kowolski and Harold. She just looks at him with her bored movie star expression and says, "Don't you think that's a little crass in mixed company?"

"Mixed company. What mixed company? A Jew and a Nazi, you mean?"

"Up yours," Harold says and everyone laughs.

Later, the Grants and the Baxters come by, each with a bottle of something. The Franconis also show up clasping a bottle of cheap tequila, though in a year, Mr. Franconi will be hauled off to jail for some undisclosed, though rumor has it, egregious act. When Harry the Dog—a large, floppy-eared stew of different breeds—and an armchair end up in the pool, the party moves indoors where the guests scatter into dark corners like shrapnel. I see their shadows, their drunken movements. I hear the ripple and cascade of their frosted laughter.

Impossible partnerships are forged, partnerships that I know then are only real for as long as the night lasts. I notice especially Maggie and Mr. Kowolski, orbiting each other with their boozy intimacy, held together, I am sure, by a gravity of their own invention. I hear the dog crying and wade into the pool to rescue him. I nearly drown in the process, fighting against his terror and apparent relief. The dog seems grateful. He puts his huge paws around my neck and desperately licks my face.

Nightfall yields a different set of rules and as if to prove it, my two brothers, Martin and Eddie, sneak off to set the lockers on fire at the junior high school that adjoins our backyard. I can see through the window of Esther's bedroom an occasional flame ignite like the butt end of a bottle rocket and disappear into blackness.

My sisters prepare suicides, a mixture of watermelon nui-nui, scotch and sangria that Esther has effortlessly pilfered from our parents' party. Esther, the oldest, dead now, tells me and Mary that the important trick to making a suicide is mixing the alcohol in equal parts.

"As old Harold would say, it's an exact science," she says. "A precise and methodical exercise leading to a delightful plane of molecular chaos." She frowns when she laughs because our father both annoys and intrigues her.

I watch her mix the potion in her careful, measured way. She has a certain expertise doing things that are not sanctioned by our parents or, for that matter, society at large. I feel privileged when she includes me in her brazen acts against authority. She has a distinct talent for making disobedience seem acceptable, even desirable. She is part soldier, part nurse. She's a warrior who carries wine and Band-Aids.

She loves the idea of jail. She fantasizes out loud about it all the time, about being arrested for protesting against the white capitalist pigs that run Corporate America. She believes going to jail is the ultimate expression of civil disobedience, which is why she idolizes Martin Luther King Jr., even though he's been dead for four years.

She hopes one day that she will go to jail for peacefully demonstrating against whatever white, corporate, racist, fascist segment of society happens to be the reigning oppressor when she is in college. She loves using the words *racist* and *oppressor*.

I imagine jail. It is gray, empty. There is no privacy. Esther and I are in there together. When I have to pee, she uses her body to shield me from the other inmates, and at night, she plots our escape.

I watch her, taking mental notes the entire time, as she makes the suicides. Her elegant, slender fingers, inherited from Maggie, are wrapped around a mason jar and she shakes the potion up with her usual dramatic flair. Her long, black hair is tied behind her head in a braid but when she prepares to take the first sip of the suicide, she untethers it and shakes her head so that her hair fans out around her.

I touch my own red hair and lament the curls, the color. Somehow I know I will never be like her. Because of this, I work hard learning

the tricks of her debauchery. I am old enough to know that while genetics cannot, certain behavior can be mastered over time.

Mary leans into the bean bag chair. She is not sure she should par-
take of the alcohol, but it is impossible to say no to Esther, who makes
all manner of illicit activities seem reasonable. Mary takes a sip, a
small one, I notice, compared to Esther's long, courageous drought,
and makes a face.

"Yuck," she says.

Mary is sweet, not a Goldblum trait, and good, not a Goldblum
trait. She seems to have few complications. She rarely complains. She
rarely gets into trouble. Unlike the rest of us, she is an average student,
dreamy and ethereal. To our collective horror, she mentions God from
time to time. She loves anything having to do with Jesus, Catholic
churches and the New Testament. This, of course, bothers Harold, a
lapsed Jew but a Jew nonetheless, but it pleases Maggie, a lapsed
Catholic but a Catholic nonetheless.

To Mary's credit, she does not gush about sin and hell and all the
other ghoulish accouterments of Catholicism, though late at night,
when I have a headache or insomnia, she will know somehow and tiptoe into my room to croon songs into my ear about heaven.

Esther laughs at the face of disgust Mary makes. It is a thick, burly
laugh. It is a man's laugh. Hearing it, I laugh too. She takes another
long sip and smiles happily after a loud, exaggerated swallow.

"Mmmmm," she says. She leans back against the wall then stands
up and goes over to the record player. She is wearing a halter top and
bell bottom corduroys. Her tiny boobs poke out beneath the flimsy cotton of her top and her pants are so tight I can see the flowered fractures
of her butt and vagina. She has a beautiful, slender body and, unlike
the rest of us, very dark skin.

She rifles through a stack of the parents' records, climbing over a
box of clothes for the Goodwill and an old dollhouse Harold constructed and abandoned years ago. She makes faces as she does this
and laments the fact that our parents have such bad taste in music. Finally, she pulls out a Petula Clark album, shrugging her shoulders,
adapting and molding her expectations to fit whatever is available. She
puts the record on and starts singing "Downtown," her body swaying
with the rhythm of the music. She closes her eyes when she dances

and watching her makes me feel a mix of complicated, embarrassing emotions that I don't yet have a name for.

She takes another sip. Then, winking at Mary, she hands me the suicide. Mary protests, but Mary's protests are rarely heeded. She is one of us, so we don't deride her. Instead, we ignore her. It is our way of loving the anomaly.

"Go on, Baby Goldblum. Have yourself some fun."

I take a long sip like Esther did, and after I swallow, I feel it rise up again almost instantly. I am able, out of a combination of horror and pride, to stave off vomiting. Esther laughs loudly but Mary's eyebrows furrow with concern.

"Go on," Esther says. She ruffles my hair and under her encouragement, I take another sip. Maybe it is the lack of food, maybe because I am so skinny, but almost immediately, I feel dizzy and loose, like my bones have become unhinged and my eyeballs unleashed into the aqueous fluid supporting them.

Esther takes me in her arms and twirls me around. I see Mary out of the corner of my eye and she has that look on her face. It is more than worry. It is an anxiety without borders. She does not like what she sees but it seems to hinge on something deeper than the present course of events, as if something more meaningful is taking place other than getting me drunk.

When Esther lets me go I tell Mary I love Esther more than anyone in the whole wide world. Esther takes me aside and says, "I wouldn't do that, Baby Goldblum, because someday I might disappoint you."

I brush her off and turn up the stereo so I can dance more. I have a vast desire to remove my clothes but when I begin to unbutton my pants, Mary tells me I had better keep them on.

Esther, meanwhile, is changing into a dress. She is powdering her armpits and brushing her hair. She puts red lipstick on and tells us she is meeting Danny at the aqueduct. She then tells us that she and Danny Franconi just went to third base. I do not, of course, know what this means because I am only eight years old. She continues using baseball metaphors as a way of telling us how intimate she and Danny are.

Mary, who is nine, holds her hands over my ears during one part of the story and all I hear, before throwing up, is the folded corners of Esther's voice rushing past me as if strapped to the sides of a speeding locomotive.

I do not drink again after that for twenty-one years, and that lapse in fortitude is only because Esther has indeed disappointed me by getting herself dead.

Three years later. It is Christmas Eve day. My oldest brother Eddie is hacking away at a large Christmas candle with the image of Jesus Christ superimposed over it. The ax he uses is impressively big, a burled mass of blackened iron and wood. Outside, smoke rises from the chimneys and a cold, driving rain pounds against the pavement, washing away my chalked hopscotch squares. I am in the cluttered garage wedged between several bicycles and a contraption Harold uses to glue the tiny pieces of his dollhouses together. I open and close the small windows on the nearly microscopic hinges of Harold's latest project, a reproduction of a southern mansion, replete with pillars and verandas. His hobby of building these dollhouses fascinates me the way most of the behavior of our parents fascinates me. It is just one more piece of evidence that they have been deposited on earth by aliens.

Harry the Dog is standing watch, his big tongue hanging out the side of his mouth while Eddie slashes the candle. Harry the Dog cocks his head from side to side and whines. "Shut up, you fucking asshole mongrel dog," I say.

I love Eddie fiercely. He is the best looking of us Goldblums, with soft, expressive features and a kind smile. He has a tough outer shell evidenced in the way he remains unfazed by Maggie's violent mood swings and Harold's melancholy. But this shell surrounds a complicated network of sensitivities and affections of which I am usually the recipient.

One day he will blow the whistle on some high-powered Wall Street executives who are ripping off a hundred or more senior citizens in south Florida and, for his efforts, will end up in a ditch bloodied from head to toe but still breathing.

On Christmas Day 1975 he is eradicating. That's what he tells me when I ask him what he's doing.

"I am eradicating," he says.

I know better than to ask him to elaborate. I suck on a hard pepper-mint candy. I watch. The ax goes up, comes down, a chunk of wax—the hand of Jesus—flies in the air. Over and over again, different parts of the body of Jesus catapult skyward until Eddie misses and his finger flies through the air and lands on the ground with a splat.

I realize he has just eradicated more than he has planned on. He faints almost the moment it happens and I pick up the finger, unfazed by the blood and the warm, wrinkled feeling of his finger in the palm of my hand. I feel in some way that I have possessed my brother com-pletely as I run through the house and find Maggie. I understand that I am the lone hero in an incident of which the retelling will no doubt be twice as dramatic as the event itself.

When I find my mother, I hold my brother's finger out to her and she screams hysterically, "Get that thing away from me!"

The finger is eventually sewn back on. Eddie loses the use of it for-ever but he is grateful to me for having helped him retain the aesthet-ics of a hand. For weeks afterward he is treated to an endless supply of ice cream and awed kindness, though Maggie has been rendered nearly incoherent and has come to rely extravagantly on the mysteri-ous little pills she keeps in the pocket of her apron.

One day, I happen upon her in her bathroom. Her hair is dishev-eled. Her face pinched. She does not know I am there. She opens the medicine cabinet, her hands trembling. Inside are dozens of prescrip-tion pills lined up in neat little rows. I feel my heart skip a beat. There is something wrong here. I wonder if she is dying.

"Maggie?" I say. "Mom?"

She turns around, startled. Then she smiles. It is a smile of kindness and superiority. It is a smile which is impossible to translate.

"Does Dr. Hearn give you all those pills?" I ask. I am afraid to ask her what I really want to know—if she has cancer or leukemia or something equally mysterious and terrifying.

"Oh, *ma petite*," she says. "There are two secrets one must never reveal. The first is one's age and the second is the name of one's drug dealer. Reputations being what they are."

She leans over, puckers my cheeks and kisses me on the lips. I smell her tonic scent and the Chanel No. 5 she dabs on her wrists every morning. I have no idea what she's talking about. I retreat from the dominion of her bedroom knowing I have stumbled onto a grave secret that she has carefully smoldered by a rare and electric little kiss on the lips.

One day later two gregarious relatives on Harold's side, both from the East Coast, stop by for the afternoon on their day's layover to Hawaii. They bring Eddie a New York Yankees baseball cap and a Star of David necklace, which he puts around his neck and never removes again. It is then that I understand the power that symbols have over my brother.

One by one, in order of age, we are:

Harold Goldblum, Margaret Magdalena Goldblum—parents.

Eddie Goldblum, Martin Goldblum, Esther Goldblum, Mary Goldblum—siblings.

Then there's me, Louise Goldblum.

Our parents are born in 1925 and 1932 respectively.

Harold Goldblum is the unwilling offspring of German immigrant parents and is raised a strict Jew in the Orthodox tradition. When the youngest of his two sisters dies during a rampant typhoid epidemic that sweeps through the Brooklyn ghetto where they live, his father, my grandfather, turns away from God forever. His mother does not, so like his own children, Harold Goldblum matures in an environment of religious ambivalence, characterized by episodes of extreme religious passion always tempered by a certain hatred for God.

In 1941, at the age of sixteen, he is accepted at Harvard with plans to earn his medical degree. He is young enough to be impressed by the upper-class snobbery of the Bostonian elite, but when he is rebuffed by the sister of a classmate not just because he is a Jew but because he is *too Jewish looking,* he is finally demoralized enough to leave Harvard in his third year and finish his education at the State University of New York at Albany.

It is there that he meets his wife, our mother, a Catholic from Pittsburgh who is the first in her family of eight girls to have a greater ambition other than to marry and reproduce. She is studying to be the next best thing for a woman at that time—a nurse—when she meets Harold in the doorway of the organic chemistry lecture hall.

After three dates he promises her the West Coast, where a job is already waiting for him at the laboratory of human virus research at Stanford University. Tired of the Pittsburgh winters, her father's alcoholic violence and the cloying scents of perfumes, hair sprays and lipsticks that have dominated her life (not to mention the threat of spinsterhood in a family of seven married sisters), she gives up her education to marry and reproduce.

Perhaps the bitterness that characterizes the marriage of our parents begins when Margaret Magdalena's mother, who has a phobia of hell, insists that her daughter be married beneath the eyes of Jesus, and Harold's mother refuses to attend the Catholic ceremony.

Since my accidental deposit on this planet, I can only say that their marriage has consisted of plate-throwing, door-slamming fights, periods of remorse followed by the anguish of missed opportunities—Harold, who bemoans the medical degree he never got and Maggie, who won't admit that she sold her soul and threw away her education in order to escape what, in truth, she could never truly escape.

Among the offspring, it is true that we all, except perhaps Mary, share one trait, and that is our ability to eat as much as we want, whenever we want without ever gaining weight. But that is as far as our similarities go. The boys look equally like our parents, Martin more so than Eddie, whose genes miraculously tricked the rest of his body into playing down the worst of their features and accenting the best. Martin is by far the ugliest of the Goldblums, having inherited Harold's potato nose and Maggie's thin, flyaway hair. He is also the most ambitious. When he is six, he builds an erector set house complete with indoor plumbing and electric lighting. Later, in a spurt of hormonal anger and indifference, he embarks on a two-year serial murder spree, shooting birds and small rodent-type animals with a BB gun and a slingshot. He spends afternoons stuffing them with the precision of a professional taxidermist. We can always tell where he is by the smell of animal flesh and blood that accompanies him from room to room, and to this day I cannot smell rubbing alcohol without thinking of small animal pelts pinned to wooden boards.

At the age of forty-two, Martin will develop a synthetic drug that mimics the benefits of certain medications found in the gallbladders of bears. This will be his effort to both atone for his past and to stop the senseless slaughter of grizzly bears, having long since abandoned the notion that there is anything noble in destroying life.

Esther, dead now, is tall and dark. She is keenly intelligent and exquisitely emotional. She feels everything intensely and angers easily, particularly when she believes she is misunderstood. For this reason, she has a tendency toward high passion and relentless overexplanation, which has the effect of wearing her opponents down. Of all us Goldblums she is the most sexual and loves to talk about it in a nasty, exciting way. Sometime after the death of Danny Franconi she vows never to marry and never to have children, and devotes her life to journalism and sex. She is beautiful in a tough way, filled with hard, inquisitive expressions and enough angles to taunt certain theories of geometry. One day she will write a story for a San Francisco publication about college kids squatting in an abandoned tenement. She will return home, like them, addicted to heroin, with a tattoo of an angel on her left arm. But within a few weeks she will be clean again and capable of writing a story that will eventually win an award for journalistic excellence.

When she is thirty-two, *The New York Times*, her employer, finally assigns her to South Africa, something she has coveted for nearly two years. The day after she is supposed to have left, she is found in a roadside motel, on the outskirts of an old ghost town in the Sierra foothills, her body in a state of repose, a single bullet wound to the head. Her clothes are found neatly folded on a chair. There are no signs that she struggled. There are no witnesses and no arrests. The case remains open, a vast, immutable desert of questions.

After we bury her, Harold insists that Maggie cover all the mirrors in the house and sit shiva with him which, in a rare gesture of partnership and respect, she does. It is no mystery that Esther is Harold's favorite.

Mary, the youngest before me and the only one beside me who escaped the strong pull of conflicting religions, is the only female I have known that, when describing her, I would use the words *love* and *respect* in the same sentence. This is not because I have never loved or respected other women but rather because I have never experienced both feelings at one time for any woman other than her.

She does not have the Goldblum height nor the exceptional lean-ness. She did not inherit any of the negative traits associated with our clan—rage, moodiness, overbearing curiosity and a savage, Darwinian sort of intelligence that enables the rest of us to bulldoze our way through adversity. But she is prone, in ways the rest of us are not, to outbursts of unadulterated empathy and long periods—a lifetime actually—of sustained kindness.

Mary is best described in this way. In October 1993, she will wrap her arms around me and whisper gently, "Oh you poor, sweet angel," not the least bit fazed by the fact that I have just been released from jail, with a bloody lip and a black eye, on my own recognizance.

2

Z e k e had no hair. Naturally I noticed this first. He had a scar over his mouth, which gave the impression of a harelip, but to my relief later that night when I decided I would fuck him, it was not a harelip. He had three gold hoops in his left ear and a small diamond in his nose. He wore black army boots. But this was not what I was immediately drawn to. On his left arm was a tattoo of an angel. I focused on it like a zoom lens.

"What are you staring at?" he said to me. He had left his table of scary-looking guys—a ragtag ensemble of goatees, tattoos and piercings—and stood at the edge of our table. He was truly menacing though vaguely familiar. I could see the fear on Alice's face as he fixed his eyes on me. In a complicated medley of shame and eroticism, I thought briefly of Mrs. Kowolski, whose large red nipples were still an inextricable part of my sexual fantasies.

"Nothing," I said. I looked down at my left hand, which was holding a cigarette, one of the new habits I acquired post-Esther, and saw that it was trembling slightly.

"Bullshit," he said. He lifted my chin up with surprising tenderness. His hand was strong and white, the veins thick with blood. It was a gesture that didn't match the threat in his voice. "You're staring at something, man. Own up."

"Your tattoo," I said. I heard my voice tremble, an egregious mistake, something Esther, I am sure, would never have done. The electricity of her, the way she voyaged fleetingly through my mind, snapped me out of my fear. My subsequent and immediate rage, buoyed by a pack of Kool Milds and several vodkas straight up, gave me courage.

"I'm staring at your fucking tattoo," I said, testing the waters.

His eyes narrowed and he looked like he might strike me at any moment. Far from being afraid, I was intrigued, a response that fascinated me. I took a sip of my drink, a puff of my cigarette and felt Esther's soul inhabit mine. I attempted to stare him down. He never relented and I felt my face turning hot, then red. I was grateful that the bar Alice and I chose to get drunk in that night was very, very dark.

"What'sa matter. You have a thing for angels?"

"No," I said.

He pulled a chair out from under the table, turned it around and sat down so that his legs were on either side of the back rest and his arms draped over the top. He never smiled though I kept expecting him to. Alice kept taking nervous sips of her drink, but it was clear that as far as Zeke was concerned, Alice was not in the room. I glanced at her and could tell instantly that she despised him. He continued to stare at me then slid his finger across my cheek. I felt something stir between my legs. It was then that Alice stood up and rolled her eyes toward the bathroom, indicating that I should follow her there.

" 'Scuse me," I said. I stood up but he grabbed my arm, twisting the skin with his hands. I did not let him see that he had hurt me.

"I'll meet you at the door in five minutes," he said as Alice marched away unaware.

I followed Alice to the bathroom without saying anything.

"Jesus H.," she said. She tapped her long, painted fingernails on the sink quickly, like she was playing an imaginary piano. She bent over and examined her teeth in the mirror, wiping away an invisible smudge of lipstick. "How come we attract all the weirdos?"

"I kinda liked him."

She looked at me to gauge the degree of my seriousness. When she saw that I was, in fact, serious, she dissolved into paroxysms of groans and eyeball rolls.

Alice is my best friend, the unfailing rock upon which I have flung myself on more than one occasion. She is everything I have never been.

Number one, she is beautiful. Her hair is blond, she has green eyes and strangely dark eyebrows. Her skin is the color of wheat and her body extremely voluptuous. She has big boobs.

Number two, she is practical and linear in all her thoughts and actions. She never gets hysterical even when situations, as far as I am concerned, demand it. This is best exemplified by her response to the time she flew to Arizona and the plane crashed on takeoff, killing three people onboard. She left the site of the crash as quickly as possible so she could catch the next plane out. Because of this steely countenance she is the one person I would like to have by my side during a kidnaping or a riot.

Number three, she has a rigid set of personal standards about which she is unrelenting and implacable. These standards are not steeped in morality, but as would be expected, practicality. For instance, she never sleeps with anyone until several months of demonstrated affection and commitment take place, after which time the party in question is expected to test for all sexually transmitted diseases and report back to her with proof of his freedom from disease. This helps explain why she never gets laid.

And last of all, she never lies, even when it would clearly spare another's feelings, because that way, she says, she doesn't have to keep track of anything. But, as if to make up for this minor streak of selfishness, she is always loyal and forgiving of others and believes that you achieve the highest state of grace when a friend begins a sentence for the first time with the words, "Don't tell anyone but . . ."

Now she looked at me, having recovered from her seizures of shock and disgust and said, "He'll hurt you, Louise. Mark my words. I bet if you asked him, he'd admit to torturing helpless little animals. Just look at him, for God's sake. He looks like the kind of asshole who uses the word *cunt* to describe a woman. I'm not kidding. This is no laughing matter. You shouldn't drink if this is gonna be the result."

"He intrigues me," I said. I lit a cigarette. "He told me to meet him outside in five minutes."

"Don't go," she said, touching my arm in a way that made me see she was serious and a little afraid for me. She had been this way for the nearly nine months since my sister died, unsure how to grapple with what she once called my alarming new penchant for one-night stands and vodka for breakfast. She had taken to inspecting me when she thought I couldn't see her, filling my cupboards up with food when I was out, leaving three or four messages on my answering machine when she hadn't heard from me in a while. She would often say, "You never acted like this before," referring to the fact that since my sister's death I had acquired a habit of being late, sleeping through entire days and picking up men with tattoos and earrings. I would hug her for this protectiveness if I were not a Goldblum. Instead, the more Alice tried to steer me from harm, the more I became convinced that I did not need to be protected.

Briefly our eyes caught in the mirror. She saw something in my expression that made her eyes flick away. She clasped her purse shut with a certain finality. On her way out the door she said, "Just don't let me find you in a goddamned alley with a baseball bat up your vagina."

I stayed in the bathroom for another minute. I smoked my cigarette and stared at my face. My lips looked drawn and colorless. I was aware of a slight smudge of darkness—not quite circles—beneath my eyes. I looked less like Esther than I would have liked, though my brain was aware that on some level my memory made her more beautiful than she actually was, more exotic and gargantuan in her excess of courage and her cravings for danger.

Before I left the bathroom to meet Zeke, I watched myself blow smoke through my nose the way Esther did when she wanted to annoy Maggie and I almost believed I was looking at her. I leaned over and kissed the mirror, leaving behind the imprint of my lips on the glass.

"See ya," I whispered.

Zeke was standing by the door of the bar when I walked out. He seemed completely unconcerned by the rain. His trench coat flapped around his ankles. His expression did not change when he saw me. He just grabbed my elbow and led me to his car.

"Where are we going?"

"You either trust me or you don't," he said.

"I don't."

"Then it should be more thrilling for you."

I got in the car with him. Old Toyota, vinyl seats, crystal hanging from the mirror. The fluorescent streetlights made his face look iridescent. The mood exacted by the car, his ghostly face and the rain pelting the windshield reminded me of the sculpture back at my studio, the one sitting there, unfinished. Incense and cigarette smells mingled with the scent of rain.

"Where are we going?"

He was driving up Divisadero and had turned left on Fell. The police traced a call Esther had made to Martin on the night of her murder; it originated from a pay phone at a liquor store on Fell not far from Divisadero. When they asked Martin what Esther had said, he smiled. "Nothing important," he'd said. "She wanted to know whether my current girlfriend had set the house on fire yet."

I thought of Esther standing there in the cold while the man who killed her bought some liquor. I pictured her calling Martin. It was not unusual for her to call one of us periodically to reveal nothing in particular. I had an image of her impatience as she stood there in the cold, smoking, tapping her nails on the phone, waiting for the man to be done with his purchase so he could take her away and fuck her.

"Do you believe in hell?" Zeke asked. He lit a cigarette. He did not use his hands when smoking. He exhaled smoke through his nose, the cigarette gripped between his lips.

"Yes," I said. I thought of the old homestead, of Esther's ghost inhabiting it completely. That was a kind of hell. I thought of the ghoulish hell that Catholics had, of all those fires and horned beasts. I thought that hell was more a state of mind than a place. "In a manner of speaking, I think there is a hell."

"You were going to make some witty comment," he said. "I can tell by the way you paused before answering. You were going to repeat something you read in a clever book on popular culture. Something like, 'Hell is a state of mind.' I can tell you're the clever type. Possibly an overachiever." He stared at me with heroic menace, taking his eyes off the road for an alarmingly long time.

"Are you going to kill me?"

"I don't usually go that far," he said. He turned right on Stanyon, then right again and pulled his car onto the sidewalk in front of a massive, dilapidated Victorian with a turret and peeling paint.

"Because if you plan on killing me," I continued, "Alice knows I'm with you and she says if she finds me in an alley with a baseball bat up my you know what, she'll cut your . . ."

"Now that's interesting," he said. He rubbed his chin, mockingly introspective. Then abruptly he opened the car door and told me, not unpleasantly, to get the fuck out of the car. I was not afraid. I don't know why, because my brothers and sisters, Esther especially, have always teased me for being the Goldblum coward.

We walked inside the entry, a spooky hallway of white alabaster and gnarled antique chandeliers that gave off a muted yellow glow. There was a library smell of books and dank air about the building that made me feel melancholy. I looked up at the elaborate staircase that spiraled into a domed ceiling. He took my hand and we walked up the stairs. I turned around in time to see one of the tenants open the door and stare at us, then close it again slowly, the hinges howling in the otherwise silent lobby.

"Casa Vincent Price," I said.

He snickered in a strange way, without smiling. His coat was wet and smelled like Harry the Dog. As we walked up the stairs I thought of all the people I knew who had died. Harry the Dog, not a person exactly but not a dog either, ran into a moving truck when I was eleven. Mr. Kowolski was electrocuted while pruning the hedges by his swimming pool. Danny Franconi died when his motorcycle went off a cliff in the Santa Cruz mountains. Then there was Esther.

"Of all the people I know who have died, not one of them has done so gracefully," I said.

He stopped for a minute and turned around. He was two steps above me, looking down at me. He appeared to be amazed, though I was not sure why. Then he walked on.

"Are you normally this weird?" he asked.

"This is one of my good nights," I said.

We got to his apartment on the top floor and went inside. He did not turn on any lights at first and all I could see was a long hallway and, at the end, a huge bay window and the lights of the city flickering through it. The same smell in his car was in his apartment, a strange, bitter aroma of spices and cigarettes. He went into a room on the left and turned on the light. I looked inside and saw an immaculate kitchen filled, to my surprise, with beautiful old furniture. Several dishes were stacked neatly in the drainer. A large, black-and-white photograph of the backside of a naked woman hung on the wall over the sink. She was lying on a bed, her hands bound behind her. He saw me looking at it.

"Lisa Silburner, nineteen eighty-eight," he said.

There were more. As we moved through the apartment, a studio furnished improbably with elegant antiques, I noticed dozens of photographs, mostly of Lisa Silburner in various states of bondage. In the bathroom there were two photographs, one of a penis, the other a vagina. I wondered if they were Zeke's and Lisa Silburner's but could not bring myself to ask, to imagine knowing.

In the main room was a large, neatly made bed. Above it was Lisa Silburner again but this time fully dressed, wearing a hat with a large flower on the front. She was smiling, her lips slightly parted and her prominent nose flaring. Her hair was red and wild. Her eyes, dark and inscrutable. She was oddly beautiful.

"Your girlfriend?" I asked.

He took his coat off and stared out the window.

"Not really," he said.

He hung his coat up in an old armoire. Before closing the doors, I saw a shelf full of camera equipment. Next to the bed was a door with a sign in bold letters: DARK ROOM. YOU FUCKING OPEN THE DOOR, I FUCKING KILL YOU.

There was a large poster on the main wall. ZEKE HEIRHOLM. JULY 13TH THROUGH JULY 19TH. Below the words was a black-and-white photograph of two hookers standing beneath a Guess jeans billboard depicting a hooker wearing Guess jeans. The Guess model did not appear to be as quietly desperate as the real hookers. Under the picture was the address of a gallery on Gough Street.

"Are you a photographer?" I asked.

He stared at me. Then he lit a cigarette and sat down on the edge of the bed. Stupid question.

"I like tying women up," he said. "It's my thing. I'm telling you that now before you take your clothes off because I'm a decent guy. But once you take your clothes off you've agreed to go the distance. I might hurt you. I haven't killed anyone. Not yet. The safe word is *cease*. You say cease, I stop. Stop does not mean stop. No does not mean no. Cease means no. Cease means stop. Do you understand? We can start slow. But we don't stay slow. Not over the long haul."

It sounded like a job interview. But I hardly knew what he was talking about. I lit a cigarette. My hands were trembling.

"You got anything to drink around here?"

He produced a bottle of something and two shot glasses. He handed me one of the glasses. There was an image of a cable car on its surface. I drank the contents. Ouzo. I thought about calling a cab. I looked at the picture of Lisa Silburner, 1988, fully clothed, of the contempt in her beautiful face.

I remembered how my brother Eddie had told me he was "eradicating" just moments before he hacked his finger off. I thought about how some things have their own momentum, their own way of launching forward, pushing aside the cluttered flotsam of all expectation. Progress is not linear, I thought.

"No black eyes," I said, unbuttoning my jeans. "I got an appointment tomorrow."

And for the first time that night he smiled.

I woke up the next morning to blinding white light, sun straining through fog, the smell of coffee, cigarettes and come. My wrists were sore from the straps Zeke had used to tie them to the bedposts. There were tiny welts on my back and legs. Despite a gaggle of past boyfriends and my recent forays into the bedrooms of strangers, before Zeke the only orgasms I'd managed were from the labor of my own hands. Now I had entered a new terrain of caustic pleasure. The hangover rounded out my terror.

I sat up in bed, reached for my cigarettes and lit one just as Zeke came into the room. He was naked and it was the first time I really saw his body. Pale, thin and hairless, its angularity was arrogant. He had large white feet and hands, with raised purple veins creating tiny crests and valleys on his skin. The goatee around his chin was reddish and stubbly. He had magnificent, unnervingly dark eyes that revealed nothing. In another time, he would have repulsed me.

"Do you know who Kevin Carter was?" he asked. He took a sip of his coffee.

I said no.

"He was South African. Many critics thought he was a brilliant photographer."

Zeke stood there, forcing me to gaze again at his strangely translucent body, its taut compartments of flesh and bone. He went to the armoire where the night before he had hung his coat and now opened a drawer. He pulled out a manila envelope and brought it back to the bed. He reached in and pulled out a copy of a photograph. It was a grim picture of a vulture patiently waiting near the fallen, frail body of a starving child. It was obvious what would happen to the girl when she finally died.

"He took this photograph and won the Pulitzer for it. After he took the picture, he chased the vulture away but he remained there crying and smoking cigarettes for a long time. Sometime later, he killed himself."

"That's an amazing picture," I said.

He threw it on the bed with disgust. "It's shit," he said. "Anyone could have taken it. It takes no great artist to shoot a picture like this. He just happened to be in the right place at the right time."

I was taken aback by his passion, the way his voice took on a new flame of intensity. He looked at me with a searing expression. "The real artist, the true artist, would have thrown his camera down and wept. It's no wonder he eventually killed himself."

I pulled the covers off the bed and wrapped myself in them. I went to the bathroom with the penis and the vagina on the wall. Before I had a chance to sit down on the toilet, Zeke was there. He pulled the blanket away from me and looked at my body with blazing disinterest. Then, as if disgusted, he turned around and left the room. A few minutes later, I heard him say, "Lock the fucking door when you leave." And then I heard the door close behind him.

I got dressed in a hurry, noticing bloodstains on the sheets and, for the first time, comprehending that the abrasions on my wrists were directly associated with the ties that still dangled from the bedposts. I felt the beginning of the dark days, the pinpoints of light obstructing my vision. I had an unreasonable urge for Maggie's cool hands, the smell of dishwashing soap, cigarettes, vodka.

My hangover—a meteor of lights flashing in the periphery of my vision—reminded me of my drunkenness the night before, sealing the sense that last night had happened without me. My body had been there. A body representing me had been tied to the bed frame. But I had not. I looked for my purse, found it and reached for the Fiorinal. I took two.

I looked around the apartment, my vision blackened around the edges by the onset of the migraine. Some camera equipment was on the table by the bed and, next to it, a notebook with the number 10 on the cover. I opened the notebook and read on the first page:

I've been noticing her. Her red hair. So beautiful. She has a friend, a beauty too, but not devastating. Not hungry. The redhead gets little attention when they are out together. But to me, she is ravenous. Something trails her, something haunts. She mystifies me. Will she acquiesce? Will she tumble? Something has been taken from her. Something is taken from all the girls. That is what makes them beautiful.

I felt the blood rush to my head, the pulsing of heat against my temples. I thought of Lisa Silburner and wondered whether he was writing about her. Or me.

Another entry read:

I think I may have found the next one. (Redhead) Her unusual beauty grows out of her coyness. She is like a fawn in the clothes of a bear. You look at her, you think, She'll break in half. She'll let you break her in half. You think, This girl is as delicate as snow. She seems hungry for annihilation. A terrible drinker. Too drunk, too easily. Silence is her best face. When she talks or laughs her expression becomes hysterical and unstable. That smile of hers. Wretched, horrid smile, like something she forces. I'll take her in B/W. Wide angle (so skinny). Catch her when she grips her head like that. She must have some terrible pain. Something happened to her. She is inconsolable. Not brave at all. Fuckable.

I closed the book, my heart pounding. I looked around the apartment, afraid suddenly that I was being watched, that maybe he hadn't actually left. The luxury of drink was not having to see. But now the curtain had been raised and my gooseflesh marched across my arms, encouraged by the horror of waking up bloody in a strange man's apartment.

I saw that the apartment was well kept and furnished in a neat and controlled way. I got the feeling that if you moved a chair even one inch from its spot, he would notice and it would make him angry. I made the bed, afraid of it. Had I slept in that bed? Had I been here at all? I went to the mirror that hung over his desk. I held up my hands to see them and feel tangible but was startled by the welts on my wrists. I remembered the pain, how it made me feel alive. More real.

I took a breath and looked around at the impressive collection of modern art, some of it by people I had studied with at school. Most of the walls though were embellished with photography. The images were spare, most black and white, the subject matter usually of people in various indoor locations. Bathrooms seemed to fascinate him but he also liked pictures of people eating food like hamburgers and fries and pie. One wall was devoted entirely to people drinking, in bars, out of paper sacks on street corners, in their own kitchens, on airplanes or in cars and trains. It was always booze. They were always people who looked like they had seen better times. They were always the desperate.

There was hardly any clothing in his closet, which gave me a strange sense of relief. There was other evidence throughout the apartment of an austere life. I looked in his medicine cabinet, taking him for the type who might like speed, little white pills, meth. But there were no pill bottles, no signs of stained mirrors, no rolled-up dollar bills. Not even aspirin. I found only a tube of Crest toothpaste, a razor and a can of shaving cream. His refrigerator was nearly empty except for a carton of milk, a carton of eggs and a block of orange cheese. All dairy products, I noticed. His freezer was filled with ice, a carton of blueberry sorbet and something wrapped in plastic with a piece of masking tape over it and the words *one mallard*. I pictured bird claws, a green neck, beady eyes. There were a few cans of food in the cupboards, but for the most part the cupboards too were practically empty. An unopened bottle of Ouzo stood on the counter next to a bottle of Joy dishwashing liquid. I had half a mind to take the Ouzo.

On the counter was an issue of *Guns & Ammo* and a book called *Thirty Ways to Skin a Cat*. A bowl of quarters on the windowsill was filled to the brim and the apartment was so silent and perfect that I had the urge to fling the coins across the room.

On my way out the door, I stopped again to look at the picture of Lisa Silburner, bound and lying nude on a bed of rumpled white sheets and blankets. It was not a picture inspired by love. I left vowing to make Zeke Heirholm just one more fuck to be forgotten.

3

T h e bright sun and taffy blue sky belied the cold that managed to worm its way under my skin. The Fiorinal wrestled with my migraine, picked it up and pinned it down so that it thumped limply from what felt like the bottom of my brain. The drug also took the edge off my dizziness, my hangover. I settled into mist. I walked through a bewildered sunshine. The nearest bus would take me somewhere. I only knew I wanted to get away. Home. I would figure out how to get there when the time came for it. Huddled against the cold, shivering, I looked at my wrists again, then planted them deep in the pockets of my coat where I touched the edges of my Muni pass. A street bum, his hair a tangled fish net, said what sounded like "Diogenes will set you free." He gazed at me, not seeing me, and I once again had the feeling that I had disappeared.

When I got on the bus I sat near an old Chinese woman whose face was wrinkled like a dried apple. She clutched a worn patent leather purse on her lap and wore a heavy brown coat and a pair of galoshes. The smell of decay and age hovered around her like a withered twin. She stared straight ahead, dignified. I watched a fly, wondering how a fly could survive such cold, travel up her leg. I remembered how my brother Martin told me when we were children that everywhere a fly went, it left behind its shit.

I willed myself to stay present, to stay there, to forget about Zeke, the ties that dangled from the bed, the orgasm. Not my orgasm, not something belonging to me which I gave up, but *an* orgasm, *the* orgasm, the rapid firing of neurons in a brain that belonged to the night, to that other place, that other body which craved—what had he written?—annihilation.

Had he been writing of me?

Getting home seemed to take forever. I had to transfer at Market and take BART to Mission. Stepping back above ground, after being in the damp, muggy subway, I felt the cold like a slap in the face. My studio, one of four in a dilapidated old building on Howard, never seemed more inviting. When I got there, I saw immediately that the door was slightly ajar so I pushed it open, unafraid. With the level of my disgrace and horror, I was not afraid of being killed by maniac robbers. But when I walked into the studio it was just Alice standing there, looking at the half-finished sculpture in the center of the room. At her feet was a plastic bag from Safeway bursting with vegetables. She was wearing some ridiculous plaid pants and a bright orange shirt. I walked in before she had time to erase the apprehension on her face. For an instant I saw the sculpture through her eyes. I could understand her concern.

"I don't get it," she said. "It's a garbage can."

"Yes, but you're an accountant so you're not expected to understand."

She gave me a dirty look. She hated when I brought up her profession as if embarking on such a course in life was something only savages did. To soften the accusation I added, "Besides, you haven't looked inside."

"But I have. I don't understand why you would put a sculpture of your sister in there with that motorcycle. None of it makes sense."

"It's not Esther, per se," I said. "It's her body. It's the garbagey way death disrespected her body."

I lit a cigarette. I was home. There was vodka. I was flush with smokes.

"Not death," I said. "The way she was murdered is what I mean. And the motorcycle. It's just about dying violently. Some people, most people, don't die in a cesspool, you know. Most people get to live a long life and then they just wither away peacefully or get zonked out on morphine while the cancer eats them up. Chomp, chomp. But others die in a conflagration of unexpected violence. It's my way of refuting the existence of God."

She rolled her eyes, disregarding me. She had a habit of shoveling my drama away with her eyeballs.

"But it's a likeness of your sister, for heaven's sake, Louise. Can't you show her more respect?"

"My sister's dead, Alice." I looked at the bag of vegetables near her feet. "I wish you'd stop trying to make me eat that shit. What's wrong with Top Ramen?"

She smiled morosely and sat down on the tattered couch I'd rescued from People's Park my first year at Berkeley and, out of a mysterious sense of loyalty, have lugged around with me ever since.

"You need your roughage," she said.

"Roughage. What is that? It sounds like a state of mind."

"Oh forget it. And anyway, I came over here to make sure you were still alive. How was it with that weirdo who I cannot believe you went home with? I hope you used a condom at least."

"He lives in a creepy old haunted Victorian with turrets. And he's obsessed with someone named Lisa Silburner. Otherwise the night was uneventful. He's a photographer."

I didn't want to tell her about the bondage thing. But more than that, I did not want her to know what I feared the most: that Zeke's cold depravity appealed to me. It was as if I had merely been passing time, waiting for him to come along and steal me from myself. I could not tell her these things because I did not understand them myself. The most confusing part was that the farther away from him I got, the weaker grew my resolve never to see him again.

Alice shrugged and half-kicked the bag of vegetables in my direction from her place on the couch.

"You probably don't remember, but I met her."

"Who?"

"Esther."

I tried to think when that might have happened. I thought back to the first time I saw Alice at Berkeley. She was reading a book called *Abstracts in Statistical Analysis*. A cigarette dangled from her lips and she wore old-fashioned granny glasses with thick, brown frames. Her blonde hair cascaded down her back. She was lying on her belly in the sun on a red-checked picnic blanket. A guy next to her was rubbing her back. He leaned over and whispered something to her and she smacked him across the face. He seemed amazed. His eyes were wide like pool balls. She sat up, speaking to him excitedly through the beautiful clenched teeth that kept her cigarette in place. Then she got up and walked away.

Two years later, after I failed my quantitative reasoning requirement, I hired a tutor. Graduating depended on passage. In she walked, dazzling me with her nearly preposterous beauty. I remembered her instantly.

"I saw you slap a guy once," I told her.

"Really?" she asked. She seemed surprised. "How unlike me."

Our association was brisk, not unfriendly but short lived, punctuated by brief spells of uncontrollable laughter and surprising moments of intimacy. Her personality was an appealing mixture of flamboyance and prudishness that I could tell baffled men and caused women to distrust her. That, and the fact that her brain got me through statistics, was the driving force behind my respect for her.

Six months before Esther's death, Alice and I met up again by chance in a Castro Street coffeehouse. We ended up talking all night. She said she admired my work and had seen my last installation at the North Beach Gallery where I regularly showed. She asked me whether I had passed statistics. I told her yes, but only because of her. After that, we met for lunch from time to time or for coffee and hot buttery croissants on cold Sunday mornings when it was clear the fog would not disappear and we had nothing better to do.

When Esther died, at my request, she came to the funeral and told the caterers where to put things, even though she had no idea where they should have gone. Maggie and Harold seemed grateful not to have to tend to such details and at one point, I saw Maggie uncharacteristically kiss Alice's cheek, a gesture which stirred up a brief, violent moment of jealousy. Later that night, after a collision with a bottle of Johnnie Walker, my first taste of alcohol in twenty-one years, I rested my head in Alice's lap and cried.

For some reason, after that Alice attached herself to me completely, passionately, phoning me every couple of days, feeding me. On bad nights, she'd arrive unbidden, as if some sixth sense made her aware that I was not able to sleep, that my head hurt, that I was lying around inside my studio like a shipwreck. She'd remark on how much I had changed, how square I used to be. Sometimes she'd just sit there and relay to me the weird stories she'd read in the newspapers: a man who assaulted his wife with a frozen squirrel; or a place near Fresno where people were constantly being kidnapped by aliens. And one night, after we had polished off a bottle of peppermint schnapps, she told me a story about a cactus that was filled with deadly spiders and how it exploded in the living room of an elderly widow, depositing millions of tiny, black, venomous spiders all over her body and killing her and her two rare cockatiels.

I looked at her now and tried to put a timeline on it. I was dismayed. It did not seem possible that she had met my sister and I said as much.

"I didn't think you'd remember, even though, as I recall, you never drank or smoked or used any brain-cell-murdering drugs back then."

"Alice, quit playing games. When did you meet her?"

"I had come over to tutor you. It was one of our last sessions and your boyfriend was there."

"Joe Torres."

"I don't know. That guy who was half Spanish."

"Joe Torres. And he was half Mexican. How come I don't remember this?"

"And Esther came barreling in, all awhirl . . ."

"Awhirl?"

". . . with perfume and bracelets and that jet black hair. God, what a beauty. And she said she'd just spoken to some visiting dignitary who asked her out after the interview and everyone laughed and Joe was going gaga over her."

She got up and went to the fridge. She looked inside, then closed the door and came back into the room. She lit a cigarette.

"I don't remember," I said. "I mean, she visited me a few times. I vaguely remember, I guess."

"You had been dating that Joe guy who was half Arab or something."

"Mexican, Alice. His father was Mexican."

"And you were so in love with him."

"Yeah," I said, because I had been and it was my first time feeling such a thing. He was only the third lover I'd ever had. He was beautiful and dignified and angry. He liked to play Parcheesi in bed and read books about Mexican cattle rustlers and California Gold Rush–era prostitutes. He did not push himself on me, the way the other two had. Instead, he drew my body out of me, he played me. He seemed to love me and then one day, he seemed to stop loving me.

"I never had the heart to tell you," she said.

"Tell me what?"

Alice went to the window and looked out. It had begun to drizzle and she traced a line in the steam that had formed on the glass. I watched her draw on her cigarette. I saw the tension coming off her back, the way her shoulders were rigid and her neck taut. For the longest time she said nothing. Then she stubbed out her cigarette and faced me. The expression on her face—it seemed like a mixture of sorrow and pity—gave me gooseflesh. I felt myself getting hot, then unbearably cold. I thought for a moment of Zeke, of being crushed beneath him. I grabbed the blanket beside me on the couch and wrapped it around me.

"We only had a couple more sessions to go and your final was coming up," she said. She spoke softly and gently, which was unusual for her. "Your sister was staying with you. God, she was fantastic. Like some warrior princess. But you know, I didn't much like her. I admired her. But there was something . . ."

"Oh?"

For some reason my heart started to make its presence known in the prison of my rib cage. I touched it briefly, felt it pumping, felt myself sustained by it. If it stopped I would die, cease, disappear. *Stop does not mean stop. No does not mean no.*

"Don't get me wrong. I liked her, you know. I just didn't really care for her that much."

"Alice, you didn't know her."

"In a way I did."

I stood up. My heart, the way it pumped, bothered me. It seemed to hinder me, to drag me down. A ball and chain, me and my heart. I thought of Joe and of the way he touched me. He had kind hands and was passionate about my body. He said my angles were daunting and beautiful. He kissed every bone and pledged himself to my skin. One night he took a Magic Marker and traced my body on the sheets.

"What are you trying to tell me?"

She peered into the garbage can where my replica of Esther lay. My heart pounded.

"I saw her and Joe. They were kissing one day. They were kissing. They weren't hiding anything. They just sat there in Sproul Plaza, kissing."

I felt the chain snap. My heart fell into the abyss.

"You must have been mistaken, Alice. Jesus."

She said nothing. I couldn't look at her.

"Esther would never have done that," I said.

Alice and I exchanged glances. She looked away first and dragged on her cigarette. Then she turned away from the statue of my sister in the garbage can.

"You're probably right," she said.

She touched the top of Esther's head. Normally I wouldn't have tolerated it—someone touching my work—but now I watched her glide her slender finger tenderly across the sculpted cheekbones of my dead sister, an inscrutable expression on her face. She walked around the entire sculpture, impervious to my glaring eyes, lost in some kind of thought.

"Your sister was beautiful," Alice said, tracing the face of the statue. "But there was something wrong, Louise. I can't put my finger on it. There was something wrong."

I felt the hairs rise on the back of my neck.

"How the hell would you know?"

She turned and looked at me.

"I saw them together myself, Louise. I'm sorry. I'm not mistaken."

"You know," I said. I walked over to her and put myself between her and the garbage can. She stepped back instantly. "There's a difference between telling the truth and having integrity. You've made that difference pretty clear to me, just this second."

"I'm sorry," she said. I knew she couldn't help it. She did not mean to be cruel. It was her honest streak, a transmitter of truth that most humans knew how to keep in check, transmitting out of bounds.

"Let's just stop this. All this talking about Esther. Jesus." I said. I went to the kitchen and pulled a bottle of vodka from the freezer. Alice looked at me doubtfully and for an instant said nothing.

"God, what an asshole I am. Louise, I'm sorry."

"Forget about it," I said. "Anyhow, I need to work."

I poured a glass of vodka and drank it down. It wasn't even noon.

"Sure," she said. "Tonight? Are we still having dinner?"

"Yeah," I said. "Call me before dark."

She left the studio. My head was pounding. I wanted to sit down and mull it over but every time I tried to get a handle on Esther fucking my boyfriend—the way it slugged me in the gut—I seemed to lose it. It was like catching molecules, this concept of Esther fucking Joe Torres, the only guy who took the time to trace my body on the sheets. The only one who drew my love out of me instead of pouncing on it and smothering it. Esther.

I looked at the sculpture. My installation had gone nowhere so far. A dead sister, a garbage can, a motorcycle. On the floor beside them was a large cardboard box filled with Martin's dead stuffed animals. Squirrels, rats, mice, frogs, a cat—roadkill he had found out on Covington Road beneath a blooming acacia tree—and a couple of gophers. Next to that was Esther's memory box, an old train case that she had entrusted to me before she left for college. The key was in its lock.

The rain had started up again and I watched the rivers of water splash against my window. The streets were deserted except for a few homeless and an old Mexican who sat under the awning of a store that sold cheap luggage and rattan furniture. His plastic palm fronds—a dollar fifty each—refused to budge in the wind.

I turned back to the sculpture. I had to make the garbage can, a circular mass of pilfered scrap metal, larger than life so that the statue of my sister and the motorcycle, both smaller than actual size, could fit inside. Esther was cast in plaster and I left her ghostly white and bald. I had erected the motorcycle from the parts of motorcycles I had found at a junkyard in Daly City. None of the parts matched so the motorcycle looked slightly askew, the tires different sizes, the seat much too big, the frame much too small.

Initial studio visits had seemed positive. Shey, my dealer, who once said that artists cannot transcribe what they see, they can only translate, loved it. But he hadn't seen it evolve. He hadn't seen the changes I had made. Neither had the curator at the De Young. It was simpler at first but was, because of my own uncertainty, becoming more cluttered and nebulous over time. I thought again of the way Alice looked at it and wondered if I was making a mistake.

I lit a cigarette and listened to the guy in the studio downstairs cut something with an electric saw. I heard the whooshing sound of the buses on the electric wires outside my window. The rain was steady and the sky beneath the streetlamps the color of slate.

I lay down on the couch and gazed at my studio. My work shed was in the back of the room, brimming with paint, plaster mix, tools, pieces of wood, panes of glass and the myriad odds and ends I had collected over the years from junkyards, landfills and sidewalks. On the wall over my bed I had hung the posters that announced all of my installations and shows, from my first feeble show at a small alternative space in Berkeley to my last one in North Beach, where one critic wrote, "Goldblum is fast emerging as the leader of a new generation of nihilistic postmodernists."

I never understood whether that was meant as praise or criticism.

On the far wall of my studio was a large piece of velvet, and on it, the tracing of a dead woman. She had fallen, jumped, been pushed— this was a matter of who you spoke to, who you believed, what newspaper you read—from the seventh-story window of the projects on Eddy Street. The night she fell, the forensics staff had drawn her chalk figure on the pavement. I watched them do it. They neglected to hose the drawing off the cement and I wondered about such disrespect and indignity.

After the paramedics left and the excitement dwindled, I went down and traced it. Whether she fell, whether she jumped, whether she was pushed, it all turned out to be the same thing. A dead woman on the pavement. I superimposed the drawing on a piece of velvet and littered it with bits of seashells, the old earrings Maggie no longer wore, Harold's cuff links, tangles of glass and rocks from the old neighborhood. It was eventually shown in a Brooklyn gallery and a positive review of the opening, along with a picture of me, was featured on the front page of the Sunday *Times* Arts and Leisure section under the headline, "California Artist Makes Waves in Brooklyn."

I remembered it, a year or so before Esther's death, flying back to San Francisco and going immediately to a party at Shey's in celebration. I remembered the brisk scent of fall in the air, how I hid my sense of amazement at all the success that had come my way because it was so private, so exquisite, like something you should never show someone lest they learn more about you than you would ever be willing to give. I remembered how I couldn't wait to tell Esther that from now on, I could make a living at my art. How she would be the only one to understand that what I felt was not triumph but gratitude.

I looked around the room, remembering that moment in time, how far I had risen and thinking how far it was possible to fall.

Hanging from the ceiling was the mobile I had made out of dozens of Maggie's empty pill bottles and looking at it made my stomach ache. *How far was it possible to fall?*

I stood up for a moment and walked to the end of my bed, staring at the table I'd constructed entirely from the glass of car windows that had been smashed open by thieves—a project which had taken me far less time than I had anticipated because I had no problem collecting the beautiful shards of bluish glass from the cars that were broken into each night in San Francisco. I slid my hands across the surface, saddened by its fragility, and the cold seeped into me as if it were an old ragged blanket left behind on a park bench.

I crawled back into bed and as I gazed at the walls, my eyes grew heavy and in moments I felt myself falling into a dreary, leaden sleep. Hours later—the sky had darkened to night and the sound of the gutters dripping indicated that the rain had stopped—I awoke and realized I must have slept through Alice's call. I heard the unmistakable sound of boots on the stairs, then a long pause just outside my door and finally a loud knocking. I looked over at the phone and saw the insistent red blink on the message recorder. Then I heard the heavy hammering against my door again and knew who it was.

I opened it and Zeke pushed me inside, slammed me against the wall and kissed me. In moments, he had torn the shirt I was wearing in half. My jeans disappeared with the same attention to violence.

"Take away the cunt and you take away the power," he said. His breath was hot, so much hotter than my own skin that it seared my cheeks. When he spoke, he did not shout but hurled his words out in a frenzy of whispers.

"You don't like the word *cunt*. You don't like things out of balance. But you crave them. I can see it in your eyes. Squalid, shabby thoughts behind all the lies of your modesty, your perfection, your misery."

As he spoke, he pushed his hand into me and I felt myself spilling over. I did not want him to know that he excited me but I had never been so excited and I couldn't stop my body from reacting in a way that made my head ashamed of it. The allure of it lay in the plate-smashing, cheek-slapping logic of it, how obviously it seemed to twist my body one way and come out another. To think *love* and act *fuck*, to move as if in a dream where the senses were muted but the awareness of them was not.

"Fuck you," I said and he just slapped me across the face, just slapped me so that tears sprang to my eyes and I thought of the safe word, *cease*, but it came at me like something I could not catch, a breeze or a mist, and I let it disappear. He went to my work space and grabbed some electrical cord. Then he tied my hands to the legs of the couch and I pictured myself years ago, dragging that couch down University Avenue and through campus to the door of my apartment, and then he was on me, forcing himself in me and at the moment he slid in, I felt a strange release, the letting go of myself. I could see my body from above, taking him in but I could barely feel it until the end when we both came in some kind of Hades of mingled breaths and sensations, our bodies merely incidental to the larger conviction that what we were doing was, in the end, not enough to shock us.

When we had finished, he immediately lit a cigarette, unleashed me and moved away. He leaned against the couch and I looked at his penis, getting smaller, gleaming with a part of me. I thought, *He just went in and stole some of me.* I had the mental image of my body getting smaller and smaller, disappearing through the opening of my vagina, of Zeke removing me from myself in that way.

"You're an amazing fuck," he said.

"Is that a compliment?"

He smiled, the cigarette between his lips. For a moment he looked just like Popeye. Then he reached out, and as he did the first night I met him at the Rite Spot, he gently caressed my cheek with his fingers. The tenderness of it made me ache. I could not tolerate his tenderness. I pushed his hand away.

"You call yourself an artist? What the hell is that?" he asked, pointing to Esther and the motorcycle in the garbage can.

"A refrigerator," I said.

"Your sarcasm is so ordinary."

"Pardon me," I said, sarcastically. Then it occurred to me that I had never told him where I lived.

"How did you find me?"

He reached for his jeans, which lay on the floor, one leg puffed up as if it were still occupied, and pulled my wallet out of the back pocket. I hadn't noticed it was missing. He handed it over.

"Did you go through my purse or something?" I asked.

"Yes," he said.

He stood up and rubbed his massive white hands over his shaved head. He went to the refrigerator and looked inside. He opened the freezer and reached for the vodka. Like most men, he had absolutely no qualms about being naked in front of a stranger. But I had already wrapped myself in a blanket I'd taken from the couch.

"Vodka and rabbit food," he said. He opened the cupboards and said, as if monumentally disappointed, "Top Ramen."

"What are you doing here?" I asked. It seemed ludicrous, all of a sudden, his being here unless we were having sex. Without the cloak of inebriation, I was afraid of him. And then I realized that it was not fear of what he might do to me but the fear of what I would allow him to do.

He went over to the window and looked out at the rain. He shivered slightly and I was aware for the first time how cold the studio was. I stood up and clutched the blanket tighter around me. I didn't care about him. I didn't care what he did. I despised him.

I left the room and went into the alcove where my bed was. I got under the covers and closed my eyes. I missed my sister so much then that I felt invisible and could imagine it, my body evaporating into nothing, leaving behind merely its warmth and a slight impression on the bedsheets. In a little while, I heard Zeke leave the studio and, for a long time afterward, it seemed that I could still hear the echo of his boots in the stairwell as he made his way to the street below.

4

T h e ranch-style house has changed very little. There's a new coat of paint, same color. The wall that separates the master bedroom from the backyard has been replaced by a sliding glass door. A puppy named Harry the Dog III has been added to the small menagerie of cats and parakeets that Maggie has collected since the departure of her children. Harold has recently invented a device to keep the frogs from entering the pool's filtering system and therefore from certain dismemberment and death.

The neighborhood looks dated, ranch-style homes having lost their relevance in an era of nineties-style Spanish tile, white stucco and arched doorways. The trees are large and loom over the street, the oleander is overgrown, the fruit orchards have long since been replaced by homes of Spanish tile, white stucco and arched doorways. Many of the neighbors have moved away and new people inhabit the old houses while the ghosts of my childhood haunt the street, triggering my memory in a way that leaves me breathless.

The entire family has gathered accidentally at the old homestead. Mary and her husband, Dan, live only a mile away. But they are always there, concern in hand, annoying Harold, who has begun to experience heart pains.

My brother Eddie is lying in his old bed with a total of thirty-two stitches in his face, having begun the process of paying for his decision to blow the whistle on the CEO of his Wall Street investment banking firm. Martin has flown in from Los Angeles for the weekend. He won't admit it, but we all know that he is trying to extricate himself from yet another woman who has fallen desperately in love with him. And Esther, with her long, jet black hair and dangling bracelets, has just arrived from Cuba in a whirlwind of cigarette smoke, brandied breath and exotic perfume, a satchel over her left shoulder and a bag of gifts for everyone. She kisses us all on the cheek and hugs us warmly, which is cause for the ripples of embarrassment that pass through the room like another presence. Except perhaps for Mary, and this new habit of Esther's, we are not a naturally demonstrative family, choosing to express our affections through clever verbal eruptions that, if necessary, double just as well as insults.

Harold has turned completely gray by now and is hard of hearing. When Esther says that *The New York Times* is sending her out of the country again, this time to South Africa, Harold leans forward and says, "South America. Will wonders never cease."

"Africa, Dad," she says. "South *Africa*."

"Oh, dear," says Maggie. "Are you sure that's a good idea?"

Eddie hobbles in from the bedroom and sits down on one of the tattered chairs near the TV. We are all silent as Esther walks up to him, takes his purple, swollen face in her hands and kisses him right on an oozing abrasion. It is the first time he smiles in a week, something which, from the looks of it, causes him great pain.

"Only you," Esther says. "You are noble in spite of your genetic heritage."

She was the one the police called first, since she lived only three blocks from Eddie's Upper West Side apartment at the time of the attack and was listed in his wallet as "closest living relative."

Now she turns around and surveys us all. She emanates such exquisite confidence and intelligence that when her eyes rest on me for a long moment, my heart surges and skips a beat. I feel my face flush and I turn away to pet the animal at my feet, a large brown cat named Stupid.

"How's my baby sister," she says once the excitement of her arrival dissipates and the attention turns toward Mary, whose third baby has apparently just awakened in its amniotic fluid and is busy kicking her from the inside, creating a miraculous visible blip on her extended belly.

Esther and I, who share a decided lack of maternal instincts, walk out back together into the cold fall air and through the gate that leads to the schoolyard. The trees have begun to turn color and the air is filmy and gray with cold. A smattering of silver clouds, like paint strokes, whisks across the sky, and beyond us the hills are dark and indifferent. Esther takes hold of my hand and brings it to her mouth. She blows on it, then kisses it and I watch the steam from her breath swirl around my fingers.

"I wanted to wait to tell you," I say.

"Oh, you didn't. Did you? Oh, hello hello! That's wonderful. My baby sister. The De Young? God protect them from your madness. Wait till I tell everyone at the newspaper. They've been following the saga of the great artist Louise Goldblum since it began in that tiny, pathetic gallery in Berkeley."

"Poor them."

"Nonsense," she says, swatting at the air as if a flying insect hovered nearby. "Do you remember how we were all sitting around on those folding chairs, smoking and pretending to know something about art, and all of sudden that guy came in from some muckety-muck New York gallery and proclaimed you a rising star?"

"He was drunk, Esther. And besides, nothing came of it. If I remember correctly the wine was a warm Gallo chablis and hardly anyone showed up except for you, a few friends and that heroin addict who wandered in out of the rain."

"Well, people have to start somewhere. You seem to forget your rapid ascendency."

"Please."

"No, I'm serious. Don't you remember how right after that you got that great group show south of Market. Oh, God, and that show in Brooklyn! Maggie still has the review and your picture in *The New York Times* taped to the bathroom mirror."

I think about Maggie taking pride in my work. She rarely mentions anything to me when I have a show, never comes to them and almost always forgets to congratulate me. But then sometimes, I will find something, a catalogue from a show or a review tucked away in some corner of the house, the date scribbled on it, a flower pressed inside.

"Tell me all about your opening," Esther says. "God. You must be so nervous."

By now we have made it to the bleachers where Esther and Danny Franconi used to spend hours French kissing and smoking pot. We sit down and there are her initials, EG, carved deeply into the wood. Beside them, bigger and sloppier, are the initials DF.

"It's supposed to be this community thing, this rotating exhibit that represents local artists on their way up. Shey says I'm considered very important these days."

"Have you slept with him?" She is suddenly pissed off. Her face takes on the lines only an angry woman can compose.

"My dealer?" I try not to laugh. "He's gay, Esther. I thought you knew that."

"Oh," she says. She seems momentarily disappointed. "I guess I forgot."

From far away, I can see our house, the trees I used to climb, a dim light shining in one of the bedroom windows. When the wind is right, I can hear the wind chime that hangs outside the living room window and I feel the emptiness of the passage of time.

"It's hard to believe," I say. "Shey has already sold the preparatory sketches. He's threatening to throw a party for me, but who knows. He loves planning parties even more than he loves having them. He keeps telling me some guy from Sotheby's is interested in my work and is promising to come to the show. But it's such a long way off."

"Talk is cheap," we both say together, then laugh. A fraction of silence, like a thin envelope of time, slides between us. Then Esther laughs.

"You are so good," she says, hugging me. "I think out of all of us, you have your head on the straightest. No, I mean it. Look at Eddie, so tortured by the world's immorality that he has to go and get himself almost killed for it. And Martin. For goodness sakes, you'd think that a scientist would know not to fall in love with a woman whose sole purpose in life is to guess the next plot twist on *General Hospital*. And Mary. Simple Mary."

We fall silent for a minute, letting the insult of her last words float away. She lights a cigarette. She looks off in the distance and as she blows the smoke out, she squints as if the sun has gotten in her eyes, though there is no evidence of sun in the sky. A flash of sorrow, or something like it, crosses her face. I see that she no longer wears the locket that contains the picture taken of us almost twenty years ago at Lake Lauganita and I want to ask her about it. Then I notice the faint hint of burnished skin around her eye, a glaze of pale brown and yellow.

"You are what I would do with myself if I could do it again," she says. Then she smiles. Darkness lifts. "I'm glad for this offspring thing, this, what is it, procreation, the advantage of seeing my face in your face. Genetics are the equivalent to mirrors. You are my second chance."

"But Esther, you're famous, you're brilliant. You're—"

"Exhausted," she says.

I want to ask her about the fading bruise around her eye but she stands up suddenly and waves. Martin is coming toward us and we laugh at the way he walks with his feet pointed out. Esther's theory is that someone saw him and invented the word *geek*. He has worn the same thick tortoiseshell frames long enough that they have already gone in and out of fashion several times. His clothes are huge on him, conspicuously outdated. When I describe him to people, I always say he is the type of guy who wears a pocket protector, even though he doesn't.

"Allo," he shouts. He holds a bottle in the air. "Let's get drunk."

When he sits down, he pulls two glasses from his pocket and fills them with the whiskey he has stolen from our parents' liquor cabinet. Everyone in the family knows I don't drink but only Esther and Mary know why, having been partially responsible for the mild alcohol poisoning that kept me bedridden for two days in the summer of 1972.

Then, like everyone does to everyone else in our family, Martin begins to discuss me in the third person, as if I am not actually sitting there beside him and Esther.

"Did you hear that Louise Goldblum will be showing at the De Young?" he asks, feigning surprise and awe.

"Yes. She's going to be famous," Esther says. "We wait with bated breath to view her postmodern whatchamacallit at the museum of old farts and boring art. She'll shock the world."

"Do you expect that she'll still deign to speak to us?"

I can see the smiles in their eyes even if their lips don't show it.

"Well, she did speak to us after she won the award for academic excellence when she graduated from Cal."

"Yes, but that was before she won that art stipend to travel through Europe."

"Shut up, you guys," I say. It is the old Goldblum trick of showering praise while making fun of the subject being praised. The fact is, I am a success, having achieved it, unlike my brothers and sisters, without the dependencies on cigarettes, alcohol, love and, in Mary's case, a tendency to procreate blindly and passionately. In this regard, I have replaced Mary as the Goldblum anomaly and am aware, on some level, that I am regarded with a barely detectable suspicion by everyone else.

"She's perfect," Esther says, wrapping her arms around me and kissing the top of my head. I can smell the aroma of whiskey on her breath and I can make out the small scar under her chin from a fall that occurred before my hapless tumble into existence.

"Louise is perfect, yes, but not so this lost piece of shit you see before you," says Martin who, it just occurs to me, is already drunk. He then launches into the embarrassing details of his latest failure at love. I watch him, trying to understand what it is that has caused gorgeous women to fall in love with him from the moment he hit high school.

It is clearly not his looks. Even he will tell you that he is the ugliest Goldblum alive. But, sitting there in the cold air, warmed more by the energy of Martin and Esther than by my flimsy coat, I realize that Martin is Harold three times over. Such excess of charm and disaster rolled into one soul is like a magnet for the heart.

He manages, like Harold, to be self-effacing and self-confident all at the same time. He seems, at first blush, shy and unassuming but he is really tantalizingly ribald and trashy. His intelligence is not intimidating though he is clearly a genius. And the fact that he does not practice medicine, but instead invents drugs to treat all manner of disease, makes him seem heroic.

"So I get home and she's evidently been involved in a head-on collision with the liquor cabinet and I say, 'Dorrie, honey,' and of course she says, 'Don't honey me, you prick.' " Martin takes a long sip of the whiskey, this time straight from the bottle. His trench coat blows in the wind around his thin body. His hair stands straight up. Mad scientist. I wonder what people passing by would think of the three of us sitting alone in the cold, deserted schoolyard, drinking a bottle of whiskey. They would not be disappointed. We are a family of eccentrics, religious mongrels, Jesus killers. We are considered by most of the neighbors as incapable of good manners and acceptable standards of behavior.

"My fucking life," he says. "I keep repeating the episodes of our parents. Over and over again. Fucking genetics. And now, I'll have to get some people at the house to clean up the mess."

Esther squints grimly into the sky. I picture Martin's simple old house in the hills above Hollywood awash in torn curtains, broken dishes, empty bottles. I think of the chaos of our own youth. I stand up.

"I'm gonna go back."

"Yeah," says Martin. "I'm gonna stay here on these bleachers and get blind."

Esther and I walk back to our house. The specter of Goldblum anarchy has silenced us.

When we get back, Eddie is lying in bed again with the television on. According to Maggie, he has developed a fascination for the Weather Channel. I arrive in time to witness a freak snowstorm in Idaho. I sit down beside him on a reclining chair. I recline, sit back up, recline again.

"Cool it," he says.

"It speaks," I say.

I watch his face for further signs of life. There are none. I am struck by the irony that the surprising spasm of genes that made my brother astonishingly handsome for a Goldblum has been dealt a fatal blow by the butt end of a gun. I realize he will no longer be beautiful. I turn and watch the snowstorm fade from the screen. El Niño has a grip on the West. Drought in the East. I recline. I sit back up. From the kitchen I hear Mary and Dan laughing and then Esther's musical voice filling the air.

"Did it hurt?"

Eddie looks at me with absolutely no expression on his face.

"Which part? When they shoved the gun down my throat or afterward, when the doctors drained the pus sacks in my ears?"

"The pus sack part."

"You know, Louise . . ." But he doesn't finish. Then I see it. His face, what's left of it, crumples and falls. I am by his side instantly.

"I'm sorry," I say, wiping the tear from his eye. "I just . . . you just won't talk. I . . ."

"It's not the pain. People always think it's the physical pain. Do you know that I shit my pants? I lost control and all I could think of was that I had joined the ranks of people who shit their pants in the face of death."

I say nothing. I hold my breath. It occurs to me; the enormity of what has happened to my brother. The thing that normally keeps me sane disappears for a moment and I am nowhere, traveling through nowhere anchored by nothing. Then I come back.

"I'm sorry," I say. I hold his hand, aware that it is the one I saved. When he sees me touching the dead finger, he smiles and reaches for the Star of David around his neck.

"I think," he says slowly, "I'm actually thinking that in a little while, soon, a week, maybe two, I'll be able to move on. But could you somehow convey to them, Maggie especially, that I just need to have my, what is it, my own private nervous breakdown?"

I nod my head. The police have not arrested anyone. According to Eddie, they have not even questioned the CEO, though Eddie is certain the orders came from him. He knows he will never work on Wall Street again, not that he wants to. Still, the notion of doors closing on Eddie, the oldest of us and the one saddled with the self-imposed responsibility of blazing trails, is asphyxiating. At least he has indicated as much.

The strange postscript to this day, which I will remember one rainy day almost a year later while hiding out in the Helen G. Urganis Camellia Garden in Golden Gate Park, is that the nurse who fell in love with my brother while he was recovering in the hospital called the old homestead that morning. And when I answered the phone she told me that for hours after the paramedics brought him in, half unconscious, on the brink of death, Eddie kept saying, "Holy smokes, Robin, they're trying to kill me."

5

"Fear is power," Zeke said. He snapped a picture of a DC-10 as it was landing. We had managed to sneak onto the edge of the tarmac at San Francisco International Airport and were lying on our backs as the planes were descending out of a thick fog onto the runway. In the tremendous roar and burst of wind each time one flew over, I felt the weight of it and imagined it falling from the sky and crushing me to death. This fantasy made my mouth go dry. I could almost touch the heat from the silver belly of the planes as they washed over me.

"Fear is like pain," I said. "It needs a brain to make it real."

He was absorbed in the mechanics of his camera and didn't look at me. His equipment was scattered around us, tripod, light meter, an empty film canister. He stood up and gauged the light, then adjusted his camera again. He sat down. He still hadn't looked at me and I sensed his deliberateness.

"Fear is defined by how much pain you expect," he said, letting his camera go and slapping me across the face. We had been sleeping together for two weeks and still I never knew when to expect the sudden outbursts of violence or the equally surprising moments of tenderness.

I reached up with my hand and covered my cheek, an act which twisted the corners of his mouth into a smile. "Or don't expect," he said, snapping a picture of me.

A plane began its descent and he positioned himself to take a picture. I watched him, the way he used a camera, the finesse of his movements. Everything about him was articulated by a certain blaze, an ambiguous energy that seemed to propel him forward. But it was clearly the propulsion of a crashing jet. Zeke would burst into flames on impact.

"The will to survive is an extraordinary thing," he said, apropos of nothing. He was sitting upright again, his arm brushing my arm so lightly that he seemed unaware of it at all. I was touched and disturbed by the guilelessness of this moment of intimacy. "But you know, there are also extraordinary situations which make this maxim untrue, irrelevant. Like the Jews who were forced to dig their own graves and then stand there in front of the trench and await the Nazi bullets. They just fell right into the graves they dug. Now that is extraordinary."

"It makes you think there's no God."

"God has nothing to do with it," he said. He scowled. "God didn't do shit to them. People did. And don't forget that."

I thought of Esther at the moment the bullet hit her brain. I had no words for the way it made me feel.

"My sister was killed," I said. "Murdered."

Roughly he put his hands over my mouth. I felt the heat in his fingers, the hard brutality of his strength.

"No," he said. "Nothing. Don't tell me. I don't want to know shit about you."

I pushed his hands away.

"The details of your life don't interest me," he said. "Only you, your body and what you'll let me do to it. That is what interests me."

"Fine," I said, but I was hurt. For a moment I didn't want to suppress myself for him. Then I thought of his capricious tempers and felt an alarming sense of arousal and comfort. How easy it was to accept such blunt, practical cruelty.

He snapped some more pictures of an approaching airplane. I watched him compose the shot, take in the light, the aspect of all that metal against the perimeters of sky. The sky was gray and opaque and a fine mist hung in the air, as if trapped, neither falling to earth nor dissipating. The plane was white, obscenely bright against the gloom.

"You have a remarkable body," he said. His voice was absolutely without passion or feeling. "You have large hands. And small breasts. I like your disproportions. They are subtle. You are subtle in your captivation."

"Is that a compliment?"

He ignored me. He put his camera down and lit a cigarette. He seemed prepared to do nothing more than that. He had a quality of stillness; a deep-in-the-center-of-the-gut sort of calm that seemed unshakable. Even his violence was metered by this primitive composure. It was the calm of the hunter, the stillness of the reverent, the silence of the insane. I was drawn to it because it reminded me of Esther, who could slip in and out of a glacial immobility like no one I had ever met.

"Who is Lisa Silburner?" I asked.

He glared at me.

"Why do you care?"

"I'm just making conversation. Jesus Christ."

"She's no one. I find beauty in objects. She is just an object. I have no relationship to her. I don't even know where she is."

I laughed. "Sounds like you got dumped."

"Don't fuck with me," he said. He picked up his camera and began to change film. "I hate it when a woman fucks with me."

"Did you love her?"

"No," he said. "I've already told you. I merely found her beautiful. She was useful to me. She was good with the lens of a camera. You put a camera on her and it was like a kiss."

"Where did you meet her?"

He stared at me angrily. I saw the bully in him. "Let me make something perfectly clear to you, okay?"

I nodded. I felt my body stir. The threat in his voice brought my body to life, threw common sense into dormancy. When he menaced, everything I thought I was made of retreated.

"You don't get to ask any questions. Questions are bullshit. They lead nowhere. Answers too are bullshit. They lead only to more questions. The process with us is simple. We fuck. You want a boyfriend, take out a personal ad. You want to fuck, you don't ask any questions, you don't tell me anything."

Just then, a 747 appeared out of the gloom. It was so low and its approach so lumbering, I believed for an instant that if I lifted my arm, I could touch it. Zeke stood up and shot several pictures. Then he dropped the camera around his neck and looked at me. I thought, by the expression on his face, that he would take off my clothes right there, that he would enact some form of humiliation on the tarmac of the San Francisco International Airport. But he simply helped me up, took my elbow and turned me toward the fence we'd climbed over to get in.

As we walked back, he stopped to take some pictures of the surrounding hills and I continued on. I started to climb the fence, and when I got to the top I saw that he had his camera trained on me and was taking picture after picture.

He drove me home in silence. He stopped the car, a brand-new Toyota Celica, clear of personal effects, and sat there while I got out. He said nothing.

"See ya," I said.

He nodded and barely waited for me to close the door before speeding off. I watched him drive away with a sinking feeling, as if I had just been marooned in the middle of a highway with no way home.

That night, I met Alice at El Rio for a drink.

The usual drunks were hanging around the bar. It was a decidedly blue-collar trashy crowd—women with lots of blue eye shadow and frosted hair teased into impossible shapes over their heads, and men with tattoos like they meant it. The men had five o'clock shadows and their eyes harbored distant memories, as weak and unsettled as their grip upon their drinks. Nestled in the back was a table full of people who looked like Kurt Cobain and Courtney Love. When Alice saw them, she rolled her eyes and popped her gum.

"They should just get over themselves," she said. She was wearing white gloves and some ridiculous dress with a high waist and Day-Glo colors. Since I'd known her, she'd always worn clothes that were over the top. It seemed counter to her professional ethos and yet somehow brilliant. She was a walking contradiction and I admired her for it. It kept her one step ahead of definition.

"You're just upset because you don't fit into popular culture," I said.

She laughed and said to the bartender, "Two martinis, arid." Then she looked at me and smiled.

"How are things with that bald-headed guy I can't believe you're sleeping with?"

"He has a name, Alice."

"Zeke? That's a name?"

"I like him," I said.

"Why? I just don't understand. Look at you, with all that beautiful red hair and that gorgeous, skinny model's body and that better-than-Streisand nose. You could have anyone. Even those one-night stands you were once so fond of seem suddenly better than him."

"Who knows why people like each other. Maybe I like him because he doesn't require much from me."

Of course I yearned for him because he would have nothing of me at the same time that he took everything from me.

"What kind of relationship is based strictly on sex?" she asked, a standard inquiry considering the source.

"You don't know the half of it."

The martinis arrived in plastic cups and we toasted the air.

"They're firing the guy in the mail room because he carried a concealed weapon in his sock," she said.

"Did he use it on anyone?"

"No. He said he was afraid of his ex-wife. Some such drivel. It doesn't matter. They were just looking for a reason to get rid of him because the real rumor, the real egregious problem, was that he had something worked out with the UPS driver to deliver certain quantities of cocaine, which he was then allegedly selling to the secretaries. You'd go into the bathroom at any time of the day and you'd hear these women snorting their brains out. It didn't bother me except for the fact that they'd be running around the office like maniacs for the better half of the day and then, later, you'd have to deal with them coming down. All that crying and remorse. Jesus."

She downed her drink and ordered another round. She was notorious for the amount of alcohol she could put away without throwing up. "Those people over there are really hideous."

I looked at the crowd in the corner. It was dark and I could not make out everyone's face. There was a large girl with ripped-up fishnet stockings close to us. She was telling a tall, bony guy, with black hair and about a dozen silver bracelets on his arm, that she had seen the face of Moses in a cloud over Provo, Utah. Another women jumped up and shouted, "Sex, schmex. It's love I'm after!"

Alice laughed. She traced the top of her cup with her finger. She appeared to be deep in thought.

"I think you oughta lose that *thing* in your studio," she said after a while.

"Thing?"

"You know, that garbage can thing."

"Oh, that thing. Yes. I was just thinking the other day, I think I'll get rid of this *garbage can thing*. It means nothing to me, or Shey for that matter, so what the hell, throw it out the window."

"I don't mean that and you know it," she said. I exasperated her all the time. "I mean you should put it aside and start working on your installation. Louise, if you blow this installation you can kiss your career good-bye. The De Young only shows dead white guys. You are their aberration. An opportunity to be seized, like an opening in hell that mysteriously leads out. O-U-T."

"I know that. Don't you think I know that? I'll figure it out. Don't you worry."

She looked at me and took a sip of her drink. "You used to be so anal, so perfect. What the hell has happened to you?"

"Death in the family," I said. I reached for my second drink and took a long sip.

"Maybe you ought to go see someone. Get some help about this. You seem to be getting, I don't know, worse."

Worse did not seem possible. I looked at Alice's clear face, a face unencumbered by grief. Her beauty was steeped in a kind of innocence and seemed to bend toward the likely possibility that even the deepest tragedy was surmountable. Her hands were steady against her drink. I looked at my own and saw they were shaking. There was no way she would understand. Still, I tried to explain.

"I just need to know, Alice, what happened. Why she went there with that guy. Why he shot her in the head. Who he was. What the hell went wrong."

"Look, I'm no shrink, but it seems to me that those are the wrong questions."

"How would you know?"

She cast me an impatient glance and went on.

"Maybe you should be asking yourself why you're drinking so much—not that I'm one to talk, of course—and why you smoke all of a sudden and why you're dating some bald-headed creep who looks like he keeps body parts in the freezer."

"No dead bodies. Just a mallard."

"A what?"

"A mallard," I said. "Dead bird."

She seemed to think this was funny and laughed long and hard. While she laughed, some urge made me look at the crowd behind us. From the shadows, wearing a strange, knowing smile, Zeke emerged. He winked at me and something in his face made me think he had planned this, knowing I would be here with Alice, perhaps following me, that all along he had been waiting for this moment to reveal himself to me. I thought again of his journal and the things he had written. *I think I may have found the next one.* He stood up and smiled. He seemed to tower over everyone at the table. A woman sitting next to him with long, black fingernails said, "C'mon, Zeke, baby, stay with Sylvia." Sylvia Berkham. I recognized her as one of Shey's newest discoveries. Her latest show—a series of abstract oil paintings—had just recently closed and according to Shey, had completely sold out. She grabbed hold of Zeke's jacket but he shook her free and headed in our direction.

"What's the matter?" Alice asked. "You look like you've seen a ghost, for heaven's sake."

I thought fleetingly of Esther, how Esther would never have revealed her feelings, no matter what. I downed my drink and ordered another one. My hands trembled. Knowing what Zeke and I did alone somehow didn't translate socially. I feared his unpredictability.

When Alice saw Zeke making his way through the crowded bar toward us, she turned to me and, exasperated, said, "Oh great."

"Well," Zeke said. "Well, well, well."

He seemed drunk. He held out his hand and Alice reluctantly took it.

"Zeke Heirholm, photographer," he said. He had slipped into a false voice, a mocking voice, the voice of a salesman and a drunk. "And you are?"

"Alice," she said, pulling her hand away.

"Swell dress," he said. "So retro."

"Likewise the hairdo," she said, pointing to Zeke's head. I looked at his scalp, at its lunar dimensions, the sway and fold of bone and skin. I was drunk. I tried to picture the aspect of a bullet hole burrowed into such a delicate surface.

"You ladies having a night on the town?"

Someone shouted, "Heirholm, stay away from damaged goods." It seemed to spur him on. He put his arm around my neck and kissed me on the mouth. I pulled away, embarrassed. When I looked up, Sylvia had molded her hand into the shape of a gun and was pointing it at me. "Pow," she mouthed and pulled the imaginary trigger.

"We were just leaving," Alice said. She gathered up her cigarettes and the loose bills on the counter. She stood up and waited for me to follow suit. I stood up too. I could not look at either of them.

"I'll join you," he said.

Alice looked at me. She raised her eyebrows. I shrugged.

The three of us walked outside into a raw, driving rain. Zeke had put his arm around my shoulder with a rare boyfriendly benevolence. I was struck by the strangeness of this ordinary gesture.

"Where to, ladies? I've got bundles of cash. Bundles. A night on the town for the ladies. What's say we head over to Gold Alley." He hailed a cab and we got in. Zeke sat between us. He kept a hand on my thigh.

"Your friends seem nice," Alice said. If you didn't know her, you would have missed the irony in her voice. But Zeke, I was learning, had a savage intelligence. He could recognize such things immediately.

"They're assholes," Zeke said. "Not friends at all. I don't have any friends." His tone was laced with a trace of regret. He squeezed my leg, involuntarily it seemed, and I hated that the truth always had its way of slipping out. I did not want to care for him.

"You should talk to them about their style," Alice said. "So eighties. Really, it's embarrassing."

Zeke smiled but it was a bitter smile, the kind you make to hide a scowl or an angry word. I could tell that he disliked Alice as much as she disliked him. I remembered his journal.

She has a friend, a beauty too, but not devastating. Not hungry. It could have been Alice. And if so, he was writing about me. *She'll let you break her in half. You think, This girl is as delicate as snow. She seems hungry for annihilation.*

I pushed his hand off my thigh. I looked out the window at the passing city. The rain had stopped. We made our way toward downtown and the TransAmerica pyramid loomed into view, shrouded by a thick mist. Two men stood on the corner of Montgomery with plastic garbage bags draped over their bodies, their expressions blank, their features dimmed by the darkness.

I shut my eyes and began to play it in my head, my rendition of what happened to Esther that night, how she found herself dead in an old motel room. Thinking it, making it up, I felt myself falling into the abyss of my imagination, the way you see people in scary movies being sucked into a spiral of dream life, farther and farther away from reality.

I saw her there, *dark, beautiful Esther alone in the playground of San Francisco. Living high and stylish on* The New York Times *expense account. She is invincible now. People know her all over the world. She is a famous reporter about to leave for South Africa where anti-apartheid violence rages, where governments are poised to topple, where she will witness it all and bring it home to us with her searing, passionate style.*

She is aware that she has reached some kind of apex in her life, a crescendo of professional acumen, but that the vacancy left by Danny Franconi's death nearly nineteen years ago has kept her on a collision course with loneliness her entire life.

She sits alone at the bar—the last place anyone sees her alive—at the St. Francis Hotel, perhaps made aware of her loneliness in the alarming and epiphanic way that the sudden desertion of self-delusion leaves you. Or perhaps she is merely studying a pack of matches, debating whether to call one of us, to go to bed, to get drunk and roll onto the plane the next day with a plunging blood alcohol level and a flask of whiskey hidden in her purse.

A man walks up to her. He is handsome, big and somewhat tough. He is, in one way or another, spectacular because only men with a cer-

*tain beauty and a surplus of self-assurance ever approach Esther. When
he introduces himself, she makes it clear right away that she is not interested in the details of his life, only whether he can entertain her, keep
her moving, take her mind off things. She doesn't say this out loud. She
never has to because the admonition is a part of every movement. Every
drag of her cigarette, every sip of her drink, every laugh that tumbles off
her lips says, Touch, but not too deeply, look, but not too carefully, talk,
but not too intimately.*

*He's a wealthy and highly educated man but also cagey and slightly
dangerous. When he suggests they go to the gold country in the Sierra
foothills, Esther contemplates it. She thinks about the long flight she is
scheduled to take the following day. She thinks about the detriment of
too much movement, drinking, fucking, driving, before a big assignment.
But she never passes on risk, never turns down something new and outlandish. Yes, she says (I see her eyes close in slow motion, the long, dark
lashes kissing the upper crest of her cheekbones, then opening again to
reveal the burnished brown of her pupils), I'll go.*

"Louise," Zeke said. He pinched my leg. "Where the hell are you?
Huh? Jesus. I'm asking you a fucking question here."

He grabbed me by the chin and pulled my face toward his.

"Hey," Alice said.

"It's okay," I said, aware on some level that her protests would only
egg him on. I brushed his hand away and to my surprise, he let go.

"She likes it," Zeke said.

Alice raised her eyebrows at me and Zeke snickered in a self-satisfied way. When we got to Bic's in Gold Alley, she stayed in the cab.

"Louise," she said, calling to me as I neared the entrance to the bar.
I walked back toward the cab and peered in.

"Tell me this isn't some bondage thing. Just tell me that, okay? Tell
me you aren't letting him hurt you."

I looked at her. I shook my head.

"Louise," she said. But I didn't wait for her protests, her protecting,
sisterly love because the thought of it, the thought of so much love got
itself around my throat and stopped me from breathing. She could not
tether me with her protection any more than I could stop following
Zeke into bars. I left her sitting there and just before entering the bar,

I heard the cab drive away down the narrow alley, sloshing its way through every puddle.

The bar was crowded. In the corner, a lone saxophonist belted out a strange, melodious song that filled me with sorrow. The opulent, smoke-filled, booze-scented air swirled around me, grabbing me by the neck and dragging me into itself. I searched the room for Zeke and found him in a corner of the dining room talking to a woman with close-cropped black hair and dark eyes. A man walked up and gave Zeke a robust but oddly obsequious handshake. The woman stared back and forth between them and regarded them with a distracted studiousness, as if looking at a painting she didn't quite understand. Occasionally she puffed on her cigarette and lifted her head to blow the smoke out.

Zeke listened with his unnerving, boulderish silence. He nodded once, then searched the room. I turned away and ordered a drink from the bar. A woman next to me grazed me with a molten stare and turned away from me to abruptly kiss the man who stood beside her. The bartender winked at me and I said, "Did I miss something?"

On the other side, three men in dark suits and skinny ties were huddled over the bar, engaged in a deep, intense conversation. I heard one of them say, "I'm gonna use the fucker for target practice."

Zeke strode up after a while, our reunification celebrated by a long, drawn-out kiss and his hand on my crotch.

"Fucking artists," he said after our lips had parted company. "I hate that you're one too. Jesus, I can't get away from them."

"Maybe you should take up truck driving then. Toss your camera equipment out the window along with that journal of yours."

"What do you mean?" he asked.

"Let's see if I can remember," I said. " 'Something trails her, something haunts. She mystifies me. Will she acquiesce?' "

For a moment his mask slipped and I saw what lay underneath—some human emotion. It horrified me to see that he was capable of embarrassment. I was jolted by the sudden truth of it. Zeke had been following me. I was the redhead, the one hungry for annihilation. But more horrifying was knowing it and agreeing to stay. When I looked at Zeke again, he had crawled right back into his skin, his shield. He lifted his glass.

"Touché," he said.

"My mother does that, you know," I said.

"What? Follow girls around hoping one day to get into their pants?"

"Speaks French when she's drunk. She loves the word *amour* and everything is *c'est la vie* this, *c'est la vie* that. You give her a couple of vodkas and it's *ou est la toilette* and *oh, mon cher*."

"Perhaps your mother and I could have a conversation one day."

"Or not," I said, eyeing him. The image of Zeke sitting across from Maggie with a bottle of vodka between them did not sit well. I could just hear her now in her Hollywood movie star accent and her B-movie drama: "So, dear, I hope you're using some sort of protection."

Zeke drained his drink and motioned for the bartender. The bartender scowled at Zeke. He made no move to come over. Zeke motioned again and the bartender sauntered over. He appeared to know Zeke. He appeared to despise him.

"We want a drink," Zeke said, enunciating every word as if the bartender was hard of hearing.

"Why the fuck do you keep coming in here?"

"Because I can."

The bartender lost his scowl and the hatred in his eyes vanished as if he had just made up his mind not to move in the direction of trouble. Nevertheless, you could still feel it between them, the way they hated each other.

"What are you drinking?" the bartender said.

"The usual."

The bartender left and a few minutes later returned with two vodkas straight up.

"On the house," he said.

"Fuck you," Zeke said, reaching for his wallet and handing over a twenty-dollar bill. "Keep the change."

I watched the bartender go over to the cash register, ring up the drink order and walk back with the change in his hand. He slammed it down on the counter and leaned over, staring Zeke in the eyes. Zeke did not budge. He returned the stare in kind.

"Fuck . . . you," the bartender said. "I don't want your fucking tip." Then he left our area of the bar.

"Must have something to do with a girl," I said.

Zeke burst out laughing.

"You aren't stupid, I will say that much," he said. He leaned over and kissed me. It was an affectionate kiss. A reward. I felt like thanking him. I felt like slapping him.

"Who?" I asked, sure that he wouldn't say anything. But to my surprise, he did.

"Lisa Silburner. Nineteen eighty-eight," he said.

"The one on your wall?"

"The very same."

I noticed a slight twitch in his eye. He pursed his lips. He sipped his drink. I had the urge to protect him then. But I also wanted to get out of his line of fire, out of his range.

"Who is he?" I said, motioning to the bartender.

Zeke looked at me and smiled sadly. He touched the end of my nose with his drink, then sipped from the glass.

"That's your last question," he said.

He looked out around the room and I saw for an instant what it was that drew me to him, because in that instant his eyes revealed a stellar insolence, an insolence so violent, so proud, so *insolent* that it could only have been born of a darkness as black as my own.

"That's her husband," he said. "Among my list of transgressions, I am also an adulterer."

Later, when we left the bar, he pulled me down the alley and pushed me against the wall across from the bar. He kissed me savagely, and it left me reeling, grasping his back for balance. How odd it seemed to balance myself against such instability. I was grateful for the wall behind me, that it kept us both standing.

Three couples stood in a cluster about ten feet away and they watched us for a moment. As they resumed their conversation, Zeke ever so gently, almost dreamily, lifted my skirt and unzipped his pants. His movements were deft and feral. Then slowly, underwater, in a fog, through a thick mist, he entered me, he pushed into me, softly, gently, slowly against the wall, his back to the three couples.

At one point I opened my eyes and I saw one of the women staring at me with wonder and also with fear in her eyes. I remembered Mr. and Mrs. Kowolski that day, twenty years ago. I remembered the sun and the gentle wake of the pool beneath my raft. I remembered the way the light was fractured by seed pods floating on the breeze. I was imbued by the blue light of Mrs. Kowolski's sad smile. The tentacles of her husband's rage reached out and wrapped themselves around my body as I stood balanced between the wall and a man on his way down.

I opened my eyes once more and I saw the woman put her hand over her mouth, not laughing but horrified, and I closed my eyes against her opinion of me, vanishing into the throat-aching, belly-churning, mind-numbing world of the past.

6

M a g g i e has become addicted to horror films. She especially likes to see them in the drive-in theater. But she refuses to go alone and drags any of us who will go along with her. Usually Eddie, Martin and I are the ones who go with her. We see *The Legend of Hell House* a record eight times.

The drive-in theater is about five minutes away from our house in a large field bordered by wild oleander and olive trees. It is called the El Monte Palms, which makes no sense to me since there are no palms anywhere in sight. During my youth it is a popular spot for teenagers to go to and get stoned, and the smell of marijuana permeates the air. It will one day become the El Monte Palms Town Homes and, in the eighties, become overrun by yuppies and BMWs.

When we go to the drive-in, Maggie brings along a tumbler of vodka for herself and a Styrofoam cooler of Cokes for us. We are each allowed to buy one treat at the concession stand before the movie. Eddie always gets popcorn with butter. Martin gets Red Vines. I can never decide. I have cravings for both salt and sweet. Eddie and Martin are patient for about thirty seconds. Then they start pestering me. This kind of pressure only makes me more indecisive. Panic sets in. Eddie orders something for me and I walk away disappointed, a failure, clutching a box of Milk Duds, a bag of peanuts, whatever he has commanded that I shall eat.

As the three of us walk back to Maggie's station wagon with its scents of Chanel No. 5 perfume, cigarettes and tonic water, Martin and Eddie pretend I do not belong to them. This has to do with the girls who hang out by the bathrooms before the movie starts. Sometimes they know one or two of the girls. In this case, they hurry by, hoping not to be seen. They would die if any girls they knew saw them with Maggie or me.

But when we get back inside the safety of the car, Martin and Eddie become boys again. They flirt with Maggie in a way I never see otherwise, as if the novelty of the giant movie screen in collusion with the black night lends itself to other curious fantasies.

It is at the drive-in that I get to see Maggie in a state of happiness. She teases us about being scaredy cats and dotes especially on the boys. Sometimes they all gang up on me, tickling me and calling me the scarediest cat of all. I enjoy this attention immensely and even if it gets to be too much, I try not to let on because I will do anything to keep Maggie touching me, to keep the sound of her laughter floating through the confines of the station wagon.

Sometimes Eddie gets up in the front seat with her and she puts her arm around his shoulders. When something really horrible happens, say one of the characters gets decapitated, the two of them scream simultaneously and throw up their hands. Afterward they will look at each other and laugh. Martin and I will roll our eyes, but only because we are expected to greet all expressions of affection with cynicism. Secretly we both like it.

But, in the end, she usually gets very drunk and we must be on guard for the hills and valleys in her mood. Generally the worst that happens is an unsettling helix of melancholy and a grave, serious happiness, as if she does not dare feel too good for too long. Often, when we drive home, Maggie zigzags in and out of the dotted lines on the road but it is of little consequence because the night is old and the streets deserted.

One night it is just Maggie and me. Without my brothers there, I feel awkward. Maggie is also very subdued. It is true that in order for Maggie and me to have a relationship, other people need to be around.

Alone together, we are miserable. She forgets to give me money so I can go to the concession stand. I have to go to the bathroom but am afraid to go alone. I don't want to ask her to come with me. It is Eddie's or Martin's job to take me.

She asks me how school is. I say fine. She turns to look at me.

"You get A's like the others?" she asks. Her question seems to surprise even her. I nod my head.

"Every one of you is so smart," she says. She lights a cigarette. The concept of having smart children seems to baffle her. It appears to be the first time she considers it. She takes a drag from her cigarette and looks out the window. A Muzak version of "Scarborough Fair" crackles over the speaker attached to the window. Maggie sips from her tumbler and when she breathes out, I smell the mixture of tonic water and lipstick that I will forever associate with her.

"When I was young, we didn't have to be smart," she says. "Not smart in a brainy sense. Smart, yes. Smart enough to get the hell out of there. But girls just didn't have to be smart."

She is very drunk and very agitated. She takes short, quick puffs of her cigarette and blows the smoke out in loud, brisk sighs. She cranes her neck out the window, as if waiting for someone.

"Smart," she says as if the word disgusts her. "Let me give you a word of advice, Louise."

She looks at me and the rays of her glance make me feel as if I have shrunk. Her anger and her sorrow tower over me, reducing me in size and significance. I am terrified. "Don't listen too loud to that brain of yours. You hear?"

I nod my head. I have the compulsion to say, "Yes, ma'am."

The movie starts. I can't concentrate on the images that cross the screen. I am thinking about my brain.

"Trust me, it will kill you. You plan your escape. You marry the first damn thing you see and your prison, my dear, is a life sentence of agony and regret." She pauses dramatically, takes a drag of her cigarette. "*C'est la vie*," she says through the smoke that bursts from her mouth.

I try to ignore her and concentrate on the screen. There is a large house and a storm is brewing outside. I see a grave and some leaves blowing around it. Then the camera takes you inside the big, haunted house where a young couple appear to be decorating a nursery.

Maggie stubs out her cigarette and takes a long sip from her tumbler. Then she gets out of the car. I watch her walk toward the concession stand. I see her talking to someone. She points around toward the bathroom and the person she is talking to walks that way. She lights a cigarette. Five minutes pass. Then Mr. Kowolski walks up. He tries to kiss her but Maggie pushes him away angrily and glances toward the car. I duck, then slowly crawl halfway back up, my nose barely above the dash. Hunkered down, I peer out the window.

After a minute or two during which Maggie says something using her long, slender arms for emphasis, they walk away toward the other side of the drive-in grounds. I follow them with my eyes until they disappear behind a truck.

I wait, thinking she'll be back in a few minutes. I try to watch the movie. Screaming has begun. There has been some incident involving a knife, and blood covers the stairs of the haunted house. Maggie does not come back. I have to pee. I consider going by myself but I remember the girl whose arms were chopped off by a drunken rapist last summer. I stay inside the car and hold back tears. I am afraid.

The movie ends and Maggie does not come back. People begin to leave the drive-in. I wait in the car for her to return. I watch out the window. I dutifully remove the speaker from the car, hang it up carefully. I get back in the front seat of the car. I have been holding my pee in for a long time. I am afraid I may wet my pants. I look at the bathrooms. Looking at them makes the urge to pee even worse. A group of teenagers walk by. One of them glares at me. He hitches up his pants and takes a hit off his cigarette.

I lock the doors and keep my eyes focused in the direction I last saw her walking with Mr. Kowolski. Finally, from the other side, Mr. Kowolski pulls up in his car and drops her off. She taps impatiently on the door for me to unlock it. She gets in the car without a word and starts the engine. We weave home in silence, Maggie staring rigidly ahead. When we get home she parks the car in the driveway so that one end hangs over the lawn.

"C'mon, baby," she says when I get out. She takes my hand and we walk up to the front door together. "I'm sorry, baby," she says and I cling to this apology the way I would a life raft in a raging sea.

7

I   w   a   s   lying on the couch when Alice marched in. She
was dressed to the nines in a leopard print miniskirt, a low-cut black
silk shirt and black come-fuck-me boots. Her blonde hair cascaded
over her shoulders like a shampoo ad. I was momentarily blinded by
her beauty.

"You're not wearing *that*," she said.

I looked down at myself. Jeans, sweatshirt, Keds. I reached over and
grabbed a cigarette.

"Shey called," I said. "There's some people from Sotheby's coming
at the last minute. And he's got those collectors from Pacific Heights,
you know, that couple who got into a screaming match outside Davies
Hall the opening night of the opera. They're gonna be there too. I just
can't face it."

"What the hell are you talking about? Jesus Christ, the party is in a
half hour. Get up and get dressed."

I sat up and drained what was left in my glass.

"Are you drunk?"

"Yes," I said.

She came over and dragged me off the couch.

"You know, you are really fucking ungrateful," she said, pulling me into the bathroom and starting the shower. "You have had such incredible success. Do you know that even my mom knows who you are?"

"Is that a good thing?"

"And yesterday, I heard some people on the bus—on the fucking Muni—talking about your work. Granted, they were incredible bores, but the point is, you cannot take your good fortune and throw it back in the face of those who have helped you. Shey has represented you for how many years . . . ?"

"Nine."

"And you go and treat him like this? You are acting like an ingrate. Now take off your clothes and get in the shower."

I did as I was told, but reluctantly. If Alice noticed any evidence of Zeke's handiwork on my body, she said nothing. Besides, she was busy looking at her teeth in the mirror. I got into the shower a little unsteady on my feet. When I looked at my small breasts, I thought, *booblets*. I could smell Alice's cigarette and I wished that the tobacco companies would invent a waterproof way to smoke in the shower.

"You're so skinny," Alice said. "Don't you ever eat?"

"If I had wanted my mom to be here, I would have invited her," I said. "As it stands now, you are getting perilously close to annoying me in that special way only Maggie can."

I heard her leave the room. I felt the water against my body and I closed my eyes. I was thinner now than Esther had ever been. I hadn't planned it that way. But food rarely appealed to me. I imagined sustaining myself forever on vodka and bar food—Chex mix, pretzels, popcorn and those little hollow orange fish crackers that left a fuzzy orange stain on your fingertips.

After a few minutes I turned the shower off and got out. The air was cold and my skin instantly turned to goose bumps.

"Alice," I practically shrieked. "Get me a drink." I dried off and went to the alcove where I slept. On the bed, Alice had laid out a simple black dress, a pair of black pantyhose and my favorite dress shoes— a pair of pointy black suede pumps. She had evidently rummaged through my drawers to find some jewelry but all she'd managed to come up with was a silver chain. I was struck by how much the assembly of my clothes on the bed looked like me, and by extension how logical it seemed to see myself as little more than air.

In a few minutes, Alice came into the room and handed me my drink.

"I'm warning you," she said. "Don't get drunk and act like an ass-hole."

We took a cab over to Shey's brilliant, enormous flat in the Castro. In the lighted window I could see a crowd of people mingling around his living room. The thought of all those people about to swarm me made me feel clammy and fueled my dread for all the parties to come: the preopening, the opening and the sodden letdown of the drunken first few days afterward. A migraine was slyly lurking at the back of my brain. Fortunately I had remembered my Fiorinal and took one, swilling the last of the drink that I had carried along in a plastic Thermos.

"C'mon," Alice said. She was excited. She loved to schmooze. She loved snotty people who had loads of money and always spoke as if they were just about to yawn. Her favorite thing was to check out the diamond rings on the women. Without the slightest bit of shame or embarrassment, she frequently spoke of owning such jewelry one day, bought, of course, by her fabulously rich future husband.

We climbed the stairs to Shey's second-floor flat in the Queen Victorian that he'd bought in the late seventies and spent five years renovating just as the Castro began to flourish. It was so exotic and fanciful that it once garnered a two-page spread in *Sunset* magazine. He chose not to hang his abundant art collection upstairs but, rather, kept most of it in the otherwise empty flat downstairs. He had installed an elaborate alarm system and so frequently forgot to turn it off before entering that the security company guarding his building no longer responded to the alarm. I admired him for not grandstanding his art and refusing to give it a special place. For a dealer, he was amazingly humble and guileless.

When I got inside, a spontaneous round of applause erupted. Alice held my hand, practically beaming.

"Honey," Shey said, running toward me and embracing me. "We thought you'd forgotten." He was dressed in white jeans and a white sweater. He had gained weight and lost hair since I'd first met him. Still, his kindness emanated from him in pleasant little waves. When you were with Shey, you wished you were a better person.

"Hello, Alice," Shey said. "Darling skirt." He leaned over and kissed her on the cheek.

"Everyone. Everyone," Shey said, clapping his hands to silence the well-heeled crowd. "Obviously you all know who this is. But allow me to formally introduce to you Louise Goldblum. I can't, I simply can't wait for her opening at the De Young. It will no doubt dazzle the pants off of you."

Shey was the only dealer I knew who could get away with saying something like, "dazzle the pants off of you." I heard the pop of a champagne bottle and everyone began clapping again. Shey grabbed me by the wrist and dragged me into his living room. I felt Alice slip away and had the image of a caboose disengaging from the rest of the train. *Bye-bye*, I thought. Shey held on to me tightly and whispered in my ear, "Girl, will you ever get your ass to places on time?"

"Sorry," I said.

"It's just that you used to be so punctual," he said. He was still whispering. "There are some heavyweights here tonight, sweetheart. You need to consider these things."

His frantic whispers were interrupted by people who came up to us and kissed him on the cheek, shook my hand, told me they couldn't wait for the opening. I had entered a dangerous vortex of perfume and jewelry. I was particularly impressed by the amount of cleavage around me. It seemed that everywhere I turned, I was staring down the tunnel of a woman's breasts, smooshed together by something tight and black. I had the perverse urge to reach out and squeeze them all.

"Louise," Shey said. "Have you met Sylvia?"

I had. I flashed on the night at El Rio, when she had molded her hand into the shape of a gun and fired at me. *What a bitch*, I thought.

"Hey," I said. I held out my hand.

She was positively bored. Slowly she reached out with her right hand and her sleeve drew up against her wrist. I saw instantly the track marks on her arm.

"Pleasure," she said. Her handshake was wet and limp.

Shey quickly shuffled me away.

"Great personality," I said.

"I'm working on her," he said.

I didn't want to burst his bubble by telling him you can't exactly *work* on a heroin addict's personality.

Shey's immense dining room was flecked with brilliant china and crystal. Bouquets of exotic flowers were everywhere. Little white lights had been strung around the dining room ceiling and gold coins hung from the chandeliers. When I looked at them I thought of rivers, stars and wind, all the things of promise and simplicity. The caterers had outdone themselves, even carving little faces into the watermelon and honeydew. It was hard to believe that all of this was done for me and that there would be more of the same to come. The prospect of it suddenly made me feel exhausted.

Shey's boyfriend, a tall, exquisite man from Zimbabwe with skin as black as midnight in winter, stood off to the side with a slight smirk on his face, as if the entire affair amused him. I felt an overriding affinity toward him and had the urge to grab him by the hand and take him to El Rio, where I imagined we would sit for hours drinking and making fun of everyone. He had a small tattoo of a spider at the base of his neck just below his collarbone and he stood absolutely still except for the wondrous movement of his smirking lips.

"You remember Nassif," Shey said as we passed. I reached out and clutched his hand. His expression did not change, and I realized that I was at the center of what he seemed to disdain the most.

It took us almost an hour to get to the drinks. That's because as we headed toward the bar, Shey had to stop and introduce me to all the wealthy collectors and art critics he had assembled in my honor. I yearned for the cold zing of vodka and the silence of my studio. I wanted Zeke. I craved the horrid consummation of our little secret.

When Shey and I finally reached the appetizers—an elaborate display of foods that appeared vaguely undercooked and too pretty to eat—I pulled away from him.

"Unhand me," I said, with more vitriol than I had meant.

Immediately he let me go, but he leaned over and said, "As you know, I don't much care for the temperamental sort."

I had to bite my tongue to keep from defending myself. *Sorry,* I thought.

I got myself a drink and tried to wade through the crowd without being stopped, but it was impossible. A collector from Texas came up to me and purred accolades into my ear. I remembered meeting him about two months ago at Shey's gallery. Shey had told me then that the man was interested in my work.

"He's rich," Shey had said. "Beguile him."

Now the collector was asking me about the installation. He wanted to know what the idea behind the work was. I focused on the tiny speck of food that clung to his cheek and tried to remember his name.

"I'm not sure how to answer you," I said, aware that I was liquored up and that the Fiorinal was coming alive. I suddenly thought of my bloodstream as a confluence of poisons.

The man from Texas looked at me skeptically and then began to tell me about his recent trip to Africa where, on safari, he shot and killed a water buffalo.

"I've had the damn thing mounted," he said, laughing. "A water buffalo. Who would have ever thought?"

I excused myself and headed for the bathroom. I kept thinking of that poor water buffalo, wondering exactly where the sport was in shooting an animal that just lies there. As I headed down the hallway, I passed Shey's guest room. The door was slightly ajar and I saw a flash of movement that startled me. I pushed the door open wider.

"Hello, Louise," Zeke said.

My heart went into overdrive. I felt the boil of a hard, fast fury spitting up out of the confluence of my poisoned blood. It was one thing to claim territorial rights over my body, to allow him to take me from myself. But it was another altogether for him to trespass on my professional landscape. This was my geography. This was what Esther liked most about me.

"Who the fuck invited you?"

"Sylvia asked me to come. She needed a date. You know how insecure heroin addicts are."

"Fuck Sylvia. *You* were not fucking invited here."

He laughed. "As if that makes any difference to me."

He walked over to me and grabbed me hard by the back of the head. He brought me to him and kissed me. It felt like a slap.

"Congratulations, Louise. You're famous."

"Fuck you, Zeke," I said. I hated the irony in his voice. The amusement. But he just laughed again.

"I had a long talk with Shey. Nice man. He has a way of deflecting negative thoughts. Like a force field of good nature."

"You should be so lucky to have someone like him to represent you."

"Tsk, tsk. Don't be catty. I'm not competing with you. Though I must say that Sylvia is hot on your scent. She really despises you. I find it amusing that it's all about professional jealousy. You artists make good theater."

He walked over to the mirror and gazed expressionlessly at his reflection. He could have been dispassionately viewing a lamb chop. He rubbed his chin, then his scalp. He reached for a cigarette, put it between his lips, but didn't light it. I thought it strange how Zeke was a well-known, successful photographer but did not seem to consider himself an artist. As if reading my thoughts he turned toward me and said, "It's entertaining to see how people—artists—like you love to hate the attention you get. I admire your ability to be so droll, so blasé, when underneath, you are teeming with self-congratulation."

I wanted to get away from him, to forget about him. But I was also drawn to him like a doe in the headlights, unable to move despite the coming onslaught.

"I'm leaving, Zeke. You should get out of Shey's guest room. For an uninvited guest, you're certainly pushing limits."

I turned to leave the room but in one quick movement, he grabbed me and shut the door.

"Don't talk to me about pushing limits," he hissed. His breathing came out hard. His face was inches from mine and his grip on me was so strong that I knew I could not break away. I felt myself getting wet and hated him, me, the appalling passion that passed between us. He pushed me on the bed so that my back was facing him. I landed stomach first and he lifted me up by the waist and bent me over. He pulled up my dress and tore at my pantyhose until my ass came free. He spread me apart and entered me. I could feel my wet surround him. He did too and I heard him laugh.

"I knew you couldn't resist," he said.

He pushed into me from behind.

"One day, when they all stop coming and your art has been proclaimed passé, you will sit alone in your studio and remember that at the apex of your career, you were fucked doggy style in your dealer's house," he said.

"Go to hell, Zeke," I said. I tried to pull away from him but his grip was too strong and, in the end, I stopped resisting and gave in to the pleasure. At the same time, I felt the fixed, crisp edge of my humiliation. How was it possible that his cruelty could spawn such desire? And yet the meaner he was, the more I wanted him, the more I craved him. I heard a sudden intake of laughter from beyond the doors and a new round of applause erupt with alarming force. Then without warning, the door to the guest room opened. I turned around for a moment and tried to spring free, but Zeke would not let me go.

"Louise," Shey said. "My god."

"Kee-rist," said the rich oil man from Texas, a man I was sure would forever remember me only as the artist being fucked from behind by some bald-headed guy.

Shey quickly shut the door and they were gone.

"Let me go, Zeke," I said. Even I could hear the despair in my voice.

"Not yet, doll," he said. "I haven't finished."

On the way home in the cab Alice put her arm around me.

"Great party. They loved you. You're a star," she said. "My best friend. A star."

I could not even look at her. I could barely stand her touch. All I clung to was the small miracle that Zeke had slipped out before Alice had the chance to see him.

I a m fifteen. My brothers are away at school. Mary has just met Dan and when Esther prods her to the point of blushing, Mary admits that she wants to wait till her wedding night to sleep with him.

Esther leaves for Columbia University in a few days. It has been six months since Danny's death. Everyone says she has recovered amazingly well. No one can believe that she has only put off college for six months, that so soon after Danny's death she is ready to begin again.

Eddie, Martin, Mary and I are not fooled. There is no question she has changed. She is too happy. Too controlled. She has grown slightly dangerous, taking risks even she would have once considered foolish.

Now, because she is leaving, she decides she has a million things to tell me. She steals a pack of cigarettes from Harold, throws a brown grocery bag with something bulky inside of it onto the floor of the backseat of the station wagon and grabs me by the collar.

"We're going to Koral Street," she says, putting the car in reverse and driving wildly out of our neighborhood.

Koral Street is where everyone goes to smoke and drink on the weekends—a long, winding road that culminates in a field of tall grass, oak trees and a few grazing cows. I have never been there and am flattered that she has decided to take me. It is a place reserved only for cool people. I am not cool.

When she parks the car, she puts the seat back a little and lights a cigarette. She pulls a beer out of her purse, opens it and says, "Go on, Baby Goldblum, have the first sip."

I am careful not to whine when I ask her why it is that she can never remember that I don't drink. She merely winks and says it is not an issue of memory but rather one of hope.

She is almost her old self today. There is that glint of hers, the unconcerned self-assurance. She tells me that she can't wait to go to Columbia. She loves New York and feels that New York was born in her through Harold. She wonders out loud whether things such as longings for certain places and tastes for certain foods are hereditary. She has already acquired a way of speaking that captivates everyone who listens to her. Her voice is rich and deep. Every word underscored by the hint of laughter and fervency. She can convert anyone. She can make anyone a believer. She can abolish the poverty of the soul.

She sighs and looks out the window. The faraway look that grew into her eyes when Danny died takes over. For a moment I feel myself fade away from her consciousness. But within seconds, she snaps out of it and smiles at me, a smile of such magnitude that I can only think the words *thank you.*

She turns to me and brushes a wisp of hair from my face.

"You are my favorite little Goldblum," she says very gravely. "And now that I'm going off to college there are several things I need to tell you."

I sit straighter. Esther is imparting advice. When Esther has something important to tell you, her face grows tighter and her eyes serious. It is wise not to interrupt her when she dispenses advice because it is clear that she believes it is just as essential that you listen as it is that she be heard.

"Number one," she says. "You should not be afraid if the popular girls still hate you when you go to high school because popular girls eventually turn into alcoholics or drug addicts or food maniacs. They will all tempt you to eat gallons of ice cream then throw it up afterward. It only leads to obesity and death. Stay away from these girls."

I nod my head. She pauses to get another cigarette and lights it off the first one. Then she throws the butt out the window and takes a deep drag, blowing the smoke out of both her mouth and her nose at the same time.

"Ignore the bigots who call you Louise Goldblum the Jew-Brain. They are simply jealous of your talents and don't understand that their Christian forebears were the ones who conceived of the crusades."

I make a mental note to look up crusades in the encyclopedia when I get home.

"Now," she says. She leans over and touches me on the leg very lightly. "About sex. Don't do it unless you mean it."

"Did you mean it with Danny Franconi?" I ask before I can stop myself.

At first her entire body seems to shut down and turn off. But within seconds she smiles sadly and says, "What I did and do has no bearing whatsoever on what you should do. Don't ever aspire to be like me." A spark of anger weaves its way into her voice and I realize she really means what she says and is not simply talking the way stuck-up people do when they pretend to put themselves down.

She reaches for her purse and opens it up. The cigarette is gripped between her teeth and she squints her eyes against the smoke. She looks so cool and so unaware of her coolness at the same time that I can't imagine not wanting to be like her.

"Open your hand," she says.

I obey. She pulls a square-shaped object wrapped in plastic from her purse. On the label it says TROJAN.

"This is a rubber."

I feel my face turn hot, then red.

"Don't blush," she says. "Penises are very real. And very lethal."

She laughs, a long and satisfying laugh. She takes a drag of her cigarette and segues into seriousness. She implores me to use one always and says that any man who won't wear a condom is not worth giving your body to.

"It's about nothing more than respect. Do you understand?"

I nod my head vigorously, understanding nothing. I am amazed at the way she talks about sex as if she is discussing last night's rump roast. It is staggering to me that someone can say the word *penis* without laughing, but even more impressive is the condom that she has magically extracted from her purse. I want to ask her where she got it but I am afraid of sounding naive, so I just stare at it for a moment and fold my hands around it. It feels mushy and it is this snail-without-a-shell sensation that scares me off condoms my entire life.

Just then a police car drives up and comes to a stop right next to our parents' car. Esther rolls down her window and at the same time hands me the beer with such clandestine finesse that I don't have time to panic.

"Officer Pete," she says. She waves her hand out the window and with her other hand points to the beer and whispers, "Lose the beer but no fast movements. Don't make it look like you're hiding something."

She speaks very quietly and calmly. I absorb this unruffled quality of hers and do what she says without a hitch.

The policeman stops the car and steps out.

"Now, Esther, don't let me find anything more'n a cigarette burning in that car."

"You know me," she says. Her voice radiates with laughter. I have a mental image, for some reason, of crystal shards flying through the air, capturing sunlight on their way down.

"You only have to catch me once," she says.

He laughs and makes his way over to the car. He is extremely tall and handsome except for a slight bend in the nose and a lip that looks as if it has met the knuckle end of a fist one too many times.

"Come meet my baby sister," she says.

He leans into the car. He smells of leather and car oil.

"This is Louise. She's straight as an arrow so don't count on ever finding her up here with a six-pack of beer and a pair of panties hanging out the window."

"Hi," I say. I am mortified by this course of events. It terrifies me that my sister is on such friendly terms with a policeman, but that she would even say *panties* in front of someone who wears an official uniform flabbergasts me. I look at the gun in his holster and wonder briefly if he has ever shot anyone.

"How ya doin'?" he says. He doesn't wait for my response. I know instantly that I am of absolutely no consequence to him. He looks at Esther and it is the same look I used to see on Danny's face whenever the two of them would rejoin the world after being gone for a few hours alone together.

"Hey, baby. How's it goin'?" the policeman says to my sister. His voice has changed. It has grown low and husky. It has the effect of sucking the air around us out of the car. For a minute it is as if the three of us have simultaneously stopped breathing. Then Esther speaks.

"I'm all right. Long time no see." She has slipped into the glass mode. She is as cool as a glacier and moves just as slowly. When she takes a hit of her cigarette and blows it out, Officer Pete doesn't move away from the smoke.

"You leaving for college soon?"

"About a week," she says.

I reach under the seat and feel the beer with my fingers. The can is still cold and moist. I have the urge to pick it up and show Officer Pete. And just while I am thinking this, he rubs his hands over Esther's arm ever so quickly. Esther darts her eyes at me. It is a fleeting glance, something I am not meant to see. This, above all else, puts me on high alert.

Officer Pete stands up. He is official again. Friendly. The air returns to the car. We are all breathing again.

"Give me a call then," he says jovially. "Before you leave."

"I'll do that," Esther says.

He peers into the car and smiles robustly.

"See ya, kid," he says to me.

We watch him drive away in silence. Esther holds out her hand and I give her the beer. She takes a sip of the beer so that Officer Pete can see her as he passes and I notice him shake his head and laugh.

After he has gone, she turns to me, as if he has never been there, and launches into some more of her advice.

"Now where was I?" she says. It is rhetorical. Esther always knows exactly where she was and where she's going. "Oh yeah. I wanted to tell you that the only person in the family you have to worry about is Martin because he has inherited Harold's propensity for sustained periods of melancholy and because he does not know the difference between a good woman and a hyena."

"Hyena?" I say, but she ignores me.

She is making Officer Pete disappear. I know I am being told, in no uncertain terms, that I should not remember what has happened, that I should tell no one.

"And most importantly," she says, "I have something for you."

She reaches behind her and pulls something out of the brown paper sack she'd thrown in the backseat. I am surprised to see her reveal her most prized possession, a small locked trunk the size of a makeup case. It is her memory box.

"This is sacred," she says, handing it over to me. "Anyone besides you who touches it will pay the consequences."

I don't ask Esther what the consequences might be since I am convinced of her ability to exact the perfect revenge on anyone who crosses her. Solemnly and with great ceremony, she lifts the chain from around her neck—the one that holds the locket with the picture of us taken years before at Lake Lauganita—and removes a small metal key from it.

"You are the only person I trust not to open it," she says.

"But Esther," I say. I am astonished. This is her most important possession. The only other person ever allowed near it was Danny.

"No buts. I have to trust someone. It might as well be you."

A small silence fills the car. I am honored beyond belief. But I know too that there is something sly and calculated about this gesture. Then it hits me. I *am* the only one who would never look inside. Before I have a chance to think about what this means, Esther smiles and sighs with what seems like contentment.

"The last thing I want to tell you is that you have talent. Everyone else in the family has acquired certain marketable skills, but you alone have talent. Your art is unique and beautiful."

As she makes this distinction between talent and skill, she traces her fingers along the letters on the beer can. I say the letters to myself as she traces them: B U D.

"Never, ever waste your talent. Do not be frivolous. Nothing matters but your belief in your gifts."

This kind of discussion embarrasses me, having never been prepared by our parents for such things as pep talks and moral support.

"I wish you didn't have to go so far away," I say.

Her face closes up. She has not been the same since Danny Franconi ran his motorcycle over the cliff six months ago, though she now claims she never loved him, that it was just her way of passing the time before the bigger things in life could take over. No one believes this, of course. We had all heard the passionate "I love you's" they had whispered to each other. We had all witnessed the fervent hand holding, the delicate, almost desperate way they looked at each other. All over town, rocks, walls and bleachers were sprayed with the painted words: D.F. LUVS E.G.

At the funeral, Mrs. Franconi hugged Esther so hard that a button popped off her dress and we all looked at one another with astonishment, because normally Mrs. Franconi hated Esther. One time over poolside cocktails, she told Maggie that Esther was a slut.

I begin to cry and tell Esther that I am going to miss her. She has not yet acquired her habit of kissing like the French do, on both sides of the cheek, nor has she started up with the hugging. She simply smiles and says she will miss me too. Then she says we had better get going. She looks at her watch. I stop crying instantly. I wipe my tears surreptitiously. A Goldblum, I remember, does not cry unnecessarily. This particular event, I gather, is not one for tears.

When we get back to the house, Harold shuffles in from his garage. He is wearing khaki pants that are much too large for him and a white work shirt flecked with paint. I notice he is wearing Converse hightops on his feet. He looks ridiculous and beautiful, the way Martin will one day look.

"Esther, Esther, come. Come here," he says when he sees us. He grabs her by the shirt. She follows him out to the garage, turning back at me and rolling her eyes. Harold annoys Esther. She is patient with him the way an adult is patient with a sick or slightly impaired child. She is always saying things about him like, "Screw loose in the head," or "Pickled brain pop."

I love Harold if for no other reason than he hardly ever seems to notice me. I crave the attention he lavishes on Esther. It is this desire to be loved by someone who cannot love me that seems to characterize my life. But I do not know this yet. Now, it is just vague, indefinable desperation.

I follow Esther and Harold into the garage. It looks as though the place has been hit by a typhoon. There are tools, dollhouses, fishing rods, bikes, balls, two refrigerators, a sewing machine—a gift Maggie got one year from a friend, which caused her to spill her drink from laughing so hard—and several stacks of books. The ubiquitous books. Everywhere, always books. Books on everything from kite building to existentialism, which I am sure Harold would argue are the same thing.

Harold drags Esther over to a spot on a workbench that sits beneath a filthy window. Through the window, I can see Martin and Eddie torturing Elaine Kowolski. They have her pinned to the ground and Martin is poking her chest over and over with his index finger. Though I can't hear a thing, I can see that she is screaming and my brothers are laughing.

"I made this for you," he says, pointing to the table. "Look at that. Isn't that fine? Isn't that beautiful?"

I stand on tiptoes and peer over Esther's shoulder. It *is* beautiful. A brick in a bowl is covered with pure white crystals, the texture of snow. Crystals cling to the bowl and lace the sides. They are delicate and dreamily capture the luminous fluorescent light from above.

"What the hell is that?" she says. She is annoyed. But Harold does not lose his enthusiasm. It is clear to me that he has acquired the habit of ignoring certain tones of voice, a tactic born from years of dodging the vitriolic verbal bombs detonated by Maggie's mouth.

"A crystal garden," he says. He gingerly touches one of the crystals, as if it is alive. "Four tablespoons of bluing, four tablespoons of salt and one tablespoon of ammonia." He picks up a bottle of ammonia beside him and shakes it. "And a few drops of Mercurochrome."

"Oh," she says. She looks back at me, rolls her eyes, smiles as if Harold is a slightly amusing idiot child.

The phone rings.

"Gotta get that," she says. She runs into the house, expertly—from years of practice—dodging the land mines of junk.

Harold and I are left standing in front of the crystal garden.

"It's beautiful, Harold," I say.

He stares at me, trying, it seems, to figure out who I am.

9

M y sister Mary drove into the city on Mondays for a pottery class at San Francisco State. I generally met her for lunch or coffee after her class. I would take the long ride out there on a series of Muni rails, eventually coming to a halt at the end of the line for the K Ingelside, where I would walk across 19th Avenue to meet her in the school coffee shop.

On Monday, I woke up on the couch with another hangover. I still could not shake the look on Shey's face when he saw Zeke and me in his guest room. The shame and humiliation was tactile, like an itchy wool sweater. I cared less about the prospect of losing a buyer than I did of losing Shey. He had brought me up in the world. He had believed in me.

I reached for my cigarettes and lit one, drawing the blanket over me and staring out at the hideous sculpture I had made. I contemplated the strange relationship between the inordinate amount of time I spent creating it and its increasing repulsiveness.

After a while, I showered and threw on an old sweater and a pair of tights. I looked at myself in the mirror. Hole in the sweater, rip in the tights, my hair disheveled and curly beyond exasperation. My eyes were bloodshot and watery and when I bent over or moved too fast, I got so dizzy I'd have to sit down. As with almost every day for the past nine months, I decided to give up drinking for good.

By the time I got to San Francisco State, a wreck of alcohol-inspired anxiety, trembling hands, butterflies flapping around my cranium, Mary was already sitting in her usual corner with a cup of tea. Placed before her was an obvious sample of something she had created in her pottery class. As I got closer, I recognized it for a slightly pitched, wobbly-edged approximation of a pitcher.

"Very moderne," I said, noting its tilt to the right.

"It is so hard to get things straight."

"Why do you always speak in metaphors?"

She smiled. It was obvious she didn't know what I was talking about. She had missed the set of Goldblum genes that determined for the rest of us a piercing talent for amusing repartee, something which eventually annoyed or aggravated everyone to whom we were close. In its stead, she had inherited such kindness that her face exuded a pale-lit virtuousness. It was not a saccharine disposition of honey sweets and fake little laughs. Mary took her kindness seriously and, being a Goldblum (starved for such things), so did I. She was lightly freckled over the nose and, for the first time, showed signs of an emerging plumpness. Her hair, once light brown, had grown increasingly dark with each pregnancy. Currently she had four children.

"Dan loves this stuff, but I think he's just being kind."

"Maybe one of the kids will accidentally break it. I doubt there's any chance it will fly across the room during some kind of marital altercation."

She ignored me. "Remember Lydia Firestone?" she asked.

"Of course. Esther's best friend. What a sad sack she was. In retrospect."

"She's in all the papers. She claims her stepfather killed her best friend. She says it's repressed memory. She saw him shoot the poor girl on a lonely stretch of Old Santa Cruz Highway."

"Ah, repressed memory. The Salem witch trials of the nineties."

"There might be something to it, you know. Some people who have that repressed memory thing can actually prove they're telling the truth. Like that Catholic guy who claimed his priest molested him. The priest confessed."

"Well, I'm not surprised," I said. "If you're Catholic it doesn't matter what you do, right? 'Cause of that confessing thing."

Mary rolled her eyes. She was the only one of us Goldblums who chose a faith in God over the certainty of a test tube. She had become a true-blue, died-in-the-wool Catholic.

"Anyhow," she said. She looked at the pitcher she had made and unconsciously, it seemed, pushed it away from her. "Lydia accused her stepdad and he's been indicted. There's gonna be a trial and everything. She says the memory came to her one day in a flash while she was driving up Old Santa Cruz Highway."

"I'll take my memory the old-fashioned way," I said. "Roiling, intense, festering with lies."

Mary smiled sadly. "Poor girl," she said, and I wasn't sure if she was talking about me or Lydia, who was anything but poor, having inherited her mother's share of a large estate and a certain, delicate beauty that made men turn to rubber.

Mary looked at me for a moment and then, making the leap from memory to the present, said, "Mom is worried about Dad."

"No, Mary, you're worried about him. Maggie would never worry about Harold."

"I just think he might have a heart attack."

"He's incapable of it. You need a heart first."

"Oh, Louise. Why are you so hard on him?"

"It's not him, per se. I mean, I like his brain 'cause I got some of it. But there's something, I don't know. His vacancy. The way he just doesn't exist in any tangible daddish way."

"Oh, Louise. He's your father."

"He's Harold," I corrected her. She was the only who did not refer to our parents by their first names.

I stood up and made a move toward the pub. When I returned with a mug of beer, Mary said nothing, but when I rested my hands on the table because of the way they were shaking, she enfolded them with her own hands and said in a gay voice, "How about coming to our house for dinner on Saturday. A nice home-cooked meal."

I thought about those four children of hers running around with their little cherub faces and their wails and screams for attention, their funky baby smells of shit and powder.

"I have a date," I lied.

"Someone special?" she asked hopefully.

I thought about Zeke for a minute, of his cruelty and of the way I was drawn to it. I had an image of Zeke, standing beneath the massive belly of an airplane, his concentration so fixed and intense that next to him, my dedication to my own work seemed merely superficial fluff.

I remembered the way Zeke pinned me against the wall in Gold Alley, his thick and veiny hands wrapped around my face, treating me to the ironic coupling of protection and violation, because that was how I felt wrapped by his body while he humiliated me before an audience of strangers with horrified O's for mouths. I remember the regret that coursed through his face the moment he came—that peculiar conclusion to male sex, set by the barricade of his passion dissipating into the distance. I thought of these things simultaneously and took a long sip of my beer.

"He's special," I said. "But I don't like him much."

Mary looked away. She seemed embarrassed.

A woman with about seven earrings in her ear came by and picked up our dishes. She picked up my empty beer cup and smiled at me like she was saying *fuck you*. Someone behind me in the next booth was passionately saying, "Christians were already beginning to loot. Twenty-four Sienna Street."

"I'm just teasing," I said. "He's nice enough."

"Don't do it," she said.

"Don't do what?" I said, though I knew where we were headed. I felt myself fitting into my armor. I felt the settling of boulders in my gut as the warbly, crooked hangover of me smoothed out into a thin, cold line of silence.

"Ever since Danny died, Esther was a loser," Mary said. "You've made her into some kind of hero. Some kind of martyr or saint. She did not love anyone. When Danny died, she buried the capacity to love with him, where it remained forever. She did not love her success, it was just something to keep her from herself. I'm telling you this because you need to be clear that following her footsteps, *becoming* her, won't bring her back." She twirled her hands in the air, a gesture of rarely exposed fervor, more in keeping with Esther's personality or

mine than her own. I tried to stay focused on this blip of familial mannerisms and said nothing.

The girl who had picked up our plates was standing before the man
in the booth behind us. He was shouting now, as if reading lines from
a script, "I have no words to describe my desolation. I ought to go after
her. To die. But I have no strength to take such a step."

"Wow, did you write that?" the girl asked, incredulous. I could
smell, even from where I sat, the thick, sudsy fusion of dishwater and
perfume emanating from her body.

"Do you hear what I'm saying?" Mary said. She reached across to
me and lifted my chin, which had sunk toward the table. I pulled back
and swiped my hands across the table as if I were brushing off imaginary dishes. I would have liked to hear them shatter on the floor. I
understood, for a moment, our parents' propensity to destroy everything that could be broken.

"For fucking God's sake, Mary," I said a bit too loudly.

I flashed on Zeke, on the red burst of his furies and tempers and I
thought of myself taking them in, swallowing them, gorging on them
as if my sole purpose in life was to ingest his anger in order that my
own would have company. I thought of all the anger in the world and
I opened myself to it and I said, "Jesus fucking Christ, Mary, do we always have to talk about her?"

The girl, who moments before had been enamored of the man behind me, flashed me a look of sheer disdain.

"What the fuck are you looking at?" I said to her and stood up, leaving Mary behind with that pathetic, tilted pitcher that her husband
would fawn over simply because he loved her.

"Louise, we need to talk," Alice said, bursting into my studio.

"We can't right now. I'm dying."

"No you're not. Sit up."

"Aren't I already sitting?"

I knew I wasn't. It was just that lying down offered no relief from the
jagged knife slowly carving away the inside of my cranium.

"I'm serious."

I peered out from under the covers. There she was in all her amazing radiance, serious, controlled, worried. I went back under the covers.

"Tell me a story," I said.

I heard her walk to the window. I heard the sound of a match being struck. She inhaled. I smelled smoke.

"Okay. But then we talk."

"Story, Alice. Story." I was desperate. The Fiorinal wasn't working. I was a captive to the pain. A prisoner dodging the ricochet of a cannon blasting within the walls of my brain.

She came back to the couch.

"All right," she said. "But then we talk."

She sat down and I could tell she was thinking. Whenever Alice was thinking, you were not supposed to interrupt her. You were supposed to sit by quietly until the thinking was completed. If you interrupted her, she flashed a look of such annoyance that you would feel the inside of your heart curl. It was better to avoid annoying Alice.

"Okay. This is a true story,"

They were all true, according to Alice, even the one about the aliens kidnapping people from Fresno.

"This guy leaves a note. He's very despondent. He decides he's gonna jump from the twelfth-story window of a large apartment complex. So out he goes, whoosh."

I peeked out at her. She was completely involved now. She especially loved making sound effects. My head pounded but I cared about it less.

"What he doesn't know is a safety net exists at the eighth floor. For the window washers, you know. And so he's falling, falling, falling, when suddenly a shot rings out from a ninth-story window and a bullet lodges in the suicide guy's heart."

"Lovely," I said. Thud, thud, thud, went my head.

"So, he dies. It turns out that the bullet was fired by an elderly man who had been pointing the gun at his wife during an argument. The question, of course, for the investigators was whether this was now a murder or a suicide, since the eighth-floor safety net would have saved the man's life and the man's life had, in reality, been ended by the shotgun-wielding grandpa."

She took a drag of her cigarette. I reached for two more Fiorinal, washing them down with a shot of vodka. If I was lucky, I had just murdered the headache.

"So anyway, the old geezer tells the police that he didn't know the gun was loaded and his wife vouches for him, saying that he always threatened her with the gun when they were fighting but that he never, ever, ever loaded it. In the end, no charges are filed against the old guy."

"Nice," I said. I felt a sudden torpid immobility. A velvet curtain was coming down on the world. Relief at last.

"So here's the clincher."

"You mean there's more?"

She smiled a greedy, impish smile.

"It turns out that the suicide was a young man despondent because his mother would not include him in her will and, knowing that his father always threatened his mother with an unloaded gun, decided to load the gun so that when his father pulled the trigger, he would kill her. But the father, yes, you guessed it, ended up killing his son, who happened to be jumping from the twelfth-story window of their apartment building, instead."

"That one's live, Alice," I said.

We did a high five. I met resistance raising my arm, as if a long, gooey tendril of gum kept it lashed to the ground.

"What's wrong with you?" she asked.

I chose not to answer because suddenly a number of options seemed plausible, not the least of which was that I was trapped between a layer of drugs and a layer of reality and couldn't tell which was which.

"I'm worried about you," she said.

"So what else is new?"

"Look, I'm serious. You haven't even started your installation. Shouldn't this stuff be at the museum by now? Shouldn't you be carving and sawing and gluing or whatever it is you artist types do?"

"Well, since you're just an accountant and don't understand—"

"You know, you never used to be bitter. Sarcastic maybe. In college especially. But lately you've developed this real nasty streak."

"It's a coping skill, like denial."

She grabbed my hands, squeezed them and looked imploringly into my eyes. I felt a moment of panic.

"I don't think it's a good idea to get mixed up with that Zeke guy. He's not your type. You need someone very, very sweet. Someone who will offset your . . . eccentricities and not excite them. Do you hear what I'm saying?"

"Alice," I said, giving her hands an adios squeeze and pulling out, "I hear what you're saying. And I promise, starting tomorrow, or maybe as soon as this headache is gone, I'll get to work. As far as Zeke goes, it's just a phase. I don't even like him."

"Then why take unnecessary risks?"

I thought about Esther then. I saw her driving in the man's car, curving in and out of the highway, touching him from time to time, laughing from time to time, high on the risk, high on the illusion that she was getting away with it one more time. I pictured the two of them registering at the motel, how he already knew he was going to kill her when he gave the night manager a fake name, a fake license plate number, a fake ID.

I had no answer for Alice so I told her that just being alive was a risk.

"Well," Alice said, "maybe I'm not talking about risks like, you know, crossing the street and getting hit by a car. Maybe I'm talking about greater risks. Risks to the soul."

"Soul? I thought you were an atheist."

"Atheism and believing in the soul are not mutually exclusive."

My head went thud, thud, thud.

"Let's take bondage, for instance," she said, eyeing me. "Now, I am not one to politicize sex. Sex is sex. I once knew a man who only came if he put his dick in a high-heeled shoe. But let's just get this straight. Bondage is the ultimate prison for a woman because it demeans and pleasures all at the same time. I ask you this . . ." She was getting excited. She lit a cigarette, dragged dramatically, said, "You tie her up, you pleasure her. Go figure. Where's the freedom?"

"Maybe for some woman, it is freeing," I said, remembering the way I escaped my body whenever Zeke tortured me. It struck me as odd that in order for me to have an orgasm, I had to vacate the premises of heart, lungs, ribs, breast, body. It occurred to me that the material was becoming increasingly less important. Who cared about flesh and bones when you could Houdini yourself into pleasure? I sat up, excited by my own ideas about Zeke.

"Give me a cigarette," I said.

Alice reached for my smokes on the coffee table. She lit one for me. I took a drag. There was a certain clarity to my intoxication.

"Listen," she said, quietly now, insistently. She had a way of speaking sometimes that drew me into her, that made me grateful she had chosen me to be her friend. I wanted to listen to her, to take her advice. I wanted to feel better. I had not felt well in a long time. When she spoke to me like that, using a voice like feathers falling on a snowbank, I wanted to comply, to follow, to fall into the soft cradle of her perfect, logical comfort. She was fearless, a mother in her protection, a sister in her friendship.

"You need to listen carefully. I will always love you. Okay? But you have to get up off that couch. You have to get ahold of yourself. You have to accept that Esther is dead."

I considered this. Suddenly it didn't seem like such a difficult thing. I looked at my hands, the barometer of my existence. If they moved when I told them to, I was alive. I moved them. But Esther was nowhere. She did not breathe. She was gone.

It seemed suddenly comprehensible. Esther was dead. I looked up at Alice. Her expression was all tenderness and encouragement.

"You are only hurting yourself," she said. "And you have talent. You have been called on by the gods of San Francisco's art world to enhance reputations. Yours. Theirs."

I nodded. It seemed all right suddenly. I knew what I had to do. Tomorrow, I would quit smoking and drinking. Tomorrow, I would start on the installation. Really start. I would tell Zeke it was over. I would go to Esther's grave and say good-bye. Kiss the corners of the tombstone, touch the hard rock, cradle the flowers before giving them to the grave. I nodded my head. Looked at my hands and wriggled my fingers. I understood.

"You're right," I said, and even my voice had a conviction in it I had never heard before.

She looked at her watch.

"I have a date," she said. "I have to get ready."

I nodded, choking back the rocks that had settled in my gut and were now trying to escape in the form of tears. I would not cry. A Goldblum does not cry. But it was a start. The granite was crumbling.

"A new guy?"

She rolled her eyes, picked some lint off the blanket.

"Yeah. I didn't even get to phase one with Sam. You know, the frank discussion of intimacy, my requirements and all that. He was too impatient. Jesus. These people are potentially spreading disease and they don't even care. It boggles the mind."

"Sorry," I said. "About Sam, I mean."

"Yeah, well, someday, maybe."

She stood up to go just as the phone rang. She looked at me with a curiously suspicious expression. I looked around for the phone, not having seen it in a couple of days. It was over by the alcove where I slept.

"Okay then," I said, experimenting with the ground. One foot. Then the other.

She stayed where she was. I went to the phone, picked it up.

"Hello?" I looked at Alice. "Hey," I said, into the phone. I put my hand over the receiver and whispered to Alice, "It's my mother." She nodded and left the studio, shutting the door quietly behind her.

I went back to the phone.

"I'll be over in fifteen minutes," Zeke said.

"Yeah," I said. "See you," I said. I went back to the couch and poured myself a drink. *Tomorrow*, I thought.

We are going to Lake Lauganita to catch frogs. Danny Franconi is driving his mother's Chevy Nova, a pack of cigarettes rolled up in the sleeve of his T-shirt. I am in the backseat with Eddie and Martin. Eddie has me pinned against the seat and Martin is performing his version of torture—poking me in the chest with his index finger, not so it hurts but so it becomes a monotony of torment. I squeal, half liking it, half hating it. In my struggle to get free, I kick the back of Danny's seat.

"Quit fucking around," Danny screams, and my brothers instantly stop. It is no mystery that we are all slightly afraid of Danny, whose father went to jail for some undisclosed act of violence and whose sister Simone got pregnant and had an abortion, refusing to deny it even when the neighbors called her a whore.

The only person who is unafraid of Danny is Esther. She laughs at him when he tries to get tough with her. She laughs now at our obedience. She is always telling me he is really a pussycat, that his tough exterior is all for show. Sometimes she tells me he's like that because he's Italian. Sometimes she says he's like that because he is lonely and angry. But it doesn't matter what she says because I am afraid of him no matter what, and whenever he looks at me directly in the eyes I blush or turn away, my heart racing.

It is late spring, the pussy willows and acacia are blooming. The air is fragrant with honeysuckle and the sky is pale blue like the underbelly of a pansy. The hills have turned the color of golden wheat and horses and cows integrate peacefully, dotting the landscape in a way that makes them look like a calendar photograph.

We drive fast down the expressway, the wind blowing in through the open windows and I can smell the musky, dirty-hair smell of my brothers on either side of me. Eddie takes my hand absently and slaps it gently between his two hands as he watches the world go by. Mary is not with us, having chosen the relative safety of a Camp Fire girl sleepover rather than risk damage, emotional or otherwise, from the army of us.

As we near the wet, dark roads close to Stanford University and the lake, Danny slows down and Esther moves over to his side. He looks at her and puts his arm around her. They kiss for so long that I am afraid we're going to drive off the road and land in a ditch. But Danny seems to have mysterious dexterity and he maneuvers the car expertly through the narrow, winding roads all the while that his eyes are glued to Esther's.

After a few minutes of this intimacy I look away. Eddie has apparently noticed nothing. He is too busy taking pictures out of the moving car with the new camera he bought using Maggie's S & H green stamps. But Martin glares at the back of Danny's head with a mixture of jealousy and loathing as Danny caresses our sister's face. When Martin sees me staring at him, he turns to me and rolls his eyes. I pick up the net I am going to catch polliwogs with and put it over my face. I roll my eyes and then go into a parody of kissy face.

We get to the lake and Esther and Danny disappear immediately, taking a blanket and a bottle of Boone's Farm Strawberry Ripple with them. Eddie carries the basket of lunch Maggie has made for us—egg salad sandwiches and Chips Ahoy cookies—and I carry the Thermos of Kool-Aid to the shore of the lake. There are polliwogs everywhere, I can see this right away, but not for several minutes do I notice the hundreds of small frogs lining the murky shore of the water.

"Holy shit," I say. I am twelve and believe that swearing makes me cool. "Look at those fucking frogs."

"Cut it out, Baby Goldblum," Martin says. He has a prudish streak that makes itself known only when we are not around our parents, since all of us believe that we have a certain duty to annoy them as much as possible by swearing, lying and generally disobeying.

Eddie is already knee-deep in the water with a net, gathering polliwogs and examining them under the blazing spring sun. He wades over to a small island of rocks and tall grasses and scoops a frog up in his hand, looks at it, holds it up in the air, palms outstretched, and watches it leap back into the water. Diamonds of light cascade from the face of his watch.

Martin, who has been killing and stuffing animals for several months, picks up a large frog, kills it through a merciless act of suffocation and places it carefully in a plastic case that he stuffs into the pocket of his overalls. He does not appear particularly happy about having to do this. But he does not seem particularly unhappy either.

For a long time, I sit on the shore drinking Kool-Aid. I breathe in the fetid, eggy smell of wet moss and slimy rocks. Seed pods float through the air. A flock of red-winged blackbirds fly overhead and I make a wish. I wish that I will be just like Esther when I am fifteen. For a few minutes I watch Eddie greedily fill a bucket with tiny silver frogs. Then I get up and head in the direction of Esther and Danny.

I don't realize until I start walking that I intend to spy. I think of the book I have recently finished reading called *Harriet the Spy*. I search for clues of their whereabouts but it is fairly obvious. I can smell the trail of Esther's perfume and once in a while the wind brings their voices to me.

The grass is high and the color of summer wheat. There are hidden rocks and snake holes to be negotiated. A few feet away is a huge rock with peace symbols and the words LED ZEPPELIN RULES and DF LUVS EG painted on it. I walk up to the rock as quietly as possible. I am too young, though I won't be in a moment, to think that people would take their clothes off in public.

But there they are. Esther is on her knees. Danny is leaning up against the rock, his eyes closed. She has his penis in her mouth. She appears to be enjoying this but I feel my stomach do a somersault. Why would anyone put that in their mouth? While I am contemplating the number of germs that must exist on the end of a penis, Esther opens her eyes and looks in my direction. She doesn't miss a beat. She pulls Danny down, to his audible protests, and covers his body with hers. I turn and make a run for it, not the least bit surprised that the sight of their commingled bodies against the golden hues of the tall grass alights in my imagination and takes wing like the flight of some exotic bird.

I race back to the shore of the lake, where Martin has collected generous amounts of dead lake creatures. He is sitting against a tree writing furiously in a journal of some sort. I come up behind him, my stomach still pitching from the idea of Danny's thing in Esther's mouth. I look over my brother's shoulder and make out the words "Evolutionary Features, Webbed Feet." There are several exquisite drawings of frogs and polliwogs.

"You're blocking the light," he says. He covers his notebook with his hands.

"So."

"So shove off."

"You shove off."

This circular conversation goes on for a while until I get tired of it. For some reason, I'm not sure why, I am angry. I want to get into a fight. But Martin remains maddeningly neutral. He will not engage. Maybe killing all those animals has its way of nullifying rage.

Eddie is sitting on a rock on the shore of the lake with a fishing rod in his hands. When I sit next to him, I sense his placidity, his happiness to be there doing nothing. He doesn't mind that he never catches a fish. But each time we come here, he dutifully throws a line into the lake. I am concerned by this non-goal-oriented behavior. I do not understand why anyone would do something just to do it.

"I'm bored," I say.

"Eat something."

"I'm not hungry."

"What is it, Baby Goldblum?" he says. His eyes remain fixed on some point in the center of the lake but he is with me all the way. "What's bothering you?"

"I'm bored," I say. I want to tell him about Esther and Danny. The incorporation of their two bodies into one has, in the end, unsettled me. It is almost as if their action has taken something from me. I don't recognize it for what it is, the permanent addition of jealousy to my range of emotions, but I'm certain nonetheless that I will never know how to explain what I feel. Nor will I be able to tell my brother what I saw Esther and Danny doing without dying of embarrassment. I have, after all, inherited something of Maggie's Catholic prudishness.

"It's good to be bored," he says. "Think of all the people in the world who are starving or growing up in ghettos and stuff like that. They don't get to be bored. They have too many things to worry about."

I think about it. The image of people foraging through garbage cans for food comes to my mind. I think of all those starving children in Africa with puffed-up stomachs and the giant whites of their eyes while flies hover around their mouths.

"Why do you always fish, Eddie? There aren't any fish in the stupid fucking lake."

"How do you know? If you don't keep after something, you never know the truth. There might be one fish in the stupid fucking lake. And if there is," he leans over and starts tickling me, "I'm gonna make you eat it."

Eddie is so handsome and so funny that being with him makes some of my anxiety disappear. We sit side by side in silence. Then I hear Esther's voice, her laughter. I turn around and she and Danny are emerging from the shade of the scrub oak. The sunlight shines down on her hair. She is always laughing with Danny except when Danny is serious. Then she is always serious. I watch them, two tiny dots in the distance, and I have the sudden revelation that Esther does not love me the way she loves Danny, that Esther has never loved anyone the way she loves Danny. The two of them are like one person, they are like the fusion of energy Harold speaks about after several martinis. They seem interdependent on each other for survival. I know of no other relationship like theirs. I don't know it yet, but I will never know anything like it again.

As they get closer to us, I try to find something that will define the fact that my sister has recently taken Danny's penis in her mouth. But there is no clue.

"Hey," Danny says. He is wearing sunglasses. His cigarettes are rolled up in the sleeve of his T-shirt. He is the only one wearing jeans. Danny would not be caught dead in shorts.

"Hey," says Martin.

"Dead shit again, huh?"

Martin ignores him.

"What do you see in all this dead shit?"

"Possibility," Martin says.

Danny laughs hysterically. A flash of worry bolts across Esther's face. She has stopped smiling.

"I'll show you possibility," Danny says. He grabs his crotch and squeezes it. He looks over at Esther and winks. She does not respond except to raise her eyebrows. I know, having spent my life around people who drink, that it is not so much Danny talking as it is the Boone's Farm Strawberry Ripple talking.

"Let me see them dead things," he says. He picks up the frog that Martin so meticulously killed. "Man, oh, man. One day that's gonna be us. All dead and shriveled up."

Martin remains absolutely still.

"Danny," Esther says. It is almost as if the sound of her voice drugs him. His entire demeanor changes. He drops the frog and goes over to Esther. She whispers something in his ear and he makes a sound like *"ay carumba."* He pushes her against a tree and starts to kiss her. Martin picks up the dead frog lovingly and sadly. His face is white as a sheet.

Esther is saying no. Her voice is unruffled, insistent and firm. But Danny won't stop kissing her. Martin continues to look at the frog, turning it over and over in his hand, touching it. We can both hear Esther's insistent no and Danny laughing, ignoring her. What happens next happens so quickly, I hardly see it take place. Martin stands up with the frog still in his hand and he races over to the tree, pulls Danny off of Esther and throws the dead frog in his face.

"She said no, you asshole."

For a moment Danny is flabbergasted. I wait for him to beat my brother up. But instead he does the strangest thing. He picks the frog up and hands it back to Martin. Martin stares at it, not comprehending for a moment that he is still alive.

"You're right, man," Danny says. "I'm sorry."

Then from the shore of the lake, Eddie stands up and shouts, "Hey, Baby Goldblum, look at this."

He holds up his fishing rod. There is a tiny fish, about six inches long, on the end of the line. It strikes me as odd that in the space of three minutes two entirely different realities coexisted on the same patch of land at Lake Lauganita: Eddie's patience paying off and Martin's courage finding reward.

Before we leave, Eddie takes a picture of Esther and me standing by the car, which she will cut out, place in a locket and wear around her neck. In the picture, we are both smiling as if nothing ever happened.

Then we all pile into the car, drenched on too much sun, a bag of Chips Ahoy and, for Danny and Esther, an entire bottle of Boone's Farm Strawberry Ripple. At one point Danny makes a sharp left turn that causes the flimsy cover of Eddie's bucket to come loose, freeing dozens of distraught frogs. As they hop frantically through the car, Danny says, "Goddamnit, I told you not to bring those things in here," and Esther turns to me and winks while she puts her index finger to her lips. She is referring to my having caught them at it earlier by the rock. It is a gesture that forces me to come face-to-face with the fact that I am, for Esther, not much more than custodian of her secrets. I am aware of my convenience for her, but would never change worlds with anyone. She has chosen me, I think. I am the only one she trusts.

T h e r e was a garden in Golden Gate Park named the Helen G. Urganis Camellia Garden after a woman—Helen G. Urganis—was raped there and sliced into four parts in 1974, the same year I had finished a sculpture of Esther made entirely of wax paper and steel wool. Maggie had taken one look at it, then at me and had said, "*Mon cherie*, I hope you aren't taking drugs."

I was ten years old.

Now I was standing before the camellia garden alive with winter blooms and slick, deep green leaves, after spending fifty dollars of the last two hundred granted to me by the corporate underwriters of the exhibit. I bought two cartons of cigarettes, a bag of Cheetos, two bottles of vodka and a box of Entenmann's cookies. After the stipend ran out I would be broke.

From the paths that wound around the camellia garden, I could see the De Young Museum, its orange hue emboldened by the late winter sun, and I kept thinking, *Holy smokes, Robin, they're trying to kill me.*

An extremely well-groomed couple passed by on the path. The woman, wearing very expensive Italian shoes and panty hose, laughed at something the man said and put her arm through his. He smiled in a way that suggested he was anointing her beauty for some higher good. I had a sudden longing to be like her, to be with someone like him, to appear as beautifully manicured. Something about them reminded me of the hysterical perfection of expertly tended lawns and gardens, the absolute public politeness of landscaping. I watched the couple until they rounded the path and disappeared from sight, and when they were gone I felt as if I'd been abandoned.

After a while, until my hands were actually blue from the cold, I went inside the museum and headed for the administrative offices. I asked a secretary if Lucille K. Johnson, who had the dubious title of curator of the Newly Emerging Local Artist Exhibits, was available. The secretary stared at me. She was blond, blue-eyed, eerily Aryan. The name plate on her desk read *Gerta Heinz*. I remembered the time Harold read Elie Wiesel's *Night* and cried for three days until Maggie told him to get ahold of his damn self. After that he went back to the garage and immersed himself in the haunting fantasy world of quantum physics, quarks and black holes as he worked on a new dollhouse.

Though I had met with her several times, Lucille K. Johnson was viciously formal and the effect was that I could never remember what she looked like or where her office was.

I was escorted by Das Führer through a blue door with the word *private* posted on the outside. As we walked down the hall to the office, the secretary said to me, "She's been trying to reach you for days, Ms. Goldblum. Days. She's been quite worried. Quite, quite worried."

"I'm sorry. I'm sorry," I said, picking up her tendency to repeat herself.

The woman turned and looked at me as if I had just told her to fuck off. She opened the door to Lucille K. Johnson's office while she knocked on it and left, closing the door quietly behind her.

I sat down in a stale-smelling office with De Young Museum posters adorning every inch of wall space. There was a picture of Lucille K. Johnson and her clone, in the form of what must have been her daughter, at the edge of the desk. There was no evidence of a Mr. Lucille K. Johnson, but there was a small photograph in an elaborate, silver frame of another woman holding a dog and smiling a generous smile. Her hair was silver and shorn in that San Francisco way that suggested feminist, lesbian, vegetarian.

I listened to her end of the phone conversation, the labor of her voice, like her hair, cropped short, the consonants especially, chopped off as if language were a merely utilitarian function and if she didn't have to, she would prefer not to speak.

"Of course, Mirna," she was saying, talking down, talking to a child, "but Mr. Seldholm insists that the Africans and the Incans are switched. . . . No, not my domain . . . no, Mirna . . . No . . ." There was a long period of silence though I could hear the tinny prattle of Mirna's voice coming through the receiver and then, without warning, Lucille K. Johnson hung up the phone.

"Well, Louise," she said, chopping off my name in a short, quick hiss of the s. "What's going on here? We expected you'd have started by now. It's only a month away. You don't return my phone calls . . ."

She was a thin, intense-looking woman with deeply set eyes and a complicated network of bones in her face. A certain, wistful beauty clung to her, as if trying to escape the prison of a bad attitude. She was dressed smartly in a pair of pinstriped pants, a white shirt and an over-size black jacket.

"I'm so sorry," I said. "My sister died and . . ."

"Oh," she murmured, uncomfortably shifting in her chair. I realized, not without my own discomfort, that I'd been using Esther's death as an excuse for a long time. She would have hated me for doing it, but I couldn't seem to stop. "I promise I'll start tomorrow, first thing. I've got everything ready."

"All right," she smiled, a thin caricature of a bitchy teacher's smile. "Felipe Gomez can help you move your things if Shey hasn't already arranged things. Here's the number." She reached into her drawer and pulled out a business card. On the back of it, she wrote down Felipe's phone number. I noticed a large silver ring with a black stone on her pinky finger. It was much too large for her surprisingly thin, dainty hands. I stared at the stone, intrigued by its resolute blackness, wishing it could be a place.

"If there's anything I can do . . ." she said.

"Oh thanks." I paused for drama. "It's just going to take time."

She nodded curtly, the half-smile vanished and for an instant she stared off into space. It occurred to me then that if I failed they'd have an excuse on my behalf. Everybody would have an excuse because I had made sure of it. They could always smile sadly and say, "Poor

Louise, she was so grief-stricken she went ahead and threw her career down the toilet." I got up to leave.

"Thank you," I said. "I won't let you down."

Outside, the air was filled with crystals of light; cold, shiny air that burned my lungs. I lit a cigarette and the smoke billowed out of my mouth in a cloud of fumes and warm steam.

I walked through the park heading toward Stanyon and Hayes streets. I smoked one cigarette after another. When I got to Zeke's building, I rang the bell. No voice came over the intercom but in seconds I was being buzzed up. I climbed the spiral staircase, breathing in that old book smell, my heart battered into rebellion by anxiety. I hadn't been back since the first night I met him.

Zeke's door was wide open. Swanky food smells met me at the door: garlic, butter, dill. This surprised me. He struck me as so hamburger noodle casserole and cheesy potatoes. But when I walked in, there he stood over the stove, an apron covering his body and a neat convention of spices arrayed at his left elbow. He did not seem at all surprised to see me.

"Do you like sole?" he asked without yet turning to look at me.

For a moment I thought he was talking about music. Blues, soul, rap, funk. But then I saw the white fish corpses on a bright pink plate, sprinkled lightly with fresh dill. I thought of Zeke, of his soul, and I could picture it, a twisted mist barreling into walls, lost among concrete and Muni buses.

"Yes," I said.

"It's a special dill sauce of my own invention. Light. With a touch of garlic. And a warm potato salad on bitter greens."

He held up a dish of what I presumed were bitter greens.

"You'll stay for dinner," he said.

"But it's only four o'clock."

He gave me a look, baffled and exasperated.

"What the fuck difference does it make?" he said. "You'll stay for dinner. Here, set the fucking table." There was no rancor in his voice. He had a way of making the word *fuck* sound pleasant. He motioned to a cupboard and I pulled out two plates, the same bright pink as the one the fish lay on. They were heavy and, I could tell, quite expensive. I opened two or three drawers before I found the silverware, baroque stainless steel with an elaborate handle pattern. I noticed a bottle of whiskey on the counter. I reached for it and picked it up, but he grabbed my wrist.

"Ow. Jesus, Zeke," I said.

"Use a glass. In my house, we use glasses."

"All right, for Christ's sake," I said.

He let go, laughing to himself, and I got a glass from the cupboard.

"I knew a man once," he said, "who made his son drink from the toilet, like a dog, just because he caught the kid taking a fucking sip from the milk carton."

"That's rich," I said. "What some people do. I heard about this guy who beat the shit out of his wife with a frozen squirrel."

Zeke laughed. I had never seen him like this. Almost normal. He picked up the whiskey and, despite his previous exhortation to use a glass, took a sip from the mouth of the bottle, winking at me in the process. He was very good at it, teasing and torturing. His apron said PHOTOGRAPHERS DO IT IN THE DARKROOM. It was so atypically nerdy. For a moment I liked him. I watched him work in the kitchen and saw that he gave to cooking the same passion and intensity he did to his photography, to sex, to the dissemination of his cruelty.

"What? Did he just throw some roadkill in the freezer one day and pull it out when he needed it?" Zeke asked.

"I can't remember," I said, thinking back to the time when Alice told me the frozen squirrel story. "But I think there had been some kind of freak frost in Fresno and all these little rodent-type animals died and this guy, pissed off at his wife, just picked up a frozen squirrel off the ground and whammo."

"Whammo," he repeated thoughtfully. "Fresno. Now that's a place for pirates and bandits. What a corrupt fucking city, man. Either the desolation draws in the shysters and swindlers or else it drives them to it. I'd like to live there."

"Yeah, maybe you could get in on some corrupt land deal involving cash from some wealthy, drug-running Nicaraguans."

He grinned and pointed a spatula at me. "Now there's an idea," he said. "You're much more interesting without all that sodden, ridiculous drama of yours."

"What are you talking about?" I felt something on the inside of me shudder. It didn't matter that he accused me of melodrama. What mattered was the accusation made me think, in an ancillary way, of Esther.

"Oh, you know, the heavy drinking, the unnatural way you smoke, like Marlene Dietrich with a cigarette holder. You ought to wrap a boa around your neck and wear false eyelashes."

"I don't think I'm particularly dramatic. My sister did die. She was shot in the fucking head. I think that might warrant some sorrow."

"How do you know she didn't do it herself?"

"Because, she was shot in the back of the head."

"How do you know she didn't want to be shot?"

"You're crazy, Zeke."

"There wasn't any sign of a struggle."

"How do you know?"

Zeke looked at me for a moment. His left eye twitched then stopped. The room seemed to lose air. Silence enfolded us. I thought of her, lying there, nude, dead, of the man fleeing in his car, not fleeing, driving normally, even somewhat carefully. Then I thought of her again, of the silence in the motel room, a silence not fractured by the sound of breathing.

"I don't know," he said. "I'm just guessing."

"Yeah, well. Unless you want to hear the story, you don't have any right to guess."

"Don't talk to me about rights."

He went back to the oven and when he opened it, a steamy draft of dill and lemon floated into the air.

"Dinner is served," he said. He brought the food to the table and lit a candle. I sat down and he pulled a bottle of wine out of the broom closet. Inside the closet, a broom and mop stood side by side, still sealed in their grocery store plastic. They had never been used. I wondered briefly how he kept his apartment so immaculate. After we had sat down he poured me a glass of wine. The sun was just setting. A chill had landed like a cool fog and I was tempted to close the window that overlooked the garden below, but I knew that even small changes and disturbances had the potential to upset him.

"Looks good," I said. It did look good, but I had no appetite.

"You should let her go, you know. Your sister. Say adios, amiga, see you on the other side," Zeke said. He was futzing with his fancy linen napkin, rolling it up then unrolling it. At first he did not make eye contact with me. Then, when he did look up, I could not tell whether he was amused or angry.

"What do you mean, exactly?" I asked. In such a short time, I was amazed at how well he knew how to upset me.

"Now that's another interesting question. What do I mean? What do I mean to you?" he said. "I think probably nothing except maybe a good fuck. I know you like it." He touched the end of my nose with his fork and winked. I felt his tension and slid my knife across the pungent meat of the fish, my heart beating.

"To Lisa Silburner, I mean the miscast father of the child, the boy to whom I must mean nothing since I am not allowed to see him, the mother having decided I'm a bad influence."

"You have a son?"

"I question what I mean to God and I think, ultimately I, you, we are simply here for Him to be. Without us, naturally, He would not exist."

"You have a son?"

He looked at me. The diamond earring sparkled in the candlelight. The room was growing darker with the fading light and I glanced around at all the expensive artwork on the walls, the rich furnishings and at the exquisite tableware. I looked at Zeke and saw instantly that his happiness had faded. Just like that, had disappeared like a vapor. The lines of indignation and fury recast his features, bringing to me the Zeke I knew and the Zeke I feared. I could not love this man. But the other?

"How is it?" he asked, pointing a fork at my plate.

I lifted some potatoes to my lips and ate.

"Very good," I said. "The fish especially."

"Then why the fuck don't you eat it?"

"I am."

"No. You're not. Eat the food. Eat the fucking food." He slammed his fist on the table top, knocking his wineglass over.

"Zeke, please." I looked at his plate. He'd hardly touched a thing.

He glared at me. Then abruptly he stood up, his chair falling behind him, and grabbed a coat from the closet. I heard him pull the door open and when he did, the candle blew out. He slammed the door and I could hear him marching away. I could hear the rage in his footsteps. I sat there for a minute longer and then I got up and left his apartment. With so much beautiful art, exquisite tidiness and the rich aroma of a dinner left untouched, it was the most desolate place on earth.

When I got home I fell into a black, dreamless sleep. At one point, I heard the door to my studio open then shut. Then Zeke was there, sleeping beside me, his arms wrapped tightly around my body. I didn't question it but I remember thinking that I had anchored him, that if he let go of me he would float away. The last image I had before lapsing into sleep again was of his white, naked body drifting above me, creating an enormous shadow over the bed.

I woke up with a start to the sound of hammering. I had met the artist downstairs only once before. He had a kind face, prominent cheekbones and sexy long black hair. He told me he had to get out of New York because there was too much cruelty and heroin to contend with. His work was muscular, large wooden pieces shaped into forbidding constructs that reminded me of shadows and jungle gyms. He had rigged it mechanically so that when you walked by them, they sighed like a breathing person. Now I wondered what he was working on. He made enough noise to wake the dead. Not Esther dead. Me dead.

The morning was bright, the raw blaze of light that only shines between storms stormed in through the windows. Zeke was gone. I wondered if he had ever really been there or if it had been a dream.

I got out of bed and walked around the hideous sculpture I had created. I was aware, on a cerebral level, of its melodrama and its hyperbole. Still, emotionally it said what I felt, even if I could not put that feeling into words.

I went over to the couch and sat down, staring at the red, digital glow of the answering machine. There were fifteen messages. I rewound them all without listening to them. I opened the freezer, took the remaining bottle of vodka out and poured it down the sink. After that, I picked up everything on the floor that wasn't attached and threw it all in a large green garbage bag. I showered. I brushed my hair. I put on some clean clothes. Then I sat on the couch, remembering the day

Esther gave me the key to her locked trunk. *You are the keeper of my things,* she had said. I remember feeling then that no one in the world loved me or trusted me the way Esther did. But I also remembered that slight feeling of annoyance. How well she knew my obedience.

I went to the alcove that doubled as a closet in the far corner of the studio and traced my fingers over the edges of the trunk, the rivets long since tarnished and the stickers faded. Standing there, I had a distinct memory of Esther's bedroom, of the way she would lie on her bed in a pair of bell-bottoms, sucking the end of a twig of hair or smoking a cigarette. I remembered the way her small, personal atmosphere smelled like musky perfumes and marijuana and I remembered the clanking sound of her bracelets when she moved. She was the gypsy of our suburban world. Everyone knew who Esther was. Her peers admired and emulated her. The adults were by turns awed, cowed or enraged by her. Alive, she was bigger than life. Death had only made her larger.

When the phone rang I let the machine answer, but the caller simply hung up. I stared at the monstrous image of Esther's bald, naked body in the garbage can, her legs flailing around the body of the motorcycle in an obscene fucking gesture. Eventually, I covered it with the top sheet from my bed and rummaged around for Lucille K. Johnson's business card. I flipped it over and called the number she had given me for Felipe. I gave him my address and told him I'd be ready to transport some of my things to the museum that afternoon. Then I extracted my installation drawings and notes from a dusty stack of papers and pored over them, realizing finally that they meant nothing to me, that they were old and academic, some mind machination of too much theory and not enough heart. I wanted to feel the panic and challenge that had driven me all my life, that had brought me, at only twenty-nine years old, to this enviable spot. But I couldn't. I didn't care.

I reached for a cigarette, forgetting I had thrown them away, and craved a drink. There was nothing to shove in my mouth, to stuff down the scream that lay in wait. I leaned back on the couch and I tried to picture the man who killed Esther. There were times I could put a face on him and there were other times when I could not. I imagined the two of them having sex, the way Esther might have sex, with desperation and passion and rapaciousness both to be fulfilled and to satisfy. I imagined her beautiful body with its tall, lanky Goldblum edges and her black hair drifting over the body of the man who would soon kill her. I imagined the way she must have thrown herself into the sex as if it were a pool of water, dousing herself over and over again with the stranger's body. I saw him too, faceless, touching her with a precision that must have simultaneously relieved and reviled her. I flashed on Danny and Esther, the way they seemed like one person even when they weren't touching. Sexual precision and expertise would have alarmed them, I was sure of that.

My eyes were closed but I heard the door open. I left them closed, afraid it might be Zeke.

"Jesus H.," Alice said. "What the hell is wrong with you?"

"Fine thanks, and you?" I said, opening my eyes.

It must have been near her lunch hour because she came toward me dressed in her usual work ensemble: today a red business suit that conveyed two meanings at once; come fuck me and don't touch me. A tiny clasp purse dangled from her elegant wrist. She had a French manicure and her long blonde hair was tied in a black bow behind her back. She put her cool hand on my forehead, asking me at the same time if I was sick. I pushed her hand away.

"I'm working," I said.

"Oh, is that how you artists do it? Jesus, you look pale. I've been calling and calling. I thought you were dead."

And when she said it, dead, I thought of Esther's nude body, lying there in its fetal position, the way the motel manager had found her. At the same time I remembered that day at Lake Lauganita when Martin suffocated the frog and stuffed it into the bib of his overall. The effect of these two images appearing simultaneously exploded in my brain and, excited, I jumped and said, "Yes."

Alice raised her eyebrows in alarm as I began to dismantle my horrible sculpture. I first took Esther, then the motorcycle out of the oversize trash bin and placed them on the ground. I went into my storage area and pulled out a large plastic garbage bag of fake plants. I placed them around Esther and the motorcycle. Then I grabbed some chalk and drew a wide circular ring on the floor near the reclining sculpture of Esther. I would have to change the expression on her face to approximate the expression of death. But I had just created an imaginary field of grass and an imaginary Lake Lauganita and that was all that mattered. I had breathed life into the empty landscape of my studio.

"What the hell are you doing?"

I ignored Alice and began wildly sketching my idea on a pad of paper.

"What are you doing?" Alice asked again. She seemed shocked but I couldn't figure out why. Wasn't this what she wanted?

"Picture this," I said. I was growing more excited by the minute. "A place called Lake Lauganita. A beautiful lake with marshland and oak trees and great big rocks and blue skies and frogs in the lake. It is idyllic and beautiful. But look closely. There is graffiti on the rocks, parts of a motorcycle are littered about, the nude, dead body of a woman lies in the grass. And all around, piles of litter, which on closer examination are the photographs of a young boy and girl, are scattered about, as if by a gentle breeze."

As I spoke, I pointed to things around the room, the nude, contorted sculpture of Esther, the misshapen motorcycle, Esther's memory box, which contained almost a hundred neatly catalogued photographs of her and Danny. As I did this, I could see that Alice was transfixed, as though she was experiencing some basic fear for the first time in her life and I understood that it was not for the project, but for me that she feared.

"Are you all right?" she asked quietly.

Sweat had formed on my face. The room seemed small and close. I felt the beginnings of a headache, points of light flashing in the corners of my vision. My equilibrium lurched and part of my body escaped, returned, escaped again.

"Yes," I said.

I sat on the couch and covered my face with my hands. Once more the image of Esther alone in that room, the bullet hole in her head, came to me. I thought fleetingly that she had asked for it, that she had wanted it, and then I brushed the thought aside.

Alice sat down beside me. She put her arm around me. I let her.

"You don't seem well. Please talk to me. Can I get you something?"

I looked at her face, so bright and concerned. I felt a sharp, brilliant angle of pain slice its way between my brain and my skull.

"Are you a magician, Alice? Can you bring my sister back?" I said.

It was bitter and Alice caught the tone first, not the words. When she recovered she softened.

"I wish it had never happened. For your sake. But Louise, honey . . ." and here she brushed my hair back from my soaked forehead ". . . she's dead. No amount of wishing it will bring her back."

"I know that, Alice. Jesus Christ. It's just that so much is unresolved. The fucking case is still open."

Alice reached for a clay frog I had made long ago and scrutinized it, though I could tell she was not really seeing anything. In a moment she set it down again and I had the sudden image of the frog Martin had killed that day at Lake Lauganita.

"They haven't found anything more?" she asked. Her voice was barely a whisper.

"No. And instinct tells me they won't. We'll never know who killed her," I said. I could barely catch my breath. I wanted a drink and remembered a bottle by my bed. I concentrated on the bottle, willing it to be full, willing it to march out of the room and meet my lips.

"You might know one day. Maybe. One day he might confess." Her voice was so gentle I felt the earth sway beneath me.

"She had so many lovers, she told me once she couldn't even remember all their names."

I thought of the many times Esther had told me not to throw my body around. Then I remembered the day at the top of Koral Street when she had said, "Don't ever aspire to be like me." I tried to put these things together, to make something whole out of them but was stopped by the sad irony of it. Another jolt of pain speared my head and I reached back and rubbed my neck.

"You haven't factored in the possibility for remorse on his part. It might make him confess."

"We'll never know, Alice, who killed her," I repeated. "He could have been anybody."

"You may never know," she allowed.

"She was leaving the next afternoon for South Africa. The next day. Why did she go to that old ghost town?"

Alice reached in her purse and pulled out a cigarette. I felt a wave of relief when she handed me one. I saw that she noticed the way my hands trembled but she said nothing. She simply put her arm around me again. I could hear her heart beating, I'd have sworn it. The room seemed to bend down, to wait for me, and I saw the sublime look of expectation on Alice's face, as if she believed I would finally, freely begin to talk about my sister's death. But the heartbeat of anticipation only swallowed me up. My mind went blank and the spheres of dizziness and confusion evened out, a long, flat line of nothing.

"I've got to get this stuff over to the museum this afternoon," I said. "I'm out of money. I need to buy some things."

Alice instantly pulled her arm away. I could feel the disappointment in the withdrawal. She looked at the room, at the parts of my installation. She sighed quietly and reached into her purse and wrote me a check for two hundred dollars. I swallowed my pride and accepted it. I was a month behind on the rent. A stack of bills lay unopened by the couch.

"I have to get back to work," she said grimly.

"Thanks," I said. "I'll pay you back."

She didn't say good-bye, just shut the door firmly. I ignored the plume of shame billowing within me.

When she had gone, I looked at the motorcycle and at Esther's body. I saw exactly how I would re-create Lake Lauganita. I went to the alcove and pulled her trunk down from the shelf and opened it. Esther's memory box. Her things. A train case full of photographs consisting entirely of pictures of her and Danny. No one else. Her and Danny making love, her and Danny nude, a vagina, a penis, a breast. Danny licking a breast. Esther licking a penis. Danny with his clothes on, petting Harry the Dog. Esther inside Danny's bedroom, smoking a joint. It was hard to comprehend such obsession, such bewitchment between two people. But here it was, proof. A hundred or more photographs of nothing more than the study of Danny and Esther. I closed the trunk and locked it.

I waited around for Felipe and the other movers to help me move my things over to the De Young, and after they had moved the motorcycle and the sculpture of my sister into the van, we drove over to the museum. Lucille K. Johnson was not there, to my relief. The guys helped me move the things into the space I was granted and, afterward, I took off to buy some supplies I would need to complete my installation. Large blocks of Styrofoam could be painted to look like rocks. Plexiglas and acrylic would make the lake. I would have to do only one edge of the lake—a shoreline and then a foot or two more of lake bed—because it was all I could afford in the way of supplies. And I would need more grasses and plants. Before heading to the art supplier, I stopped at El Rio for a drink. It was a reward. For the first time in months, it seemed, I was feeling better. Just one drink, I told myself. That would be all. And then, I would stop for good.

12

L y d i a Firestone is Esther's best friend. People mistake them for sisters all the time. They are a sight as they douse their thirteen-year-old selves with perfumes and makeup and take off down the street. Boys hang all over them and act stupid, pushing them and grabbing them so they can cop a feel. Lydia and Esther whisper and giggle all the time. I swear I will never be like that. But I am secretly jealous and think they are the two most beautiful girls I have ever seen. My reaction is the beginning of my ability to show scorn when I feel rejected or alienated, the fledgling growth of my porcupine's quills.

Lydia and Esther spend hours on the phone with each other. I am allowed to sit in Esther's room while she talks to Lydia (though never when she talks to Danny), as long as I promise not to make a sound. I listen carefully. They always seem to be laughing or swearing. They discuss marijuana with the same seriousness as they discuss boys or the development of their breasts. Sometimes Esther talks in code. She says, "You know, *the thing*," or "He *you-know-what-ed* it." I am careful during these moments not to move, not even to breathe for fear of being summarily ejected from the kingdom of her room.

When Esther speaks on the phone, she lies on her back on the bed, one knee crossed over the other, and she twirls her hair, shouldering the phone with her neck. Sometimes she brazenly lights a cigarette and puts it out in an ashtray she hides in her drawer. During these moments of extravagant disobedience, she motions silently for me to open the window. As far as I'm concerned, this is as sophisticated as it gets.

Whenever Lydia and Esther are together, Esther ignores me or makes comments to prove to Lydia that I am just her nerdy little sister and not really someone she likes. They often break out into peals of laughter at my expense. Sometime later, always unpredictably, Esther might ruffle my hair and say, "No offense, kid."

Whenever Danny Franconi is around, Esther stops laughing and whispering. She listens intently to every word he utters. They touch each other like grown-ups. He puts his arm around her or they hold hands. They go over to the schoolyard and carve their initials in the bench. They smoke cigarettes and French kiss all the time.

One day Esther and Danny deign to take me to the movies with them. I climb into the backseat of Danny's mother's car. It is not clear to me whether Danny is driving legally. I swear he is only fourteen, but I don't say anything because I want to go to the movies. But first, we have to pick up Lydia Firestone.

Lydia's father died of some terrible, rare disease, which, according to her, came upon him suddenly and involved a lot of snot and bleeding and loud moans from behind the closed door of her parents' room. Sometimes, late at night if I have just waked from a bad dream, I begin to think I may have contracted the disease and will be dead by morning. I have the peculiar propensity to obsess over death, and am especially good at imagining myself in the dying body of other people. I spend more time than it must be healthy in the dying body of Lydia's father, anticipating death.

As we drive up to Lydia's mansion in the hills, I think of the disease, of her father's death. Then, as I invariably do every time Lydia enters my consciousness, I think of the mystical extremes of her family's wealth. The mansion is an ugly, modern building with lots of windows and rounded stucco walls the color of cowhide. Lydia's mother and stepfather designed it and I often see one or the other of them inspecting it with a critical but slightly self-satisfied expression.

The ceiling and walls inside are simply bare, exposed grids of steel and wood. It looks like it hasn't been entirely built yet, but Lydia says it

is supposed to look that way. There is absolutely no smell in the house,
unlike our house which always smells mildly of smoked fish, onions
and cigarettes.

Lydia's mother is from England. Her accent makes her seem exotic.
I approach her with the deference and awe I would a movie star. She
is tall and slender with a mane of dark hair that she teases into a small
hump at the back of her head. She has one glass eye and when you
look at her it's hard to decide which eye to make contact with. Her
voice is warm and furry but she is elegantly and alluringly cold. You
never hug Lydia's mother. You do not touch. She is like rare china.

Her husband's name is Dick. I distrust him immensely and stay as
far away from him as possible without being rude. Only later, when I
am old enough, will I make sense of the way Dick tickles Lydia when
he thinks no one is looking and the way he stares at Esther, with his
mouth formed into a half-moon grin and his eyes shaped into narrow,
sleepy crescents.

The day of the matinee, Danny, Esther and I climb the steel staircase to Lydia's bedroom and walk in on her pulling up a pair of underwear. I see a glimpse of her pubic hair, dark and matted. She does not
seem the least bit fazed at having been caught with her pants down
and continues dressing casually, standing in front of one of her closets
in her underwear and a T-shirt.

"Where's the Dick?" Danny asks. "Did he get lost upside something?"

"Fuck off," Lydia says unconvincingly.

Esther grabs the locket with the picture of us and the key that hangs
around her neck. She twists them up and down on the chain. Then
she reaches under Lydia's bed and pulls out a locked trunk the size of
a bread box. It is exactly like her own box. She opens it with the key
from around her neck. Inside is a bag of marijuana and a water pipe.
She begins to fill the pipe with pot and in moments is taking a hit. The
water gurgles pleasantly at the end of the pipe. Esther holds her breath
in for a long time. When she exhales, no smoke comes out.

Danny takes a hit and then Lydia, who is still in her underwear,
takes hers. When she is finished, she looks at Esther and raises her eyebrows and, when Esther nods, offers it to me. I blanch. I manage to
mumble, "No thanks." I want nothing more than to get out of this

house of steel girders and into the dark movie theater where I can get lost in the luxurious anonymity of the dark.

After about five minutes, Danny starts telling us about his father, who is in jail for some undisclosed reason, a secret that not even Esther will divulge, no matter what. He says that his father had to join a gang in prison so that no one will butt-fuck him. He actually says "butt-fuck," a concept which horrifies me.

He says that the prison is surrounded by barbed-wire fences that will electrocute anyone who touches them and that guards wielding shotguns are positioned atop the prison grounds in towers. He tells us these things in a way that transfixes both Esther and Lydia, but I think he is being overly dramatic. I think he is lying. I roll my eyes. I go to the window and look outside to show him I am not impressed. He stops talking for a minute and walks over to me.

"What the hell is wrong with you?"

Lydia giggles but Esther remains transfixed, as though her mind has yet to move on past the things Danny has said about his father. I feel my face prickle and begin to turn red.

"Nothing," I say. I turn back toward the window.

"Listen, you little smart-ass," he says. He grabs me by the arm and turns me around. Instantly I pull my arm back. "Don't turn away from me when I'm talking, you hear?"

I say nothing. I wait for Esther to come to my defense. She never does.

"No one turns away from me when I talk about my dad. You hear me, you little brat?"

I nod my head. I'm afraid I might cry. Esther loads the water pipe with more marijuana and Lydia goes over to the closet and finally pulls on a pair of Levi's cords, extra-wide bell-bottoms. Danny sort of pushes me and then he goes over and sits by Esther.

"Jesus Christ, you got some rude family members," he says.

Esther looks at him apologetically and he grabs her face and plants a hard kiss on her mouth. "You are so fucking beautiful," he says.

It is another day in a long, hot summer. We are in Esther's bedroom. Danny is playing the guitar and Eddie is weighing some marijuana on the scale he got for Christmas. I am cutting pictures from magazines, pictures of household items and furniture. I admire these objects because they are unblemished by the torrents of our parents' brand of love. They remain still, perfect, unbroken. I long for such things. I carefully organize the pictures by where they might go in a house. So far, I have several items for the kitchen, the bathroom and a baby's room. Behind the closed door, we can hear them in the kitchen. Maggie is saying, "How do you want me to say it? How the hell do you want me to say it. I tiptoe, Harold, tiptoe around your damned feelings . . ."

"Bigfoot," Harold screams. "It's the tiptoe of Bigfoot."

Something crashes. Esther says, "Teapot, third shelf near the fridge."

Eddie shakes his head knowingly. "Wrong," he says. "That was the sugar bowl, hutch against the wall, top shelf."

"Nope," I say. "The pitcher Mary got Maggie for Christmas."

Esther and Eddie look at me. They think about it. After a minute, they both know I am right. I am always right, having developed the unusual ability to detect, from the sounds they make shattering, what has just been thrown across the room.

"You guys are weird," Danny says. He puts the guitar down with a thud. I am grateful for this. He has no musical gift whatsoever.

"Oh, brother," Eddie says. "I wouldn't talk."

Danny looks like he wants to use Eddie's face for target practice.

"What do you mean by that?"

Eddie, who is older though smaller than Danny, looks visibly afraid. But he has courage, which is why one day he will end up almost dead in an alley after having rescued a colony of elderly people he had never met from the rapacious greed of his Wall Street employers.

"You're the one with the father in jail for murder and a sister who can't keep her skirt down."

In one swift motion—it occurs to me that he is like a cat—Danny picks up the guitar and smashes it over my brother's head. Esther sits up, her eyes bursting open. The action has created a wind of some sort. I notice that my clippings have flown all over my corner of the room.

"Jesus," Esther says. "Danny, for heaven's sake."

Danny retreats at the sound of Esther's voice, contrition spreads across his face. It appears that Eddie is unhurt but in a state of mild shock. The guitar is fine too. Esther turns to my brother, the scarlet of high passion in her cheeks.

"Eddie, you know better than that. Jesus, Eddie. How could you?"

Eddie looks at Esther in disbelief, but I have known for a long time that when it comes to choosing sides, Esther will always choose Danny's.

"Fuck you," he says finally. He is clearly hurt. The words come out more plaintive than anything else.

From out in the other room, we can hear Harold shouting, "Look, Maggie, we don't have time for this. David and Irene will be here in a few minutes. Go wash your face. You look like you've been hit by a truck."

Something crashes but doesn't shatter.

"Brass candy bowl, telephone table," I say.

Everyone looks at me like I'm crazy.

Later, when the Kowolskis get there, our parents are happy, even lovey-dovey. Maggie puts her arm around Harold. Her eyes are wide and glittery, so I know she's been into her pill bottle. Harold leans casually against the wall with a drink in his hand. He is telling the Kowolskis about Danny smashing Eddie with the guitar. For some reason, the adults think this is funny. Mrs. Kowolski says, "Good thing he wasn't playing the tuba," and they all burst out with laughter. It sounds like bullets.

I leave through the back door, determined not to watch them ease into inebriation and destroy things around the house. Outside, the air is warm and dry. The sun is sinking and a slight hint of chill seems to wait off somewhere near the horizon. Soon it will be fall and I breathe deeply, trying to smell the change of season. I have taught myself to be aware of small things that enhance sight. I understand, on an intuitive level, that interpretation relies upon the careful honing of all the senses and that everything I make with my hands must express this. I am eleven years old.

I walk through the schoolyard. I don't know where my brothers and sisters are. I haven't seen Martin for days, and no one seems to know whether he is away on a camping trip or staying with some friends. Mary and Eddie went somewhere on their bikes. For her birthday, Mary has just received a brand-new bike with a long white banana seat and a sissy bar the height of which you can adjust, up or down, depending if you are riding alone or giving a friend a lift. I saw her and Eddie taking off down the street and could hear for a long time the flap, flap, flap of the playing cards Eddie attached to Mary's bike spokes with a wooden clothespin.

I head for the aqueduct that runs beneath the schoolyard. It is empty this time of year and people use it as a garbage can for the things they no longer want. I go there often, looking for things I can use later when I am building a piece. I still have no idea that the strange and, to me, magnificent structures I build are sculpture.

I climb down the thick metal rungs that lead down the steep, concrete embankment. Already, I see a spoon glinting in the sun and go over to pick it up. I turn it over. It says *sterling* on the back. It is a beautiful spoon, with ornately inlaid flowers on the handle. I put it in the front pocket of my overalls, Martin's hand-me-downs, and keep searching, my eyes to the ground.

I continue walking until I near the opening of the tunnel. There are several tall, leafy bushes sprouting out of the concrete near the tunnel. I see the head of a Barbie doll in one of the bushes and go to retrieve it. That is why I happen to be hidden when I spy Danny and Esther, sitting in a huddled mess inside, but near the entrance to the tunnel.

Danny's knees are drawn up and his arms are wrapped around them. I can't see his face because it is buried in his arms. Esther is leaning back against the wall, looking up at the curved ceiling of the tunnel. She wipes her eyes. In a moment it becomes clear to me that Danny is crying and that Esther is crying with him. Esther puts her hand gently on his arm and leans over. She whispers something which I don't hear. But I hear Danny say, "I know, I know."

I am amazed to see Danny like this. It is counter to everything I know about him, every expectation I have for his behavior. I watch the two of them mourn some mysterious death or birth—some cryptic emotion—and it is staggering to me how intimate they are, how much like one person they seem, how totally absorbed they are by the moment. I am astonished to see how consumed Esther is by Danny's sorrow, as if it is her own.

Through our parents I have learned that intimacy, unlike warfare, is an unnatural act between two people, so this unity is new for me. I hide in the bushes, clasping the head of the Barbie doll. It is not the first time I have felt my difference from the rest of the world, but it is the first time I have lamented it. Until that moment, when I witness the huddled solidarity of Esther and Danny, I believe that my alienation is a gift. Now I see it as something else, not a curse exactly, just something to bear, like a birthmark or freckles, something to have forever.

When I get home everyone is having a good time. Mrs. Kowolski has her arms around Harold's shoulders. Harold is flushed and moisture dresses his forehead. They are dancing to Frank Sinatra. I can smell the overbearingly sweet scent of her gardenia perfume and I stare for a moment at the silver bracelets that jangle from her wrists. She is wearing a black midiskirt and shoes that look like the Pilgrim's shoes you see in cartoons. Her black hair is teased into a high bouffant.

Mr. Kowolski and Maggie are at the table, the picked-over remains of the hors d'oeuvres between them like some sort of offering. They are leaning forward and Maggie is speaking so intensely that a vein on her forehead is engorged with blood. Mr. Kowolski is nodding his head up and down vigorously. From time to time he looks up at his wife, then returns to my mother. On the counter is the pitcher Mary got Maggie for Christmas. It is broken in three or four large pieces.

I go to Esther's room. Her smell is everywhere and I breathe it in deeply. I wonder if I smell like her. I smell my skin but don't recognize Esther anywhere in it. Scattered throughout the room are the pictures I had been cutting out of magazines—dishes, lamps, wineglasses, pitchers, a crib and wedding crystal. I look at them for a full minute before I start to cry. It takes a long time for me to calm myself.

13

F i v e drinks later I got home to find Zeke sitting on my couch.

"How did you get in?"

He stared at me blankly for a minute. He put his cigarette in the ashtray and picked something off his tongue, flicking it across the room. He was wearing his long trench coat. He ran his hands over his shaved head, picked up a glass and drained whatever was in it—vodka I assumed.

"Never mind that," he said. "More importantly, where the hell have you been?" There was a flame to his cheeks, a crazy beauty about him that transformed me. I wanted to give everything to him, my lips, my breast, my cunt. I lit a cigarette.

"I'm not the one who left in the middle of dinner last night," I said. I had a slightly sour taste in my mouth and a cranium containing cotton and knives that rattled around whenever I moved. I reached in my purse and pulled out a Fiorinal. I was running low. That meant I'd have to call Maggie soon for more supplies.

"Oh, that." He waved his hand through the air in indifference and picked up a bottle from the floor. He unscrewed the cap and poured some into his glass.

"I asked you how you got in."

He looked at me as if realizing for the first time that I was actually in the room. He smiled. He approached me slowly and kissed me tenderly on the lips.

"Don't be mad at me," he whispered. "I made a key. You don't mind, do you?"

I reached out and he handed me the vodka. The veins in his hand were thick with blood and his fingers seemed larger and stronger than I'd remembered.

"A key? Isn't that just a trifle domestic?"

He ignored me.

"What happened to that sculpture of yours? The garbage can and the naked chick?"

"It's part of my installation. It's over at the museum."

He grunted.

I took a sip of my vodka and sat down on the couch. I had not taken my coat off yet. My hair and my feet were wet from the drizzle that had begun as I walked home from the bus stop. I reached into my coat pocket and pulled out a cigarette.

"Why do you play stupid games with me?" I asked.

"Because you have given your assent to them."

"Oh? What? Did I sign a contract?"

"I like your sarcasm," he said. "It's at odds with that sweet face of yours."

"You're full of shit, Zeke. My face isn't sweet. It never has been."

He came over and grabbed hold of me. He lifted me up and brought me to the bathroom. Grasping my chin with his hands he forced me to look in the mirror.

"Goddamnit, that's a sweet face," he said. He sounded genuinely angry. "Don't fucking contradict me."

"Okay," I said. I could feel that warm, strange surge between my legs.

"When I give you a compliment, you say, 'Thank you, Zeke.' "

I saluted him in the mirror. Then I looked at my face and decided privately that it was anything but sweet. It was not Esther's face, stern, hard and beautiful. It was a small face, lightly freckled, thin with an inkling of the Goldblum potato nose. It was a face that had none of the entrenched sorrow of its siblings or parents but seemed to be leaning into sorrow, afraid of it, waiting, waiting for it, not ready to accept it. Just waiting. It was a face of tired eyes and lips waiting to tremble, lips waiting for the reprieve of tears.

"Some of my pictures are up at the Joseph Gallery in North Beach," Zeke said. "The opening is tonight. Come with me."

"I can't, Zeke. I gotta work on this installation. They're champing at the bit at the De Young."

"It's just the fucking De Young," he said, but I could tell he didn't mean it. "Come with me tonight, baby. Then I promise, I'll leave you alone."

"What pictures?"

"Just some pictures. C'mon."

I looked around the room, which seemed strangely desolate now that the garbage can with my sister and Danny's motorcycle were gone. All that remained was the chalk circle I had drawn and Esther's trunk of photographs.

I pictured the large blocks of Styrofoam I had bought, sitting inside the silent museum, waiting for me to carve them into something real. I thought of the dark, silent museum and the loneliness of a project in its infancy. For a moment I grasped what it was that had always driven me to create things from nothing. The putting of life into objects offered me the possibility of attaching to something else, something outside all the hulking, lurking things in my head that by turns haunted and delighted me. To breathe life into the dead body of my sister took her death temporarily out of me, where it had been nesting, and put it into another sphere altogether. It might be morally superior to be humbled by my sorrow but the thought of hurling all that pain onto the retina of strangers was infinitely more satisfying.

I thought of Esther. I looked around my studio and saw the ashtrays everywhere filled with cigarette butts and a stack of empty vodka bottles that I'd neglected to toss. The message light on my answering machine was flickering insistently. The stack of bills lay on the floor by the couch.

"Okay. Let me change, though. And shower."

"You look fine. Let's go."

I looked again at my face in the mirror, at the mysterious, biological construction that continued to take place, changing and rearranging me. I tried to understand what it meant to think *me* as I looked at that face in the mirror. Now that the monolithic brilliance and beauty of Esther was gone, I had nothing to weigh that face against. The force of her absence had left me floating, insubstantial and lost.

We got into an old beat-up BMW and pulled away. When I asked him where his other cars were, he shrugged. When I asked him who the BMW belonged to he mumbled something incoherent. We drove through the wet streets at top speed. Several times, Zeke almost crashed the car. I took sips from the bottle he had taken from the studio. I smoked. We passed people on the street and I watched them walk, huddled beneath umbrellas and raincoats. Street signs flashed through the rain, a drizzle of reds and greens and yellows, and the white buildings of the city seemed to tower over us at drunken angles, the street to curve and snake dangerously before us. I imagined myself as Esther, running through the world at risk, turning a blind eye to the death that stalked her. I wanted to die like her, in a maelstrom of unabashed violence.

But then at Market, near Powell, Zeke charged through a stoplight seconds before it turned green. We barely missed colliding with a large, souped-up sedan that had the words *Yo* and *Zihuatanejo* plastered to its hood in Day-Glo colors. My heart stopped beating for that brief moment when the car threatened to barrel out of control on the slick pavement as Zeke slammed the breaks on. To the fading sounds of "Fuck you, asshole," Zeke sped away.

"Jesus, Zeke. Are you trying to kill us?"

"It's called jumping the green," he said with a diabolical smile. "You know, like landing before you actually leap, leaving a room before the door opens, anticipating life before it happens."

I took a sip of the vodka to quiet the beat of my heart.

"Known fact," he said, pointing his cigarette at me and taking his eyes off the road for an alarmingly long time. "People who jump the green meet their maker at an early age."

"Thanks for the warning," I said, hoping he'd concentrate again on driving.

In the end, he did slow down. We drove up Columbus and wound our way into the complicated network of streets in North Beach. Zeke drove the car up on the sidewalk of a residential street and killed the engine. We got out and he guided me through the crowds on the sidewalk into a small gallery off an alley.

There were twenty-five or so people milling around inside, clasping glasses of champagne. Several people came up and shook Zeke's hand. When Zeke introduced me, they smiled as if we'd already met, as if I had done something to embarrass them. Then it dawned on me.

"Show me the pictures," I said.

"In a minute. There's some other things I want to see first."

"Now, Zeke."

"Tsk, tsk, little girl," he said. He swatted me on the ass.

I pulled away and walked around the gallery until I found them. There were three of the airplanes he had taken that day at the airport, the silver bellies of the planes at first indistinguishable, looking vaguely obscene, like giant, deformed penises. Then beside them were several pictures of me, two at the airfield, the one he snapped a second after slapping me and the other while I climbed the fence, but this one was taken with a wide-angle lens at a slow speed so that I was more movement than form, lost along the long, chain-link fence.

But the others, the ones that were causing Zeke's friends to stare at me with curiosity or familiarity, were the black-and-white series of me asleep—taken no doubt that first night I'd slept with him—curled up on my side, welts on the backs of my legs. In one of them, my hand was up near my mouth so that it looked like I was sucking my thumb. My hair was tangled, covering my breasts and parts of my back. My ribs showed. My toes were slightly curled. There were several dark spots on the sheets. Blood.

I stared at them for a long time, feeling nothing but a strange, clinical curiosity, seeing my body as if it were not my body, amazed at how long and thin I was, how white my skin seemed against the white sheets, how thick and unruly—*arrogant* was the thought that came to me—my hair looked. I was struck by the haunting beauty of the photograph, not that I, its subject, exuded beauty, but that my vulnerability—the subject's vulnerability—contrasted so brutally with the welts and cuts on her body. It was not the nudity that shocked and alarmed me—that seemed to shock and alarm everyone who looked at the pictures—it was the way the body seemed indifferent to the violence meted out upon its skin.

Then at once, I felt a rage rise to the surface of my skin, my skin turn hot and red. Tears welled up in my eyes. Someone said, "Hey, aren't you the chick in the pictures?" I wanted to tear the pictures off the wall. A tall, thin man with gray hair beside me said, "Posed or real?" I reached for the cigarettes in my pocket and lit one on my way out the door. When I got outside I felt the bile rise in my throat and bent over to let it out but nothing came.

I stood up and gazed into Washington Square. I saw a gang of kids smoking near a fire that burned in a rusty steel garbage can. A homeless man shuffled past, pushing a shopping cart. Two women kissed and held hands by a large tree. I forced myself to think of these things, to picture them over and over again, the fire, the kids smoking, the homeless man, the lovers, and in that way I made it home and into bed without getting sick.

I woke up to the sound of a blender. It was the ancient, familiar sound of my childhood: the sound of Goldblum pool parties, frozen drinks that made the adults act insane, that threw them into corners of unnatural intimacy. It was the sound of Bloody Marys in the mornings, gin fizzes for the Christian holidays, dark, kosher wine slushes for the uncelebrated, unrequited Jewish holidays. It was the ambient sound of my youth, the way music might call up for others the auditory memories of childhood.

"What the—"

"Here. Now drink this. I won't take no for an answer."

"Alice, what the hell are you doing here?"

"You don't return my phone calls."

She handed me a glass of something that looked suspiciously like a daiquiri. I sniffed it.

"It's a smoothie," she said.

"A whatie?"

"Yogurt, ice, orange juice, strawberries, bananas. Drink it."

I tipped it to my mouth. It tasted wonderful. Cold and sweet and slightly thick. It made me believe in the future.

"Mmmm," I said, wiping the frosty foam from the top of my lip.

"Where the hell have you been?"

"Zeke," I said.

"He's killing you, Louise. Have you seen yourself lately?"

I thought of my reflection in the mirror yesterday. I thought *me*. "He's not killing me. I'm killing me."

Alice looked at me. Standing there at the foot of the bed with her arms folded rigidly in front of her, she reminded me of a drill sergeant. She sat down on the edge of the bed. She reached out to touch me but I moved away. I saw how it made her stiffen, how she reared back without actually moving her body.

"Your sister Mary called and asked me to check on you. She says your mother and father are worried."

"They don't worry, Alice. They brood. Or they tap into rage. But they don't worry."

"Look, I wouldn't know. All I'm saying is Mary called and asked me to check on you."

"So you've checked."

She stood up and went to the window. After a moment, she opened it and the sound of the street, the buses and the car horns barreled in like a burst of dammed water unleashed. I heard a woman's shrill laugh and then the foghorns breaking the sounds of the street in half.

Alice turned around to face me.

"I saw the pictures, Louise."

"Pictures?"

"At the gallery in North Beach."

"You were there last night?"

"Contrary to your opinion of me, Louise, I don't live in a cultural vacuum. I saw the posters downtown. Zeke Heirholm. The weirdo my best friend is fucking. You tell me nothing. So I thought I'd go see for myself."

I rolled over away from her. I was not prepared for the embarrassment of it. It was not the sickly white of my body, the bones showing through the skin. It was not my nakedness but the blood, the bruises that embarrassed me. Seeing the marks on my body—that body of the other me, the me of the night—had made me feel one degree more than naked. I could not face Alice because if given the chance she would forgive me. She would want to take me in her arms and soothe me.

"Listen to me," she said. She reached over and my skin rose to gooseflesh where she touched me. "You need to get some help. This is more than just about Esther."

"Leave me alone, Alice."

"Louise, do you want to end up like your sister? Is that it?"

I sat up in bed.

"Yes," I said. "I do. I want to end up like my sister. Six feet under. Okay? Is that what you want to hear?"

"Louise," she said. Her eyes looked dark and mournful. I could feel the pity come off her like waves of sonar. Her eyes filled with tears, but she didn't cry.

"I can't stand your pity, Alice. Just take your pity and your prim, chiffon, bouffant, retro, prissy self out of my bedroom. Just leave me alone. Just leave me the fuck alone."

She stood up as if I'd slapped her. Then her face settled, like the conclusion of an avalanche, and I saw in her expression the hardened epilogue to our friendship.

"If you think it's pity, you're wrong," she said. It was a whisper. Her cheeks were suffused with color. Her lips trembled. But she had her dignity and she had being right on her side. She stared at me sadly for a moment then left the room, and I heard the door open then shut quietly behind her. I got up and shut the window and fell back into a dark, brooding sleep filled with shadowy images of Zeke and Esther.

I knew it was not fashionable, what I was trying to do, that the renderings were too close to reality in a time when reality was increasingly represented by abstract figures and images. Still, I didn't care. I felt, I believed that I was solving the riddle of Danny's death and Esther's death, of what I had always believed was a relationship between them, his death propelling her toward her own. I hoped, at the very least, the critics would give me the approval of a retro label and leave me be. And then I thought of it. Critics. And I actually laughed. I didn't care anymore. It was too much work to care.

When Zeke showed up, I was a sip from finishing my third drink and halfway through a pack of cigarettes. He let himself in the door and sat on the couch.

"I'm sorry," he said.

"No, you aren't."

"You're right." He lit a cigarette. "I'm not exactly sorry. I was afraid maybe I'd pushed it a little, so in that sense, yeah, I'm sorry."

"Oh," I said. "So you were afraid of losing me."

"No," he said.

"Do you think of me as growing attached?"

He smiled. "In the way of the black widow, maybe."

He took a long drag of his cigarette and brought it to his mouth. All of his movements seemed measured and calculated to be beautiful and intimidating. He squinted and blew smoke out of his mouth. He was beautiful but in the way certain horrifying, destructive things—things like explosions and infernos—are beautiful. And his intimidation had the opposite effect on me. It made me feel fearless and willing. I saw possibility in his browbeating and bullying. It was like an opening into the future, a door slamming on the flat, smug face of the past.

I drained the vodka and threw the bottle at him, barely missing his head. This sobered us both for a moment.

"You humiliated me, Zeke," I said quietly.

"That was the point," he said even more quietly. Then I saw that he *was* sorry, that this was a game to him too. In the instant of his apology—because that was as long as it lingered in his eyes—I recognized something of myself: that part of me that was faking it. He seemed seconds from lapsing into tenderness and the thought of it irritated me. Then he stood up, to my relief, and said, "Let's get the fuck out of here."

I looked at him for a long moment. His skull glowed in the iridescent lights that shown from the street below and I thought of all the metallic, luminous things that resulted from Harold's experiments. I pictured my own work, the unfinished installation sitting in the dark untended, and a kind of torpid indifference took over.

"Why should I go anywhere with you?"

Zeke smiled. He raised his eyebrows and I felt my rage rise up again. The smugness. How I hated him. He came over and knelt before me. He glided his large, bony hand across my cheek and then cupped my chin in his hands. He kissed me hard, without apology or passion, and I realized suddenly that Zeke embodied all my artistic cravings. He was the nightmare. But he was the relief too. I remembered when we were young that Martin had once said when you were hot it was better to jump into a cool dirty pond than into no pond at all.

I stood up and headed toward the door.

"Lock it behind you," I said.

Zeke snickered with satisfaction.

No rain. A cold winter sky with slivers of light doubling as stars. Moonless. Our breath was a tangle of steam on the air. I lit a cigarette.

"I want to show you something," he said. "A place."

As usual he had parked on the sidewalk. We got into a new-looking Mercedes-Benz.

"What's with the cars, Zeke? Do you steal them?"

"Yes," he said and started the ignition.

"Doesn't that bother your conscience in the least?"

"I return them," he said. "It's my way of redistributing the wealth, of, how would you say it, bridging the gap between the haves and have-nots."

"Does jail mean anything to you?"

"If you mean, does it scare me, the answer is no. And besides, I never get caught. I never will. Go on and check out the backseat."

I turned around and saw, lying across the seat, a fur coat.

"Gruesome," I said.

"Yeah, but rub your hand over that fur and tell me it doesn't feel nice."

I reached back and glided my hand over the fur. It felt nice.

We drove through the Richmond, by the Irish pubs and trendy breakfast joints, past Green Apple Books and Clement Street Bar and Grill, then farther out to the netherworld of Chinese restaurants and corner liquor stores. The air was so dry and cold you could almost see it, like a pane of glass always in front of you. At Park Presidio he turned right and soon we were on the bridge.

"Did you do it to Lisa Silburner too? Display her naked body all over the city?"

He glared at me and reached under the seat and pulled up a bottle of something. Whiskey.

"You ask too many questions. Some questions just shouldn't fucking be asked. You might think you're smart and maybe you are . . ." And here he shrugged as if considering it. "But you don't know shit when it comes time to leaving well enough alone."

"Zeke, this isn't normal. People *do* have conversations, you know, they do talk to each other."

"Yes, but what you want is conversations on your terms. You follow a paradigm which says you have to do things a certain way. You have this idea in your head about what is and isn't important information. The only way this benefits you is to send you marching in the wrong direction. You are spending time, a lifetime maybe, barking up the wrong tree."

"Bullshit, Zeke. Two people sitting in a car exchange information back and forth. It's not that difficult. You say, 'How are you,' and I say, 'Fine,' and it goes on and on like that for a while. Then we talk about other things and it progresses along some kind of linear path."

"You are barking up the wrong tree, sweetheart. Information ain't linear any more than this path we're on right now is linear. You have the wrong idea about the things you think you need to understand."

He opened the bottle of whiskey, took a sip and handed it to me without ever taking his eyes off the road. The night was black, the roads nearly empty. We were crossing the bridge, a speck of light in a universe that, according to Zeke, was not linear.

I remembered the day Harold had shown Esther the gift he had made for her. The crystal garden which, as far as I knew, was still there, growing out of control in the garage, taking over the abandoned dollhouses, rusting bikes, fishing rods, refrigerators. I remembered Danny smashing his guitar over Eddie's head. I remembered Maggie's tail-between-the-legs adultery and the shameful way she skulked around the El Monte Palms Drive-In with Mr. Kowolski. I recalled the day I heard that Mr. Kowolski had electrocuted himself and the first thought I'd had before good manners took over to censor it: *Adios, prick.* It all seemed oddly linear to me, but also like a straight line curving around the dimensions of our dysfunction, stringing us along. A rope tow gone haywire.

"My sister was shot," I said. "Some man, we don't know who, took her to a motel and they had sex and afterward, he shot her."

Zeke looked at me, and in the weird fluorescent light of the bridge, a halo of darkness surrounding the distance, his face was drawn and pale. For a moment he looked like he would explode and deteriorate like fine dust before my eyes.

Then his face became his face again, the bald head, the scar over his lip, the earrings, the strange, furious beauty.

"I don't need that information to understand you," he said. "But you insist on shoving it down my throat."

I wanted to claw his eyes out.

"Give me another sip," I said. "Jesus fucking Christ."

He put a tape in the car stereo and began to sing along with the Gipsy Kings' Spanish version of "My Way." His voice was surprisingly good, strong and deep.

"You speak Spanish?" I asked.

"Only phonetically," he said and continued singing.

We ended up exiting the freeway and driving down a country road, two lanes through rolling hills that eventually gave rise to a redwood forest, shrouded in mist. We turned off at a road that said, SAMUEL P. TAYLOR STATE PARK, and below that, CLOSED IN WINTER. He turned off the lights and drove slowly until he hit a locked gate and a park head-quarters booth. When he turned off the ignition, a resounding silence filled the car. We had drunk enough that I no longer felt the cold. Still, when I got outside, my shoes loudly spanking the gravel path, I reached for the fur coat and put it on. When Zeke saw me in it, he laughed out loud.

"You look like a marmot," he said.

"I knew if I waited long enough you would one day compliment me."

Snickering, he grabbed his own coat, a thick, green army jacket with a big hood, lined with imitation fur.

"Are we going to Freddy Kruger's house?"

"That would be too obvious," said Zeke. He looked above him at the trees and I watched a plume of steam from his warm mouth spiral upward into the cold, starlit sky. "The kind of killer you'd want to find here would be someone not intending to kill. Somebody with a lot of pent-up sexual frustration who just got dumped and accidentally heard us fucking. Something like that."

We were smoking and walking, listening to our footsteps on the gravel. The ground was wet and the air humid. Ferns and redwoods looked twice their size in the shadows and the earth smelled rich and spicy. We passed a dozen or so deserted campgrounds and began walking down a narrow trail, farther and farther into darkness. It had been a long time since I'd heard anything of the road.

"Are you going to kill me?" I asked. I hadn't been scared until I said it. I remembered how I had asked him the same thing the first night I went home with him. Somehow it had seemed different. Saying it then had made it an impossibility. Saying it now brought the possibility to life.

He didn't respond.

I took the bottle from him and drank but he found my hand beneath all the fur and took it, squeezing it hard. Then, all of a sudden, he took off running and I watched him disappear in the fog. I heard his feet and then they stopped. I stopped, my heart beating wildly. I began to walk slowly forward, and the earth around me seemed to bend forward. I clutched the bottle, took a sip, clutched it some more. I felt how drunk I was, as if it had just then saturated my bloodstream. I wondered, perhaps irrationally but perhaps not irrationally at all, if he was going to kill me.

I walked on. The silence sounded like the inside of a conch shell and roared around me like wind. But there was no wind, just stillness and fog, the occasional drip of water.

"Zeke," I said. I couldn't see him anywhere. I felt bleak and lonely. Something huge and nameless wrapped its giant hand around me and I felt myself being smothered by it. I could see myself, floating above, wrapped in the animal fur, floating far away. I saw the image of my sister, the one I had imagined over and over again, the indignity of her nudity, the single bullet hole in her head, the motel room and her clothes lying neatly on the chair. I got into the head of dying the way I once used to with Lydia Firestone's father and felt it, what Esther felt like dying. I might have died for an instant.

But a hand covered my mouth. I heard my muffled scream and shut my eyes. I dropped the bottle of Jack Daniel's and heard it fall to the ground with a muted clunk. Zeke pushed me into the woods off the trail and threw me down. I felt myself fall, as if in slow motion, and braced myself for the pain of it, but the monstrous fur coat buttressed me and I landed with a soft, gentle thud. I saw Esther then, with her jangling bracelets, and I could smell her exotic foreign scents. I felt her wrap her arms around me and say, *Genetics are the equivalent to mirrors. You are my second chance.* For a long moment, I was her and she was me.

Then I opened my eyes and I could see Zeke's face, a face transformed by obsession and yearning. He held my wrists down and kissed my lips, calling my name out in his gnarled voice and then he let go of me to unbutton his jeans, to hold my body as he entered me. I felt the warmth of him, the smell of his whiskey breath on my breath, our breaths commingling into steam and heat in the cold air and I closed my eyes.

Wrapped in the fur, I felt like an animal and could see them, animals in the woods copulating in the shadows, the hard, animal thrusts of sex, the urgent fucking of animals. That was us and the thought of it made me come.

When he had finished, he lay against me, breathing hard. I could feel something like a mixture of gratitude and disgrace in the way he held me. There were tears in my eyes, but I wasn't crying. He wiped them away.

After a while, he broke the edge of night's humility, fraying the darkness and the silence with a whisper shackled by its own terrible sadness.

"I'm sorry," he said.

And I knew—I believed—he was referring to Esther.

14

W e are at Lake Lauganita. It is midsummer and the lake is dry. Green, vomity mounds of algae cling to the rocks. Mosquitos fly spastically in the scattered pools of remaining water. They are multiplying before our eyes and at certain times, when the wind is down, you can hear them, like a sonorous drill off somewhere in the distance. We have not been back here for two weeks, not since the day Esther placed a poem, a dried rose and a seashell at the base of the rock against which, long ago, I had caught her with Danny's thing in her mouth. I am older now since that day three years ago, and somehow the leap between ten and thirteen is larger and fundamentally more powerful than any leap of age so far. I understand things more clearly. It is as if a fog has lifted. So I grasp the mind-altering potency of things like blow jobs and drugs even if I have no experience with them. Now, at the dried-up lake, I am beginning to understand something of the mystery and enormous power of death.

Esther and I are alone. We decide not to walk out to the rock on which Danny and Esther's initials are embossed because of the heat, even though this is why we've come, to pay homage to a rock that is more than a rock. It is a temple, a shrine, the holy monument to their shared bodies, their unified minds, their combined souls. It is a testimonial to the mysterious fact that under certain circumstances two people together are infinitely better than one alone.

I watch Esther and hopelessly look for clues as to what I should do, the things I should say. There are certain things I know about Esther, facts of her life that define her, and I latch on to them now in order to keep her from slipping away from me.

I know, for instance, that she has just finished reading *The Stranger*, in French, and that she and some of her friends have recently been experimenting with ideas of existentialism and a godless universe. They speak to one another in a mixture of surprisingly conversant French and slang English. *Je suis fucked, Tu es fucked, Nous ons fucked.*

They spend long evenings out by our parents' pool, smoking cigarettes and drinking red wine. They are always at our house because our parents are too wrapped up in their own thing to object to their teenage daughter and her friends drinking and smoking and taking illegal drugs on hot summer nights at the old homestead. It is just another of the things that will take me a long time to figure out is not normal.

Esther and her gang also regularly swap recipes for new and creative ways to mix hallucinogens without actually dying. They take drugs nonchalantly, practically without joy. When they are high, they are a generally serious and thoughtful bunch, except for the boys, who get rowdy and filled with desire.

They speak about sex openly and share partners, though this is something that Esther is singularly against. She would never share Danny with anyone and, by the same token, it is inconceivable to her that she would let any other boy touch her body. In matters regarding fidelity she is uncharacteristically old-fashioned and remains that way until Danny is lowered into the ground.

Now she sits and writes the words *godless fuck* in the sand. She has not cried once, not once, but her countenance has gone steely and remote. Thankfully, she exhibits none of the forced bravado of a survivor. The tortured smiles. The vows of strength. Still, no one who knows her will mistake her grief. It is thorough and complete. It has drowned out the color in her face, has stolen her appetite, has profoundly silenced her so that when she speaks you have to lean forward and listen carefully to what she is saying. She is never quite sober, but she is not drunk either. She seems to have achieved a working kind of inebriation, a perpetual gloss of emotions that are neither stony nor blubbery. Though none of us know it, least of all Esther, she is walking through the doors of a new life.

She sits on the shore of the empty lake and throws small, smooth pebbles into the muck. A few birds alight on the branches of a brown, dry bush and she throws pebbles at them. With disinterest she watches them fly away.

"Fuck," she says.

I remain absolutely still. I do not know what to do with an Esther felled by sorrow.

"This is the only time I'll ever say this. Do you understand?" she says, turning on me suddenly with her dark eyes.

She appears to be begging me to understand. I understand nothing except that two weeks ago, just before dusk, Danny Franconi and his best friend, Jack Lombardi, who everyone just called the guy with the harelip, took several hits of acid and went for a spin on their motorcycles. In an attempt to avoid a deer, Danny drove himself over a sheer cliff and landed a hundred feet below with a broken neck and massive internal injuries. His death was instantaneous. Esther refused to look at the body, saying, with the coldest, most ferocious voice any of us have ever heard, "If you all think that mess of blood and brains and intestines is Danny, you've lost your fucking minds."

"There wasn't a fucking deer," she says now. "Do you understand?"

I gaze at my sister's eyes, trying to harvest her meaning. I shake my head.

"Lombardi said there was no deer. He made it all up. He said Danny just drove over the edge."

I had a hard time understanding what she was saying. That's because a Goldblum, I knew, might throw priceless antiques in a fit of rage or torture others for no apparent reason. But the notion of a Goldblum hurling himself or herself over ledges was unheard of. It seemed impossible, therefore, that anyone else could either.

"Why?"

She glares at me and doesn't answer.

"I mean, why did the guy with the harelip make it up about the deer?"

"Oh shit," she says. She stands up and throws a handful of pebbles into the lake. "Why do you think?"

"Did Danny kill himself?"

"I don't know," she says. "Yes," she says and her voice is so plaintive and desperate that I know right then and there that this will never end for her. I know it just by looking at her that Esther's bewilderment will keep Danny alive forever. She has entered a room. It is a room with Danny's image on every wall. It is a room that fits against her body like armor. It has no doors, no windows, no escape latch. It is a room where living people go to live their lives as if they are dead.

She sits down again and lights a joint. Without thinking about it, she hands me the joint and, not wanting to say no, I take it and hold it between my fingers for a minute and pass it back. She doesn't seem to notice that I have not taken a hit and it occurs to me, rather irrelevantly, that she has never really comprehended that I don't drink or smoke or do drugs. It is just like her to think that the things she does everyone does, as if not to participate as she does is unheard of. I feel a moment of irritation but quickly brush it off.

"Fuck," she says again.

I don't know what to do. It is a Goldblum trademark to be exceptionally bad at comforting people who are hurt or suffering. Except for Mary, who has inherited compassion despite her genes, we are a fumbling and embarrassed tribe around the fires of grief.

"Esther," I say, and at the sound of her name she looks up, startled. Unexpectedly her face crinkles up like a baby's. It is as if her face were made of glass and an object has been hurled through its center, shattering it into a thousand shards. She begins to cry. It is a loud, terrible sound I have never heard before and I am momentarily reminded of a show I once saw on PBS with Muslim women trilling at the funeral of a family member. I look around me, afraid someone is nearby and might mistake the sound of her cries for a woman being murdered. But there is no one around for miles.

She screams and cries for several minutes, ultimately grasping hold of my shirt and laying her head in my lap. I feel the warmth of her breath on my legs, the heat emanating from her scalp, and in a burst of unadulterated anguish and misery I kiss the top of her head and breathe in the vanishing scent of her capacity for love.

"Oh God," she says, her voice muffled by the cave of my legs. "How could he fucking do this to me? We were it, me and him, that was it for me. That was it."

A f t e r the fur fuck, Zeke dropped me off at the studio and said he'd be right back. I saw him drive off down the street, the muddy fur coat in the backseat, and turn right on Mission. About a half hour later I heard his heavy boots on the metal staircase and the key he had stolen from me and copied turn in the lock. Once inside, he went to the sink and poured himself some water from the tap. For several minutes he sat smoking on the couch. I pretended to be asleep, tucked away in my alcove, but opened my eyes occasionally to find him looking anxiously out the window. About fifteen minutes passed when he seemed to decide that everything was all right, that he hadn't been caught returning the stolen car and the police were not after him. I took a perverse kind of pleasure watching him, imagining he was sweating it out; watching his fear.

He stubbed his cigarette out and crawled into bed beside me, smelling badly of cigarettes and leather, whiskey and me.

"Your feet," I said.

"What about them?"

"Move them."

He kept them where they were, next to my legs, and I pictured his long white toes. In a few minutes, he was snoring.

When I woke up the next morning, the lingering smell of a freshly lit cigarette was the only evidence that Zeke had just left my studio. I went to the window and watched him walk down the street. A bus passed him and he ran to catch it at the next stop, flicking a cigarette behind him just before the doors swallowed him inside. I turned away only after the bus itself vanished from my view.

I put on some sweats and left the house, not bothering to brush my hair or shower. The air was brittle and I regretted not bringing a heavier coat. I lit a cigarette and walked toward 16th and Mission. People were just waking up, the storefronts emerging from behind their metal roll-away barricades.

I tossed my cigarette and went below to the BART tracks and waited for a train. The walls of the station were covered in advertisements. One of the ads pictured a couple, presumably parents, sitting at either end of a table with their dinner in front of them. Between them a place had been set but the chair was empty. The caption read, "Do You Know Where Your Child Is?" Below that were the words "Partnership for a Drug Free America." Looking at it reminded me that Mary and Dan were coming to the city tonight to take me to dinner. *Do You Know Where Your Sister Is?* The thought of it sent a bolt of panic through me.

The train came and after a transfer and a bus ride through the park, I was standing in front of the De Young museum, a stone's throw away from the Helen G. Urganis Camellia Garden. I hesitated going in. The separate parts of the installation were all there in the gallery. An oily feeling of dread washed over me. I tasted vodka in my throat. I thought of Zeke and me fucking each other like animals in the woods the night before and I could smell my stink mingling with the partnership of our bodies' emissions. I wished I had showered. I ran a hand through my hair but it didn't get very far.

When I went inside, I had to push my way through a throng of tourists to get to Lucille K. Johnson's office. She was on the phone but when she saw me, she quickly hung up. She was as tight-lipped and closed as the first time we met.

"We're glad to see you begin work," she said, her tone overly polite, her words clipped and abrupt. "Let me get you the key to the space. You'll be able to work with relative privacy. Felipe's crew erected some walls. No one will see you. But you'll hear the visitors walking by on their way to the permanent collection."

As she said this, she opened a filing cabinet and brought out a large tin cookie can and opened it up, extracting a key. She came around from her side of the desk and put her arm under my elbow, guiding me out the door. We walked through the crowds together in silence but when we got to the newly erected walls and the doors with the padlock on them, she leaned over and said, "Your project is quite a bit different than I remembered it from the preparatory sketches, which I understand were sold fairly quickly."

"Yes, well, it continues to change," I said. Then I started in on the bullshit. "I don't see my work as stagnant, stopped in time, but something that evolves through time. Nothing I do is ever finished. It changes just as I change and the world around me changes."

"It must be nice," she said. "Not to have to finish something. Not to put an end on it."

I looked at her to see what she knew about me but her expression seemed to be mired in some deep, personal disaster. It crossed my mind that she had cancer or some other terminal illness. When she opened the door and let me pass through before her, she seemed to snap out of her thoughts.

"Well," she said. "I hope it's not radically different, at any rate. We did invite you based on your past installations. We understand, of course, that things change, that as the artist grows, so too does his or her work. But we also have certain ideas about what we like to show in this particular milieu, this emerging artists exhibit. We hope that you don't stray too far from your original intent. You understand."

She was positively official. It made my skin crawl. I reached into the pocket of my coat and fingered my cigarettes. It occurred to me that she didn't have a terminal illness, she simply didn't like me or my work. I thanked her and watched her leave the room.

I turned to look at my things. I had left Esther leaning against the motorcycle and just before going home, had stuffed some of the reeds I had bought at the flower mart into her clenched fist. I had quickly pieced together the Styrofoam perimeter of Lake Lauganita. Felipe and his crew had helped me put the massive blue acrylic lake that I had constructed the day before inside the perimeter. I could still smell the paint drying on the large Styrofoam rocks. Stacked against the wall were the boxes of Martin's dead animals and the plants and reeds I would station around the lake. I had brought the train case of Esther's photographs with me and set them down at my feet.

I looked at the area and my eyes seemed to open past the physical limitation of iris, pupil, cornea so that I was able to see, for an instant, a geography that was different than the reality of the space which lay before me. This was a trick of mine, something I'd been born with — to see objects in spatially reconfigured ways, to reinvent visual reality even as I stared at an old paradigm. I rarely used measuring devices. Something akin to it was already built into my vision.

I disassembled everything, naturally, and moved it around to best maximize the space, to fill it without crowding it. I stacked the Styrofoam rocks against the far wall. Before I had left the other day, I had spray painted DF LUVS EG, and LED ZEPPELIN RULES on one of them just as it appeared on the real rock at Lake Lauganita. I began to place the rocks around the landscape in a way that suggested the haphazard effects of nature, the chaos of being strewn to the earth as if without design. I then began to lay the grasses, reeds and bushes and when I finished that I moved the sculpture of the motorcycle to the southernmost end of the room and lay it down. Then I put Esther's body at the other end of the landscape, partially hiding her behind one of the rocks and a tangle of reeds so that when someone entered the display from this side, they would not see her until they had made a full circle around the perimeter of the display. On the other hand, they could start from the other end and see her first. It was — I decided — going to be their choice.

I opened Esther's trunk of photographs but did nothing with them for the time being. Then I took Martin's taxidermy and placed the animals around the landscape in a way that suggested the natural way they might try to camouflage themselves. I was counting on everything but the motorcycle and the pictures to blend into, rather than stand out, from the landscape. The stuffed animals had held up quite well over the years and I thought, for a moment, how smart and exact my brother Martin had been and always was.

I worked for several hours, not conscious of time passing. Not aware of time at all. When I got tired, I stopped and leaned against one of Felipe's makeshift walls. I knew it was against the rules but I lit a cigarette and was aware for the first time of the crowds brushing past me. Sometimes people knocked on the door. Sometimes they tried the handle. I heard a kid say, "Pee-youuu, it smells like stinky cigarettes."

I sat for a while like this, mesmerized by the sounds of people swelling around me, remembering Lake Lauganita, the hum of its birds and insects and grasses, the lapping of the water against the shore, the feel of the coarse, pebbly sand beneath my feet. I could see the two of them, Esther and Danny, taking off hand in hand through the field, leaving my brothers and me to the Kool-Aid, the egg salad sandwiches, the torpid heat. I saw myself as I had always been, the Goldblum observer, the chronicler of our lives. I had been Esther's tireless defender and admirer. The keeper of her secrets.

I began to do it again, make up the missing details of Esther's last hours on earth. I pictured her driving in a nice car, a luxury car that would hug the road and absorb the curves and stomach-wrenching hills at rapid speeds, at speeds no doubt entirely suitable to Esther's need for high adventure. I saw them driving there beneath the moon's glow and the canopy of oak trees. He must have touched her occasionally and I pictured his hands, not unlike Zeke's—large, defined and beautiful. I imagined him leaning over and kissing her while rounding a particularly harrowing bend in the road. They talked about things that didn't matter. They bantered in a highly charged, sexual way, using words with double meanings. Perhaps he was not quite as articulate or clever as Esther was, but few people were, and so she helped him out once in a while in a way that would make him feel like he was the cunning, inventive one.

I saw them entering the small town of Angels Camp, passing all the monuments to Mark Twain and the frog-jumping fame he brought to the town a century before. I imagined Esther enjoying, in a distracted, clinical way, the Gold Rush–era buildings and the syrupy quaintness of the town in the glow of the occasional streetlamp. I pictured the man bringing the car to a halt in the parking lot of the Frog Jumper Inn and I could hear the silence that would move instantly into place, the deafening roar of it. The unsettling darkness pounded them like something material and physical, and out of it the harsh silver light of the stars appeared, seeming at once both impossible and logical. I felt then my sister's moment of uncertainty, the awkward precedent to that moment a short time hence when she would feel his lips on her body.

It was something I myself had never felt until Zeke—the uncertainty of a stranger's lips on your own, the absolute, tidal thrill of it, the way seconds before impact a thousand possibilities burst forth, none of which makes any sense until afterward, when you have survived it and you think without really thinking it, *Ah, so he did not kill me.*

The fact was, I knew only a few things for certain, details the police and the forensic staff and the coroner could provide. I knew, for instance, that her blood-alcohol level had been three times the legal limit. Traces of cocaine and another undetectable substance were found in her blood as well. She had been shot once in the back of the head, from close range. There had been no struggle, no hairs or skin beneath her fingernails. Her clothes were not ripped. DNA tests had been done on the semen found on her body but no matches had ever been made. Her clothes, a pair of jeans, a black sweater, black boots, a pair of panties and a bra, had been neatly folded and placed on the chair by the bed. Next to the bed, on a nightstand, they found her address book, her airline tickets to South Africa, a pack of Kool Milds and some loose change. Three hundred dollars plus all her credit cards had been left behind in her wallet. There was an empty bottle of vodka and one empty glass. Another glass, wiped clean of fingerprints, had stood on the dresser, still full of vodka. The police assumed it was his.

When we got her personal items back, I went through her purse and found a small locket, without a chain, in a zipped compartment. Inside was a picture of Danny standing next to his motorcycle, a cigarette dangling from his mouth. The locket with the picture of me and Esther, taken that summer day long ago at Lake Lauganita, was not there and had never been found. There was also a poem by Rilke, folded up into a neat square, but it had been written a long time ago. The edges of the paper were worn, the ink faded.

All of a sudden from the park's full green
Something, you can't say what, has been rescinded,
You feel it drawing closer to the windows
And growing silent. Fervently and keen

Resounds alone the rain-note of the plover,
Like some Jerome, so tensely from the brush
A sense of zeal and loneness arches over
Out of this single urgence, which the rush

Of rain will slake. The walls of the great hall,
its pictures, have retreated like a hearer
Who must not overhear what we are saying;

The faded tapestries which line them mirror
Those afternoons of twilight mootly graying
In which we were afraid when we were small.

There had been nothing, besides her death, of course, out of the ordinary. There had been no clue as to who had killed her. The
anonymity of her sex life had worked well for the killer. She never told
anyone who she fucked. I thought for a moment of my boyfriend Joe
Torres. My first love. I remembered what Alice had told me, how Esther had been fucking him.

A group of rowdy boys passed by the walls of my space and banged
on the sides. There arose, as they passed, a cacophony of profanity and
the particular inner-city slang that seemed to me a kind of sad salad of
musical notes. I contemplated for a moment how to translate the
sound of their voices, the testosterone violence of their hardened youth
into sculpture, but I could come up with very little. In another time I
might have had more inspiration.

I looked at my watch and stamped out my cigarette. I was already
late and I knew Mary and Dan would be waiting for me. On my way
home, I noticed the first lights of the Christmas season shining
through the gloom.

When I got to the studio, I was relieved, then perplexed, that Dan and Mary weren't waiting for me in the hallway. I started to unlock the door but it swung open of its own accord. Mary was on the couch. Dan stood off to the side, trying to look interested in the outside of my freezer door. When Mary saw me she hurried over to my side and said in hushed tones, "There's someone here. He says he's your fiancé."

"Shit," I said.

"Howdy," Zeke said, emerging from the bathroom still zipping up his pants.

"He let us in," Dan said, trying to sound casual. Zeke and Dan stood side by side in the kitchen. Seeing them, I realized they were the antithesis to each other. Where Zeke was wildly beautiful, scarred with strange tattoos, starved for an indiscernible god, devoted to darkness, sex and death, Dan was neatly groomed, blandly handsome, shirt tucked in, pants perfectly creased, faithful to Jesus, the pope and the president.

I turned to Zeke and eyed him but he simply laughed and put his arm around me. "I didn't know you graduated with honors from Berkeley. Mary told me that you never used to smoke or drink. Is that true?"

His tone mocked lightly but if you didn't know him, you wouldn't have noticed.

"Zeke tells us you two got engaged last night," Dan said. I could see the degree of his concern by the deep furrow of his brow.

"He's lying," I said.

"Louise, honey," Mary said. "You didn't forget we were coming over tonight, did you?"

"No," I said. "I just got tied up at the museum . . ."

Zeke laughed out loud. "Appropriate choice of words, my dear," he said.

"And then I had trouble catching a bus. I just need to take a shower. Zeke wasn't staying anyway, right, Zeke?"

"Actually, sweetheart," he said, "your sister invited me to join you."

"Oh," I said. "Good. Let's go then."

The three of them stood there staring at me. Zeke seemed amused but Dan and Mary had that gentle concern in their expressions, something they used to develop whenever Esther showed up but was now reserved for me. I realized I must have looked like a disaster, filthy from the physical work at the museum, my hair matted, my clothes a mess. But the thought of showering and leaving Zeke alone with them for one more minute caused an unwieldy panic to rise up inside me. Still, I had no choice. I tried a smile.

"You look like you could use a drink," Zeke said. He was acting ridiculous, robust and overly attentive. He sounded like a commercial spokesman. I smiled again, reached for my cigarettes and said in the same tone, "Then why don't you fix me one, *honey*."

He bowed. He winked. I thought, *Cease, you fucker.*

He brought me my drink gallantly—my knight of booze and perilous copulation. Armed as such with my vodka and a cigarette I shut myself in the bathroom and locked the door. I felt, rather than heard, the silence. Then I became aware of the faucet dripping and the muffled sound of laughter from the studio below. With the first sip of my drink, my body flushed with warmth, my face grew hot and I opened the window, shocking my skin with the cold December air.

I pictured Zeke out there with Mary and Dan, frightening them with his bad manners, his antisocial behavior, his shaved head and its lunar proportions. Alone, in the darkness, Zeke seemed an organic, integral part of my existence, an extra, necessary limb, something essential to breathing, to not dying. But in the context of my other life, the Goldblum life, where I belonged by the sheer accident of genetics to Mary Goldblum, Zeke was a disaster, a freak. Zeke did not belong there.

As I turned on the shower, the thought of Esther came streaming in. I saw her there, lying in the motel room, dead for twenty-four hours before anyone found her. I tried to piece it together. There were no answers. No clues. No one saw her with a man. No one saw anyone leave her room. But she'd had sex, apparently willingly. And she'd thought enough to fold her clothes up neatly on a chair beside the bed before fucking him. Or had he done it later, after he had undressed her, after he had killed her?

I tried to force the inclination to fill in the gaps out of my mind. But they came in a rush and I could no more stop them than I could stop anything—my fierce attraction to Zeke, my desecration of Esther's memory through my installation, the dinner I would have to sit through tonight.

A knock at the door caused me to jump and spill a little of my drink on my bare skin. I watched the vodka make a tear and roll down my belly. The room was filling with steam.

"Louise, honey." It was Mary.

"Yes," I said. "What?"

"Well, the reservations are for seven-thirty. I'd hate to be too late."

"Oh, I'm sorry. I was just . . . thinking."

I got up and put my hand under the showerhead. There was a moment there when I felt the ground leave me and a ripple of vertigo tip me to the left. I looked down at my body, how thin and white it was. How easy it would be to break it.

Later, after I'd showered and put on something demure—a plain black dress, tights, black shoes—we all piled into Dan's Toyota and drove the short distance to a small, family-run Mexican restaurant in the outer Mission. We always went there. It was Dan's favorite restaurant and I understood why. It was the kind of place that offered slightly exotic food in a slightly exotic environment without actually intimidating anyone who ate there. When you were finished you could feel good about having tasted another culture without getting your feet too dirty. But Dan was like that. I didn't fault him. His roots were Catholic, small Midwestern town, one church, little scandal. One did not experiment with Dan. One felt safe with him.

We were seated at a big table in the back, next to walls painted from floor to ceiling with a rich mural of the Caribbean. The waitress was a large woman. She wore traditional garb and a vibrant red carnation in her black hair. But her feet were swollen and when she stood up from behind the counter to greet us, I could see that her back ached.

We ordered drinks: Zeke and I margaritas, Dan and Mary Cokes, and then our dinners, a zesty mess of foods fried in oil and hot sauce. The room itself smelled delicately of corn tortillas and butter. The alcohol I had drunk blunted everything so that the world was vibrant and colorful, and at the same time edgeless and unintimidating. If I could have, I would have stopped at one drink to enjoy the simultaneous expansion and deadening of the universe. But I couldn't seem to stop.

Mary took a sip of her Coke and looked at me and Zeke carefully. Zeke's happy boyfriend act had slipped a little, maybe from the booze, and though Mary lacked the Goldblum wit and shrewdness, she was a good judge of character. Where the rest of us categorized people by their intellectual capacity, Mary went straight for the soul.

"Zeke," she said.

He looked up as if startled. He didn't quite know what to make of such ready kindness in one voice.

"Where are you from?"

"Here and there," he said. "Military brat."

Mary nodded her head. "There was always something romantic about that. We all were born and raised in the same place. Always saw the same faces, knew the same people."

"Yes," said Dan. "But stability is important."

"Oh, I know," she said. "But still."

"Don't romanticize it," Zeke said. He appeared calmer than I'd ever seen him, cowed by some long-lost urge to be polite. "People romanticize what they don't understand. That's why Hollywood, for instance, is so sinister. It's the selling of lies on a grand scale. People eat it up. Moving around teaches you to create your own reality. It's a question

of necessity." His face was flushed. He was evidently moved by something he said or thought.

"I didn't mean anything by it," Mary said. I could see that she felt
bad for having roused his emotions.

But Zeke raised his glass in a toast and smiled. It was a Zeke I didn't
know. A generous, affable Zeke. A Zeke who could clearly charm and
delight but who was also vulnerable and hurt. It was a better Zeke. A
Zeke I didn't want.

"My mother and father are divorced now," he said. He had put his
hand on my thigh, had found a hole in the tights, was inching toward
my crotch. "But they live next door to each other in Phoenix. My
mom takes care of my dad when he's sick. Get a load of that." He
laughed and motioned to the waitress for another drink. He did not
see Mary and Dan raise their eyes at each other, but I did. I knew to
expect it.

"Two more," he said.

"Where did you two meet?" Dan asked.

"At the library," Zeke said. "We both reached for purgatory at the
same time."

Dan and Mary stared at him.

"Dante. *The Divine Comedy.*"

"Cut it out, Zeke," I said.

"All right. The truth is we met in a bar. The Rite Spot."

He shrugged as if to apologize. His sheepishness was at complete
odds with the tattoos, the shaved head, the earrings. But they were buy-
ing it, or at least Dan was. I would have too. The tough with the heart,
the sweetheart with the tough exterior.

But I knew he was acting. And lying. That all of it was a farce. The
military brat story, mother and father in Phoenix, it was all bullshit. I
knew this because he had his hands up my crotch, his fingers inside
me as he was talking and he was trying to make me come. He knew
where to touch me and how to do it. In the end, I pushed him away.

"Cut it out, Zeke," I said. But I felt it anyway, the way I disappeared
so effortlessly into the comfort of my humiliation, vanishing into the
syrup of my own weakness. It was a relief really to know that his fingers
came away wet.

When his food arrived, he put his finger in the guacamole and made a show of sucking it off.

"Very good guacamole," he said. "This is a fine restaurant."

When we walked back to the car after dinner, Mary shivered and wrapped her coat tighter around her. I had my secrets to keep me warm, the violence and shame of Zeke. A cold wind had picked up. It felt like pricks on my skin. Zeke and Dan were ahead of us. Zeke had a good two inches on Dan and was gesturing wildly at the sky. Occasionally you could hear his voice, deep and drunk, but not his words. His gait was expansive and his long trench coat whipped around him in the wind. From behind, he looked like the mad conductor of some ghostly orchestra.

"He certainly is . . . interesting," Mary said.

"That's not what you really feel, Mary. Why don't you just say what you really feel?"

She put her arm around me and held me close.

"I want you to be happy," she said. "I want you to grieve for Esther and get it done with so you can move on and stop being someone you aren't. This girl with the cigarettes and the booze and the fuck you's, this is not Louise. It is Louise trying to be Esther and doing a lousy job at it."

"I am not trying to be Esther."

"You could never be. You have a heart made of warmth and hope and a brilliance and a talent that no one in our family, certainly not Esther, ever had. But it has disappeared behind those Kool cigarettes and that—what is his name, Zeke?—behind his odd behavior. Really, Louise, he reminds me of something the cat dragged in."

"Mary, I don't think I want your advice right now."

But she held me closer and put her forefinger over my lips to silence me. Her eyes were filled with admonition and pity. I saw instantly in the tight weave of her face that I should obey.

"Esther was self-destructive. She was not a bad person but she did not love herself and she did not love anyone else. Whether the one was the result of the other, I don't know."

"You're wrong, Mary, she loved me. She loved me especially."

"She loved only Danny. After he died, she stopped loving at all."

"You're wrong. We had a special bond."

Mary stopped walking for a moment and looked up at the sky as if searching for the words she wanted to say. She put her hand in my hand and continued walking. Her mittens felt warm and furry. I thought of our cat Bilbo Fucking Baggins, who I especially loved because he ran into glass windows with alarming frequency and fell asleep atop fences only to roll off and land on the ground with a startled thud. He died when I was fourteen.

"She loved only Danny. After Danny died she acquired a bad habit, and that was to make everyone feel as if they were the only person that mattered to her. It was her way of getting away from the fact that she could never love anyone after Danny died."

I remembered Esther sitting beside me at the lake, her head in my lap and her words, *We were it, me and him, that was it for me. That was it.*

Zeke turned around and motioned for us to hurry up. I looked at him, at his white skin, his large head, and felt the way I did when Esther died, as if I would be riding on a long train, through a dark tunnel, forever.

When Mary and Dan left, Zeke came upstairs with me. I felt him hounding me with his desires. I thought of the safe word. *Cease.* It rolled through my head, then disappeared.

"Nice family," he said.

"Like you care."

"I do and I don't. It's interesting to see your context."

"Why did you tell them all those lies?"

"They were half-truths. You have a negative way of looking at the world."

"I'm tired of this game, Zeke. I know what you get out of your half-truths."

"Oh yeah? What do I get? Go on. Be clever. Tell me some mumbo jumbo you read in your fifty-dollar psychology book at that fancy college of yours."

"Control," I said. "That's your thing. You keep a person guessing so you can control them."

"Your problem, Louise, is that you expect everything to travel forward, for truths to unfold in a fashion commensurate with your need of them."

"You're drunk."

"And? Your point, please?"

"It's just that you're so snotty. I'm going to start calling you Professor Fucking Zeke."

He smiled. He sat down on the couch with his coat still on, his hands in the pockets. He closed his eyes, leaned back and tilted his head toward the ceiling. The room was exceedingly quiet. A single lamp burned on the glass table I'd made from the shards of car windshields, casting a sad brownish glow into the studio. I could hear the wind roaring against the windows and I could smell the smell of us, a musky tangle of scents amid cigarettes and tequila. I was very drunk.

"I want you to picture something, okay?" he said.

I was lying on the floor, staring at the ceiling, trying to block Mary from my mind.

"Imagine," he said. "An arc in the sky."

I imagined an arc in the sky and Mary vanished. The arc I imagined was lit by bright lights. It flashed on and off like a neon sign. It was a beautiful arc. I swung from it.

"Imagine now an arrow flying along the trajectory of the arc. From the beginning, point A, to the end, point B."

The arc lost its lights. It was now a dark crescent in the gloom. An arc that began at one point and ended at another. The arrow traced its trajectory, moving forward at unfathomable speeds.

"Imagine a point along that arc, say point C," he said. He had moved off the couch now and was walking slowly through the studio smoking, his lips gripping his cigarette, his hands thrust into the pockets of his coat. I looked at him. He was beautiful.

"At some point along its course that arrow must pass through the precise point along the arc, point C. Can you see it there, at that point?"

"Yes," I said. I felt hypnotized by the arc, the arrow stopped briefly at point C, his voice droning on and on.

"The paradox of movement is this," he said, kneeling over me. "That any object in flight must pass through and therefore briefly stop and exist at each point along the arc. This means simply that move-

ment is nothing more than a series of stops and starts through points
along the path."

He was breathing hard as he rubbed his fingers along my lips.

"You sound like my father," I said. "He used to bombard us with
meaningless crap. Crap, crap, crap. What do I care about some out-
moded, outdated paradox?"

"You know what, little girl?" he said. His voice was filled with a rare
tenderness and a grave kind of sorrow. Such mutiny from Zeke's normally calculated emotional landscape made me go silent, made me
listen.

"You," he said, "are so desperate to know who I am because when
you can't point a finger at me and define me it scares you. It's like
everything else in your life. You can't pinpoint the exact source of your
grief. You can't stop it from eating you alive. You want answers. You expect them, like a petulant little girl at the candy counter. You want
your bonbons."

"So."

"So it's you who is out of control, not me trying to control you. You
should know by now that life is not a seamless road where all your mys-
teries are resolved effortlessly along the way. There is no such thing as
forward movement without a billion unscheduled stops along the
way."

He lay down with his head against my waist. We were a T on the
ground, not intersecting, not quite touching. I fell into the rhythm of
his breathing and closed my eyes.

"I could devour you, you know," he said matter-of-factly.

17

B e f o r e she is hired by *The New York Times,* Esther
pitches a story to a magazine in San Francisco about some rich college
kids who drop out of UC Berkeley and live in the abandoned projects
on Eddy Street. They are multicultural, the offspring of liberal subur-
banites. It is an experiment. A disregard for the bourgeoisie, a way of
embracing the life of the street. It is an experiment guided by the intellect and therefore certain to succeed. Esther is convinced that only
endeavors bordered by emotion are doomed to failure. It is the brain,
she believes, the intellect, which guarantees success.

She is excited about the story. It is a concept close to her heart. She
has always held a certain disdain for the tennis-playing elite, the country club set who move themselves into harbors of safety and live alone
among themselves, preferably behind gates, where the only color allowed is on the faces of the help.

Esther says she will spend a few weeks living among the students,
none of whom are more than two years younger than she is. She will
uncover their radical philosophies, report on their attempts to live
without jobs, without the constant flow of their parents' money, without the values of the monied classes. She will detail the society they
have established, the class and social structure that has emerged. Es-

ther believes there is no such thing as a classless society. Even the best-intentioned societies fall into a class structure, she says, because there are always some people who find themselves longing to be like others.

Maggie and especially Harold are worried when she gets the assignment. I see it in their faces when she comes bounding into the room, breathless with the glow of achievement. I am home from school, sitting on the couch with them, watching them get slowly drunk when she tells them.

"Isn't that a little dangerous?" Maggie says, lighting a cigarette.

"Nothing could be as dangerous as growing up with you," she snaps back.

Both of them seem to get momentarily smaller. They are hurt, especially Harold, who favors Esther and lights up when she enters a room. The thought crosses my mind, even though I laugh when she says it, that she has a cruel streak. A rare spurt of pity wells up for my parents when I see how Esther's remark has wounded them. An unusual desire to defend them flares briefly before the floodgates of memory unleash themselves to drown it out.

Esther ignores their protests and is gone the next day. Within a week, I receive a letter from her. She swears me to secrecy. I cannot even tell our parents where she is. She writes about the filth and the beauty, as though they are interchangeable. She sends a photograph of her and a group of people standing in front of a tenement wall. Someone has painted, in fat letters and bright colors, the words DEFEND YOUR RIGHT TO SQUAT. Esther has her arms around a handsome man. He smiles ironically into the camera. She does not. Weeds grow around their feet. The two of them, amidst the ruins, look like a pair of deities. I understand. Beauty and filth. Interchangeable.

There are ten or so of them, squatting among several other tribes comprised of the homeless, the drug addicts, the disenfranchised. Esther says they call them Reagan's Army, the homeless lunatics set free by budget cuts. Her group, the one she is with, are the only ones squatting voluntarily. It is as much protest as desire. There are armies of outcasts, she writes, that have nothing to do with budget cuts.

Esther's tribe has commandeered the southeast corner of the eighth floor. They call themselves the Rasta Posse. They wear their hair in dreadlocks and mohawks and listen to reggae and punk rock. Tattoos adorn their arms and ankles. They shoot speed and heroin in one of the rooms, which they call the safe room. The group itself is broken into a loose system of couples, but there is nothing necessarily permanent about relationships and from time to time a peaceful transfer of bodies takes place. "You can fuck anything when you're loaded," she writes.

She sends me her notes, tells me where she is, what it's like. I read that Esther is accepted almost immediately and within days is shooting heroin and panhandling on the street corners. She takes up with one of the guys, the one in the picture—a mixed-race, UCLA transfer student disgusted by Hollywood, and now disgusted by the elitism of the UC campus system in general. The two of them spend hours inside the room they have commandeered as their own, drawing pictures on the wall, having sex and shooting up. It is then that she gets her tattoo of an angel. She writes that she is careful. They clean their needles with bleach. They use condoms. But I don't see how they can remember the details. "Time," she writes, "has stopped."

She is gone for almost a month. Her notes stop arriving. She could be dead for all I know. The family has lost contact with her though Harold drives up to the city on several occasions to try and find her. He even contacts the police and persuades Maggie to put posters with pictures of Esther up on street corners, around telephone poles, at Muni stops. But Esther is never found. I do not, out of a sense of loyalty, tell our parents that she is on Eddy and Scott, in the projects, shooting heroin with a Los Angeles anarchist. I can't. I am sworn to secrecy, a Goldblum sibling code. You do not ever break this code. It is something we have had since birth, something Esther says is in our genes. Our collective secrecy is what gives us our power, she says.

Still, it is something that worries me no end. I go to sleep wondering if I'm being foolish. I wake up each day wondering if I should tell our parents. Before she left, Esther said she would not be gone more than a month. Already it's been two. I am afraid to confide in Harold and Maggie. I am afraid not to. I lie in my apartment at UC Berkeley, a naive freshman unaware of the dynamics of rebellion. I am not sure how to proceed. *She is just across the bay*, I think. *I can rescue her.* But I find I can no more do this than tell our parents. I am caught between my loyalty for Esther and my fear of her. I am trapped.

Then one day out of the blue she shows up at our parents' doorstep. Miraculously, because this rarely happens, I am home from school for the weekend. Sunday we are going to celebrate Eddie's birthday. When I open the door, I see a red truck disappearing around the corner.

She has lost so much weight she looks like a cancer patient. Her hair is knotted. She has evidently stopped washing it. The tracks on her arms are visible, and there are a couple of sores around her mouth. She looks like a street person. I feel a moment of sheer panic, the desire to run away. This is not my sister. My sister would never look like this. I am as drawn to racing through the door and shutting it firmly behind me as as I am to rescuing her.

"Yo," she says, "man."

She trips over the doorstep.

"Where the hell are they?" she asks.

"Everyone's gone to The Echo for a drink. It's Eddie's birthday tomorrow."

"Oh shit," she says. "For real?"

She smells so bad I have to take a step back. I repress the urge to gag and am horrified that the scent of my sister, which for years has sustained me, at this moment disgusts me. I wish for a moment that I had not come home for the weekend, that this would be a story I would hear about later after it was all over and in our sick way, we could laugh about it. But the thought instantly shames me. This is Esther, after all, beautiful Esther. You do not leave Esther in need, no matter what.

She sits down amid the turmoil of books and papers and begins to cry.

"God," she says. "I am fucked up."

"Esther," I say. "Why did you stop writing? Dad's been looking for you. He's gone to the city three or four times. He even notified the police. They've put up posters. You swore me to secrecy. Jesus, Esther. What the hell?"

"Dad?" she says. She seems incredulous. Then I realize I have not said "Harold." "Oh, it's Dad all of a sudden, is it?" Her eyes blaze with madness and hunger and coming down from whatever drugs she's been on. "You know what your problem is, Louise? You're a goody fucking two-shoes. You're perfect little Louise Goldblum and you make me sick. Sick. I've always thought you were too goddamned perfect but now the proof is in the pudding. Dad. Dad. Dad. I despise you and your lame-ass so-called art."

Her words sting and I don't know what to do with them. I am prickly at the skin over the idea that a Goldblum child, and Esther no less, could say something for which there is no emotional repository, no refuse bin or flame to destroy it. How, I wonder briefly, do you store such hatefulness? How do you forgive it? But then I look at her, at how skinny she is and how lost she seems. Amazingly, I am able to forget her vitriol and move on. She is visibly shaking and crying. Snot is running out of her nose. I realize Maggie and Harold can't see her like this no matter how looped they will be when they get home. I wish Eddie or Martin were here, but they are getting drunk with our parents. Mary, I realize, would be a bad idea so I don't call her at Dan's house, where she spends more and more of her time.

"Get up," I say.

She is shaking. I lean over and pick her up. I drag her to the bathroom and turn on the shower. I actually take my clothes off and get in the shower with her because she is almost dead weight, and I can barely hold her up. I wash her hair but it will have to be cut because the knots cannot be brushed out. I wash her arms, her legs, her vagina. I wash her ears. She does not fight me. She is half-unconscious.

"Esther," I whisper over and over again. I am more scared than I can remember. I know nothing about drugs or what happens when a person has been poisoned by them. I do not yet realize she will need to be checked into a detox center. I finish washing her and drag her out of the shower. I dry her off and go to Eddie and Martin's old bedroom and pull whatever I can that looks like it will cover her off a hanger. This is not difficult since the closets are stuffed with clothes, many of which I have never seen before.

She is very sick now and pissed off. She shakes uncontrollably and calls me terrible names, names that cut to the core of me: "Goody two-shoes." "Fucking virgin." "Miss Priss Bitch." I am trying to decide if I believe drugs make people spew forth their real feelings or if they make people say things that are not true. I am pondering this when Esther vomits on one of Harold's books, an obscure scientific treatise entitled *The Aftermath of Knowing: Evolution and Behavior.*

It is at this juncture that our parents burst through the door, followed by Eddie and Martin. They are all loaded. I realize this immediately, but when they see me, then Esther, then the vomit, they all sober up, at least for an instant, until they dissolve into an anarchy of emotions.

"Jesus, Mary and Joseph," Maggie says. She actually does the sign of the cross while holding a burning cigarette between her fingers.

Harold is dumbstruck. He brushes a bony hand through his thinning gray hair. His face turns pale. He is, as he has always been in times of crisis, completely ineffectual. Martin says, "What the fuck," but it is Eddie who comes to my rescue.

"What happened?" he asks me amid the screams and hollers emanating from the hallway. Like the time he hacked his finger off, I feel the insular world of Eddie and me, how clearly we are the duo of sanity in the midst of crisis.

"I thinks it's heroin," I say. "Look at her arms."

"Jesus. Fuck. Okay," he says. "Maggie, get something to clean this puke up. Harold, why don't you pull the car up from the street. Martin, help me get her to the car."

Perhaps Eddie is too logical for comprehension because everyone falls silent under his commands. But in seconds, they all fly into action, except Maggie, who stands there staring at Esther's barf as if it will tell her something about the situation. I am grateful for Eddie. I feel my throat constrict. I want to cry, a Goldblum sin. I do not indulge, though relief has raised my skin to gooseflesh.

Then, as if in the wake of some natural disaster, they have all vanished, leaving me behind to cope with the silence, the destruction, the terror. It is my choice not to accompany them. I have no wish to see Esther get her stomach pumped or whatever it is they do with drug addicts who are close to death.

I clean up her vomit, strangely immune to it. It is a mess. It must be erased. I find an empty spot on the couch, between an aging calico cat who used to bite me when I petted him and a stack of *Scientific American* magazines, and sit down. The echo of Esther's venom remains.

Miss Priss Bitch, Goody two-shoes, I despise you, you and your lame-ass so-called art.

The amazing thing, the aspect to all of this that fascinates and intrigues me, is that six months later, after she has recovered and has resumed her usual binge drinking in lieu of total drug addiction, Esther writes a story of her experiences for the same magazine she contacted to begin with and ends up winning an award for her efforts.

But, of course, with Esther, all things are possible.

18

I woke up to sunshine and the sound of an electric saw. The studio was so cold that I could see my breath. I rolled over, imagining the artist downstairs with his gentle, breathing sculptures and his proud Indian cheekbones. I envied him his obsession for chopping things up. Destruction. The tearing down to create anew. I listened, enthralled by the demolition and eradication. I thought, *Adios, adieu, auf Wiedersehen.*

I covered my head with the blankets, willing the sun to disappear. But in a few minutes, defeated, I got up and made a pot of coffee. As I stood by the window drinking it, I watched people board the buses that would take them to work. A woman in a fur coat dragged a Christmas tree down the street. A man with a fishing hat and no teeth stood on the corner panhandling. People ignored him. I consumed the loneliness of the street. It went inside me, this loneliness, and detonated. I left the window.

Zeke must have left sometime during the night. The empty studio was not much comfort. I remembered reading once about phantom limbs, how people who had lost an arm or a leg still felt them from time to time and I was reminded of the way I felt about Zeke.

I poured another cup of coffee, drank it down and got dressed. I decided I would go over to the museum and finish the installation. I was amazed that I would be done with it two weeks ahead of schedule. Somehow I had managed not to disappoint Lucille K. Johnson. It was a miracle and the idea of being almost finished lifted my spirits.

I made my way over to the park, but instead of getting off in the Haight and transferring to a bus that would take me to the De Young, I continued on the Muni and got off at Embarcadero. I hadn't seen Alice for a few days. Strangely, she had stopped calling. I walked with the commuting crowds through the cold streets. Everywhere I looked people seemed miserable and alone. I walked to Embarcadero Three and rode the elevator to the twenty-first floor.

I never much liked going to her office. It was stuffy and filled with people wearing suits and scowls. There was a new receptionist every time I went there but they all had the same demeanor. They seemed uniformly pissed off that they had to sit behind a counter and answer phones. They were all young and pretty and had hungry looks in their eyes, as if they were waiting for a rich man to rescue them from the indignity of having to wear panty hose every day.

I got off the elevator as a group of young men swarmed from the inner sanctum and headed toward me. I was reminded of the migration of large animal herds.

"Hold the door," one of them shouted but it was too late. He gave me a dirty look when the elevator doors shut but I ignored him and walked up to the receptionist.

"May I help you?" she said. Her voice had the perfect pitch of snottiness and exhaustion. A *Glamour* magazine lay open in front of her. She was reading an article with the headline, "How to Have the Perfect Orgasm."

"I'm here to see Alice Bronson."

"And your name?" She eyed me from head to foot.

"Louise."

"Have a seat," she said, gesturing to a corner of uncomfortable-looking chairs and a coffee table bearing copies of *Forbes* and *The Wall Street Journal*. The firm reeked of conformity and big bucks. I thought of my brother Eddie living this kind of lifestyle in New York before it almost killed him. I could not imagine him in a suit and tie. I had a mental image of him returning home from work one night, frustrated by so much obedience and throwing the cat out the window or tearing the walls down with a sledgehammer. Then I realized it was not something Eddie would do. It was more in line with Esther's personality. Or mine. The new improved edition of me.

I was lost in this thought when Alice, in her decadent version of the business suit—a tight red miniskirt, low-cut jacket and pearl earrings—emerged from the intestines of her banking firm.

I stood up.

"Hey," I said.

"What's up," she said. Her voice was cool. She seemed vaguely annoyed.

"Just thought you might want to get some coffee or something."

My hands were trembling from lack of alcohol and I thrust them into the pockets of my coat.

"I don't think so, Louise. I'm busy."

Her voice had taken on a tight quality. Her words were clipped and I remembered once back in college how she had called her boyfriend from my apartment. I was in the other room and I couldn't hear what she was saying, only that her voice was cold and abrupt. When she came back her face was pinched and she smiled in a pained way. "No matter how much it hurts, it's the better part of self-preservation to set an asshole free," she had said.

"Are you mad at me, Alice?" I said now, looking at her distant expression.

She folded her arms. I could feel the receptionist staring at us. Alice took hold of my elbow and escorted me to the elevator banks. She lowered her voice. It was calm and steady, which made me suddenly very nervous. I felt like my insides were sweating.

"It's not anger, Louise. It's just that I think you take our friendship for granted. I love you, you know that. But lately, you haven't been returning the favor."

"I don't know what you mean." I looked over at the receptionist, embarrassed by Alice's unusual public display. But the receptionist had gone back to her *Glamour* and was chewing thoughtfully on her lower lip.

"I never would have pegged you for the ungrateful type," Alice said. It was almost a whisper. "You didn't used to be, at least. It was the quality I admired most about you. Your sarcasm was always a decoy where you hid your humility. Now you're just bitter and you seem to have forgotten the importance of saying thank you, even if you don't mean it."

"What?" I said. I realized how serious she was.

"Look, Louise," she said. She had pressed the elevator button. "I have tried to help you. You don't want my help. I have tried to be your friend. You don't want a friend. You are rude to me, you take the things I give you and pooh-pooh them and you choose to sleep with some asshole photographer who likes to beat you up, take your pictures and display them for the entire world to see."

I felt the color rise to my cheeks. She was so calm that anyone walking by might have suspected she was talking about a stock portfolio. I was instantly angered. I felt it boil to the surface of my skin and turn my cheeks red.

"Why should you give a shit who I sleep with? You're not my mother."

"I don't give a *shit*," she said. "Not anymore. That is the difference between being a friend and being an acquaintance. It is what you want."

"Why does everyone think they know what I want?"

"We're all just filling in the gaps," she said. "Because you obviously don't know and wouldn't tell us if we asked."

The elevator came. The doors opened to an old man with an immaculate suit who leaned on a cane. He stared at us. The doors began to close. Alice held her hand out and the doors popped open again. The old man inside seemed to have the patience of Buddha, but there was something slightly unsavory in the way his eyes glinted at the sight of Alice's breasts.

"You're ruining your life, Louise," she said.

"Oh, yeah? Why should you care anyway?" I said, thinking in the twisted way I had become accustomed to that a good friend would just let you do what you did.

She shook her head. "I don't care," she said quietly. Sadly. "Not anymore."

She walked away and I stood inside the elevator. The old man leaned forward on his cane and winked at me. The walls moved in closer. A stab of light exploded in my peripheral vision like fireworks, giving birth to hundreds of shards of light. I rubbed my eyes. We hit ground and I stumbled out onto the street, blinded at once by the raging force of a locomotive smashing into my brain. I had left my Fiorinal at home. My hands shook. I thought of Alice. *Fuck her*, I thought.

Then Esther's image came to me. I stopped, kicked the pavement. My head ached. I couldn't stand the prospect of going over it again in my head. . . . *So there she is. Esther. Dark, beautiful Esther alone in the playground of San Francisco. Living high and stylish on an expense account. She meets a man in the bar of the St. Francis, where she is staying before she will leave for South Africa.*

I began to walk through downtown. There were no people about, just a few messengers riding like maniacs on their bikes, nearly clipping the bumpers of parked cars and averting disaster with the empty buses at the last minute. It was like a schoolyard before the bell for lunchtime rang. I imagined them all, the overworked, underpaid secretaries in front of their computers, the overpaid executives saying such unimportant things with such grave importance. I had never needed a real job because I was always winning scholarships, grants and stipends and later selling my work enough to keep me going. But now I was broke. And the prospects for money were dim.

I walked on in the cold. Christmas decorations had suddenly sprouted like weeds. It depressed me to no end. I clutched my head, prayed for the end of sunlight, for the dark ages, the ice age, the age before fire.

Then I couldn't help myself. I was like those people with an obsessive-compulsive disorder washing their hands over and over again. I couldn't stop thinking of Esther's death. I started to do it again, to see it again.

She arrives at the motel, aware on some level that she has gotten herself into something perhaps a little too dicey even for her taste. She refuses to think that harm will come to her, but the thought lurks there nevertheless beneath her carefully cultivated inebriation.

The man goes inside the motel office to check in and Esther, wondering fleetingly if she will make it to the plane that will take her to the valiant, unspeakable chaos of South Africa, clings to a memory. It is of Danny, his hands gripped around his face, crying. It is the fleeting memory of the caving in of Danny's soul as he leans despondently against the wall of the concrete tunnel. Esther reaches for him in her mind, then turns away, willing the man who has brought her to this cheap motel to hurry up, to annihilate her and her memories before they destroy her.

I wound my way to Union Square and looked at the Christmas windows along with all the tourists. The street people were thick and unruly. I watched one mean, skinny man with purple lesions on his face spit at an elderly couple who refused to give him money. I felt a mixture of rage and pity for him. But I also felt the same for the fur-clad woman and her husband as they turned away in outrage and fear.

I finally went to the bar at the Hyatt and ordered a Bloody Mary. There were mobs of tourists at the hotel. I was surrounded by money on tables and the confusing, dizzying myriad of foreign languages. A few obvious regulars were hunkered down in the corner playing chess, oblivious to the mayhem. Near me a table full of blond, husky Australians was discussing American football with delighted disdain. I sat alone and sipped my drink. Within moments a woman a few years older than I claimed the seat next to me.

She smelled faintly of gardenia. She wore her blonde hair in long braids. Her features were sharp, so ugly they bordered on beautiful or perhaps so beautiful they bordered on ugly. The men in the room and those who walked by seemed to be drawn to her, confused by her, their expressions slightly baffled and awed as they passed her or turned away. I was not sure whether she was a local or a tourist.

She looked over at me and nodded gravely.

"Bloody Mary," she said to the bartender. "Extra tabasco."

She drank it greedily when it arrived, then put it down on the counter with a thud.

"Jesus," she said. "Tourists."

"Yeah," I nodded.

"Too much damn polyester," she said, taking another sip of her drink.

"And dead animal wraps."

She laughed without the slightest trace of enjoyment. The hard edge to her was offset only by her peculiar beauty and the fact that she was apparently loved by someone. She sported a large diamond ring on her left middle finger.

We both downed our drinks as if some alliance of desperation and frightened energy propelled us forward. When the bartender brought us another round she offered to buy. I wondered briefly if I was being picked up.

"I am so goddamned tired," she said.

"I know what you mean."

It was bar talk, meaningless, circular. But then she said, "You look just like this chick I knew. But she was a brunet. Her name was Esther something. Esther Goldberg, something like that."

For a minute I was unable to say anything.

So there she is. Esther. Dark, beautiful Esther alone in the playground of San Francisco.

I took a sip of my drink. I lit a cigarette.

"Goldblum," I said. "She's my sister."

"No kidding," the woman said. Her face changed with the smile. It didn't exactly light up, but it became less austere. "How the hell is she? Man, she was something. Crazy, crazy girl."

"She's dead," I managed.

The silence fell then, as it always did, and the woman looked at her glass. She ordered us another round immediately, an action I thought quite admirable and forthright given the circumstances. Had I been in her shoes, I liked to think I would have done the same.

"How? It wasn't drugs, was it?"

"No," I said. "She was killed. Murdered. Uh, some guy, we don't know who, shot her in the head."

"Oh, man."

We said nothing for a long time. But I knew from my few meager attempts at talking about it that the news of death, especially violent death, killed chatter. We were surrounded by the din of the hotel, the clatter of glasses and the startling insult of Esther's early death.

"How'd you know her?" I finally asked. For a wild moment, I had the overwhelming urge to reach for her, to grab her and touch her. I saw myself grasping her around the neck, clutching her, smelling her, anything to glean, in some way, what she knew of my sister. She was a link I had not counted on, the unexpected surprise, like finding money in the street.

"We were squatting together at the housing projects. She was working on that story for some magazine. I finally read it. Long after I got clean. I always thought it was so amazing how well she captured our experiment, the philosophy and the terrible way it deteriorated. She took our lives and made them her own, became one of us."

"She came back pretty messed up. Three months of detox. But she wrote the story. She won an award for it."

The woman beside me didn't seem to hear me and I felt momentarily adrift, cast out by her seeming indifference to what happened to my sister afterward. I studied her face, its eccentric beauty, and tried to imagine how my sister saw her, whether Esther chose to include her in the article she wrote. I couldn't remember reading about someone like her and I made a mental note to go back to the story, stashed away in a drawer at my studio, to see if I could find this woman in its pages.

"The experiment was a failure," she said. "We didn't have any right to destroy our lives that way. Not all of us got out of it alive, you know. I always wanted to find your sister. I always thought another story, a follow-up would be good. Three of us died, you know. Two OD'd and there was one suicide. Two are still on the streets and three of us made it out. I always thought that would be interesting, following up on it. A better story really. We were kids. We really fucked things up. We took our privilege and flushed it down the toilet. Only three of us, not counting your sister, made it out."

I could see that this was the experience of her life, the one event that she would gauge every action by for the remainder of her life. It seemed that nothing else meant as much to her. I felt a kinship to her, not just because she knew Esther, but because she was locked in the past.

"No one at home understood Esther when she did that. But I think I do," I said. I was smoking furiously, drinking fiendishly. I felt sweat under my breasts, on my neck.

"Well, listen. What better way to live a different sort of life?" said the woman. She too drank with a fervent determination, as if it might be her last one for a long time. "A hundred different lives, for that matter. Just adopt the chaos, the happiness, the fears, whatever, of other people's lives."

When I reached for my drink, my hands were shaking.

"Do you think my sister was like that?" I asked. I hadn't planned on the tone of my voice being so sharp. It caught the woman by surprise. She looked at me with a careful expression.

"I didn't know her," she said. "We were like planets orbiting around each other. I don't think I knew any of them."

The sadness in her voice took me down a few notches. Still, after what Mary said the night before about Esther—how Esther made everyone think she loved them when in fact she loved no one—and now this suggestion that Esther adopted other people's lives with relative ease, rattled me. There was a mysterious kind of truth to it that jarred what I knew, had always known or wanted to know about Esther. She was brilliant, beautiful, she loved me more than anyone.

A good-looking, preppy man and an elderly couple arrived. The man leaned down and kissed the woman beside me. I heard him whisper, "You promised." The elderly couple were dressed to the nines. The woman had a fur wrap around her.

"Gotta go," the woman who knew Esther said, leaving a twenty on the bar. She began to walk away but then circled back quickly, her eyes blazing with a searing, unidentifiable intensity. She touched me on the arm.

"I'm sorry," she said. "I'm really sorry. It was all a terrible failure. Misguided youth."

I nodded. The man—probably her fiancé—and the elderly couple, after whom he bore a faint resemblance, stood off to the side impatiently. I watched them walk away, and when they got outside they passed the window, my existence already gone from their memory but for a fleeting moment when the woman looked in at me, smiled sadly and waved with a gloved hand. I finished my drink. I could not remember feeling so bleak.

I went back to my studio, slowly boarding buses, walking up hills, around pedestrians, into traffic as if I were moving underwater. The world was muted and I had the feeling that I was separated from it. If I reached out, I would actually touch the glass that kept me apart from everyone else.

I couldn't stop thinking about Esther. How at the age of twenty-seven she had been nominated for a Pulitzer Prize. How she loved people feverishly. And how she dated expensive men, men with shady connections who drove Mercedes-Benzes with tinted windows.

I remembered the passionate way she traveled throughout the world, dissecting every inch of it, uncovering the greed, the avarice, the corruption of humankind, but also revealing the humanity of humanity. And as if being in strange places all the time was not enough variation for her, she loved changing her appearance. From one month to the next, she never looked the same. She'd go to Cuba and return with blonde hair. She'd return from Paris in some exotic, couture fashion piece more appropriate for a museum than a body. But she was Esther. Always Esther.

I said her name over and over again and then I thought of her lying there, dead, startled by her own death, her spirit perhaps hovering above, wondering how in the world she had failed to escape this final mess. Or not. Maybe she had known, on some level, that he would kill her. Maybe she had wanted it. One of the detectives had said she looked so peaceful, lying there on her side in the fetal position, a slight smile on her lips, her clothes folded neatly on a chair beside the bed. She had not been expecting it, he'd said. Our mother and father took comfort in that and so too, eventually, did everyone else. But not me. I could not imagine an ill-prepared Esther.

There had been no struggle, no pain. One bullet and all light had been extinguished.

I pictured them now as they drive under the cold, moonlit sky, through the rolling hills, dotted with oak trees and large rock formations. *The landscape romances her. She is captivated by the moonlight on the lonely landscape, by the man beside her. But then a glimpse of memory, a touch of Danny whispers through her; she longs to see him. Sorrow eclipses her face. She brushes it away, a physical gesture, swiping her hand at the air.*

They drive fast until they come to Angels Camp. He pulls into the gravel parking lot of a tiny motel above a creek. The air is chill, you can almost see the cold but it is a cold that summons the image of spring, a fragrant cold filled with possibility. They get out of the car and Esther goes over to the edge of the steep ravine that towers over the creek. She can smell the scent of snow melting from the Sierras in the distance. She hugs herself against the cold.

The man is smooth. He is wearing leather gloves and a camel hair coat. He puts his hand gently on her back and guides her to the room. They unlock the door and Esther sees through the darkness to the bed, the chair she will put her clothes on. She senses that this is her last night on Earth. She thinks fleetingly of Danny. But of no one else. Not me. Not our parents, the siblings, Lydia Firestone. No, it is only of Danny who she thinks.

Lost in the imaginary re-creation of her death, without realizing it, I found myself standing in front of my studio. I fumbled for my keys in the cold, my hands burning from it, as I rifled through my too-large bag. My breath came out in billows of steam and I remembered once how my mother, in a rare burst of sentimentality, said that when you saw your breath against the cold, it meant that you could be sure your soul was keeping alive the fires of your dreams.

I unearthed my keys from the black hole of my bag and went upstairs. The message light on my phone was blinking. It had been a while, I realized, since I'd played them. I hit the rewind button and listened, half expecting to hear Esther's voice. One was from Lucille K. Johnson, wanting to know if I was coming today, the sharp tone of disapproval in her voice. There was a message from Maggie, her dry voice, roughened over the years by so much booze and pills and cigarettes, exhorting me to come home for the weekend. She missed me. She rarely called and when she did lately it was always to ask me to come home. I did not know what to do with a mother who longed for me. It was never what defined the two of us. Mary had called too, asking me to call her, collect if I had to. There was nothing from Zeke.

I went into the alcove and buried myself in the covers. I slept till morning.

"Microfiche."

I opened my eyes. Zeke was standing over my head, dangling some papers.

"What?" I pulled the blankets up higher to cover me. I felt both shy and ribald with my body around Zeke and I knew that the degree of either depended on how much I had or hadn't drunk.

"The wonders of a little bit of information, a librarian and microfiche. Who says we need computers?" He dropped some papers on my belly. I recognized them immediately as the newspaper articles on Esther's death written up in the local *Palo Alto Times.*

The daughter of a Stanford researcher was found slain last Friday at a small motel in the Sierra Foothills. Esther Goldblum, 32, a reporter for *The New York Times* who in 1985 was nominated for a Pulitzer Prize for her coverage of the anti-apartheid movement here and in South Africa, was shot once in the head after an apparently consensual sexual encounter. There were no witnesses to the murder, which took place some time after 11:00 p.m.

I sat up in bed. I was trembling from the cold. And from something else. Nerves maybe.

"I thought you didn't care."

"No," Zeke said. He sat down on the edge of the bed. "You're just confused over what aspects of things, what details I do care about."

He looked at me and I saw it immediately, the way his desire changed his face, opened it but also drew it tighter. At the same time that desire softened his eyes, his lips grew angry. I saw that his desire was opening and closing his face, bringing him nearer to me, forcing him farther from me. He looked at me. He seemed to be trying to find something in my face. He looked baffled for a moment, and I saw again what he was like without the mask or the shield. I wanted to reach out for him, to take him in my arms. To beg him to stop.

But he must have sensed this because roughly he pulled the blankets down and put his mouth over my right breast. He sucked hard on the nipple, bit it, rolled his tongue over it. He moved over to the other one and did the same. He smelled of whiskey and cigarettes. He pulled back, tore the blankets off me, spread my legs apart.

"An apparently consensual sexual encounter," he said without any emotion at all. He unzipped his pants, pulled out his cock and leaned over, shoving it in my mouth. I heard myself cry out.

"You've consented," he whispered grotesquely.

In a short time his body tightened and he spasmed without making a sound, as if to orgasm itself was to surrender, as if keeping himself quiet eliminated part of the disaster of his capitulation, the humility of raising the white flag. As if to say without quite admitting it, *I am done. You own me now.*

He got off the bed, leaving me with my desire and my humiliation intact. He zipped his pants up. He left the room and in moments I heard the shower running. Ten minutes later, he was back. He picked up the newspaper articles that had been tossed to the floor and began to read. He adopted a TV newscaster tone. I was helpless.

"Lydia Firestone, a friend of Goldblum's for over seventeen years, said it was not uncommon for Goldblum to take off in the middle of the night with a stranger. 'Taking risks was the key to Esther's success. We all thought she was a little insane. It's not surprising she would die this way. Some might say she deserved it.' "

He looked at me and raised his eyebrows. "Bitch?" he asked.

I nodded.

He continued. "The victim's father, Dr. Harold Goldblum, a research scientist at Stanford University, refused to comment at length on his daughter's death, saying only that it was a great tragedy and a tremendous shock for the family."

Zeke paced the floor as he read. After the last sentence, he put the paper down as if exasperated.

"The family *refused* to comment? Do you want to comment for me, Louise? You've wanted to talk about it since we met. Go on, then, talk about it."

"Please, Zeke," I whispered.

"Tell me about the tragedy. Tell me about your sister. Tell me about all of it, including this, what's her name, Lydia Firestone."

"Go to hell, Zeke."

"Oh, so now you don't want to talk about it." He threw the newspapers to the ground. He seemed angry now and I marveled at the meteoric alterations of his moods, the way he could turn them on and off at will.

His badgering had the strange effect of making me feel superficial, as if wanting to discuss my sister's death was like discussing the weather or another woman's looks, catty, meaningless. I hated him.

"Get dressed," he said. "If you don't eat you'll erode away to nothing."

After I showered and dressed we walked out into the cold December air. Someone had put a huge picture of Frosty the Snowman up over the building next door. Christmas lights, some of them still lit in the morning light, skirted the roofs of buildings.

"Fucking Christmas," he said. "You're Jewish, right?"

"Half."

He said nothing. He walked on.

"Lisa Silburner was . . . is . . . was Jewish."

"And you?"

"Nothing. I'm nothing."

We walked north up Mission to a tiny hole-in-the-wall diner filled with Nicaraguans. We sat down. The waiter came up and said hello to Zeke. They conversed in Spanish for a while. A woman brought us two cups of coffee. The waiter left.

"My entire life," Zeke said, "I'm trying to put my finger on the pulse beat of Christmas."

"And?"

"Makes no sense. What is it with the lights? I don't know my Bible, but did Mary and Joseph, like, decorate the manger?"

"Yeah. I think it's somewhere in the New Testament. Look up Christmas in the index."

"There's an index?" He laughed.

It was impossible, I realized, to carry on the charade constantly. Was this our first conversation? *If Alice could see us now*, I thought. A bitter taste, like parsley, came to the back of my throat.

My throat constricted, closed. I realized I had a habit of losing people. Or of never having them in the first place. As with Zeke. And just as I thought of him, he reached out and touched my hand as it trembled on the table.

"Girl," he said. "You are not healthy. You need some food."

I felt it go through me, his touch. I felt the other side of Zeke, the netherworld of Zeke. The Zeke of humanity, pathos and pity. I could not bear the thought of being loved, not even by this mongrel of love. I felt something lodge in my throat and the walls close around me. The world swayed. Zeke let go. And then mercifully the food arrived, mercifully hot, filled with the fiery green peppers of Nicaragua. I took a bite, ravenously. I swallowed almost without chewing and in this way, as the spices burned the back of my tongue, my mouth, wound their way down my throat, I could find an excuse for the tears that formed in my eyes. I could find a way to stifle the scream.

A f t e r our breakfast, which I ate ravenously, Zeke and I walked. We walked silently through a city mired in Christmas and cold wind. The air was fragrant with the scents of coffee beans, baking bread, the sea. I could smell the onslaught of another storm and waited for it impatiently. I wanted to drown, to be drowning in the things that existed outside myself. I wanted to immerse myself in Zeke's body, in the shame of us, in vodka and cigarettes. I wanted to be swept away by a torrent, a flood of rain and Zeke and drunkenness.

We walked through the Mission, past the only McDonald's in the city, up toward Market Street. We caught a bus to the Haight—the doors of the bus opening and the city sucking us into a vortex of cold air—and got off near the park. We walked the Haight, stepping over heroin addicts and dodging the hordes of European tourists that traveled to San Francisco in winter. Zeke stopped at one-dollar book stalls and the tables of jewelry hawkers, looking but not looking.

We did all of this silently, in unison, as if our thoughts had been strung together by lights, as if the lights were guiding us. In time we entered the park and walked slowly along the paths. We never touched. We spoke very little. A child rode by on a Big Wheel and Zeke made car sound effects as he passed. His trench coat wrapped around him in the

wind, the wind rode the top of his bald head. He shivered, hugged himself tighter in his coat. Clouds darkened the skies.

Our silence filled me with loneliness and I swallowed this loneliness whole, filling myself with it, lining myself with it, choking on it. I
craved the emptiness of us together, the indentation in the air, the
crater we made in the wellspring of normal humanity, a humanity that
gave the impression at least of connection, joy, substance. The two of
us, the eked-out, carved-out vacuum we left behind as we dented the
air, that hole in which nothing but our own silence and detachment
existed, left a trail, a luminescent bridge of nothing. I found myself
burrowing into our silence like some rodent, fearful of the light but
afraid of the predators of the dark.

We walked through the pockets of gardens, many of them boney
and deadened by winter, the plants dazzled by rain and frost into a
kind of panting hibernation. I accepted the baffled voicelessness of the
park and Zeke's lonesome silence. I loved Zeke in this absence of him,
this turbulence of our combined emptiness. I thought that as long as
we didn't touch, as long as we didn't speak, the scream that lived inside
of me would subside. We could pass our lives walking through America in this shroud of silence, not touching, falling in love with our
muted selves, captives of our unuttered lonesomeness.

We walked together, as if by some design, into the arboretum, opening the door, shutting the door, walking silently among the mist, the
heat. It was empty, all good people earning livings or staying at home
by the fire, living decent lives.

We wound our way around the effusive tropical plants. They wore
their beauty on their sleeves. They shocked, dazzled, hypnotized. The
rain began and we were miraculously tropical, warmed in the cata-
comb of mist and narcotic beauty.

At the end of the gravel path, we stopped near a bench and the rain
came down against the white arboretum walls in droves, beating senseless the beat of my heart. I felt bludgeoned, empty, alone, the beauty
taunting me, the scents of gardenias and jasmine poisoning me. Zeke
took me in his arms, wrapped me in his coat, kissed the top of my
head, pressed himself against me, alerting me to his hardness, to his
wanting me, to that forlorn desire of his, the desire that slammed doors
and stole cars in lieu of loving.

I let him kiss me. It was a kiss of such loneliness that I took it with greed, ate it, swallowed it. I might have loved him then, in the instant of that kiss. Then the scream began to rise and I reached for him, knelt on the ground, put my mouth around him to shut me up, to drown it, that love. But he pushed me away, gently, without his usual anger. The perfume of the flowers entered me, rode the crests and valleys of my veins, consumed me.

Zeke sat down on the bench, sat me on top of him and unbuttoned me, removed my armor, put his mouth to me. I felt the scream rise up against the odious, wondrous pleasure of it. I looked at my hands, at the way the skin became translucent in the overbright glow of the greenhouse. I calmed myself and understood the way he loved me in that instant, like a baptism of desperation and desire, a wave filled with broken shells, washing over my body. I thought, *Stop this, don't love me.*

And still we had not spoken. I could not speak. I could not stop him. And then I gripped his head. I ran my hands over the planet of his skull, the odd formations of bone not protected by hair, of bone so easily shattered, so easily broken and he kissed me like that until I came, quietly, silently, without words, without words.

Later, I sat inside my walls at the De Young, the smell of Zeke on my body, and stared at the monster. It was in final form. In imagination lay the substance of experience. In the lake, in the motorcycle, in Esther's deadness, in the mounds of earth, the stuffed animals, the rocks made impure by graffiti—LED ZEPPELIN RULES, DF LUVS EG—lay the sum of my experience.

I lit a cigarette. I smoked. I remembered. The lake with its emboldened hues, the way the sun made dots of spectral light on the white caps, the smell of fresh reeds, rotten eggs, the sight of my sister, alive, brimming with life, fucking, eating, drinking, loving.

I had never liked Danny. But she had. He had given her life. He had taken her from the madness of the old Goldblum homestead. He had given her reason to survive our parents and their endless drinking and dish throwing. When he died, Esther merely became one of us, unprotected children scrambling to make sense of our pathetic lives.

And there she was, dead. She had not survived after all.

I stubbed out my cigarette just as the flimsy door to my makeshift barrier from the world opened. I turned around, startled.

"Mary," I said, realizing instantly that it was Monday and I had missed our lunch at San Francisco State.

"Am I disturbing you?" she asked. She stood by the door, the embarrassed intruder.

"No," I said. I smoothed my hair, took a clandestine look at myself. I was fully dressed. Jeans. Shirt. No bra but no bruises either. It was the best I could hope for. "Shit, Mary, I'm really sorry. I totally forgot."

She held up her hand to stop me from further blubbering.

"I'm just glad to see you working."

It was at that point that I realized she hadn't quite seen the breadth of my installation. My stomach flipped. I felt a moment of nausea. I was always forgetting that family lurked everywhere—the harshest judges. The most easily offended.

She peered around the room. Taking her time. I could sense her uncertainty. Her fear. Her kindness was like a wall. It precluded knowing my work too intimately because underneath it—and she must have known this—she knew my demons. They were, after all, hers as well, existing on some subordinated level, beyond all that church-going, baby-making joy. I thought of her producing another half-Goldblum. *We all have our addictions*, I thought.

"Is that supposed to be Lake Lauganita?" she asked.

"Bingo," I said, pleased. "How'd you know?"

"That rock over there. *Zeppelin Rules. DF Luvs EG*. It's a dead giveaway."

"Do you suppose it's still there? The rock."

"I doubt it, what with the condos and all."

"Condos?" I asked. I had heard they were going to develop Lake Lauganita but it seemed impossible that they actually had. I didn't want to know. Couldn't know. "C'mon in. Have a look around."

Sufficiently diverted, she had a look around. She remained quiet. I couldn't tell what she thought. My heart beat. Eons passed. The dark ages, the ice age, the industrial revolution, beatniks, hippies, punk rock. She lifted her eyebrows at the motorcycle, said nothing, walked on. When she got to Esther, she said nothing. She merely took her glasses off, wiped them on her sweater, put them back on and came back around to the front where I stood, holding my breath, turning blue, cursing my imagination for having spoken so profanely. Fuck you brain, heart and soul.

"Are those Martin's dead animals?" she asked.

I nodded.

"And Esther. Is she dead?"

"Sleeping, if you wish."

She sighed, exasperated. She was only one year older than me. A lifetime away.

"Well," she said. "I don't know that it does much to honor her death. But, then, it's your interpretation of events."

"Conglomeration of events. The path winds around the lake. Nothing is linear. Things happen in a lifetime. It's all out of order. That's why you get Martin's murderous heart throughout the landscape. You can start over here, you see, and Esther appears first. It doesn't matter which way you walk. I have no interest anymore in piecing the events together as if they exist on a chain. There is no point A. No point B. There's simply an arc, filled with pit stops. It all just happens. It's called chaos."

Mary looked at me, her expression slightly alarmed. "I don't know what you're saying. Relax. Your face is turning red."

But I couldn't relax. I had tried to arrive at some semblance of order in the installation. Only I had failed. I could see this now. I had made it too real. I had left out too many things. I had included the wrong ones.

"I didn't ask you to like it, Mary. It's mine. It's the vomit of my imagination. You aren't expected to like it."

"I didn't say I didn't like it. You're overreacting . . ."

"It's no mystery to me, Mary, that most people, without possibly even knowing it, are afraid that their hold on reason is very precarious. I am obliged to challenge that precipice of sanity."

"Yes," she said, coming closer, placating me, hypnotizing me with her concern.

"You resent being asked to look at our lives in this way."

"Honey," she said. She was on me, enfolding me. "It's okay."

"No," I said, pushing her away. "It's not okay. None of this is okay.

Don't you understand that we were forced, from the very beginning, to sidestep broken glass? We weren't even in diapers and somehow we knew instinctively that if we didn't watch our step our feet would bleed."

It was the most I could manage. I could not put the pieces together, the connection between the moments of my life: a pool party in which Harry the Dog nearly drowns, a deserted roadway where Danny Franconi kills himself and a dingy old motel room where Esther gets shot in the head. I could not put together the plate-throwing madness of our parents, Mrs. Kowolski's tits—her smashed-in face—and Zeke taking me in a gulf of silence among the garishness of tropical flowers. And yet somehow I knew it was all a part of the same path that led me to regurgitate my monster on the floor of the De Young Museum.

I looked at Mary and I saw the indefatigable serenity in her eyes. I could not comprehend this. I wondered if there was a God only for certain people and the rest of us were left to flounder needlessly in the pit of uncertainty and grief. Why was it that she had survived?

"Mary, I need to be alone now," I said. The headache had come on me with the force of a blunt object against my brain. I saw my brain, running from the pain, hiding like a frightened child in the back of my cranium. Poor brain.

"Good-bye, Mary," I said. I picked up my things and walked through the door, leaving her behind the walls that barricaded the monster from the world.

When I got home Zeke was sitting there smoking a cigarette, cutting something into the back of his hand with a razor. He looked up at me and smiled.

"Hey," he said.

"Don't be nice to me," I said. "Just fuck me."

20

E s t h e r and I have come here alone. There is a strange man, a naked man—no, he is not naked, he is wearing a suit, a paper-thin, skin-colored suit. A gas mask covers his face. He jumps from bush to bush. He sees us, runs the other way, toward the road. In moments we hear the squeal of brakes, a horn honking. Then nothing.

"Do you suppose he's been killed?" Esther asks. She laughs. Weirdos, as long as they're not sex weirdos, don't frighten her. In fact she has an affinity for weirdos, feels impervious to their whims, their potential to hurt, kill, maim, destroy. She believes weirdos are the underdog, to be protected or at the very least left alone.

I, on the other hand, do not like weirdos, sex creeps or otherwise. But that is because I am the Goldblum chicken shit.

The lake glimmers red under the hot sun. I feel my version of Goldblum skin—white, tender, easily shocked—turning pink. Esther just gets darker. She says all the time that her existence merely proves Maggie was fucking the milkman. She often jokes like this in front of Maggie.

She gets away with it too. She is the most unshakably ribald member of our clan. She circles our world like a whip, calling things as she sees them. She is fearless. No one chastens her. No one says a word and that is because everything Esther says is tinged with a kind of truth. Refuting her would merely be a form of self-indictment.

We walk away from the shore of Lake Lauganita toward Esther and Danny's rock. Esther is here to perform some kind of ritual. She has taken a year off between high school and college because when it became clear that Danny Franconi was not going to college, at the age of thirteen or fourteen she promised she would spend a year with him before going away.

During their year together, she and Danny never spent a moment apart. They smoked pot endlessly and thought that no one ever saw them screwing each other anywhere they could—behind bushes, in the backseat of our parents' parked car, in the nearly dilapidated tree fort. When they weren't having sex, they played endless rounds of backgammon and drank coffee, strong with lots of sugar. Sometimes they would take Mrs. Franconi's beat-up old Chevy Nova that barely ran anymore and disappear for days at a time. Mrs. Franconi would invariably show up at our house screaming that it had to stop.

"This has to stop, Maggie," she would scream hysterically and our mother would calmly, deftly pour her a glass of sherry, get her slightly drunk and hand her the keys to her own car saying she didn't need it. Mrs. Franconi, drunk by then, would refuse the keys and the two of them would spend the next few days doing their errands together, driving to the market in Maggie's station wagon, having apparently found an amiable truce in the shared disaster of their wayward children.

Eventually, Danny and Esther would return sunburnt, with sand in their hair or leaves in their clothes, reeling from too much happiness and guilt, cowed by their extravagant excess, until it dissipated—it always did—and they reached for it again.

But now, in two weeks' time, Esther will be off to Columbia University in New York. And she must say good-bye to Danny in a number of ways, not the least of which is to perform a ritual at their lovers' rock.

"He's not doing well," she says.

"I guess he wouldn't be."

"What he doesn't understand is that he is the only one for me."

"Then why won't you let him come with you?"

She has never explained this to anyone. Now, she stops, folds her arms, thinks. Moves on again with abrupt determination. "Because he would be a distraction."

"Maybe he thinks it's other boys," I say. I like my daring dip into the adult world of relationships, the hinterland of sex and jealousy. I am and will remain a virgin for three more years. Esther, however, has been sleeping with Danny since she was twelve and he thirteen. Now, seven years later, I am waxing philosophical on a subject about which I know nothing. I feel myself blush. *Shut up, you fool,* I think.

We get to the rock—ZEPPELIN RULES, DF LUVS EG—and Esther pulls out a dried rose, a tattered piece of paper with what looks like a poem written on it and a seashell. She sits down, using the rock as her back-rest and pulls a joint out of her pocket. She lights up.

Sitting beside her, I take in her musky Esther smell, the scent of marijuana, incense, fragrant lotions, shampoo, a vague, slightly pun-gent odor of sweat and skin. She shakes her hair free, takes a hit off her joint, looks toward the sky and falls back, sliding against the rock until she is on the ground, facing the clouds.

"God," she says. "It just doesn't get better than this. But here I am, knowing it gets better. Better and better. I love him, you know. But I want a taste of freedom. To get away. To study. I can't imagine any-thing better right now than a good book, a glass of wine and a ciggy. I want to meet new people."

She is stoned. This is how Esther is when she is stoned. The world is an open sea and she is a woman with fins.

"What do you see in him anyway?" I ask. I have always wanted to know. "I think he's a creep."

She sits back up, smiling slightly. I imagine she must be thinking about the way they have sex endlessly, nonstop, copiously, with an amazing voraciousness. They are at it all the time. Animals. Every-where, shameless. You can hear them sometimes, behind doors, in the backseat of a car, in the aqueduct, on the rubber raft in the pool, on a bench in the pool house. It is slightly obscene, slightly unsavory. It is also titillating and staggering. It is pure suburban anarchy. Every time any of us hears it, we roll our eyes and move away. My brothers espe-cially find it disgusting and embarrassing and sometimes, if they are in the mood, they'll scream at them to put a lid on it. But nothing stops them. We could walk in on them and they would keep going.

Our parents merely turn the other way. It would, after all, be hypocritical for Maggie to say anything. She knows we are on to her and Mr. Kowolski, and Maggie, in spite of being a drunk and an adulterer, is not a hypocrite.

I am waiting for Esther to tell me that sex is the thing that she loves most about Danny when she turns to me and says with dead seriousness, "Danny has saved me, Baby Goldblum."

I don't understand this. It is a consensus among the Goldblum siblings, Mary included, that in fact Esther has saved Danny. That without Esther, Danny would be a thief, a drug addict, a boy who handily pummels men twice his size with his bare fists, a jailbird, or possibly just plain dead.

"Explain," I say.

She looks at me, surprised, as if there is no need for explanation.

"Look," she says, sitting up, getting excited. "You know what it's like at home, right?"

I nod my head, though I can't be sure if she's referring to our parents' alcoholism, their endless fights, Harold's obsession for dollhouses, Maggie's obsession for Mr. Kowolski and popping pills or the fact that as offspring we have always been made to feel like genetic insults, intrusions into our parents' true desire to end forever their lineage.

"Okay. All right," she says, getting animated. "So the homestead is in turmoil. Things are flying. I go outside. U-Haul whips around the corner. I'm maybe six or something and this weirdo clan of Franconis moves in. And this guy, Danny, takes one look at me, walks over to me and says, 'Want to see my woinkee?' and he peels his pants away and shows me his cock."

I laugh. It is funny. I am also embarrassed. The word *cock* makes me feel slightly dizzy.

"You gotta understand how something like that could appeal to me."

"I was two," I say.

"Yes, you were," she says, rubbing my hair. Curly red hair. Dopey Goldblum nose. I am not worthy of her. "But, of course, it was more than that."

I watch a red-winged blackbird take flight. There was a time when

Martin would have swung a BB gun over his shoulder and taken aim. Pow.

"Since I can remember, we've done absolutely everything together. Everything. We scoured the neighborhood together, we shoplifted together, we ate, slept, peed, got sick together. We did everything together. We were, we are, a world of our own. Nothing, no one can penetrate it. Not even them."

I know by *them* that she means the adults, our parents, Danny's parents, the Kowolskis, everyone who has ever spent an evening getting blind drunk and stupid in our backyard.

"He saved me," she says. Tears spring to her eyes. I am reminded of the many times she has cautioned me against crying, so I am quite amazed by this display.

"I'm going to miss him. But it's a test of sorts. You understand. I have to know that I can survive without him too. Do you understand?"

I nod my head. But, of course, I have no idea what she's talking about.

"If I can survive without him while I'm away at school, if he can live without me, then we have the right to be together forever. I just have to know. Can I fend for myself?"

"Esther," I say. I am shocked. Of course she can fend for herself. She's Esther Goldblum, fearless devil goddess of suburbia.

She looks at me, her dark eyes glistening. She is radiant. She is brilliant with love and passion and hope. She is standing on the crest of the world, preparing to take flight.

"No need to continue, Baby Goldblum. I know what you are about to say. But you have no idea how deeply I have leaned on him. How much he has kept me free to live. Now I have to learn to do it alone. The only way I can marry him, be with him, whatever, is to be away from him for a while. I can't shake it. It's a truth. It has to be."

With that she gets up, places the rose, the seashell and the poem beside the rock, kissing the poem first before laying it down. Then she looks up to the sky, murmurs some incantation which I cannot, am not, supposed to hear and she is finished.

"It is so fantastic," she says.

She could be referring to any number of things. What it might be is irrelevant. She is happy. So happy for a Goldblum that I wonder why I've missed this aspect of her personality all along. She is taking wing, embarking on a new experiment. She is in love. She has been protected forever from the damage of growing up in an unpredictable world. She is perfect, brilliant, a pearl inside a world of her own creation. She is the mistress of her life, taking the rapids on a river that flows from her own imagination. Nothing can stop her. She is free. And she is in love. She has the best of all worlds. I stare at her, astonished. She is the Goldblum gem, the light among the ashes. I love her. I love her.

But, of course, it is only two days later that Danny drives his motorcycle over the abyss and cements his lasting and successful effort to make Esther his forever.

The phone would ring. We'd stop what we were doing, usually fucking, and look at it. Then we'd get back to whatever we'd been doing, fucking, drinking, inventing new ways to verbally insult each other.

One day he hauled an old black-and-white television set in. We watched *The Odd Couple* reruns. Zeke would say, "Felix is a fag." We watched *Gilligan's Island* reruns. Zeke would say, "Ginger and Mary Ann, what a pair of sluts." We watched *The Brady Bunch*. Zeke would say, "Which one of the Brady boys did you want to fuck?"

One day, we watched an *I Love Lucy* rerun where she got tied up by the twins she was baby-sitting. Zeke didn't wait for it to end. He tore the sash from the blinds, bound my wrists, held them up against the wall and tacked them there with a knife. Then he fucked me, the knife hanging over my head precariously, daring me, daring me to move.

So it went.

One day, after a particularly violent session involving candle wax and a blindfold, Zeke stood up and lit a cigarette.

"What do you suppose is happening out there?" He gestured toward the window.

"Same old shit. Gunfights, robbery, mayhem. Nothing like the peace in here."

He grunted. His skin appeared even whiter than I remembered. But his body was still broad, hard, indestructible. I knew it as if I had studied it, as if it were the road map to my increasing isolation and drunkenness.

"Isn't it your turn to get the cigarettes?" he asked.

"No," I said. I poured myself a drink, looked at the clock, couldn't make the time out, couldn't see. I knew I had to get to the museum before the end of the week. The show, the demon monster, opened the following Monday.

"What's today?" I said.

"Jesus," he said, laughing scornfully. "Get the fuck outta bed. You look like shit."

"Oh, baby, I love it when you talk dirty."

He laughed, sucked on his cigarette, blew the smoke out. He was naked. I hadn't seen him wearing clothes for a few days. I lifted the blanket off me. Naked. A few bruises. A little dried blood.

"Really. I'm ashamed of you," he said. "Let's get out of this hole. Jesus. You look like crap."

He seemed agitated. Upset. We had, over the last week, fallen into a sort of torpid domesticity, rarely leaving the house, ordering food in, walking around nude except for socks on our feet. There were empty containers that once held Chinese, Thai and Italian food all over the studio. Those days, I could tell, were coming to an end. He was Zeke again. Insatiable, inscrutable, a pissed-off mongrel dog. He needed the world. He needed to mark his territory.

"Zeke, did you ever notice how limited your vocabulary is. Shit. Crap. Fuck. That's about the extent of it."

He walked over to me. He glared at me. I was sure he would hit me or spit on me.

"Get the fuck out of bed," he said. "You look crappy, like shit."

I stood up and watched him snicker at his own stupid cleverness. But then I decided he was right. I did look like shit. I would try out a shower, see how it felt. If it worked out all right, I'd stick my head out the window, and if all went well, then I'd agree to go out, maybe as far as El Rio for a drink.

I turned on the shower. I heard Zeke in the main room throwing things around. I heard him talking. The phone.

"Goddamnit, Seth. I gave you those pictures, entrusted you with them. Now I see . . . No, look, Seth, you don't have any fucking respect. You hear me. No respect." I heard the phone fly across the room.

I closed the bathroom door. The irony was too much. It was an irony that could break me apart, tear me from limb to limb. I thought about it. Respect. I laughed. What did Zeke know about respect? I jumped beneath the drumbeat of water.

I stared down at my body. What a mess. So thin. So white. I saw that there were bruises everywhere, on my thighs, knees, forearms. My wrists were raw. I looked like a suicide. But the important thing, I reminded myself, was that I hadn't thought of Esther in days. In fact, I was sure, I would soon be over her. I would soon move on.

I began to get excited thinking of the things I would do now that I was better. I decided I would quit smoking first. Next, I would get rid of Zeke. I would call Mary, apologize, call Alice, apologize. Go home, say hey to my parents. Maybe fly down to L.A. and extricate Martin from another dangerous love affair with a TV sitcom starlet. Visit Eddie in Daly City. Say, Hey, how are ya?

The water felt good. I was feeling better than I had in days. I wondered if Zeke had moved in. I leaned out of the shower, screamed out his name. He appeared in the gloom of hot mist.

"Did you move in or something?" I asked.

He just glared at me, called me a name, left the bathroom.

Later, we were walking down Mission Street for the BART tracks. Something about getting some pictures back from someone named Seth at a restaurant downtown.

I said, "Fuck downtown, I'm not going."

He grabbed my ass in the middle of the street, an ass that had just that morning lost its virginity. The pain of it brought tears to my eyes. I stifled a cry.

"You're going," he said.

We got on the train. I sat beside him. He was enraged about something. It was a rage I had never seen. Why now was I just noticing it? When had the stew begun its boil?

"What's wrong?" I asked.

He said nothing, stared straight ahead. A vein bulged in his fore-head. He put an unlit cigarette in his mouth and sucked. A lady sitting across from us looked at Zeke, clucked her tongue, then looked at me. For shame, for shame, her eyes said. I checked to make sure I was dressed, that the small red welts and burns were covered. She grabbed her purse, stood up and went over to the next car.

When we got off at Montgomery, Zeke didn't even leave the station before lighting up. He grabbed my elbow—apparently I wasn't walking fast enough for him—and guided me up the escalator. I could hear a train above on the Muni tracks screeching to a halt. The sound of doors opening. The train taking off again.

When we got out to the street, Zeke guided me to a small restaurant on the corner of Market and Montgomery. Inside, it smelled like pas-trami, croissants and hot coffee.

A guy in a white apron stood behind the counter adding something on a calculator and writing in a ledger book. When he looked up and saw it was Zeke, he carefully closed the ledger and, very carefully, said, "Hey, Zeke."

"Fuck you," Zeke said. "Give me the fucking negatives."

"I told you, man, I gave them back to her."

"Seth, you better have the negatives and those pictures or I swear I will fucking kill you."

I moved back against a wall, uncertain what to do, putting my back against it and feeling its sure weight holding me up. I noticed that there were only two customers in the restaurant. A man in a business suit wearing glasses with a briefcase at his feet was sitting with a very frail-looking blonde woman wearing a pink skirt and a white silk blouse. The man stood up, made for Zeke. Like he had something to prove. It was a mistake.

"Everything all right here, fellas?" the man asked.

Zeke turned around, walked up to him, towered over him. Zeke had a good five inches on him and the fearlessness of an animal, rabid, panting. He said, "Another word, I kill you."

The man began to fumble for his cell phone but Zeke merely took it out of the man's hand, went to the door and threw it on the sidewalk.

"Fetch," he said.

The pale woman stood up. She ran out the door and the man followed. Zeke went to the door, closed it, turned the sign around so it said CLOSED and came back to the guy behind the counter. For a moment I wondered if Zeke was going to kill him. It seemed like something out of a Mafia movie, surreal, ridiculous, terrifying. I saw on the far wall, behind the counter, a telephone and wanted to run for it, to call for help. But I couldn't seem to move. I was stuck to the wall, certain it was the only thing holding me up.

"Seth, I oughta fucking kill you. But I won't. You're her fucking brother and because you share the same fucking blood, I won't kill you. So, I'm only asking now, polite-like. You see. I'm no thug. I've got a college education. I'm from a wealthy family. Manners and reputations have been inbred. You get those fucking pictures . . . no, no, you let her keep the pictures. You get the fucking negatives and I'll say thank you and leave you be."

"I can't do that, Zeke. I'm sorry."

And at that, Zeke picked up a glass jar of biscotti and hurled it across the room. Though he aimed at the opposite wall, I instinctively ducked. His face was twisted in a rage I had never seen. I thought he would cry. Tears filled his eyes. I had an uncharacteristic urge to go to him and put my arms around him.

"He's my fucking son. He's my fucking son. I gave you those negatives out of a sense of fucking loyalty. You're betraying me, man. He's my son."

"Zeke, look, man, you oughta just go. Okay. I'm sorry. Lisa's afraid of you. I can't help that. And you know her husband. You know he'll just call the police again and have you arrested again. I'm sorry."

Zeke stood there, blinking. Unsure, it seemed. If he had been a cartoon figure, smoke would have blown from his ears. But then I looked again. He seemed suddenly frail, weak. Something seemed to have been let loose. But in seconds again he changed. In a fury, he picked up a tray of croissants, hurled them across the room. If it hadn't been so awful, I might have laughed watching all those froufrou French pastries flying through the air.

"You tell her I'll fucking take him away from her. I'll find them both and I'll take him away."

Then he stormed out. I forced myself to step away from the wall that had been supporting me. I began to follow him out but turned around first and stopped, looking at Seth. He was shaking his head. He looked upset. Sad. Disgusted. But not afraid.

"Are you Lisa Silburner's brother?" I asked.

He looked up at me as if he just realized I was there. He nodded sadly.

"I'm sorry," I said.

"He's crazy. It's not your fault." Then he started toward the hurled biscotti and said, "I'd watch my back around him."

I walked out of the restaurant. I looked up and down the street. Zeke was nowhere in sight. I didn't see him again for three days. I stayed in bed. I listened for the key in the lock. His absence made me desperate. When I slept it was fitful and I always woke with a racing heart and sweat-soaked sheets. I drank myself into a frantic patience. "He'll be back," I said to the walls over and over again.

"Get up," he said. "We've got some ghosts to kick up."

Zeke was standing over my bed. He was, as usual, smoking a cigarette. In his right hand he held a bottle of vodka, gripping it around the neck.

"I can't," I said. "My show opens tomorrow. I need to sleep."

He kicked the side of the bed.

"Get up," he said.

"If I get up will you leave me alone?"

He smiled, which I took as a yes, and I obeyed.

I followed him outside where the air was still, the sky a deep blackish purple. The cold hurt my lungs. I lit a cigarette and got into the old beat-up Toyota Zeke had driven the first night I met him. I did not feel like I was inside my body, but at the same time I felt an exact, mechanical precision to my movements, a clarity of momentum that seemed to propel me forward in spite of myself. I thought of it, the idea of having a self, of being a self, and wondered over the ownership of Louise Goldblum. Was it fair to say that I owned myself?

I watched Zeke and appreciated again his cryptic beauty, the marvelous way in which he could both repel and draw me. It seemed like ages ago that I last saw him in the restaurant downtown, hurling pastries across the room. It seemed ages since I'd met him and I realized that our life together meant nothing really. No event seemed to carry a single meaning.

I had reached the apex of aversion, the exact place where the desire to know something, anything, had metamorphosed into a strong reaction against knowing it. I did not care about Zeke and Seth and Lisa Silburner. I did not care about a son, the son. There was no truth. I needed to know nothing. I had lost all desire.

We drove through the nearly deserted streets south of Market and onto the freeway, going north toward the Bay Bridge. Zeke lit a cigarette and settled back in the car seat.

"You all right?" He didn't look at me so I knew he meant it.

"Yeah," I said.

He took hold of my hand, squeezed it. I saw the way he squinted as if trying to hide something.

"Do you remember the safe word?" he asked gently, giving my hand another squeeze.

I nodded. For some reason, I felt a lump in my throat. Maybe tonight he would try to kill me. I looked forward to it. Something, something to wake me up. Or else to let me rest.

He pulled his hand away.

"There are so many things that mystify me," he said. "I sit around sometimes for hours just thinking about them, these stupid, imbecile things. Aspirin. How does it find the pain? Phone lines, how do they really work? If you can fax a piece of paper to Hawaii, why can't you fax yourself?"

"It's just idle thoughts," I said. I was bored. I didn't care.

"Yeah, because beneath the surface lurks all the Nazis, the infanticides and the unjust wars, Darwinian evolution bent out of shape by humanity. A nest is built on the ledge of a street sign and just before spring a guy on a skateboard tears it down. What do you do?"

"You dream of one day faxing yourself to Hawaii."

He gestured to the backseat where a bottle of whiskey poked out of a canvas bag. I reached for it.

"Do you think she might have planned it?" he asked.

"What? Who?"

"Esther. Do you think she might have planned her death? Not in the conscious sense, but maybe in the way alcoholics drink until they die, not exactly killing themselves with a gun or something like that but doing it slowly, with a slavish devotion to their booze and all the while, back in the deepest recesses of their brains they're thinking, *Die faster, buddy.*"

"Maybe," I said, not even sure that I had said it all. I cleared my throat. I wanted to take advantage of this, of Zeke talking to me about Esther. It was the first time he seemed interested. And this interested me. Of everyone I knew, Zeke seemed the most likely to understand how breathless her death had made me. So I spoke fast. Sputtered. Gestured strangely, like a victim of nerve damage. "I've wondered. She lived dangerously. Why would she go with some stranger to some motel in the middle of nowhere? Maybe she wanted it to happen. I think maybe she wanted it to happen and in the split second before she disappeared from the planet she thought, *Uh oh.*"

He snickered. But I knew he was with me on that one. He understood regret. He lit a cigarette and handed it to me. Then he lit one for himself.

"Would you go there? With someone you didn't know?"

And when he asked it, I knew where we were headed.

"Stop the car, Zeke," I said.

He laughed. "You're very smart. Very intuitive. I never understood why you talked so damn much when all you ever really needed to do was listen. It's a gift of yours. A kind of ESP. You know things before they're even spoken."

"I said stop the fucking car."

We were on the freeway, doing about eighty.

"Don't you think it's about time you faced those niggling little demons of yours?"

"I have never been there," I said, aware that my voice sounded shrill and that I was wringing my hands. "Eddie went with our parents. He identified her body. I don't want to go there."

"Yes, you do," he said. He reached out for the bottle. I did not, not immediately, hand it over.

"Zeke, please. Take me home. I don't want to go there." A little train of terror was making its way across my body, raising my skin to gooseflesh. I thought of it, *cease,* and imagined saying it. But the word seemed unutterable, like an apology when you didn't really mean it.

"Too late," he said. "Your search ends with me. Or begins with me. Think of me as your guardian angel. With me you brave the path to truth and knowledge."

He laughed in a sinister way and reached for the bottle. When I let it go, I felt as if I had let loose a life raft in a raging sea. I felt the perilous sway of surrender again, the hallucinogen of being pulled along, against my will, without the ability of fight.

I needed to see where she died. I dreaded it. I had to go. I couldn't. But it was not my choice. I was not me. Someone else lived inside, something else allowed itself to be swayed, swindled, cheated into the midst of Goldblum history.

We drove in silence for a long time and then we were driving through the lonely stretch of Highway 4 that I had visited in my imagination so many times before. I saw what Esther saw, the silent oak and rock-specked land of green hills and owls and mule deer and coyotes howling. I rolled the window down and breathed the same air Esther must have breathed just hours before her death.

And then it came back to me, no matter how hard I tried to keep it at bay. I saw her. *Beautiful Esther sitting beside the man who she had met in a bar in San Francisco. The man is cool, almost steely and handsome with sharp features and deep-set eyes. He is rubbing her leg as he drives and I feel what she felt, that thrill, the dark surrounding her, the emptiness of her life surrounding her, the death of Danny surrounding her, these things like arms around her, strangling her.*

They drive on the road, the same winding, narrow road that Zeke and I were now traveling over, and the man reaches for Esther's hands. They exchange a glance and Esther feels her heart skip a beat, the surging of blood between her legs. She is afraid for an instant as she recognizes her danger. She is momentarily philosophical regarding her own death.

Zeke pulled over and stopped the car, interrupting my thoughts. The road was completely deserted. He got out without speaking and urinated against a tree. The baseness of it struck me. How hard Zeke could be, how feral. When he got back into the car, he smiled at me. It was an uncharacteristic gesture.

"You are very beautiful," he said.

I thought, *Fuck off.*

"Do you want to know why you stay with me?" he asked. He had yet to start the car.

"No."

"Because you recognize in me the pleasure one can get from suffering. The difference between us is you won't admit it. Me, I know it. I make a game of suffering. You, you take it too seriously."

"Yeah, well your sister wasn't erased off the fucking map in a motel room."

"Look, I'm not interested in competing for the most miserable on planet Earth."

"Conversations with you go nowhere."

"That's because you expect them to go somewhere, as if words can have any kind of real destination. You believe that everything is linear. That everything has a beginning, a middle, an end. You don't like to come into things in the middle, go back to start, et cetera, et cetera."

"You don't even fucking know me." I was angry. I could feel it in every cell, every follicle, every corner of my body.

"I knew you the moment I laid eyes on you. Trust me. There are hundreds of you. You all have the same expressions in your eyes: hunger, longing, desire. You are not unique, Miss Goldblum. Not unique."

He started the car after taking a sip from the bottle. He had won again and as usual I had not seen the battle looming, had not, in fact, understood what the war was about. But he had won again. He could remove my skin without removing my clothes. I detested him.

After an hour or so, he slowed down and it was only after a police car passed us that I could marvel at Zeke's radar. He had capacities for detection that I would never understand, that, as an artist, I was profoundly jealous of. I lit another cigarette, one of my own, and swallowed some more booze. I wanted to disappear, thinking of my installation sitting there in the darkness at the De Young. I was embarrassed for myself, for it, for the maudlin display of all that indignity. *Someone should destroy it*, I thought.

We finally emerged from the foothills into a long straightaway. The darkness was impenetrable. We were the last people on the planet and we were drunk, filled with unrequited screams.

Then, without warning, we were in a small town, the narrow road lined by quaint turn-of-the-century buildings. I looked at my watch. It was only 10:30 P.M. but the streets were nearly deserted. Several boys, all with long, scraggly hair, were hanging outside the hardware store with their skateboards and their cigarettes. Zeke drove slowly and at the first intersection turned left.

I saw it immediately, the green neon sign, the lettering, some of which had burned out and had not yet been replaced. I read it. THE ROG HOP ER INN. The Frog Hopper Inn.

Zeke pulled into the nearly deserted parking lot and turned off the car. He looked at me.

"Ready," he said with a ghoulish sort of excitement. Instinctively I looked at his crotch. Hard-on.

I got out of the car. I heard the faint tremble of a small creek and went to the edge of the parking lot and peered over a steep ravine. I could see nothing but I smelled the sweet scent of pine and sap and wet earth. Esther had probably stood here, probably drunk, the way I was now. I breathed the air the way Esther must have. I zipped myself into her skin and felt the worn-out, tired old bottom-of-the-barrel estrangement that marked her life. A shudder—for a moment I even thought it must have been her spirit—rippled through my body. I stomped the ground. My heart beat unmercifully.

Zeke came up behind me and pretended to push me over the ledge, catching me before I fell. I had imagined it that way with Esther too.

"Always watch your back," he said.

He laughed, then went back to the car and grabbed his camera case. He reached for a pack of cigarettes in the glove compartment. Then we walked to the door that said OFFICE on it and went inside. It smelled like cigarettes and worn furniture. An old man with a prominent nose and tired, rheumy eyes eyed us suspiciously. His gaze landed on me and tarried there for a long time. Then he turned his stare back at Zeke, taking in the bald head, the tattoos, the earrings.

"Help you?"

"We'd like a room," Zeke said.

The man said nothing for the longest time. Had he been the one who'd found her? I had the urge to run out the door, and it took every bit of effort to remain standing. I imagined that every weirdo who came in must have reminded him of Esther's death. I was certain that for this man, we were all potential murderers and victims. Esther's death couldn't have done much for business.

"All right," he said, shrugging his shoulders as if having decided to plunge off the edge of a cliff. "But no bullshit, ya hear. I got enough troubles around here, I don't need some goddamned Nazi causing any more."

"I'm not a Nazi," Zeke said calmly.

The man grunted and handed Zeke the registration forms. I noticed that Zeke wrote down our names as Mr. and Mrs. Smith. He requested room 17, the one my sister was killed in. I said nothing, paralyzed. How had he known?

We walked silently across the parking lot, the gravel beneath our feet making that pleasant crunching sound. The air was bitter cold and I shivered. When Zeke opened the door, I hesitated for a moment before going in.

I thought about it, them, that night.

The man shuts the door behind him, he takes Esther by the waist and kisses her. She responds, but something in her heart has grown cold. He is holding her too tightly. There is something after all about him that frightens her. She no longer wants to be there, but she doesn't want him to see her fear, so slowly she undresses, as he asks her to, and carefully lays her clothes on the chair. He thinks her body is beautiful. He wants to possess it. He has forgotten the woman, the Esther behind the body. That is why he will be able to shoot her once in the head as she lies there curled up after sex.

He kisses the nape of her neck, breathing in her smell, the scent of her that he will steal from me for the rest of my life. He touches her bony, brown body, traces the tight lines of her thin Goldblum frame, a thinness that borders on obscene except for its one saving grace—the ability to be both inordinately strong and disastrously frail.

He thinks of her grace as he kisses her lightly between the legs. He is consumed by it, he wishes to possess it, because he does not know virtue within himself. He knows that when he first laid eyes on her, he would kill her, only it is just now becoming real for him. He must own her.

Zeke came up behind me. He put his arms around me. He kissed me.

"I have a weakness, you understand, for beautiful women."

"Don't be nice to me, Zeke."

He seemed surprised.

"Why are we here?" I asked. I kept thinking about the old man at the motel office. Of his ancient face, his ancient suspicion, his hatred for us.

"We're looking for Esther," he said.

"I want to go home."

"Too late," he said.

He kissed me lightly on the back of the neck. He touched me with a certain calculated tenderness. Then, without warning, he pushed me on the bed.

"Take your clothes off."

I did nothing. I could hardly breathe. *Cease, goddamn you.* I gulped air. Said nothing.

"Fine," he said. "Fine."

He was cold, mean. A vein pulsed in his forehead. He took a knife attached to his belt loop and unhinged it. I lifted my hands for some reason to shield my face, but he just laughed and cut my shirt open. I looked down at my breasts, startled. Poor breasts.

"Take off your pants or I cut them off too."

I stood up, both repulsed and aroused. I unbuttoned my jeans but apparently not fast enough for Zeke. With the knife in his mouth, he kneeled down and wrested them off me. The pointy, sharp end of the blade pricked my thigh. A spot of blood. My heart quickened. He slammed me back on the bed.

"What the fuck is wrong with you? Why don't you fight back? Say something."

I stood there, aroused and disgusted, the wet between my legs getting wetter as the humiliation and self-hatred grew deeper, gathering steam. I hated him. I hated me.

"You stupid fuck," he said, slapping me across the face so that I fell back into the worn, shit-colored bedspread on the bed my sister died in.

It was then that the image of Mrs. Kowolski suddenly came to me. I saw her red tits. I remembered the way her husband had slapped her. I remembered the way she had forgiven him by letting him come into her body. God, how I hated her, him, the whole lot of them. I thought of our parents. Of their boozy, pathetic lives. They were culpable too. *You killed her too*, I thought. And the thought of it, of them, of that life, drained me even more, took something from me. I felt it—whatever *it* was—recede from me. I saw a candle flicker and go out.

"Turn over," Zeke said from a long way off, from the other end of a long tunnel.

I lay there. I did nothing. Zeke smashed me across the face, but oddly it did not hurt.

"Turn the fuck over or stop me," he shouted. It was a lament, a protest, a wail. I heard demons in it. I heard the bottom of sadness and regret.

I did nothing, so he slapped me, this time across my lips. I tasted blood in my mouth. Tears sprang to my eyes. He rolled me over and tied my hands with a rope that he must have extracted from his camera case.

I wondered fleetingly whether he had been the one who murdered my sister, but I knew he was not her type. She would never have gone away with someone so obvious.

"The safe word. Say it."

"No," I said. "Never." It was a voice from another body. Not my body. But the body of a girl who had taken over control of mine.

He took out his camera and began to take pictures.

"Say it," he hissed. "Jesus Christ, say it. *Cease.* Say it."

But I remained silent, accepting the indignity, accepting the pain. I deserved it. I flashed on Esther, on the idea that she had been unaware of her impending death. Did she feel the bullet rip into her brain?

"Say the safe word. Say it," Zeke said, pleading.

He crawled on top of me. He was sweating, with an unnameable emotion. I could feel his emotions at my back, like a brick, weighting down the pressure of his hard, enameled body on me so that I could hardly breathe. For an instant, I thought I might die there too.

"Say it."

He picked my head up by the hair and turned it so that I could see his face.

"Stop me." He was begging now. But I couldn't stop him, it, this. I couldn't because all I could think was that she really was dead. I had survived, I would survive, but she, Esther, the strongest, smartest, most worshiped Goldblum had not.

"Never," I said.

Then it was like my brain disappeared, like blacking out only still feeling the presence of my skin against the sheets, his penis in my ass, ripping me apart, and me, above it all, seeing the sign outside flashing on and off, THE ROG HOP ER INN, seeing my body, my blood on the sheets. I took it all in, dispassionate, from above, while her, that other Louise, lay on the bed, embracing disgrace.

Then it was over. I felt him pull himself from my ass, a searing, hot pain darting at the tips of my nerves. He left me and I felt oddly emptied out. I breathed. He got up and quickly dressed. I saw that he had gone too far, even for himself. I saw that he had gambled and lost. He could not meet my eyes.

"Shit," he said. He wiped his face. "Shit, Lisa, you dumb, cold bitch."

He stared at me for a moment as if seeing me for the first time since we arrived at the motel. I could see his eyes fill with something like remorse and guilt. It was not me he wanted to erase after all. I remembered the picture of Lisa Silburner on the wall of his apartment and the way she stared with defiance at the camera.

I dressed slowly. Zeke gave me his sweatshirt to wear while he wore only a T-shirt that said DISCOVER MEXICO on it.

We left not even an hour after we got there. Zeke drove slowly. We didn't speak. I saw in the mirror that my eye was turning black, my lip was swollen. Zeke would not look at me. We had both failed. He had not destroyed his demon either.

"I am not Lisa Silburner," I said lamely, knowing he had confused us, understanding how easy it could be to do such a thing.

He said nothing. Those were the only words spoken on the long drive home.

When we got back to the city, it was almost four in the morning. He dropped me off and I didn't have the heart to look at him, to commit his face to memory. I didn't even say good-bye. Going to the scene of Esther's death had taken everything out of me. I remembered what Zeke had said about the destination of words. And then I understood why I had always turned to art instead.

I climbed the stairs to my studio and I sat on the couch, drinking until there was no more booze left. I watched the sky grow lighter and lighter until it was irrefutably another day. Finally, I put on a coat and headed for the museum.

When I got there, Lucille K. Johnson had yet to arrive. Nevertheless, her assistant gave me the key, which I'd left behind in my studio. She stared the entire time at my face, the bloodied lip, the black eye. I must have stunk. I must have looked terrible.

I let myself into my installation and shut the door behind me. I looked at my re-creation of the lake. I went over to Esther's nude body and kneeled beside it. It was all I could do because I had never said good-bye to her. With Esther, you were never allowed to say good-bye, and so you believed in the undisputed truth that she would be with you always. And if she loved no one other than Danny, then it did not matter because we loved her, we loved her, each of us, somehow knowing that when Danny died, Esther was lost to the world. We loved her in desperation because none of us had ever had the chance to love another soul the way she had loved another soul. We loved her out of jealousy, out of fear, out of sorrow. We loved her because we could have been her. We loved her because we were not.

I picked up the face, the perfect replica of Esther's face, and felt the lack of her in its hard surface and unblinking eyes. I let her go and sat against the wall. I sat there crying. I couldn't stop crying. I bit my nails, crying. I must have cried for a very long time, thinking it was not right that she was dead. She could not be dead, it made no sense. I had again the image of Esther at Lake Lauganita after Danny died, of my inability to comfort her or understand the expanse and breadth of her grief. I thought of the sad, reckless lonesomeness, not just of her life, but of the lives of all the Goldblums who resided in that war-torn, cluttered, disorganized shelter we called the old homestead.

Later, when the firemen came, I watched quietly as they doused my installation, most of which had burned or been ruined by the smoke and the water. And when the police showed up and arrested me for starting the fire, I told them that I didn't know how it had happened, that as far as I knew, I hadn't even been carrying matches. They just rolled their eyes.

"Okay, ma'am," one of them said, taking hold of my elbow. "Whatever you want to believe's okay with us."

And I just looked at him, wondering what the hell he knew about me.

All of a sudden from the park's full green
Something, you can't say what, has been rescinded,
You feel it drawing closer to the windows
And growing silent. Fervently and keen

Resounds alone the rain-note of the plover,
Like some Jerome, so tensely from the brush
A sense of zeal and loneness arches over
Out of this single urgence, which the rush

Of rain will slake. The walls of the great hall,
its pictures, have retreated like a hearer
Who must not overhear what we are saying;

The faded tapestries which line them mirror
Those afternoons of twilight mootly graying
In which we were afraid when we were small.

R I L K E

I t was Mary who collected me from the San Francisco County Jail, temporary home of hookers and crack addicts. She drove me to the old homestead with her careful, honest compassion. She loved me. I saw this. When we got inside our parents' house, the war-torn isle of lost innocence, she took me straight to my old room—that half-assed add-on in the back—and put me to bed, pointing to a bottle of aspirin, a cold compress for the eye and the remote control to the television.

Eddie and Martin had been summoned. We were all together, all, that is, except Esther. They, my parents and siblings, shadowed me. I could detect in Eddie a certain awe. Their collective good manners made me feel slightly sweaty. They were afraid of me.

For the first week, I did nothing but lay in my old bed, smelling the scents of the house. Fish, onions, cigarettes, gardenias and brewing coffee. Over and over in my head, like the proverbial broken record, I kept thinking, *The rog hoper, the rog hoper.* It seemed odd to me that the mascot of my life had become the hairless, amphibious frog, the unfortunate victim of high school dissecting lessons, Martin's taxidermy and the sometime emblem of the Old West. I tried to find meaning in this but I could not. And still, I kept at it like a mantra, *the rog hoper, the rog hoper,* the words themselves like a salve to the way my heart beat if I let my mind wander too far from the bed.

Each day, Mary would come into the room quietly and leave things like hot teas and magazines. Sometimes she would bring in toast and soup and ginger ale. Most everything remained untouched. I would wake up and yesterday's tray would be gone, replaced by a new shift of comfort foods and mindless women's rags. "Hot Orgasms—How to Have Them, How to Make Them Last." "Vacation Diets." "Summer Flings—Have You Cheated on Your Man?"

At night, without a bloodstream saturated by vodka and whiskey, I sweated profoundly and dreamed of strange places that I had never been to but that seemed vaguely familiar. There was always plenty of sand and water and large mansions not unlike the dollhouses that Harold built. I thought often about sneaking into my parents' liquor cabinet and not kill myself, just make myself disappear. My hands trembled so badly in the mornings that I wished for just one sip of whiskey to calm them. But my embarrassment kept me from doing it. The memory of Mary's face when she came for me at the jail kept me from drinking. I could not live through another expression such as hers on that day, a mixture of raw sorrow, pale disbelief, indescribable fright.

One morning I woke up and Eddie was sitting on a chair in the corner of the room. He had recovered well from his injuries. His beauty now had a certain burly character to it, marred as it was by a deep scar above his left eye and a lip that still looked split. He sat there rubbing the floral fabric of the chair and I realized I hadn't noticed the chair in my room before then. But I was not alarmed. It was like that at our house. Furniture, books and knickknacks came alive at night, and while we slept marched from room to room.

He was reading a book: *The Selfish Gene.*

"Hey, Baby Goldblum," he said.

"Hey."

He began to read. "Another common sexual difference is that females are more fussy than males about with whom they mate."

"Coulda fooled me," I said from beneath the blankets.

"You've never had a flair for drama, Baby G. I'm impressed."

"If you're talking about my sex life, I wasn't looking to increase the gene pool. And if you're referring to the museum, no one seems to understand that I meant to do it. As a part of the installation."

"No one around here has any sense of art."

"Or humor," I said.

It was the first time I had said much of anything since my enforced deposit back at the old homestead. Now I sat up and looked around me. Nothing had changed. It still looked as if a tornado had done the decorating, a puzzle undone. There were books stacked up all over the place, an eclectic mixture of science, art, fiction and history. *The Incas, Fusion and Energy, Kandinsky and Abstract Expressionism.* Esther's copy of *The Stranger* written in French. *L'Etranger.* In one corner of the room was a basket of shoes—snow shoes, antique baby booties, shoes made out of porcelain. Even a pair of shoe bookends.

"What is this?" I said, gesturing to the typhoon around me.

Eddie looked at the room and shrugged.

"Why," I asked, "have our lives been so cluttered? Why have we been surrounded by so much junk?"

"Is this a philosophical question or merely one of logistics?"

"Eddie," I said. "I nearly set a fucking museum on fire. Do you really think I'm interested in logistics at the present?"

He put his magazine down and got into bed beside me. I put my head on his arm, which he wrapped around me, and we lay like that quietly staring at the ceiling, an entire re-creation of the solar system that Martin had painted for me the year he gave up killing small mammals and reptiles.

"There seem to be two kinds of people on the earth," Eddie said. "Normal people. And by that I mean people who don't show any outward appearance of insanity, a position in life that allows them to gossip about other people. And then there are the people like us, who seem to have been born with the inability to act normally or to keep insanity behind closed doors. We are the group that the normal people gossip about. We need each other, you know. Think about those two little yuppie shits across the street. Without us, what would they have to keep them agog?"

"Agog?"

He shifted his position slightly and ignored me.

"Have you ever heard of the term *nurse logs?*"

"No," I said.

"I was just reading a book in Harold's garage about the forests of the Pacific Northwest and there was this one, tiny, innocuous paragraph about nurse logs."

"Yes, I've noticed that about tiny, innocuous paragraphs. They're always the best ones in a book."

Eddie nodded and continued. "Nurse logs are these trees that have fallen in the woods, dead trees out of which new life springs. They are essential. Without them nothing else in the forest would grow. It's like it takes a dead thing to make a live thing."

"Are you trying to tell me I'm a dead tree in the woods."

"Actually I was thinking more of Esther."

I felt my stomach do a slight flip at the mention of her name and immediately changed the subject.

"Do you know what a rog hoper is?" I asked.

He turned and looked at me, his face a blank.

"Oh, never mind," I said.

For some reason this made us laugh. It was the dual, hysterical laughter I remembered sharing with Eddie when I was little. It was the kind of laughter that would burst from us at the dinner table, especially when Harold had had too much to drink and began lecturing us on quantum physics or the time-space continuum, as if we cared. Or when Esther began wearing a bra. Now that was funny, the way she took to see-through blouses and a certain change in posture that accentuated her growing *booblets.* Or when Martin, oblivious to the notion that there were natural obstacles to one's geography, would walk into walls.

"So tell me, Baby Goldblum. Who was this Zeke guy?"

At the mention of his name, I felt myself fill with the desire to drink. Instead, I lit a cigarette and lay back down. I inhaled and let out several puffs of smoke before I could say anything.

"The literal truth to your question is, I don't know. I don't know where he came from, who his family is, how old he is, where, if at all, he went to school. I don't have his stats."

I thought of Lisa Silburner, the son, of Seth, Lisa's brother and of Lisa's bartender husband. I remembered the picture of the penis and the vagina on the wall of his bathroom and the dead mallard in his freezer. But they seemed like illusions now.

"Strange," Eddie said. He reached out and I handed him my cigarette. He took a long drag and handed it back. Outside I heard the cooing of doves. The sound made me cringe. I wanted to tell Eddie about Zeke. All at once it seemed important that someone know. But know what? What was there to tell? I could not imagine trying to explain what I had never understood to begin with.

"It is strange," I said, practically whispering. My mouth felt dry and when I dragged on my cigarette, my hands trembled. But I felt a compulsion to go on, to divulge what I had kept secret for so long.

"There's another answer to your question," I said slowly.

Eddie remained perfectly still. Mercifully I heard the doves outside fly away. The forlorn flap of their wings disappeared, leaving me feeling more empty but equally more desperate not to feel that way.

"Zeke was like a craving, like a sneeze that never comes. I needed him. It's so hard to explain."

"Yeah," Eddie said. "It's okay."

But it wasn't okay. I sat up and stubbed my cigarette out. My heart beat fast and hard but it felt good.

"Because there were times when I was sure I loved him, and there were times I despised him. I miss him in this sick, desperate way. But if I saw him again I would probably cower behind a couch or something. At least I think I would. What matters is that I don't know what I would do. Before Zeke, it seemed like there would never be a question. I would know just what to do and what not to do in any given situation."

I was surprised at the breadth of my answer and the strange, frantic way I spoke but also at how good it felt. It was the most I had said at one time since my release from jail. Eddie seemed surprised too and it was evidently this surprise that urged him onward.

"Why did you set it on fire?"

I looked at him, trying to decide if I should say what he wanted to hear or the truth. Then I realized I didn't know what either of those things was, so I just said, "It disgusted me. When I looked at it, I was sick to my stomach."

"Harold wrote the museum a check, you know, for the damages. They've dropped the charges."

I gazed at the mess around me and rolled the words over in my head. *They've dropped the charges.* As if dropping criminal charges should ever have anything whatsoever to do with me. The idea that I was someone for whom charges had been dropped burrowed its way through my brain and sank like a lead weight in my gut.

"Jesus," I said.

Later I actually made it out of the room for a meal, my first with the family since my fall from grace. Along with the blood relations, Dan was there sitting beside Mary. They must have had a baby-sitter for the kids because the usual chaos of their presence was absent. Instead, the table was enveloped by an awkward stillness and the kind of calm that I've always associated with tranquilizers.

"Sarah Biv named her son Roy G.," Martin said.

Sarah Biv was his new assistant at the lab at UCLA. Martin was apparently smitten with her, having moved on to the relative emotional safety of forging liaisons with married women.

"That's ridiculous," said Harold.

"I think it's clever," said Maggie.

As if by mutual understanding, they never agreed on anything. I looked around the table at my family with a strange, unusual clarity. I zeroed in on Maggie.

She had not aged well. When had she gone from the most beautiful, dramatic queen mother on the planet to this sad, aging alcoholic?

I remember the brown leather boots with the platform heels, the sexy miniskirts and her long white legs. Later, she would often wear mididresses and palazzo pants with yellow tassels and jackets with leather fringes. Her lipstick was always pink, her eye shadow tended toward blue and when she was in the mood she wore thick, false eyelashes that put me in mind of spiders.

On Saturdays she had her hair done at George Andrews Salon of Beauty, and while it was drying in the weird space-hat hair dryer with the tiny holes in the thick brownish plastic, a large woman with the biggest bouffant I had ever seen painted Maggie's nails, always bright red or orange.

She was so glamorous. I remember the other neighborhood husbands, Mr. Kowolski in particular, holding her hostage in the corners of the house, whispering into her ear things that made her laugh. But it was always a laugh which held formality and reservation in its pulse, a laugh which made it clear that she belonged to no one and would stay that way. Even while she was out screwing Mr. Kowolski, it was obvious she belonged to herself alone.

At the pool parties, which marked the passing of my childhood the way church or family picnics might mark the lives of what Eddie considered normal children, I remember watching her move about with her characteristic aloof grace, a bikini showing off her flat stomach and her long, graceful legs. The other women always wore one pieces and when they saw her they would acknowledge with disappointment and irritation their own stretch marks and tummy rolls. Esther was the one who pointed out for me the connection between the bottle of pills she kept within arm's reach and her beautiful body, her raging rhythms of elation and agitation, her long, slender fingers trembling as she reached for a drink.

Now, she had finally stopped using the red henna in her hair and the color, perhaps worn by so much sun and chlorine and coloring, was flat, brown, uneventful. There were streaks of gray at the roots. The high drama of her cheekbones, her curved lips and green eyes had given way to a more sedentary spectacle of grief and hard living. She looked merely sad, and watching her clutch her fork while consuming tiny bites of her food, I realized I had spent my life ignoring her, writing her off as frivolous and cold.

"I'm sorry," I said, the words slipping out of my mouth accidentally.

Maggie and Harold both lifted their eyes and gazed at me. Harold turned away instantly, embarrassed because most things that did not have a concrete explanation embarrassed him. But Maggie remained set on my face, her expression a complicated mix of anger, pity and forgiveness. "It seems to me," she said, though not angrily as I might have expected, but with grave sorrow. "It seems to me that we have had our share of excitement around here without you adding fuel to the fire."

Eddie snorted but Martin actually laughed.

"That's an unfortunate cliché, my dear," said Harold.

I began to laugh too but I wasn't sure, it felt so much like crying. Dan stared blankly around at all of us as if he had missed a joke, but Mary looked glum, you might even say brokenhearted.

"Shit," Maggie said. Tears welled up in her eyes. "The joke is always at my expense. But in case you haven't noticed, we are one daughter short around this table, and of the two remaining, one is a convict."

"I'm not a convict."

"You need a conviction first," said Harold.

"They aren't pressing charges, right?" said Eddie

"Roy G. Biv. What a fucking retarded name," said Martin.

We were filling up space left by the allusion to Esther. Mary and Dan, serenely, said nothing. I remembered one Christmas, while everyone else was getting drunk, Mary pulled me aside and said, "They drink like that to forget that what they fear the most are their own deaths."

Harold lifted his head from his plate and looked out over his brood with grief and amazement. I waited for him to stop the chatter, silence the masses, restore order, realizing we had never relied on him for that, that no one in our family, save Eddie, could channel our family's energy into a single trajectory. And even Eddie's claim to such magic was flimsy and sporadic, dependent only on the severity of the situation.

When Esther died, when we first heard of it and all gathered at the doomed homestead amid the clutter and the chaos, it was Eddie who organized the events, the burial, the service, the gathering of friends and the other mysterious people in our clan, people I knew little about but who were associated with us through bloodlines and the ancient histories of our parents.

There was an aunt, mother's side, who had left her husband in Pittsburgh and started a new life in Sacramento, where she sold herbs and potions in a tiny shop near the river and lived with another woman in a nebulous relationship about which no one asked. The aunt and uncle from the East Coast, father's side, who once a long time ago gave Eddie the Star of David necklace, were also there. But there were no grandparents, all of them dead before my time, and the other aunts and uncles from Maggie's side were only shadows, a bloodline lost to me, vapors in a vaporous past.

I watched Harold Goldblum, the embodiment of a lifetime of disappointment, gaze at his progeny and his wife and I felt what I had spent a lifetime avoiding: the rock-bottom anxiety of his failure. I remembered how just a year or so before Esther's death, I had flown home from Brooklyn and landed gently in the embrace of the art world as if on a bed of feathers. I marveled for a moment at the ease with which the pursuit of my own ambitions had produced its fruit, and how deadly that fruit had become, how much I had most likely lost.

"Excuse me," I said. I felt swallowed by myself. It was not, after all, just Esther's death that I had tried to outrun. I could see this now as plainly as the champagne stains on the ceiling and the priceless antique tea set lying in halves on the shelf behind Harold's chair.

The next morning, after a terrifying dream in which Zeke stood in the kitchen of a plantation mansion, opened a can of tuna fish and said, "Perhaps your mother and I could have a conversation some time," I went out into the yard and sat on a chaise lounge by the pool. There was a prism of dew drops bejeweling the mottled patches of grass, gerbera daisies and cosmos that marked the graves of all the Harry the Dogs.

The forlorn cooing of the doves depressed me but the air was filled with a premature hint of spring, like a window through the doors of what was proving to be another cold, wet, dreary winter. Black squirrels skittered about the deck looking for birdseed loosened by the feeder that hung in the tree above them and, inexplicably, a lit candle on a rusted wrought-iron lawn table flickered in the gloom. I lay there for several minutes before I noticed that Harold, in the same terry cloth robe that I wore, was sitting in another lounge chair behind me, beneath an old clothesline from which Eddie had once jokingly hung Martin's dead animals using Maggie's wooden clothespins around their hardened limbs.

"Morning," I said. "I didn't see you there."

"No. You didn't."

I reached into the pocket of the robe and pulled out my cigarettes.

"It's so funny to see you smoke," he said.

"Funny ha ha or funny weird?"

"Well, if pressed, I would say funny ha ha. It just doesn't suit you. It would be like putting the jacket from that book—what was it—ah yes, *Bridges of Madison County* on the cover of a treatise on astrophysics."

It was just like him to come up with some obscure metaphor and yet it made me laugh. I saw, out of the corner of my eye, a slight smile on his lips. It was a sly smile, the kind Martin used all the time to capture one or another of his women. I could see that on Harold its magnetism had worn itself a little thin.

"Tell me," he said. He looked around him as if to be sure that no one was near. "Why did you set that thing on fire?"

I was startled by his bluntness, not a defining characteristic of his and yet now, in the gray, dim cold, it suited him somehow. I admired it, I suppose, because no one else besides Eddie had the guts to ask me the question, even though I knew they were all dying to.

I thought about it for a minute. I realized that with Harold, I worried more about the things I said to him, worried more about how he would take them. "I was mad," I said. "I was mad, if you want to know the truth, that Esther went and got herself shot and left me behind."

"Yes. I understand," he said, sinking back into the rubber tubing of the chaise lounge as if the air had been let out of him.

"I didn't even get a chance to know her. I don't even know who she is."

"She is the mystery in this family," he said, and I noticed how we had slipped into the use of the present tense.

"Did she love anyone?" I asked, putting her back in the grave.

Somehow, the cold air, the hint of spring through the window of winter, the fact that we were exiled, for our own reasons, on a pair of plastic chairs by a pool filled with leaves and outfitted in our ridiculous matching terry cloth robes made it possible for me to ask that question. In any other situation, I would have been embarrassed. It was not a Goldblum trait to speak of love.

"Your mother used to say, right away after Esther was born, that God forgot, when He was handing out the hearts, to give one to Esther."

"God, schmod. We're a pack of crazy scientists with a renegade Catholic. What God?"

"Oh, I don't know. Sometimes God serves a function. I agreed with her, by the way."

"With who?"

"Your mother. Not about God forgetting to give Esther a heart but about the imperfection of creation, evolution, the things that do and do not get handed down through the genes. She was perhaps the smartest of us all but she did not have what people like to call compassion. Whereas Mary, who ended up with the greatest heart, did not collect the same genes that created Esther's nearly perfect mind."

"What about Danny? She loved Danny."

"In certain schools of scientific reasoning, we are lucky if we can find an anomaly because the anomaly helps us reevaluate the way we process and analyze certain information. It is by finding the anomaly that we can usually find our answer. The anomaly to Esther's personality was the introduction of Danny Franconi. And I think, to a large extent, because she was so smart, she knew that in Danny she had finally found what had been missing her entire life. The ability to care for someone else. She was, before him, almost autistic in her inability to show emotion, to feel all those ambiguous things that other people call emotions. And then along came Danny, so needy, so tough, such a rich, mysterious combination of attributes that I dare say he knocked her out of her cocoon."

He was silent for a minute. I heard him move, the squeak of the lounge chair.

"In retrospect, of course, he needed her just as much. I never believed the nonsense that his fall had been an accident. Never."

I could not remember hearing him speak like this. The scientist gone poetic. He grew silent, in that barren, cold way of his, retreating back to nowhere into his shell, and I saw him as the old gray man that I had always regarded him. I could not remember receiving one kiss from him. I could not remember one convincing hug. I stood up and walked over to him, the tie of my robe trailing behind me like a tail.

"Dad," I said. I leaned over to kiss him. He lay there, immobile, his eyes closed, his face impassive. He did not show any signs of having been kissed. He neither received nor refused it. My father was a scientist whose favorite daughter had been killed. I knew that this exchange was the most I could expect.

W h e n they all began to realize that I would not go up in a conflagration of remorse and self-pity, Eddie and Martin both left. Eddie had found a new vocation, teaching, and had taken to it like a frog to water. He was not afraid, he confided in me, of poverty. He rather liked not having so much money. He had found something simple, something that did not require a daily spilling of metaphorical blood on the carpet of a New York City financial district high-rise.

I watched him drive away toward Daly City, where he lived in a ticky-tacky house with the nurse who brought him back to life. I envied him the house, which blended in with all the other houses on that hill because there was nothing to distinguish it from the others.

I personally shuttled Martin out of town to the airport. Our parents were hesitant to lend me one of the cars but Martin convinced them that I had reformed. He actually told them to relax, driving cars into walls was not my thing.

"Remember," he said, winking at them, torturing them with the memory that I had nearly burned down a museum. "She likes fire."

"That wasn't necessary," I said when we were outside. "Who came up with the idea of torturing them in the first place?"

"It was before you were even a zygote that Esther said, and I quote, 'Bible schmible, let's disobey our parents.' "

"You were just children."

"That's irrelevant. It was fun. They had parties involving watermelons filled with gin and an arsenal of cigarettes that they put in brass cups on the coffee table for the taking. We had to keep them from setting the house on fire. It was our duty to be disobedient after so much fucking responsibility. It's in all the psychology books, you know."

"How come everyone has to be so clever and sarcastic?"

"It was the seventies. We had no defense against platform shoes, *The Partridge Family* and bean bag chairs. Insanity breeds sarcasm. It could have been worse. We could have been like those reactionary neighbors around the corner who handed out silent majority buttons."

I remembered them. The Danielsons. They had two boys who were forced to wear crew cuts and were not allowed to play with us. One day Mr. Danielson told Harold that our lawn, dying at the time, was a disgrace to the neighborhood.

"It's funny how I remember Harold and Maggie," I said.

"Drunk?"

"Yes. But sometimes they seemed all right."

"They were insane, Louise."

"They loved us, though."

"In their spastic way, I guess," Martin conceded, calmly pointing out a large moving van that I was about to rear-end. I swerved just in time and got into the next lane over. The traffic was light. We were passing the turnoff to Lake Lauganita.

"Remember Lake Lauganita?" I asked

"Yeah," he said. "All condos now. Some development called Shadow Acres on the Lake or some shit like that."

"That's what I heard. I haven't seen it. It seems so hard to believe the lake is gone."

"I think about Lake Lauganita and all I can think about is Danny and Esther," said Martin.

"Did his dad ever get out of prison?"

"No, but that's because he was never in prison. He was in a mental ward. I think he died there. Schizophrenia or something."

"God, my past is full of lies."

What was real? For a moment I even wondered if Esther was real. I remembered what Alice had told me. That she had seen Esther with Joe Torres, the only boy I'd ever loved. That could have been real.

Martin said nothing but I could see he wanted to. I watched him turn toward the window and I tried to reconcile his dishevelment, his intensity and the adult nervousness with the Martin of my youth — the one who could calmly suffocate a frog in one minute and in the next happily eat an egg salad sandwich.

"When I finally accepted that memory is part myth, part fantasy and part truth, I think I began to realize that the future didn't really matter," Martin said.

"But if you really believe that, then why not just blow your brains out?"

"I think I believe it in the Zen way, not the Nietzsche way. Its a coping mechanism. What is, is. I do the best I can. You can look at Ecclesiastes the same way."

"That's very strange, Martin. I believe you just mentioned something having to do with the Bible."

"Whatever works," he said. "At least I'm not setting museums on fire, eh?"

"Fuck you," I said, though we were not angry.

We were nearing the airport, an expanse of flat land that, from the freeway above, appeared futuristic. I tried to remember the day Zeke and I snuck in and took pictures on the tarmac. I tried to remember the way he slapped me unexpectedly, then took my picture, then displayed it to the world.

For a long, breathless moment as I veered toward the connector road that would drop us into the airport, I saw her sitting there on the tarmac, the tall, thin woman I had let myself become, the small, sad girl who had allowed for, who had made room for that kind of sexual violence. It struck me as pathetic that it took me this long to realize you can't hide from the vagaries of life, even behind the obliterating shield of a slap in the face.

●

I spent the next several days roaming through the house. I visited Harold in the garage where he had begun work on a new dollhouse. It was exquisite. Extremely intricate and detailed. I watched him work, his surprisingly dexterous fingers lovingly gluing parts of an elaborate banister together, pasting wallpaper in the tiny bedrooms, adorning the rooms with beautiful, hand-carved furniture—chairs and beds and couches that fit in the palm of my hand. Everything was tidy and perfect. There were never any people inside. No noise. No mess. It was in such stark contrast to our own house, our own lives that I got immediately lost in the fantasy of such order and perfection.

During the day, when the sky began to fill with the cold, slate gray clouds that characterized the season, I would often find Maggie sitting out by the leaf-strewn pool, covered in a blanket with a Disney-themed print, Mickey Mouse and Donald Duck. She would gaze at the garden gone to winter death, the leaves blowing across the yard, smiling or frowning at her own thoughts. More often than not, she wore a startled expression, as if her thoughts continuously surprised her, as if she were entering some new, surprising emotional terrain, the geography of which both upset and tantalized her.

Sometimes I would find her sitting in her bedroom in a tattered rocking chair asleep, a mystery book on her lap or beside her on the table. There was always a drink nearby, half finished, though I could find no trace of the brown, child-proof bottles of Xanax or Valium that littered her bedroom and bathroom when I was young.

I had no idea what I would do next, where I would go. Though he had left several messages with Maggie, I could not bring myself to call Shey back—to seek redemption. I had spent the last few years of my life as the privileged darling of the emerging art scene, and though on some level I understood that most people actually had jobs and families and responsibilities, it had never really sunk in. For the first time in my life, I was aimless.

Often I walked through the schoolyard. The old wooden bleachers on which Danny and Esther had carved their initials had been replaced by more permanent metal ones, chained to a post, impossible to mar. I walked to the edge of the schoolyard, to the perimeter of the aqueduct which at one time was easily accessible. Now a chain-link fence, topped by curlicues of barbed wire, ensured that no one would explore the netherworld of concrete, dripping water, rusty pipes and other people's lost things. It occurred to me that the world was getting smaller and more impenetrable, that new devices were being created all the time to ensure that no one explored the environment too deeply. Or destroyed it. The irony was not lost on me that the bitterness and cruelty of barbed wire had come to mean preservation.

One night at dinner, my parents and I sat around an overcooked rump roast and lumpy mashed potatoes, evidence that I had inherited Maggie's ineptitude in the kitchen, when Harold suddenly put his fork down and looked up at us, a confounded expression on his face.

"What is it, Harold?" Maggie said. She seemed alarmed.

"I was just thinking about something," he said. He picked up his fork and shook his head, then went back to eating his dinner, his expression grave and perplexed, as though he just realized something tremendously important.

Later, I stood in the kitchen drying the dishes that Maggie had washed in her slatternly way, leaving little specks of the dinner on the plates and forgetting to wash the undersides even though they'd been stacked one atop the other.

"He's getting old," she said. She was speaking about Harold, her husband.

"He always seemed old to me."

"Now he's started with that thing he does at dinner."

"Thing?"

"He drops his fork or stops chewing his food and stares into space with that look in his eyes."

"What look?"

"It started after she died. It gets worse. I'm afraid . . ." She stopped talking and I recognized the unmistakable intake of breath that I myself took when I didn't want to cry. "I'm afraid it will just get worse and I'll have to spend the rest of my life looking after him. Wiping his mouth and his nose . . ."

I was certain—I hoped—that she did not mean to be nasty.

"David Kowolski asked me once if I loved your father. I told him that Harold got me out of Pittsburgh. What more could I expect?"

"Mom, please."

I could not stand living with the anomaly of an unkind mother. She looked at me, and as if reading my mind she said, "I don't mean to be cruel. Things just didn't turn out the way I'd planned."

"That's the problem with planning things."

She went back to the dishes. Then, exhausted suddenly, she turned off the water, took her apron off and walked out of the room. I followed her to the living room where she sat on the couch. I noticed a bottle of peppermint schnapps and a brandy glass. She reached over and poured herself a drink.

"I don't understand, Louise, why you would do such a thing."

"I don't know," I said. Then I felt it again, that rising anger, the need to be heard. "Look, when Esther died, no one around here said anything. It was like it never happened. A fire seemed somehow appropriate."

"But Louise, destroying your work like that."

"It wasn't my work I was destroying," I said.

She waved her hand in the air, a characteristic gesture that meant to express impatience. Her typical flutter of disregard. But the expression on her face was bewildered and I had a flash of pity for her. I could see the passage of her life, one big loop into dissatisfaction and loss and I understood that her aloofness was just her way of coping with one more disappointment. I had not failed her by setting a museum on fire. Esther had not failed her by dying. She had made the wrong choices to begin with. And then life itself had gone ahead and failed her. I watched her wash her misery down with a long sip of peppermint schnapps and I felt close to her when, in that moment, I recognized how much alike we were, how thoroughly we craved the ability to evaporate into the thin air of inebriation.

The next day, I woke early and already Harold was in his garage. I went in with two cups of coffee and set one down beside him. He was involved in the painstaking task of gluing tiny little floorboards down on a tiny little staircase. The night before, after his private epiphany at the dinner table, he had retired to the garage to stain each of the floor-

boards. It seemed like an awful lot of work but I admired his en-
durance. It was the one shred of proof I had that he started and finished things, that he was good at something and cared about it.

"The second law of thermodynamics states that the entropy of an
isolated system never decreases with time," he said, speaking for the
first time since I entered his private kingdom of beautiful homes and
perfect lives.

"Entropy," I said. "Remind me."

"Disorder. Chaos."

"Ah yes. Of course." I smiled, remembering his drunken soliloquies
at the dinner table of our youth.

"Common experience tells us that disorder will tend to increase if
things are left to themselves. Leave a house alone without repairs and
you see what happens, the grass is overtaken by weeds, the paint peels,
the pool fills with leaves and frogs."

"Entropy."

He smiled grimly.

"You can fix the house up, say, stain the floorboards of the staircase," he said, holding up the last floorboard as if to illustrate his point,
"but the energy you use on the repair simply reduces the amount of
ordered energy available. The more energy spent, the more chaos."

"The second law of thermodynamics," I said.

"Precisely," he said and he glued the remaining floorboard down. I
understood that the lecture had been for my benefit. His logic had always been mysterious to me yet somehow I always got his point. In his
screwball scientific mind, I had been forgiven. What I had done by
burning the installation was out of my hands, on account of the second law of thermodynamics. At least according to him. And he, at
least, forgave me.

After another cup of coffee and breakfast, which consisted of three
Oreo cookies and a tuna sandwich, I wandered into Esther's old bedroom. Her canopy bed had long since been dismantled and her closet
had been overtaken by clothes that must have belonged to Maggie.
The dresser by her bed was still there, replete with smiley face stickers
plastered on top. There had once been a lock, keeping snoopers out of
the top drawer, but it was no longer there, only the holes in the wood
left behind by the screws that had once held it in place.

I opened the drawer. An assortment of tools and some nails and screwdrivers rolled around inside. There were some old papers clipped together—Esther's report cards from junior high school. She got A's and B's in every class except biology, in which she received a D in both seventh and eighth grade. I wondered briefly whether this was a protest against Harold, who loved her too much.

There was a note attached from an English teacher named Mrs. Peterson, who I too had taken English from.

> Esther has remarkable skills with literature and language. Her grasp of difficult material is excellent. Her attitude in class, however, is inconsistent and participation is erratic. The other students look up to her, and often her behavior affects the performance of others. B+

I found a stack of notes in a small plastic makeup case. They were mostly on torn bits of paper. I recognized Esther's handwriting but no one else's. *D. is freaking out. He can't understand why I study so hard. I'll have to take care of him my entire life.* Then in someone else's script, Lydia Firestone's I assumed, was this: *Let's get high at lunch.* Next to that was a crude drawing of two stick figure girls smoking a joint. Esther had written back. *I think Todd is doing too much LSD. Let's ask Sherry what she thinks.* In the margin she had written, *The Eyes of Dr. T. J. Eckleberg. Define implacable!!!*

I put the notes and the report cards back in the drawer and gazed at the room. It had been taken over by Harold's elaborate computer system and his books. I read some of the titles. *Theories of Personality, Physics, The Selfish Gene, The Collected Works of John Donne.* I was stumped by his eclectic tastes. Startled by the last one I saw. *The Story of O.*

On the desk next to his computer equipment stood a small glass bowl filled with rocks and shells. I assumed they had been Esther's. She had a passion for beachcombing, an obsession with finding shells. A framed picture of the First Harry the Dog was next to it, beside a binder that was labeled "The Infamous Adventures of Ellie Allbright and Blue Fuscue" in Esther's handwriting. When I opened it, all I found were several pages of equations, an alien and indecipherable language in Harold's neat, small handwriting. There was a Father's Day card but it was signed from Martin.

Esther, I realized, had all but been erased from her room. But it happened long before she died, I was sure. My own room, I discovered, had been taken over too by beverages and household items like toilet paper and dishwashing liquid that Maggie bought in bulk at the Costco in the neighboring town. And the same thing in various forms had happened to Mary's room and to the room Eddie and Martin shared. I saw how the inhabitants of the house—our parents—and their aged lives and needs had taken over, like a sort of domestic fungus, usurping the old lives—us—who had lived there. The smells were the same, the structure of the house was the same, even the paint and the carpet and most of the furniture was the same. What had changed was the presence of the inhabitants, the soul, the spirits of us.

When I thought of this, an immense sadness rose up inside me before disappearing into a shower of light behind my eyes. I rubbed my eyes to stop the light and realized I was in for a migraine. I felt the tentacles of it sweep across the back of my head and launch across my scalp before settling in its slow, syrupy way into nausea and unbearable pain.

I headed for Maggie's room, certain that she would have some drug or another to alter the course of my headache which, with each second, continued to escalate. The pale, wintry gleam of the sun shone in through her windows, which she had left open, as if just moments ago she had been gazing out into the yard.

But she was asleep on her bed, her age more pronounced in slumber, as if only in sleep would she let her defenses down and then only because she had no control of the matter. A mystery book—*The Lost Body*—lay on her chest and two cats, both of whom I'd never seen before, were at her feet, fast asleep.

The house was silent except for the sound of the wind chimes out back blowing in the cold wind and the wind itself, which howled through the chimney. It was a barren, lonely sound and I felt something inside me tremble as the memory of Esther came to life despite her erasure from Goldblum territory. I could picture the way she filled up a room, the way no one had to be bored when she was around. Her death seemed wildly impossible to me. I looked at Maggie's drink, half empty, on the nightstand and for a minute was tempted to take it. And along with the temptation came the overriding desire for Zeke. I traced this odd process of reasoning, from Esther to alcohol to sex, but I didn't get too far with it when Maggie woke up.

She woke slowly at first but when she saw me she sat up quickly, her book flying off her chest, and fussed with her hair. Her mouth must have been dry because she swallowed a few times before saying anything.

"What's wrong?"

"Nothing," I said. "I was just sort of walking around."

She found this funny and laughed—her dry, ironic laugh that for me had always been impossible to decipher.

"What's so funny?"

"Well, darling," she said, reaching for a cigarette on the bedstand. "It's not like we have a mansion here. Let's face it, the grounds are fairly squalid. I can't imagine where you'd walk around, exactly."

I heard in her voice that old habit of hers, how she spoke dramatically, often in italics, as if she were some old-fashioned movie star. So when she said, "I can't imagine where you'd walk around," her voice took on a slightly lilting, pompous accent. She lit her cigarette and puffed on it with her usual flair.

I flashed on watching her when I was a child and remembered the combination of reverence and apprehension she inspired in me. She was exotic and arresting, as beautiful and elegant as she set her mind to being—and just as damaged and irascible when the correct confluence of chemicals mixed it up in her system. She loved center stage, something as off-putting to the women as it was enticing to the men. She was an enigma, fiercely Catholic when she needed the presence of God, otherwise adamantly pagan in her parties, her attire, her infidelity.

"I've been walking in Esther's old bedroom. Looking for things," I said. I rubbed my head. A conglomeration of molecular-like spots flitted about in the periphery of my vision.

"Oh?" she said. She picked at some invisible thread on the blanket still on top of her.

"It's almost all disappeared."

"Your father," she said, as if this would explain everything.

"I have a migraine. I'm wondering if you have anything."

She looked at me for a moment, contemplating something, then stood up, adjusting her shirt and pants, smoothing them down with her wondrous elegant mannerisms. She slipped on a pair of pink, Zsa Zsa Gabor–type slippers. They were furry and had a hole at the tip for her toes. I noticed her toenails were painted red but the paint had peeled and chipped in places. She beckoned me into the bathroom, "Come, *ma petite,*" and with a sly look on her face took my hand. I felt as if I were being lured into the lair of an opium addict or some equally dangerous, exotic renegade from society. She opened the medicine chest and there the dozens of prescription pills were lined up, crowding out the face cream, dental floss and toothbrushes.

"Jesus," I said. "Some things don't change."

She smiled and I remembered the time Eddie chopped his finger off and how for days afterward Maggie stumbled around the house smoking furiously and popping pills.

She began searching the labels for a remedy for me and eventually she pulled two white pills with Fiorinal spelled out on their surface and another small pill that she didn't bother to explain to me. She filled a glass with water from the tap and handed it over to me. I swallowed the pills dutifully.

"Come. Lie down," she said.

I followed her to the bed and lay down beside her. I closed my eyes. The pain had moved to a spot just behind my left eye. It rushed at me in waves, an undulating sort of spear into my brain that had its own rhythm. I concentrated on the rhythm while I felt the smooth, liquidy heat of the drugs even it out. In a few minutes I was loopy, and though the pain began to subside, I knew on some level that it was still there, hiding behind the fog.

"I'm wasted," I said. "Why did you get me so high?"

Maggie laughed. She leaned over on her side and faced me. I could not move. She put her hand on my forehead. It was cool and dry. I remembered the way she would place her palm on my forehead when I was a child, the cool reassurance of her hand, the smells she brought with her of tonic, lipstick, dishwashing soap. I grabbed her hand. Sinking, I held it.

"You always craved being touched. That is, until we beat it out of you," she said without the slightest trace of irony.

"Esther used to pull you aside and say things like, 'Now, Baby G., a

Goldblum does not cry.' Or she would say, 'Don't let them hug you, they may squeeze you to death.' Not a chance one should take given the risk. Poor girl. She was so afraid. I always told your father she was born without a heart."

I thought I might have said something, but I wasn't sure. What I heard in my head were the words, *Esther was never afraid of anything.*

"But you are mistaken," Maggie was saying. "Esther had the most to fear. She was running from something her entire life. It took me a long time to understand that it was just her own shadow."

"Danny," I said. It was all I could manage. The drugs had taken my voice box, absconded with it, buried it deep in my ribs.

"Well, of course. Danny's death. He was the only one who could get her to sit still. None of us could understand it. He was a *hoodlum*, for crying out loud. He was not smart the way you kids are and he had that crazy family. But the two of them. What a mysterious thing. It was beautiful and terribly, terribly upsetting. Of course he needed her as much as she him. You can't imagine what we did when we found out. They were only twelve years old, you understand."

"Found out?"

"Oh, you know," she said. She reached beside her for a cigarette. "The sex. And the drugs. They started so early."

"You taught us," I said. But I must not have said it or else she ignored me. She rolled on her side again and faced me.

"Don't pull away," she said. Her breath smelled of lipstick and tonic and faintly of stale vodka. She stroked my forehead very gently.

"We never got to know each other, did we?" she asked. I shook my head. I was not in pain anymore and I felt an overbearing sense of gratitude toward her. I was momentarily adrift in gratitude and the desire to sob. Her hands continued to stroke my forehead ever so gently.

"I spent my time with Esther and Eddie and then Martin. You and Mary, even though it was only two, three years later, you two just arrived too late for me. Things had changed so much by then. Or maybe the problem was they hadn't changed at all. Your father and I, kaput. *Au revoir, amour.* Well." She swirled her cigarette in the air, making a figure eight over and over again. I noticed the skin on her elbow sagging. "Do you suppose, if I had asked more, if I had been more *curious*, you wouldn't have done it?"

I tried to sit up but the effort was too much.

"I don't know," I managed. "It might have been too late anyway."

She said nothing but nodded her head. I saw the light catch a small tear at the corner of her eye.

"It didn't turn out the way I had hoped," she said. "I can't seem to care the way I'd like to. I am more like Esther, I suppose, than I would like to be. It was me who handed that coldness down to her. And that rigid, amoral beauty."

The solitary tear escaped and slid down her cheek. I closed my eyes. What I struggled against the most in that moment just before passing out, what I fought the hardest against, was knowing that I loved her. I loved her. How could I not? That bag of bones. That sack of regret. I loved her.

In moments I drifted off until, at last, I lost consciousness thinking, *Define implacable.*

I slept in her bed all day. At dusk I awoke and was flattened by the loneliness of the gray sky outside my mother's window. I rolled over, still drugged it seemed, and slept through the night. I had moved hardly at all. Maggie must have covered me with a quilt. In the morning, there was no indication that she had slept beside me.

I w a s sitting out back by the pool. The yard was a disaster. In one corner, like some diorama of urban blight, three of Harold's dollhouses stood rotting. Weeds had sprung up around them. One of them was missing part of a roof, another leaning heavily to one side. I half expected to see miniature drug dealers and crack addicts skulking around.

I smoked cigarette after cigarette, gazing into the dreary sky, my hands shaking from too much coffee, not enough booze. Without the alcohol I sweated through sleep, the sheets soaked. My dreams were vague and filled with Zeke and Danny and Esther. In the morning my head pounded, my mouth was dry. But I had begun to see things more clearly. Literally. It was as if the material world were coming alive after a year of dormancy.

As I was contemplating a massive tree I used to climb, studying it, thinking of nothing more than the leaves, the bark, the shape and angle of the branches, Mary walked out back. She was wearing a ratty-looking coat that she drew tighter around her as she sat down on a lawn chair opposite me.

"Hi," she said. She smiled. It was like seeing land after being adrift at sea for years, like the first star to come out at night. Her kindness was magnificent, of another world. You could trust Mary with your life and she would preserve it for you until you were ready to reclaim it.

"Hi," I said. I smiled. I still had not spoken to her about what happened, why I did it. I still had not thanked her for rescuing me.

"You're okay?"

I nodded. For a moment I could not find my voice. I put my cigarette out and lit another.

"You look better. The black eye is turning yellow."

"The color of baby diarrhea."

She laughed.

"Almost," she said.

We locked eyes. I saw it there, all the love I'd never asked for, sitting there in the dark hue of her irises. If her eyes had been a place, I would have crawled into them, never left, set up shop, and remained protected by that love. As it was, I could barely accept it. But I didn't turn from her either, which struck me as a personal improvement, and when she stood up and sat on the edge of my chaise lounge, I accepted her hands as they brushed my hair back. She leaned down, kissed my forehead.

"I love you," she said. "Don't forget that."

"Hard not to," I said. Boulders tumbled. I gripped my stomach, trying to quiet the avalanche. I did not want to cry. I would not cry.

"They're glad you're home."

"Maggie and Harold are never glad about anything."

"You're wrong, Louise. They love you. You just don't see it. They don't show it the way you want them to. They can't. They are . . . disabled. They are broken-down people. But it doesn't mean that they don't love you."

"So I should accept it, their weird-ass brand of love? Is that what you're saying?"

She nodded.

I thought, *Whatever, what fucking ever.*

She stood up and went over to the edge of the pool. A new storm was coming. The pool would get filthier with every storm until the season ended. Then Harold would grudgingly hire someone to clean up the mess. I thought about entropy, chaos. I thought how much it must have killed him every spring to make that phone call.

"Remember when we first got the pool?"

"Yes," she said. She smiled. It had been exciting. Everyone in the neighborhood got swept up in the excitement. It was one of the first pools on the block.

"Remember after the pool builder guys poured the cement, before we even filled it, Maggie and Harold and the Kowolskis got some lawn chairs and a backgammon board and went down into the deep end to play?"

"Yes," she said, smiling grimly. "They brought down that table with the umbrella on it."

"God, did they get blind that day. Remember how they couldn't get out? How I had to go down there and show them where the steps were?"

"Mmmm," she said. "You were always rescuing the dog or one of us. Remember Eddie's finger? And the time Esther came home from those projects? Mother always brings these things up. She says, 'What would we have done if Louise hadn't been there?' "

"Not no more."

"You will again. It's your nature to rescue the Goldblums from themselves."

"Didn't do much good for Esther, eh?"

"Well," Mary said, returning to her lawn chair and sitting down. "No one could have rescued Esther. Danny did for a while. But you know what Danny did."

"Yeah, the fucker took her with him."

We were silent for a moment. The sound of a cooing dove somewhere in the distance got under my skin, withered me, made me desperate to be somewhere, anywhere that doves did not exist. It was such a sad and terrible sound, the sound from my youth, the one thing I heard when the battles ended and the wounded—Maggie and Harold, my brothers and sisters—lay sleeping before dawn, before another day of war.

"I'm sorry, Mare. I'm really fucking sorry," I said. "I can't say it's something I'm proud of. I feel like shit about it. God, when I think of it, I just cringe."

"Well, you're a Goldblum. You're allowed one escape into madness.

Esther took hers and lost. But Eddie survived. You'll survive. Martin and I, we have yet to have the requisite Goldblum nervous breakdown."

I laughed. "Shit, Mary, Martin has a nervous breakdown with every new relationship."

We both laughed now, because the thought of Martin, with his geeky walk, his brilliance, his moodiness and his women *was* funny. We laughed because we knew Martin would survive despite it all.

"Listen," Mary said. Her eyes glittered. I thought she might cry. "If it ever happens to me, you'll be there. Yes?"

I nodded.

"Now what about this boy?" she asked.

"Boy?" I had no idea who she was talking about.

"This bald-headed fellow."

"Mary," I said, stifling a laugh. "It's an impossible association. You simply cannot use the words *boy* and *Zeke* in the same sentence."

I thought fleetingly of Zeke, of the wind blowing through his trench coat, surfacing his head. I thought of his insanity, his loneliness. But I thought too that unlike Danny, he had not been able to destroy me, only to slow me, to send me to a temporary grave.

"Are you still seeing him?"

"Presently? No. I'm sitting here recovering from a black eye and a bloody lip. Strictly a matter of geography. He's there. I'm here."

Mary made a face. She hated my sarcasm.

"Besides," I said, "it's a lot more fun sitting around this chaos contemplating the fact that I almost burned down a museum."

"Louise, it's not funny," Mary said. Her anger was sudden and sharp, like a spark plug firing.

"I'm not trying to be funny, Mary. It's called a coping mechanism. Booze is no longer a part of the equation. My decision. So what else is there if not sarcasm?"

She glared at me. "Perhaps a shred of humility." She stood up. "Then maybe some forgiveness."

She walked into the house. I watched her back disappear into the darkened Goldblum vortex, the hurricane that sucked the life out of its victims.

I looked up at the tree. "You're an asshole, Baby Goldblum," I said to it. "A real asshole."

I took a rusty bike from the garage and rode through the old neighborhood. Soon I was headed up toward Koral Street. I remembered the time Esther took me up there, introduced me to condoms and a policeman named Officer Pete. It was funny how time brought clarity to some things. I understood now with certainty her terrible secret, the desperation that made her, a teenager, sleep with a cop who was fifteen years older than she was. It seemed startling now. The gauze of my naiveté had kept me blinded from the implications of such an act. Now I saw it, the monster emerging at last from beneath the bed.

The rain hadn't begun but the sky was growing darker. The bike was a clunker, only three of its ten gears functioning. It was a Wicked Witch of the West bike and as I rode, I resisted the urge to sing songs from *The Wizard of Oz*. "*If I only had a heart.*"

Finally the bike and me, in my weakened state, couldn't go any farther. I hopped off, lit a cigarette. I wouldn't make it to the top after all. I was relieved, actually. As I began to turn around, a bright red Porsche sped by me, came to a screeching halt, then did a three-point turn in the narrow street and headed right for me.

"Oh my God, Louise. Is that you? Oh my God."

"Oh, shit," I said. "Lydia. Wow."

Lydia Firestone. I hadn't talked to her since the funeral. I tried to turn away from her so she wouldn't see my black eye. I remembered what she had said about Esther in the newspaper. *It's not surprising she would die this way. Some might say she deserved it.*

"Wow, what happened to you? Boyfriend beat you up?" She laughed.

"As a matter of fact . . ."

The smile faded from her lips. It was fun to torture Lydia. She was never any match for Esther and years later, when their friendship died, I could see why. One word. Vapid.

"C'mon," she said. "Get in."

"Can't," I said. I pointed to the bike.

"You're not going to ride that thing, are you?"

I mentally rolled my eyes. Then I looked at the bike. She had a point. And it wasn't like we needed it. There were three or four others like it in the garage.

"Can you drive me home?"

"Sure," she said.

I leaned the bike up against an overgrown hedge. Somehow, it looked beautiful there. *Au revoir, la bicyclette.*

I got into the car and Lydia sped away, toward the hills, away from my parents' abode. I said nothing. She knew where I lived. She and Esther spent their entire high school years getting high in Esther's bedroom, stealing booze and probably pills. One time Lydia got so drunk I had to help Esther hold her up while she barfed over the toilet.

"How ya holdin' up, kid?" she asked.

Kid? I felt like punching her. I recalled something I had read once about Vice President John Nance Garner in 1939 going up to King George the VI, slapping him on the back and saying, "How are you doin', King?" Lydia's bad manners had the same effect. Laughable. Absurd. But cutting too, something malevolent and intentional about them.

"Well, you can see by my appearance that I'm holding up quite well."

She smiled. She wasn't sure how to take it. I wasn't sure why I hated her so much. I tried to focus on her lecherous stepfather. We are all our parents' creations. I felt the pathos rise, the hatred dissipate. She did not kill Esther. She merely blabbed to the newspapers. She was merely not a good friend.

"Well, I have something for you. It was Esther's. Don't ask me why I have it but . . ." Her words trailed off. I watched her for a minute as the past rose up and swallowed her whole. Yes, it had been magic, for a time.

We drove deeper into the hills, the road getting narrower and the trees hanging over in an eerie way. Enchanted forest. I waited for the Tin Man or the Scarecrow to emerge. I searched the leaf-choked gutters for Dorothy's shoes. I would put them on, click three times and go home, but it would be a different home. It would look like one of Harold's dollhouses. And the clutter would be the graceful clutter of a few books, some pieces of mail, perhaps an old shawl draped over the rocking chair. A fire would burn in the fireplace and Maggie would come out of the bedroom, a protestant, cheerful and loving but above all else practical, not prone to outbursts of unexplained emotion. Harold would be wearing a Brooks Brothers suit, having just come home from a highly successful day at the office. He too would be a protestant. A protestant pediatrician. And we would all be there, Esther alive, gathered around the fireplace, discussing things such as gardening techniques or whether the stock market would hold out until the recession ended. There would be cocktails, one apiece, and hors d'oeuvres. Perhaps a maid, someone who has been a part of our family since we were children.

Suddenly we were stopped in a narrow driveway. You could see nothing of the house behind the gate. We got out of the car and Lydia opened the gate. Behind it was a small, quaint cottage, made of wood shingling and white shutters with a beautiful dark blue door. As we walked inside I asked stupidly, "Do you live here alone?"

"Sometimes with Jack."

"You don't mean the guy with the harelip who was with Danny the day he decided to hurl himself into eternity?"

She looked at me sharply. "It was an accident," she said.

"Yeah, and I'm a protestant."

"Louise, it was an accident."

"Why do you keep repeating the same old mumbo jumbo? Everyone knows he killed himself."

She looked at me for a moment with a spark of anger. "No they don't," she said.

"Sorry," I said. She went to the freezer and pulled out a bottle of vodka. My heart pounded. I felt the rush of love.

"Drink?" she asked.

The thought crossed my mind that I would just have one drink and be on my way. Then I thought of Esther, the gunshot piercing her skull. I thought of Danny hurtling off the side of a cliff into the unknown. I thought of Zeke punching me in the face and then of me— finally of me—allowing him to do it.

"No thanks," I said.

"Oh, yeah," she said, laughing. "The Goldblum fuddy-duddy."

"No, that's Mary. I'm the Goldblum coward and resident square."

She laughed again. It seemed odd that you could go back to the past, see people you haven't seen in a long time and they would remember you the way they always knew you. It had the effect of momentarily erasing the last year of my life, as if none of it had ever happened.

She poured herself a hefty drink. I salivated. I noticed how much she gave herself, how much remained in the bottle, where she placed the bottle in the freezer. I watched her take a sip.

"You have something for me?" I asked.

"Come," she said.

I followed her down the hallway and into the master bedroom. I saw a pair of men's sneakers on the floor, a couple of free weights and a pair of boxer shorts. There was a picture of Lydia and the guy with the harelip—Jack—on the dresser. She opened the drawer to the dresser and I noticed a gun nestled in a pile of lace panties. She pulled out a small box and quickly closed the dresser drawer.

"I forgot that I had this. I don't know how I got it and from time to time I thought about sending it to you. We shared everything, you know. She was the sister I never had. At least for a while, before Danny and all that. But she would never have parted with this. I don't know why I have it."

She handed me the box and I opened it. Inside was the locket Esther used to wear around her neck. I opened the locket and there it was, the picture of us taken at the lake that summer. I gripped it, enfolded my hands over it. I felt a wave of relief. I studied our miniature faces, our miniature smiles. Our heads were so close together it was almost as if we were joined there. Except for our hair we looked so much alike. I thought of the mystery and awe-inspiring power of genetics. I thought of Esther as she had once been. I closed my eyes against the memory of it and against the torment of her death as I put the locket around my neck. The strong, sure weight of it there reassured me.

Then I thought of our parents sitting around at the old homestead, squashing their grief with their addictions, whatever they could come up with, to kill the pain. And it was there, in Lydia Firestone's bedroom, with the gun in her dresser, the jockey shorts on the ground and Esther's locket firmly in place around my neck, that I saw the enormous tapestry of anguish and misfortune that, for a lifetime, had woven itself around the hearts of them, my parents.

W h e n I returned I saw an unfamiliar and somewhat beat-up-looking car parked in the driveway, and when I walked up to the house, I could hear Maggie's voice through the open window. In the kitchen, Maggie was saying, ". . . must have been horrible for everyone. We're deeply sorry. Deeply embarrassed. We had no idea, of course, how *tired* she must have been."

Alice was sitting opposite Maggie, nodding her head politely. When Maggie saw me she said, much too buoyantly, "Hello, dear." Alice swung around, looking cowed and apologetic. She stood up but when I made no move, she sat back down.

"Hello," I said. I felt my cheeks flush. She hadn't been to the old homestead since Esther's funeral and I was suddenly embarrassed. Embarrassed that Maggie had Alice cornered with her Bette Davis affectations and her cigarettes. Embarrassed that I had been such a terrible friend to Alice. Embarrassed about setting fire to the museum. It was as if Alice was part of my real life and this house, this mother and father, were not, so that looking at her I felt the full weight of what I had done.

"You look good," she said. I knew she was telling some part of the truth. Alice had very little time for formalities. Alice never lied.

"I feel all right," I said. "Did you rent that piece of shit out there?"

She nodded, smiling slightly. "Rent-a-Wreck."

I walked over to the table and grabbed one of Maggie's cigarettes. I glanced at her as I did, but she didn't seem to notice. Her expression was wracked with misery and sadness. I wondered briefly about her galaxy of emotions. I thought of my own face and wondered if it would one day betray me in the same fashion as hers did. I lit the cigarette. I used my free hand to cover the aged, wrinkled hand of my mother and she looked at me, surprised. She brought it up to her mouth and kissed it. When we parted, I still felt the thrilling little sting of her kiss on the back of my hand.

"I figured you'd come here," Alice said. "I called last night but your mom said you were asleep. That it was perfectly all right for me to come over."

"Do you want some eggs or something to eat?" Maggie said.

"No thanks," I said.

An embarrassing silence opened up between the three of us, like a gaping hole into which all of my actions seemed to tumble. A billboard announcing my past transgressions would have been less painful.

"So, anyway, I stopped by your studio and picked up the mail. I wanted to drop it off to you. And I wanted to see how you were."

I smoked in silence for a minute. Maggie stood up and began banging around in the cupboards.

"You want to go somewhere?"

"Sure," she said, pulling her purse over her shoulder and standing up.

We left the house eagerly. When we got outside, Alice put her arm around my shoulder briefly. It was an unguarded moment. I was grateful. The thought went through my head that she still loved me.

We drove to a Denny's about five miles from my parents' house, on the other side of the freeway. The restaurant was situated between two car lots. We went inside and from where we sat I could see across the four-lane road to the Shangri-La Motel and Ed's Drive-U-Rite Truck Rental. The area itself was marked by an indistinct seediness, not like a red-light district or a slum, but the kind of low-rent dishevelment peculiar to suburbs. Overgrown weeds, strip malls, auto body shops and fast-food restaurants gave the area a comforting anonymity. If you were running from the law, you could hide here as long as you did nothing to draw attention to yourself. I stored this realization away for future reference. Just in case.

I stared longingly at the Shangri-La Motel—what dereliction could tempt me there?—before turning back to Alice, who was hoisted mid-sentence on a long monologue having to do with someone at work embroiled in a sex scandal.

". . . and he said to Mr. Gamble, and I quote, 'No sir, I did not fuck her, for Christ's sake.' Can you believe it? Mr. Gamble, he's about a hundred and seventy years old, about fainted." She began to light a cigarette but an overweight, motherly waitress appeared out of nowhere.

"Sorry, kid, no smoking." She pointed at a sign on the wall with her pen, a red circle with a diagonal slash superimposed over a drawing of a cigarette.

"Well, all right then," Alice said. I could have hugged her for her icy-smooth transition from chronicler of sex scandals to pissed-off miss priss. I laughed. Alice suggested a smile but with her eyes only. She made a show of putting the cigarette back in the pack.

"Can I place my order?" she asked in a snotty voice.

"Hey, kid. I don't make the rules. I just enforce them."

Alice ignored her.

"I'll have the eggs, scrambled, side of hash browns, two sausages, coffee."

I ordered French fries.

When the waitress left we laughed and then, afterward, that horrible silence enveloped us.

Finally Alice cleared her throat.

"This was taped to your door," she said. She pulled an envelope out of her purse. I immediately recognized Zeke's handwriting. For some reason, my hands trembled as I grabbed it from her and shoved it in my back pocket.

"Thanks," I muttered.

"So. How are you?" she said, cutting to the chase at last.

"You know," I said. "I'm okay. I'm not sure it's the best thing, really, to be staying at my parents' house. It's so cluttered, so cloying."

I could hear the way I'd picked up Maggie's exaggerated inflection, italicizing words as I went along.

"Are you coming back to the city?"

"I don't know what I'm doing. I've been practicing at insomnia a little. Warding off Bacchus. Smoking."

"I saw Zeke a couple of times," she said. "He was waiting outside my building one day. Like he followed me there or something."

"Wouldn't surprise me," I said, trying to sound nonchalant.

"He was looking for you."

"Did you tell him where I was?"

"God, no."

The food arrived and after the waitress placed it before us, we both stared at it. A look of incomprehension passed over Alice's face, as if she didn't quite know what the plate was doing there. She furrowed her brows and picked up her fork, taking a tentative bite of her eggs. In seconds, she took another bite and then another, reaching over for the salt and pepper. She ate the way she drank, unabashedly, without any consideration to being politically correct. Her motto was, The stiffer the drink, the bloodier the meat, the better.

"He seemed really pathetic. Bent out of shape. Like he was hurting," she said between bites of her sausage. I pushed my French fries around my plate. The thought of Zeke bent out of shape and hurting seemed absurd. A living, breathing oxymoron. Like seeing John Wayne weep.

"He begged me to tell him where you were. But hey, I never liked the guy to begin with. I never said a word. We ended up having a drink together. Strange guy. I can see it now, what you saw."

"Oh yeah? Explain it to me, 'cause I'm still trying to figure it out."

She laughed, her mirthless laugh. "Well, he has that godless kind of ability to pull you into his nihilism. Like you could go to the end of the earth with him and maybe never come back but the trip would make the risk worth it."

"I never really analyzed it, but in my mind Esther's death had something to do with it. Like every time I thought of her going off with that man and getting killed, I just wanted to be with Zeke."

"Because," Alice said, "it's the nature of Zeke's personality to annihilate the personality of whoever he's with. Give someone the right set of circumstances and that could be a very pleasant thing."

"Did you fuck him?" I asked.

She stopped eating, fork in midair, then smiled slyly.

"I thought about it," she said, removing the vestige of a sausage from her fork with her mouth. "But you know my criteria. Can you imagine Zeke agreeing to all those blood tests?"

It was the first time I could remember laughing in a long time. But then the strangest thing happened. I started to cry. And once I started, I couldn't stop. I kept thinking about Harold, sitting there in his garage making houses and Maggie, alone beneath her Mickey Mouse blanket, a warm vodka at her elbow, and then I'd think of Esther, of the eternal loneliness that drove her to the brink and back on a daily basis until one day she never made it back. Then I thought of me and how I had missed out on innocence. How even such a simple thing as a picnic to Lake Lauganita had been fraught with death and sex and love and violence, how this cauldron of stew had been on a slow boil for as long as I could remember and that I had not, as yet, hoisted myself over the sides, escaped.

Alice reached over and grabbed my hand, and I felt myself not pulling away but instead reaching out to her, gripping her the way I had gripped the ends of Zeke's earth, only now it was different, now it had a different shape to it altogether, a cohesion and not, as with Zeke, the bursting apart of bodies, of ambition, of dreams, of love. I sobbed so hard that I could feel the stares of the other customers, and when Alice came over to my side of the booth and put her arms around me as if to shield me from all those eyeballs, I was grateful enough not to push her away. I felt myself sinking into her giant breasts, my head resting against their warmth and comfort, and into them I said, "I am so sorry, Alice," and she just kissed the top of my head, saying, "It's okay, sweetie, it's okay."

Afterward, Alice drove me home and stayed with me long enough to pack my things and take me back to the city. I said good-bye to my parents, hugging first Harold and then Maggie. They seemed bewildered that I was leaving. Harold started to call me Esther, then caught himself. He asked me to look in on Eddie once in a while. He put his arm around Maggie, who seemed suddenly very small, very old. I kissed her on the cheek.

"I'll call you," she said with determination.

We took off for the 280 Freeway, but instead I asked Alice to drive for a while down Foothill Expressway. It was inevitable that I should see the lake before leaving and with the inevitability came a sense of purpose and clarity. I wondered if it was just the booze leaving my system. I felt something like my old self again.

The sun began to disappear, in and out of a bank of large, forbidding rain clouds. By the time we took the exit, a few scattered raindrops had begun to fall. As Alice skirted the narrow roads shrouded in ferns and large towering trees that led to the lake, I noticed a FOR SALE sign for a town home at Shadow Acres at the Lake.

When we arrived, Alice said she would wait in the car, citing the rain as her excuse. But I knew Alice. I knew her manners, her sensitivity. I figured I could learn something from them.

I got out of the car, which was parked in a new parking lot. When I was small, we parked in a patch of dirt off the side of the road. I came across a large, wrought-iron gate with a guardhouse. Beyond that, the small lake gave off a fragile, silver glow in the gloom. To the right of the guardhouse was a footpath and an unlocked gate. I walked in under the watchful eye of the bespeckled old guard.

The gentle, rolling hills that surrounded the farthest shore of the lake were now dotted by row upon row of town homes, each painted the same pale peach color with white trim. They were all capped by red tile roofs and each had the same tree planted in the front walkway in a giant pottery urn. To the left of the lake, the area where Esther and Danny spray-painted their names on the large rock, where they used to sneak off to make love while my brothers and I caught frogs, were more town homes, situated side by side in neat rows of three. They were identical to the homes on the hill, but many were still for sale. A large banner draped across the front of the model home promised "Peaceful Living on the Lake."

A small boat launch had been built at the edge of the lake, and in the center of the water a floating raft bobbed up and down in the minute wakes caused by the wind. I also noticed a lifeguard post and beside that a bungalow with a thatched room upon which was posted the rental fees for paddle boats, rowboats and beach towels.

I walked to the shore of the lake, the rain now insistent, and kneeled down so that I was eye level with the lowest tier of town homes, across on the hill. I kneeled there for several minutes, by then soaked through, before I realized that I would have no epiphany regarding Esther, that nothing about the place even resembled the shabby hideaway lake of polliwogs and frogs that occupied my youth. Try as I might to conjure up the image of my sister, she eluded me. Kneeling there, drenched to the core, I could barely remember what she looked like. I had no way to grasp her personality. It was as if she herself had decided to stop haunting me and pulled back, lifting her spirit farther into that netherworld of old souls and vapors.

As I was about to leave, the guard emerged from his house, holding a flimsy umbrella, a cigarette clenched between his lips. He appeared tentative, one foot still inside his little old house, one foot outside.

"Hey, girl," he said. His voice was shrill. "You all right, girl?"

I stood up and turned to face him. He was a small man with errant tufts of gray hair bursting from his scalp. His long rain poncho hung on him like an ill-fitting muumuu, clinging to parts of him, flying off others in the wind. He was appropriately strange-looking for a job that required the ability to sit for long periods of time with nothing to do, and I wondered what he thought about all day long, what menace of memories haunted him.

"I'm okay," I said.

"You'll catch your death," he said, pointing to the air, the rain, the invisible temperature.

I thought about it, catching my death. What a strange saying, as if death were like the flu except with more severe and far-reaching implications.

"Yeah," I said, more to myself than to the old man, who, having apparently come to the conclusion that I was harmless, if not a little strange, returned to his lonely exile inside the booth.

Before leaving, I took one last look at the lake and again felt nothing. It was the first time that I did not experience blinding pain at the mere thought of my sister. On top of that, I had, for the space of a second or two, a clear image of who she really was, and it occurred to me that had she not been my idol, I would have seen right through her. I would have seen the vacancy of her soul and the sad way she kept running around in circles, accumulating professional successes and one-night stands in lieu of love and friendship. In the end, the pain I felt was not for me, but for her.

I got back in the car. Alice lit two cigarettes and handed me one. I smoked on it and sat back in the seat.

"Let's go," I said.

She pulled away and soon the San Francisco skyline came into view, a shimmering necklace of buildings bursting through the shadows of rain.

A   n o t i c e   threatening eviction unless I paid the
rent was taped to my door. Just as I unlocked the door, my neighbor
came running up the stairs, two at a time, with a brown box.

"This came for you," he said.

I took it from him and thanked him but he lingered for a moment.
He was a beautiful man, and I felt like I was seeing him for the first
time. The bones in his face were sharp and angled and I wondered if
he really did have Indian blood in him as I had always assumed. He
had a long, handsome nose with a bump in the crook and large, red
lips. His eyes were almost black but seemed to exude an eternal sort of
kindness, like Mary's eyes.

"Listen," he said. "I read about what happened in the newspaper."

I felt my face flush.

"Don't worry about it. I think it's a rite of passage or something," he
said. "I mean, I drove my motorcycle through a little gallery in
Tarzana. I don't know why either. Too much to drink, I guess." He
shrugged.

"Thanks," I said. I took the package from him and opened the door
to the studio.

"No one will forget who you are, that's for sure," he said, grinning, though not unkindly, as I stepped inside.

The studio was cold and damp. I could see the steam from my breath. I looked at my hands and wondered if they would ever make art again. I plugged a little space heater into the wall and sat beside it for a few minutes, opening my mail. Aside from the stack of bills, there was a letter from the museum, prefire, congratulating me on my installation and telling me how excited they were to be showing the work of an emerging artist such as I who had demonstrated prodigal talent and so on and so forth. It was signed Lucille K. Johnson, but it was a form letter, the signature preprinted. I crumpled it up and threw it in the trash can. Someone had also sent me a copy of the newspaper article, something that up till then I had avoided with scrupulous energy.

Artist Ignites Own Exhibit

Artist Louise Goldblum was arrested yesterday at the De Young Museum after setting her own exhibit on fire.

Goldblum, 30, whose work has been hailed as innovative and disturbing, was taken into custody shortly after the fire was extinguished. She was released a short time later after the museum agreed not to prosecute, pending financial reparations by Goldblum.

"The entire installation was destroyed," said curator Lucille K. Johnson. "Fortunately the museum itself did not burn down and nothing else was damaged."

The exhibit, part of a series of young, local artists whose work previously has appeared in a national or international setting, was apparently a re-creation of the artist's childhood environment. It featured the nude likeness of a dead woman cast off in the weeds, a motorcycle and several mounted animals.

About a dozen photographs, apparently of Goldblum's sister who was murdered last year, and an old box survived the flames. Many of the photographs portrayed Goldblum's teenage sister and a boy engaged in intercourse.

"We had no idea that the installation would be as risqué as it was because we initially invited Louise based on some work we had seen in Brooklyn and elsewhere, work that was much less controversial," said Johnson.

Witnesses said Goldblum had several bruises on her face and neck, including a black eye at the time of her arrest. Goldblum was not available for comment.

I lit a cigarette and, before extinguishing the match, burned the article in the ashtray. Then I turned to the brown package with a mixture of cold curiosity and fear. I saw, from the return address, that it had come from the museum. But I was unable to open it.

After settling in with a cup of coffee and a pack of cigarettes, I took the letter from Zeke that Alice had given me from my pocket and opened it. A stack of negatives fell out of the envelope. I held them up to the light and saw that they were the pictures of me he had taken the first night I had slept with him and the last night at the motel where Esther was killed. There were some photos too. There was one of me, one I don't remember, standing beneath a plane about to land. My hair was wild, unruly in the wind. I was staring out into the sky, the plane behind me. I looked small and frightened, so unlike Esther that I had a jolt of our separateness. I read the note.

Dear Louise:
I am sorry.
Zeke

So taciturn. So tongue-tied. Poor Zeke.

The next morning, I tidied up the studio, showered, changed and went downstairs to catch a bus. I spent the day roaming the city. Maggie had given me enough money to get through the month and Mary had loaned me a little bit for loose ends. I ate lunch at a Vietnamese restaurant near City Hall, savoring the sticky noodles and the pungent sauces. I felt I hadn't eaten in days and the flavors were sultry and exotic.

The sun had come out, a brilliant yellow, but the air was cold and the wind hurt as it blew against my skin. Homeless people wandered around searching trash bins near Fifth and Market. The arcades were full of seedy-looking characters and kids ditching school. Two Muni bus drivers were leaning against a stalled bus smoking cigarettes while nearby, a woman with severe eczema screamed obscenities at a wall.

I began walking up Hayes Street, then at Gough caught the 21 and got off at Stanyon. I walked through the nearly empty park, bundled against the cold, past the arboretum where Zeke, for all his madness, had loved me for a few moments—where I had let him love me.

I made my way up to the De Young. I stood at the edge of the Helen G. Urganis Camellia Garden. I thought of the girl who had been raped. I thought of Esther. I remembered her the way she was, with that long black hair and her alarming, exotic insolence. I thought of the way she laughed. I thought suddenly of Harold, silently, privately in his garage loaded with all that flotsam, crying over Elie Wiesel's *Night*.

The tips of my fingers bristled with that peculiar, bone-chilling San Francisco frigidity. But I felt alive. I could see the shapes of the trees, the peculiar winter solitude of the park. I stared for a moment at the implacable beauty of the De Young. And I thought again of Harold, realizing that perhaps it is your aloneness that allows you to make reparations to the one who needs forgiveness the most. To yourself.

Exhausted, I went home and slept.

When I awoke, I remembered the package that my neighbor had given me. I reached for it and opened it. Inside was Esther's memory box and an envelope. I opened the envelope, my hands trembling. It was from Lucille K. Johnson.

Dear Louise
This is all that was left of your installation.
Sincerely, Lucille

I opened the box and found about ten photographs of Esther and Danny making love. There was one picture of Esther standing naked by the window in her bedroom at the old homestead, her body barely developed but her pose so womanly. Even in the stasis of the photograph, she exuded a certain aplomb and self-determination. A certain forward momentum. I closed my eyes, and then I began to think of it, to let it wash over me, my imagination, her death. *So there she is,* I thought.

Esther. Dark, beautiful Esther alone in the playground of San Francisco. Living high and stylish on a New York Times *expense account. She meets a man in the bar of the St. Francis Hotel where she is staying before she will leave for South Africa. The man is handsome, big and somewhat tough. She is not interested in the details of his life, only whether he can entertain her, keep her moving, take her mind off things. He's wealthy and highly educated but also cagey and slightly dangerous. When he suggests they go to the Gold Country, Esther, never one to turn down something new and outlandish, says as long as they are back in time to catch her flight, she'll go.*

On their way there, they stop for some liquor. This is on Esther's insistence. The man does not drink. He only gives the illusion of drinking. In fact, the man is cool and calculating. He likes being in control. He senses immediately Esther's love of risk. He knows he will get a good fuck out of her.

They drive under the cold, moonlit sky, through the rolling hills dotted with oak trees, trees that have the shape of freaks and monsters. Large rock formations protrude like bald heads from the green hills. Esther is entranced as much by the man as she is by the landscape. A glimpse of memory, a touch of Danny whispers through her, she longs to see him. A pang of guilt. She thinks his death is her fault. She knows it is. She longs, in the abstract, for her own death because there is enough Christian in her to believe they will meet up again in the afterlife, that only there can they forgive each other, love each other, protect each other.

Esther and the man continue on until they come to Angels Camp. The conversation up till then has been limited to vague, sexual innuendo, demure hand-holding, gestures of sexual promise. When they arrive in town, the man guides the car directly to the Frog Hopper Inn. It is a tiny, well-kept motel above a creek. None of the letters are missing from the sign and a quaint stone frog with a statue of Samuel Clemens standing guard greets them as they turn into the parking lot. The lot, Esther notices, is nearly empty.

The air is chilly; you can almost see the cold, but it is a cold that summons the image of spring, a fragrant cold filled with possibility. While the man is registering his alias—Steven Aldercroft—Esther waits near the car. She hears the gurgle of a small stream and walks to the edge of the steep ravine that towers over the creek. She can smell the scent of snow, melting from the Sierras in the distance. She hugs herself against the cold and waits for the man who has said his name was something else, something she can't quite remember because she has had so much to drink and because it doesn't matter anyway.

Before he joins her at the edge of the ravine, Esther doubts for an instant the wisdom of coming here. She regrets already the hangover she will have on the flight to South Africa and laments the fact that the only cure will be to drink more. She foresees the difficult few days before her system will stabilize again from the jet lag, the booze, the indistinct memory of fucking a strange man in an old, worn-out Gold Rush–town motel.

The man sees her standing there. He comes up behind her and pushes her, then grabs her. She lets out a little scream but he is smooth.

"Always watch your back," he says.

He is wearing leather gloves and a camel hair coat. He puts his hand gently on her back and guides her to the room. They unlock the door and Esther sees through the darkness to the bed. Then her eyes drift over to the chair that she will put her clothes on. Oddly, she senses that this is her last night on earth. She thinks fleetingly of Danny. (Of me? Of anyone else?) No, it is only of Danny whom she thinks.

The man comes up behind her. Esther, startled, jumps, then laughs. She does not want him to see that she fears him. He begins to remove her clothes, gently, sweetly. He tells her, in a whisper, that she is beautiful. So, so beautiful. She responds. She thinks her instincts are wrong, that in fact, the man is safe.

It is when they fuck that she gets scared again, because he pins her roughly to the bed and penetrates her before she is ready. He tears into her and tells her she is a stupid whore. When he comes and pulls off of her, she feels humiliated and rolls onto her side, fighting tears, fighting her fear. But it is futile because no time passes before the man shoots her in the head and kills her, not even giving her the chance to have a last meaningful thought.

I had the idea of a cold drink. Its harsh, tasty zing on the back of my throat. I thought of myself—I could see my shape from the back—sitting at the bar at El Rio getting blind. I thought of Esther the day she had taken our picture at Lake Lauganita. My grief glowed inside me.

I got up and turned off the light. I shut the window. I was making my way to the alcove, to sleep, when I heard the key turn in the lock. I stopped, heard the door open then shut quietly. When I turned I saw the shape of Zeke, cloaked in his trench coat and heavy boots. I saw the smooth, lunar shape of his skull from the glowing streetlamps outside the window.

"Hey," he said.

I was not surprised to see him there. I felt no alarm. I realized on some level that I had been expecting it.

"Key privileges are over," I said. I turned on the lights. I held out my hand and he reached into his pocket and gave me my key. It was strange how his personal anarchy was countered by civility, as though his entire personality was based on a system of emotional checks and balances.

"Great show at the museum, Louise. I wonder about you sometimes, whether you don't do things in a calculated way to benefit from them later. This will always be with you now. When you do make a name for yourself—and you will because you have talent—the antics of your past crimes will only enhance your celebrity."

He was neither being cruel nor sarcastic. The invariable flatness of his tone suggested an unbiased examination of the events of my life. I realized he viewed life in clinical terms. He was still very much a mystery to me.

"I can only hope for such luck."

He smiled. He was beautiful.

"Have you ever heard the term *arrow of time?*" he asked, dragging deeply on his cigarette and squinting against the smoke.

I said nothing. I just wanted him to leave. I could not see myself, after everything that had happened, resisting him. He was harder to give up than booze.

"It is something that gives direction to time and distinguishes the past from the future. This is not my theory, mind you. It's been bandied around in physics for a while as a way to open up dialogue on things like the beginning of time, the beginning of the universe."

He stood up and went to the freezer. When he saw there was no vodka inside, he said nothing, but I saw him raise his eyebrows, surprised.

"Anyhow," he said, turning to me and meeting my eyes for the first time. "There are three different arrows of time. But I think the one that would interest you most is the psychological arrow of time."

"Zeke," I said. "Give me a break already. Jesus."

"This means simply the direction in which you feel time pass," he said, ignoring me. "Where you remember the past but not the future."

"So? What makes you think I give a shit about any of this . . . any of your stupid theories anyway?"

"Because time is your primary preoccupation. You might say you're a time traveler, that up till now your goal has been to elude the damages wrought by the passage of time."

"Zeke," I said exasperated. "What is it that you want from me?"

He stood up and came over to me, wrapping his giant hand around the back of my neck and pulling me toward him. I struggled against him but he was stronger than me and in seconds we were kissing. He had his hand up my shirt and I felt myself swaying into his mind-numbing scent, the smells of earth and incense and the delirious way he siphoned desire out of me and forced it into him, into us. I felt myself plunging into his nowhere, deserted by the terrible way he seduced me. He began to take my shirt off and I saw Esther then, lying there, dead, the gambles of her life finally not paying off. I saw too that I was an imposter, that I was nothing like Esther, that I would never be like Esther, nor should I want to be like her. Zeke began to rip my jeans from me and it was finally at that point that I said it.

"Cease," I said.

And he stopped immediately. He looked at me for a long time, as if to determine whether or not I was serious.

"Please, Zeke. I want you to go."

His eyes filled with a special kind of sorrow, and I saw the vague gray of his damaged soul. I thought it would kill me. I couldn't bear it, I had to get away.

I walked out of the room and into the bathroom, locking the door behind me. I turned the shower on full blast, a stream of hot water.

Downstairs, I could hear the faint sound of a piano and a man singing. I pictured my neighbor, the diamond in his nose and his kind smile. The wind blew against the windows and burst through the shafts and chimneys of the building like the labored breathing of an old house.

I stepped into the shower and, at the same time, I heard the door close and the sound of Zeke's footsteps in the stairwell. As the water pelted me I remembered the Lake Lauganita of my youth. I could see them as if we were all there again, my brothers, Esther and Danny. I could feel the dry heat, hear the chorus of mosquitoes, bees and grasshoppers. I could taste the egg salad sandwiches and feel the shock of ice-cold Kool-Aid on the back of my dry throat. I heard our shouts and our laughter and the way it had always been tinged with an edge of sorrow and wanting.

I stood there beneath the hot waves of water for a long time, waiting for relief and consolation, the balm of peace, a life without anguish. I knew somehow that it would be a long wait, but that I should wait, that I should be patient.

About the Author

Leslie Schwartz is a freelance journalist and editor. Her short stories and articles have appeared in various publications, including the *Los Angeles Times, Self, Sonora Review* and *Yellow Silk. Jumping the Green* won the James Jones Literary Society award for best first novel in 1997. She lives in Los Angeles with her husband.